continued . . .

"Readers rejoice! The Mackenzie brothers return as Ashley works her magic to create a unique love story brimming over with depth of emotion, unforgettable characters, sizzling passion, mystery, and a story that reaches out and grabs your heart. Brava!"

—*RT Book Reviews* (Top Pick)

"A heartfelt, emotional historical romance with danger and intrigue around every corner . . . A great read!"   —*Fresh Fiction*

THE MADNESS OF LORD IAN MACKENZIE

"Ever-versatile Ashley begins her new Victorian Highland Pleasures series with a deliciously dark and delectably sexy story of love and romantic redemption that will captivate readers with its complex characters and suspenseful plot."   —*Booklist*

"Mysterious, heartfelt, sensitive, and sensual . . . Two big thumbs up."
—*Publishers Weekly,* "Beyond Her Book"

"When you're reading a book that is a step or two—or six or seven—above the norm, you know it almost immediately. Such is the case with *The Madness of Lord Ian Mackenzie*. The characters here are so complex and so real that I was fascinated by their journey . . . [and] this story is as flat-out romantic as any I've read in a while . . . This is a series I am certainly looking forward to following."   —*All About Romance*

"A unique twist on the troubled hero . . . Fresh and interesting."
—*Night Owl Reviews* (Top Pick)

"A welcome addition to the genre."   —*Dear Author*

"Intriguing . . . Unique . . . Terrific."   —*Midwest Book Review*

Titles by Jennifer Ashley

TIGER MAGIC

JENNIFER ASHLEY

BERKLEY SENSATION, NEW YORK

THE BERKLEY PUBLISHING GROUP
Published by the Penguin Group
Penguin Group (USA) LLC
375 Hudson Street, New York, New York 10014

USA • Canada • UK • Ireland • Australia • New Zealand • India • South Africa • China

penguin.com

A Penguin Random House Company

TIGER MAGIC

A Berkley Sensation Book / published by arrangement with the author

For information, address: The Berkley Publishing Group,
a division of Penguin Group (USA) LLC,
375 Hudson Street, New York, New York 10014.

ISBN: 978-0-425-25121-8

PUBLISHING HISTORY
Berkley Sensation mass-market edition / June 2013

PRINTED IN THE UNITED STATES OF AMERICA

10 9 8 7 6 5 4

Cover art by Tony Mauro.
Cover design by George Long.

CHAPTER ONE

"No, no, no, no, not *today.* You can't do this to me today!"

But the car died anyway. It throbbed onto the shoulder of the empty highway, bucked twice, and gurgled to silence.

"Aw, damn it." Carly's four-inch heels landed on the pavement, followed by tanned legs and a tight, white sheath dress. She glared down at the car, the Texas wind tugging her light brown hair out of its careful French braid.

She would have to be wearing white. Carly jammed her hands on her hips and skewered the Corvette with her enraged stare.

Take the 'Vette, her fiancé, Ethan, had said. *It's a big day. You want to make an entrance.* She'd been in a hurry to get on her way out of the city to the gallery where she worked, so Ethan had pressed the keys into her hand and pushed her out the door.

Carly had agreed with him—the artist they were showcasing liked classic cars, and he was doing an exclusive with her boss's gallery in the little town northeast of

Austin. Buyers were already lined up. Carly's commission could be enormous.

If she could get there. Carly kicked one of the tires in rage, then danced back. Her shoes were substantial but that still hurt.

Perfect. Ethan could be generous—and he had the filthy richness to do it—but he also forgot little details like making sure cars got tuned up.

"His lazy highness can just come and get me, then." Carly went around to the passenger side of the car and leaned in through the open window to grab her cell phone from her purse.

Today. This had to happen *today*. Still bent into the car, she punched numbers with her thumb, but the phone made the beeping noise that indicated it was out of range.

"No effing way." Carly backed out of the car and raised the phone high. "Come on. Find me a signal."

And then she saw him.

The man stood about ten feet from the car, not on the road but in the tall Texas grass beside it. That grass was dotted with blue, yellow, and white flowers, and this being summer, the grass was also a nice vivid green.

It wasn't every day a girl saw a tall hunk of a man, shoulders broad under a black and red SoCo Novelties T-shirt standing by the side of the road. Watching her.

Really watching her. His eyes were fixed on Carly, not in the dazed way of a transient wandering around in an alcoholic haze, but looking at her as no human being had looked at her before.

He wasn't scruffy like a transient either. His face was shaved, his body and clothes clean, jeans mud free despite his having walked through the field. And he must have walked through the field, because she sure hadn't seen him on the road.

His hair . . . Carly blinked as the strong sunshine caressed sleek hair that was orange and black. Not dyed orange and black—dye tended to make hair matte and stark. This looked entirely natural, sunlight picking up highlights of red orange and blue black.

She knew she should be afraid. A strange guy with tiger-striped hair popping out of nowhere, staring at her like he did should terrify her. But he didn't.

He hadn't been there when Carly had first stopped the car and climbed out. He must have arrived when she'd bent over to get the phone, which meant he'd seen every bit of her round backside hugged by her skintight white dress.

This stretch of road was deserted. Eerily so. The streets in Austin were always packed, but once outside the city, it was possible to find long stretches of highway empty of traffic, such as the one Carly drove down to get to the art gallery every day.

There was no one out here, no one speeding along the straight road to rescue her. No one but herself in now-rumpled white and the tall man staring at her from the grass.

"Hey!" Carly shouted at him. "You know how to fix a car?"

He didn't have a name. He didn't have a clan. He'd had a mate, and a cub, but they'd died, and the humans who'd held him captive for forty years had taken them away. They hadn't let him say good-bye, hadn't let him grieve.

Now he lived among other Shifters, brought to this place of humidity, heat, and colorful hills. He only felt completely well when he was running in his tiger form, way out in the backcountry where no one would see him. He usually ran at night, but today, he hadn't been able to stay in the confines of the house, or Shiftertown. So he'd gone.

He'd left his clothes hidden behind a little rise at the side of this road. Connor was supposed to pick him up, but not for a couple more hours, and Connor was often late. Tiger didn't mind. He liked being out here.

He'd dressed, walked around the rise to the road . . . and saw a fine backside sticking out of a bright red car. The backside was covered in thin white fabric, showing him faintly pink panties beneath.

Below the nice buttocks were shapely legs, not too long, tanned by Texas sun. Shoes that rose about half a mile made those legs even shapelier.

The woman had hair the color of winter-gold grass. She had a cell phone in one hand, but she waited, the other hand on her shapely hip, for him to answer her question.

Tiger climbed the slope from the grass to the road. She watched him come, unafraid, her sunglasses trained on him.

Tiger wanted to see her eyes. If she was going to be his mate, he wanted to see everything about her.

And this woman would be his mate. No doubt about that. The scent that kicked into his nostrils, the way his heartbeat slowed to powerful strokes, the way his body filled with heat told him that.

Connor had tried to explain that mating didn't happen like that for Shifters. A Shifter male got to know a female a little bit before he chose, and then he mate-claimed her. The mate bond could rear its head anytime before or after that, but it didn't always on first glance.

Tiger had listened to this wisdom without arguing, but he knew better. He wasn't an ordinary Shifter. And this female, hand on one curved hip, wasn't an ordinary woman.

"Can you put the hood up?" Tiger asked her.

"I don't know," she said, frustrated. "This car is different from anything I usually drive. Hang on, let me check."

Her voice was a sweet little Texas drawl, not too heavy. A light touch, enough to make warmth crawl through Tiger's veins and go straight to his cock.

The woman found a catch and worked the hood open, then dusted off her hands and peered at the inner workings without comprehension. "Classic car, my ass." She scowled at it. "*Classic* just means *old.*"

Tiger looked inside. The layout was much different from the pickup he and Connor had been tinkering with all spring, but Connor had been teaching Tiger a lot about vehicles. "Got a socket wrench?"

When he looked up at the woman, he saw her staring at him from behind the sunglasses. "Your eyes," she said. "They're . . ."

"Yellow."

Tiger turned away before her scent convinced him to press her back against the side of the car and hold her to him. She wasn't a female someone had tossed into his cage to trigger his mating frenzy. This was his mate, and he didn't want to hurt her.

He wanted to take this slow, woo her a little. Maybe with something involving food. Shifter males around here liked to cook for their mates, and Tiger liked the rituals.

She opened the back of the car and found a toolbox, which did have a set of socket wrenches. Tiger took one and reached inside the car, looking for the silence within himself that would lead him to the problem. He seemed to be able to sense what was wrong with engines, and how to coax them back to life. He couldn't explain how he did it— he only knew that cars and trucks didn't watch him, or fear him, and he could see what was wrong when others couldn't.

As he worked, the neckline of his T-shirt slid down, baring the silver and black Collar that ran around his throat. The woman bent over to him, the top of her dress dangerously open, the warmth of her touching his cheek.

"Holy shit," she said. "You're a Shifter."

"Yes."

She lifted her sunglasses and stared at him. Her eyes were clear green, flecked with a little gray. She stared at him frankly, in open curiosity, and without fear.

Of course she wasn't afraid of him. She was going to be his mate.

Tiger met her gaze, unblinking. Her eyes widened the slightest bit, as though she realized something had happened between them, but she didn't know what.

She restored her sunglasses and straightened up. "I've never seen a Shifter before. I didn't know any of y'all were allowed out of Shiftertown."

Tiger picked up the wrench with one hand and moved

the other to the timing belt chain, which had come loose from the gear. "We're allowed."

The repair needed both delicacy and strength but Tiger finished quickly, leaning all the way inside and letting his fingers know what to do. He backed out and closed the toolbox. "Start it now."

The woman eagerly rushed to the car, slid inside, and cranked it to life. She emerged again, leaving the car running, while Tiger scanned a few more things. "The timing belt will hold for now, but the whole shaft is worn and could break. Take the car home and don't use it again until it's fixed."

"Terrific. Armand is going to kill me."

Tiger didn't know who Armand was and didn't much care. He carried the toolbox to the back for her and closed the small trunk, then returned to close the hood.

He found her smiling at him on the other side of the hood as it came down. "You're kind of amazing, you know that?" she asked. "So what were you doing out in that field? Were you running around as a . . . Let me guess. Tiger?"

He let his lips twitch. "What gave it away?"

"Very funny. I've never met a man with striped hair and yellow eyes. Call it a clue. Anyway, you're a lifesaver. I'm Carly, by the way." She stuck out her hand, then pulled it back from his now-greasy one. "Hang on. I think there're some wipes in here."

Carly leaned in through the passenger window again. Tiger stood still and enjoyed watching her, and when she straightened, she knew he'd been looking. "Like what you see?" she asked, her voice holding challenge.

Tiger saw no reason to lie. "Yes," he said.

"You sweet-talker." Carly pulled out two damp wipes for him.

Tiger took them and wiped off his hands. Wet wipes were familiar, at least. Whenever he'd been working on the truck, Connor's aunt always made him clean up with them before she'd let him back into the house.

"You need a ride into Austin?" Carly asked. "It's still thirty miles from here to the gallery, so I'd better take this car back to Ethan's and not risk it. Ethan loves this car. Like I said, Armand's going to kill me, but I'm so late now, it's not going to matter."

"Yes."

Carly sent him a wide smile. "Yes, you want a ride? Or are you just being polite while I ramble?"

"The ride." He could call Connor with the cell phone they made him carry when he got back to town. He couldn't miss this opportunity to get to know his mate.

"Man of few words. I like it. Ethan, my fiancé, can talk on and on and on about his family, his business, his day, his life—Ethan. His favorite topic."

Tiger stopped. "Fiancé."

"Do Shifters have fiancés? It's what humans call the man they're going to marry."

Tiger wadded up the now-dirty wipes in his big hands. "I didn't know you'd have a fiancé."

Carly opened the door of the running car as though she hadn't heard him. "Get in. Ethan's house is on the river—it's a ways from Shiftertown, but I can always get you a taxi, or one of Ethan's many lackeys can run you home."

"Why are you marrying him?"

Carly shrugged. "Girl's got to marry someone, mostly so her older sister stops mentioning it every five minutes. Ethan's a good catch. Besides, I'm in love with him."

No, she wasn't. The slight motion in her throat, the scent of nervousness as she replied gave away the lie. She didn't love him. Tiger felt something like triumph.

He got into the car as Carly slid into the driver's seat inches away from him. Her fingers ran over the steering wheel as she made a competent U-turn on the still-empty road, and she drove, somewhat slowly, back toward Austin.

Carly tried to talk to him. She liked to chatter, this female. Tiger was fine with sitting back and listening to her, scenting her, watching her.

As they neared the city and the road started getting busier, Carly lifted her cell phone and called the man named Armand. She explained she'd be late, then held the phone from her ear while a male voice on the other end spoke loudly in an unfamiliar accent. Carly rolled her eyes at Tiger and smiled, unworried.

"Bark's worse than his bite," she said, clicking off the phone.

"I know some wolves like that."

Carly laughed, her red mouth opening. Tiger leaned in closer to her, not hard to do in this coffin of a car, and brushed his scent onto her.

She glanced at him, again with the puzzlement of knowing something had happened but not sure what. "It's dangerous for a woman to give strange men rides. I wonder why I'm not worried with you."

Because you're my mate. "Because I'd never hurt you."

"Well, you can't, can you? That's why you wear the Collar. Keeps you tame. Shifters can't be violent with it on."

Tiger could. This Collar was fake. It didn't have the technology or Fae magic that would send shocks through his system if he started to attack.

They'd tried to put a real Collar on him, and Tiger had nearly gone insane. They concluded that Tiger should wear a fake Collar—not that the humans realized it was fake—and proceed from there.

This Collar would not stop Tiger from scooping up Carly and running off with her if he wanted to. He could sequester her, mate with her, soothe his need for her until they both collapsed in exhaustion.

Or he could be kind and wait for her to get used to him.

Carly kept up the conversation all the way through midtown traffic and up the hill north of the river. She pulled into a drive that arced in front of an enormous house, the mansion white with black shutters and black trim. Carly parked the car and emerged, and Tiger got out with her.

Gates on either side of the house led to the backyard, and Carly opened one, beckoning Tiger to follow. Tiger got in front of her and went through the gate first, his Shifter instinct urging him to make sure the way was safe for her.

The backyard overlooked the river and the hills opposite it, where similar houses had a view of this one. A stair ran down the side of the hill to a private dock, where two boats bobbed.

A row of glass windows lined the back of the house, but the glare of the sun and tint of the windows kept Tiger from seeing inside. A man with pruning shears looked up from a bush at the corner of the house, then stood up in alarm as Carly reached for the handle of one of the glass doors.

"Ms. Randal, you don't want to go in there."

Carly turned to him in surprise. Tiger tried to get around Carly to enter the house first, but she was too quick. She was opening the door and walking inside before Tiger could stop her, and he had to settle for following a step behind her.

What Tiger smelled inside the house wasn't danger, however. It was sex.

He saw why when he and Carly rounded a wall behind which stretched a huge kitchen. Cabinetry in a fine golden wood filled the walls, the long counters shiny granite. It was clean in here, no dishes cluttering the counters, no one cooking something that smelled good, no chatter and laughter as a meal was prepared.

A woman sat on top of the counter with her blouse open, her skirt up around her hips, high-heeled shoes on her feet. A man with his pants around his ankles was thrusting hard into her, holding her legs in black stockings around his thighs. Both humans were grunting and panting, and neither noticed Carly or Tiger.

Tiger stepped in front of Carly, trying to put his huge body between her and the scene. Carly stopped, her purse falling from nerveless fingers to the floor. "Ethan." There was shock in her tone.

The man turned around. Tiger was growling, feeling the distress of his mate, the animal in him wanting nothing more than to kill the person who'd upset her.

The man jumped, his mouth dropping open, then he

stumbled over his pants and had to catch himself on the counter.

"Carly, what the *fuck* are you doing here?" His gaze went to Tiger, whose fingers were sprouting the long, razor-sharp claws of the Bengal. "And who the hell is *that*?"

CHAPTER TWO

Carly's anguish hit Tiger in a series of waves. Shock, anger, and then a pain so harsh the edge of it hurt him.

Tiger reached for her, but Carly snatched up her purse and swung away, blinded. She ran from the room, out of the house, and back into the sunshine.

The house's windows let Tiger trace her progress through the backyard and around to the front. She slammed her way back into the Corvette, started the engine with a roar, and shot around the circular drive and out into the street.

Leaving Tiger alone, unable to comfort her.

He turned instead to the source of Carly's distress, the man called Ethan. Ethan glared at Tiger, outrage in his eyes, and snarls built in Tiger's throat.

The young woman Ethan had been with—*unknown, not part of this*—scrambled from the counter, her skirt catching on her black thigh-high stockings as she righted herself. A flash of yellow satin panties broke the monochrome colors of her outfit before the businesslike gray skirt shut it out.

The woman buttoned her blouse with agitated fingers. "Shit, Ethan, you said she'd be gone all day."

Ethan dragged his gaze from Tiger, took a step toward the woman, half tripped on his pants again, and leaned down to drag them up. "Lisa, wait . . ."

"You said she knew. You said she was cool with it."

The woman grabbed her purse and started for the sliding glass door. Tiger remained in front of it, growling.

The woman looked up at him, and a bite of primal fear entered her eyes. She didn't know what Tiger was, but something inside her knew a predator when she saw one. She stood a moment, indecisive, then pivoted and ran out the other side of the kitchen toward the front of the house.

"No," Ethan called. "*Wait.*"

He frantically zipped and buckled as he swung around to follow her and found himself up against the solid wall of Tiger, who'd stepped in his way.

Tiger smelled Ethan's outrage and shock, but no fear and no shame. "Who the hell are you?" Ethan had to crank his head back to look at Tiger, but he had an arrogance that would make an alpha smack him down just to make a point.

The front door slammed open, the young woman fleeing. Ethan grimaced as he heard her car start, then turned even more rage on Tiger.

"Carly's sleeping with *you*?" he demanded. "You can tell that slut for me she can give me back every penny I've ever given her."

Feral anger rose inside Tiger in a wave. Living outside the cage, experiencing new sensations and feelings had dampened his rages a bit, but hadn't erased them. Nothing ever would.

This man, this pretend-mate of Carly's, had hurt her. He'd not done it with calculation, but with careless cruelty. Now he twisted the fact that Carly had walked in on him while *he* betrayed *her* to make the betrayal her fault.

Tiger's reactions were more basic. He saw a source of pain, and he eliminated it.

His snarls grew in volume, a sound so deep it was felt more than heard. The glass-fronted cabinets rattled, and dishes behind them took up the dance. The kitchen windows caught the vibrations and rumbled in response.

A glass cabinet door shattered and broke. Ethan gaped at it, then back at Tiger. "You're paying for that."

"Mr. Turner." The gardener who'd tried to stop Carly from entering the house now stood in the kitchen's open door. "He's a *Shifter*."

"Is he?" Ethan peered up at Tiger again, taking in his Collar. He started to smile. "Son of a bitch. Carly's doing it with a Shifter? She won't have *anything* left when I'm finished with her. Teach her to mess around with me like that."

Killing rage beat through Tiger's blood. Ethan was a small, sniveling creature, smelling of deceit, and he dared to threaten Tiger's mate.

Tiger slammed his fists to the kitchen counter, a polished slab of granite. It broke into two giant chunks.

"Here . . . you . . ." The gardener held his rake in front of him, a tool Tiger could snap between his fingers.

Now fear appeared in Ethan's eyes but still not enough. "Get out of here, or I'm calling the police."

Tiger barely heard him. Because the man was so weak, Tiger's need to protect Carly would be slaked with something simple, like breaking Ethan's neck. Ripping him apart and painting the walls with his blood wasn't necessary. Not this time. He reached for Ethan's throat.

Fear at last radiated from Ethan, sickening waves of it. Tiger smelled the man's bladder fail him, and then Ethan turned and ran.

Running was a bad idea. It woke Tiger's need to hunt, to kill, the instinct to track through the jungle something for his dinner.

Ethan ran into his living room. The place was filled with furniture, all of it white. Tiger threw things aside to clear his path, chairs and the sofa crashing to the floor in pieces. Ethan dashed into a smaller room, darker, with a desk and a computer. And no escape.

Tiger barreled inside like silent death, while behind him,

the gardener shouted, "I'm calling the cops! I'm calling the cops!"

Ethan yanked open a desk drawer and scrabbled in it. Tiger picked up the desk and threw it aside. The wooden thing crashed into the wall, smashing desk, wall, and computer.

Ethan came up from a terrified crouch, something black in his hands. There was a loud bang.

Fire bit into Tiger's gut, but he plowed on, kicking aside the remains of the desk.

Bang, bang, bang. Three more bullets entered Tiger's body. The pain finally cut through his rage, and he looked down to see blood dripping over the front of his shirt.

Tiger hadn't been shot in a long time. The humans who'd tried to tame him in the basement had used tranqs at first, and they'd had to shoot him several times before Tiger succumbed to the drugs. Then they wondered, *How many bullets would it take to slow him down?* And they'd tried it. They'd discovered it took more than the four small ones Ethan had just pumped into Tiger's front before he felt it.

Tiger reached for the pistol.

Five, six, seven. The bullets hit Tiger one by one, pain escalating. Tiger snatched the gun from Ethan's hand and broke it in half.

Ethan was screaming now, his terror beating against Tiger's pain. Tiger lifted Ethan by the neck, higher, higher. The man gave Tiger one look of intense fear, and then he went limp, eyes rolling back into his head. Tiger shook him, and Ethan's head lolled. He was still warm and alive, but unconscious.

Disappointing. Tiger dumped Ethan's body on top of the ruins of the desk and turned to leave. Blood slid down the shirt and his torso behind it, pooling in his waistband. Kim was going to be angry at Tiger for ruining the shirt. She always shook her finger at him when he got his clothes too dirty.

The gardener jumped out of the way as Tiger came out of the office. The man still held the rake, ready to swat

Tiger if he came too near, but Tiger ignored him. The gardener had done nothing to Carly.

Tiger pressed his arm to his abdomen as he found the front door of the house, left open by the other woman's swift exit. He staggered out on weakening legs, vision blurring.

Dimly, he heard the wail of sirens, growing louder as he stumbled down the long driveway and out into the street. He saw and smelled other humans popping out of front gates to peer at him, reminding him of prairie dogs he'd seen while he'd roamed, peeking up out of burrows to check whether the way was safe.

Shiftertown lay to the east of this place, so Tiger turned his steps that way, feeling the warm asphalt through the soles of his shoes.

The sirens grew louder. Tiger remembered how afraid he'd been when he'd first heard them charging through the city, how Connor had explained what they were and what they meant. Police, fire, ambulance. Get out of the way, because someone needed to be saved, or someone needed to be hunted.

Hunting should be silent. Predators had to stalk, to move silently, to find their prey and strike before the prey knew they were there.

Five police cars charged up the hill toward him, followed by a small red truck, lights blazing. They cut off Tiger from progressing east, but he could climb walls and cut through yards if he had to.

Tiger turned in through a gate to another house, scattering two more men with garden tools. Behind this house, the river gleamed at the bottom of a hill, a better way to escape than the roads. He could swim down the river, pull himself out near Shiftertown, and make his way home from there.

Police cars hurtled through the gates after him. Tiger jogged around the house, heading down the slope, his breathing labored now.

The river flowed, cool and sweet, at the end of the path at the bottom of the hill. The water would feel good on his wounds. Tiger would wade in and then just float away, dreaming of Carly and her scent, her red-lipped smile, and her eyes assessing him without fear.

Another loud bang ripped away his daydreams. Pain tore into the base of his spine, and Tiger's knees buckled.

He landed facedown in a lawn of green grass, the blades tickling his nose. "Carly," he mumbled. "Carly."

A boot landed on his backside. A man pulled one of Tiger's hands behind his back, and a cool cuff touched his wrist.

Bound, chained, trapped . . .

Tiger rose, the Shifter beast tearing out of him as he went up, and up, and up. The bloody mess of his clothes fell away, and the cuff shattered and fell to the grass.

He roared his Tiger roar, opening his mouth filled with fangs, his in-between beast huge and deadly.

A barrage of guns pointed at him, including a large air rifle loaded with a tranquilizer.

Tiger went for the man with the tranq. Too late. The dart entered Tiger's already battered body, and the quick-acting tranquilizer made him stumble. But it wasn't enough. Never was.

"Takes two," he said, his voice clogged, clawed hand reaching for the rifle. "Maybe three."

The man had already reloaded. The second dart hit Tiger's throat, right above his Collar. A third one entered his thigh, shot by a second man, and peaceful tranquilizer poured into Tiger's blood.

"Good shot," he said, or thought he said, then he rushed to the ground at sickening speed.

Tiger woke flat on his back, both wrists enclosed in the hated steel, hands bound to rods on either side of him.

He roared as he came awake, jerking the cuffs and chains, which wouldn't break. They'd used metal thick enough to withstand a Shifter. He opened his eyes to find himself in a bed, surrounded by white curtains, white walls, machines, tubes, and soft sounds of beeping.

Panic wedged in his throat. The compound, experiments, pain, fear . . .

He roared again, frantically banging against the cuffs. He'd thought himself safe in the strange place called Shiftertown, but now they'd sent him back, had trapped him again. No. No. *No!*

"Easy, lad."

The voice cut through Tiger's panic, promising strength. A hard hand pressed his chest, and Tiger tried to rise against it, jerking at his restraints. He had to get out. *He had to get out.*

"I said, *easy.*"

Tiger stared up at the hard face and intense blue eyes of Liam Morrissey, leader of the Austin Shiftertown. Liam was a Feline, his wildcat smaller than Tiger's, his human body smaller as well. Tiger could defeat him.

But the usually laid-back, unhurried Irishman locked his gaze with Tiger's. He wore the hard resolve of a man who held together a band of Shifters of three species and protected them against all comers. His scent and look willed Tiger back down in the bed, and Tiger found his panic lessening.

When Tiger's vision cleared a little, he saw three men in black uniforms standing like columns at the foot of his bed, their faces blank. They held automatic rifles, loosely, but Tiger knew they were willing to shoot to kill as soon as someone gave the order.

"You stay down, lad," Liam said, his Irish tones laced with steel. "You understand me?"

Tiger dragged in a breath. The fear hadn't left him, but he knew he had to obey Liam or the men in black would bring up the weapons and fill Tiger's body with bullets, too many to withstand at once.

Tiger managed one nod. His fists stayed balled, but he stopped pulling at the chains.

Liam's hand remained on Tiger's chest. "Good lad. You

need to stay still to heal. You *stay still,* and everything will be fine."

"Carly," Tiger whispered.

Liam leaned to the bed without lifting his hand from Tiger. "What?"

"Carly. Where is she?"

Liam shook his head. "I don't know who that is, but you've been whispering her name. Someone from the lab?"

"She's my mate." Tiger could barely speak, his voice grating and strange, but it felt good to say the word. "My mate."

Liam blinked slowly, once, but he didn't let his body move. "You need to stop talking and rest now."

"She's hurting."

Liam leaned closer, speaking so only Tiger would hear him. "Was she at this house you broke into? She get caught in the cross fire?"

"Find her."

"You have to give me a bit more to go on, lad."

"Carly." Tiger dimly remembered the name the gardener had used. "Randal."

A machine above him clicked, and the meds or whatever they'd given him coursed through his body again. Darkness rushed at him.

Tiger tried to reach for Liam, but he couldn't move his hands. He had to settle for pinning the alpha with his gaze, something Connor had told him never to do. "Find my mate," Tiger rasped, and then nothing existed.

The red 'Vette's door hung open, Carly's foot out on the driveway. The rest of her remained behind the wheel, she staring at the blankness of the garage door as more tears slid down her face. The rearview mirror showed mascara smeared into black smudges under her eyes and streaks of it tracking her cheeks.

Carly had driven blindly around the city before ending up in front of her house, but she didn't want to go inside right now to the silent, empty place. She didn't want to be alone, but she didn't want to call her mama or her sisters and tell them what had happened. Not yet. Her energetic sisters and mother weren't home anyway—they'd gone to Mexico for days of shopping and sampling every kind of tequila they could find. Carly had decided to give the trip a miss so she could stay behind and help Armand. If she called them, they'd exclaim in sympathy and anger and give her lots of support. When that happened, she'd lose it completely.

She'd tried to go see Yvette, Armand's wife. With Yvette, Carly could pour out her heart and find sympathy, but also sage, clear-eyed advice. Yvette knew the world, and she'd tell Carly what to do.

Except Yvette hadn't been home. If Carly had stopped to think about it, she would have realized that. Yvette was at the gallery helping Armand, because Carly wasn't there for the big exhibit opening. Armand was probably even now firing Carly.

And Carly didn't care.

Nothing mattered right now. Not her sitting in her driveway in a car that wasn't hers, not her mascara-blotched face, not the black lines that dropped from her cheeks to her pretty white dress.

She'd been so sure of Ethan, her future cut-and-dried. Ethan had been the antithesis of Carly's father—her father had never held a job for long, gambled away money he did have, grew angry at Carly's mother if she didn't hand over most of what *she* earned to him. When her father had lived with them, Carly's family had moved constantly, never able to stay in one house long. And then one day he'd gone. He'd vanished one afternoon when Carly was twelve, walking away from his wife and four daughters, leaving them with unpaid back rent and a mountain of bills—after withdrawing all the money they did have out of the bank account and taking it with him. He'd never come back, hadn't wanted to see his daughters, had agreed to the divorce from afar, and had vanished from their lives.

Ethan represented stability, ambition, a man who wouldn't

lose everything on the next turn of a card or on a horse that had long odds to win, who wouldn't leave a wife high and dry. Carly's father had been quicksand—Ethan was a pillar.

But now that pillar had crumbled, plunging Carly into pain and uncertainty. Ethan hadn't endangered her financially, but he'd betrayed her trust and had slapped respect in the face.

How long had he been screwing other women? From day one? Had Carly been so blinded by her need for Ethan's stability that she hadn't noticed?

And to have his betrayal thrown in her face in front of a helpful stranger, that hot-looking, weird-eyed . . . Shifter.

"Oh no." Carly scraped tears from her eyes with an already sodden tissue. "The poor guy. I left him in Ethan's house."

She'd have to go back. This was Ethan's frigging car anyway. Much as she wanted to run it off the road, or maybe push it into a deep, muddy creek, she had enough sense to know that Ethan would sue her for it. He liked to sue people.

Carly dragged her foot back into the car. Surely the Shifter-man with the multicolored hair would have left, caught a bus, called a friend.

But she thought of him and his slow stares, his not-quite understanding of what she was saying to him. She'd left him defenseless with Ethan, and Ethan didn't like Shifters.

Carly started the car.

"Are you Carly?" a male voice said almost in her ear.

Carly bit back a scream. A dark-haired man peered in through the open driver's-side window at her, regarding her with a pair of very blue eyes. Behind him stood another man, just as tall but without as much bulk, younger. A flash of black and silver showed above the T-shirt of the man staring at her, a Collar. He was Shifter.

"Is the tiger-man all right?" Carly asked him, wiping her eyes again. She had no way of knowing if this Shifter knew hers, but she was worried about him. "Did he get home?"

The Shifter blinked once in surprise, then he masked

that surprise like a master. Carly had worked for a while now in the art business, which involved selling high-dollar goods. Those who bought and sold learned to school their faces and words in order to make the most profit or spend the least amount of money, but their body language could speak volumes. This man was telling her he knew all about body language but could manipulate it to serve his ends.

"I'm Sean," the man said. "You need to come with us to the hospital. Tiger's been asking for you."

"Hospital?" Carly gasped. "What happened?"

"Tiger got himself shot, that's what happened," the Shifter said, his Irish accent becoming more pronounced. "Seven times, right in the gut."

CHAPTER THREE

"*Seven*? Oh my God, is he all right? Where is he? I'm sorry. I'm so sorry."

Surprise flickered in the blue eyes again. "Why are you sorry? Did *you* shoot him, lass?" A tiny bit of anger also touched him, a flash that told her that this man would be dangerous when he was angry.

"He was hurt because of me, wasn't he?" Carly cried. "Where is he?"

The passenger door opened, and the younger Shifter slid inside without asking permission. "Follow Sean. He'll get us there." The young man closed the door and touched the dash in wonder. "I've never been in a 'Vette before," he said, his accent as Irish as the other man's. "Wicked, this is."

"Come on, lass," Sean said and unfolded himself to walk to a motorcycle parked behind her. Though not as big as Tiger, Sean moved with ease that belied his strength, the balanced grace of a cat.

He started the motorcycle and waited for Carly to back out of the driveway before he started down the street in front of her. Carly's hands shook a little, but her tears had dried. Concern for Tiger cut through anger at Ethan.

"I'm Connor, by the way," the young man said as she started to follow Sean. "Still a cub, but getting there. You ever want to sell this car to me, we can negotiate."

"It's not mine," Carly said.

"No? Whose, then? Think they'd be willing to sell? If not to a Shifter, I can find someone to be an in-between."

There was nothing at all wrong with Connor, but Carly's temper splintered. "It belongs to a two-timing, gutless, son-of-a-bitch-bastard-asshole, and I wish you'd steal the damn thing from him!"

Oh, that felt good! Carly laid her head back on the headrest, clutched the steering wheel as she floored it down a hill after the motorcycle, and let out a long, heartfelt scream.

"Whoa," Connor said. "Take it easy, sweetie. Maybe I'd better drive."

"No way," Carly said. "He told me to take the 'Vette so I'd be out of the way when he did it with his bitch, and so *I'm taking the 'Vette*."

She peeled around the corner after Sean, laughing as the car hugged the road and accelerated at the same time.

Connor's eyes, blue like the other Shifter's, rounded. "Are you saying your mate cheated on you?"

"He's not my *mate*. No way, no how, never, ever. And that's exactly what he did. Hang on."

The road made a sharp turn, and Carly took it fast. The Corvette, made to race, slid around without a waver. "Woo!" She pounded the steering wheel. "I love this car. Way better at getting me excited than Ethan ever was."

Connor laughed. "I like you, human woman."

Carly's anger flashed, sharp. "If Ethan hurt the tiger, I'll kill him with my bare hands."

"That's the spirit," Connor said. "Tiger will live. He's tough. But he needs you, I'm thinking."

"Did he tell you what happened to him?" Carly asked,

her anxiety for Tiger cutting through her anger again. "How did you find me?"

"He's not up to giving out much detail," Connor said. "But once we pried your name out of him, it didn't take our Sean long to figure out where you lived. He's a wizard with computers, is Sean."

A Shifter computer geek. What a day.

Carly blew out her breath and made herself follow Sean the rest of the way without antics. She needed to get to Tiger and make sure he was all right. The fact that the huge, strong man had been shot, hurt, made her heart race and her mouth dry. He needed to be all right.

The small hospital outside the city limits to which Sean led Carly served a large portion of the population on the south and east side of town. Carly parked as close to the front door as she could. Connor got around the car faster than she could register and opened the door for her, helping her to her feet. Ethan had never done that.

Sean waited for them outside the front door, on his phone. "We're coming. Just keep him quiet."

Carly heard the exclamation on the other end before Sean closed the phone. He said nothing to Carly or Connor but strode in through the front door ahead of them.

Inside it was as crowded as Carly would have guessed from the packed parking lot, with mothers and kids waiting to be seen, nurses hurrying through halls, and the admin desk serving a long line of people. The smell of antiseptic covered the odors of worry and illness.

Sean moved without stopping to a back corridor then continued down it and onto an elevator, pushing the button for the top floor. When they stepped off the elevator at the top, Carly heard the noise.

The roar began at the end of the corridor, a wash of sound that flowed to them past every room and the nurses' station to the bank of elevators where Carly stood. The nurses' station was deserted, but a knot of people clustered at the other end of the hall.

Sean said something under his breath as he picked up the pace, but Connor, behind Carly, didn't keep his voice down.

"He's going to get himself killed, he is."

Sean kept walking, his broad back upright, moving swiftly. Carly jogged on her high heels to catch up.

The faces of the nurses and orderlies that turned to them were filled with fear. Three hard-faced men in black uniforms tried to intercept Sean, and another shout rose inside the room.

"You threatened him, didn't you?" an Irish voice said. "Are you that stupid, then?"

The men looked like private soldiers or security guards in all black fatigue-looking uniforms, but their hands and thick belts were empty. Carly saw why when she peeked around Sean into the hospital room.

The floor was littered with black detritus that Carly couldn't place at first, but then she saw they were pieces of automatic rifles, radios, and other things too broken to identify.

The roaring came from inside the room, followed by a repeated clank of something metal. Sean blocked most of her view, but Carly could see enough to make out the giant bulk of Tiger, barely covered by a hospital gown, on his feet, one hand fisted. He was pulling, pulling, pulling at the metal bar on the bed to which he was chained.

Near him were two more Shifters, one with a shaved head and tattoos wherever Carly could see skin, the other a Sean look-alike.

The tattooed man deflected a blow from Tiger's free fist in a practiced move. Enraged, Tiger struck out again, and the tattooed man blocked, twisting Tiger's arm behind his back. A spark jumped in the Collar around the tattooed man's neck.

"What in hell happened?" Sean demanded.

"Fucking guards happened," the tattooed guy snarled. "Nurse wanted to change his IV, the three boy wonders stuck their guns into him to hold him down while she did it. He broke out of one cuff. Guess the rest."

"Spike, let him go," the one who looked like Sean said. "Tiger. *Stop.*"

The last word reverberated through the room. Everyone stilled—guards, Spike, Sean, Connor, the guards, nurses, and orderlies behind them.

All except Tiger. He kept banging, roaring, his eyes yellow with rage. The Collar on his neck was silent, no matter how much he struck out or tried to rip his wrist from its restraint.

That didn't make sense. The Collars were supposed to shock the Shifters, Carly understood, if they ever got violent, to protect humans from their immense strength. The Collars went off in reaction to adrenaline and intent to harm, or so she'd heard. If a Shifter wasn't trying to hurt anyone, the Collar wouldn't do anything. They were meant to keep the Shifters peaceful, not to punish them all the time.

Tiger's Collar lay quietly, looking no different from Sean's or Connor's. That meant Tiger wasn't angry or trying to kill anyone.

He was scared.

They'd chained him to the bed and prodded him with guns, and this after he'd been shot. No wonder he was going crazy.

Carly ducked under Sean's arm and moved into the room.

"Lass, no," Sean said sharply, but Carly didn't stop.

Tiger yanked again at his bonds, and this time, the entire metal slat broke free from the bed. The slat danced at the end of the chain, Tiger still cuffed to it, as he swung around.

The Shifters near him leapt back. Tiger roared, a strange, animal-like sound in a human throat. Blood blossomed on the front of his gown as he hefted the bar like a weapon, crimson stains spreading. *Shot seven times.*

"Tiger!" Carly shouted into the noise.

Tiger's roaring ceased as though someone had hit a switch. The rod and chain clanged with the bed slat once, then went silent.

Tiger shoved his way past Spike and the other Shifter without seeming to notice them and reached for Carly. Carly stood her ground as Tiger clasped her by the shoulders, the chain and bed slat bumping gently into her back. He looked down at her with eyes tight with pain, the yellow gold tinged with red.

"I'm here," Carly said, touching one of his hands. "You okay?"

Her words and breath cut off when Tiger slammed his arms around her and pulled her against him. He buried his face in the curve of her neck and gathered her close.

"Carly." As though gaining strength from the name, his arms tightened around her, his voice rasping. "Carly."

"It's all right." Carly lightly smoothed his hair, finding it warm and soft. "I'm all right. But you're not, are you?"

Tiger held her in silence, his face against her neck, breathing in long, shuddering breaths.

"We need to take him into custody," she heard a man say behind her.

"No," the Shifter who seemed to be in charge said firmly. "The man's bleeding half to death. I had him settled. If you pull another weapon on him, it will be *me* breaking the guns."

Carly tried to loosen Tiger's hold, but he didn't let go. "You need to let them patch you up," she said to him. "Seven shots. Damn, Tiger, how are you still standing?"

"Shifters heal fast," Connor said.

The head Shifter growled. "Connor, *out*."

"He's not going to hurt me," Connor said. "I'm a cub, and a friend. He's not going to hurt Carly either, obviously. It's just trackers, Guardians, Shifter leaders, and dumb-ass security that upsets him." He came up to the two in a locked embrace. "You should see her car, Tiger. Classic Corvette. It's way cool. Let them sew you back up, and maybe she'll give you a ride home in it."

Tiger turned his head on Carly's shoulder to look at Connor. "I saw it. Helped her fix it."

"Oh man," Connor said in dismay. "You got to work on it? I have so much envy."

"Tiger came to my rescue," Carly said. "He performed a miracle."

Tiger lifted his head, his eyes quieter now, and touched her face. "He hurt you."

Carly shook her head. Ethan seemed unimportant at the moment. "He's an asshole. What happened? How did you get shot, for heaven's sake? I didn't mean to run off and leave you. I'm so sorry. I was upset."

Tiger cupped her face, rubbing his thumbs along her cheekbones. Not speaking, just gazing down into her eyes.

"Did *Ethan* shoot you?" Carly asked, her anger rising. She knew Ethan kept a gun, not because he shot for sport or anything, but because it made him feel superior to the rest of mankind.

"Doesn't matter," Tiger said.

It did matter. Carly's rage surged like a tide to cover her hurt and grief. "I'm gonna *kill* him. He screws around on me, then he shoots my friend for trying to help me. Don't worry, Tiger, by the time I and whatever lawyer I hire get finished with him, he'll be happy he can scrape what's left of himself off the sidewalk."

Her warmth and strength flowed into Tiger like a bright light. He'd been buried in darkness and pain, the guards jabbing with the guns awakening memories he'd long wanted to bury.

They'd taken his mate, they'd promised to take care of her, and she'd died. When he'd demanded to see her, more and more frantic, they'd beaten him back and threatened to kill him.

The memories of the past had fused with the reality of now, and Tiger had known in his heart that Carly, his beautiful mate, was dead. Liam had lied, Sean had lied, the guards had lied. They'd taken her away, and she was dead . . .

Memories slid away. Tiger had Carly *here,* her scent like a bite of cinnamon, her face petal-soft under his fingertips. He leaned to her to inhale her again, exhaling to leave his mark on her. *Mine.*

"Tiger," he heard Liam saying. Liam, the leader, the man he'd been told to obey.

Liam was a strong alpha, and the Shifters under his command felt the weight of his orders. Tiger had watched them all, even Liam's father, become slightly lesser in Liam's presence. Tiger was supposed to as well—if he obeyed Liam's orders and showed fealty, he could live in this Shiftertown in peace. Any challenge, and Liam would have to take him down.

Liam hadn't actually said all this specifically, but Tiger knew. Tiger knew everything Liam was thinking, because Liam's body language, no matter how subtle, revealed every thought.

Carly's body language showed only distress that Tiger was hurt. She didn't give a rat's ass about hierarchy, or who was alpha, or that she should bow her head and keep her gaze averted from Liam as a submissive must do.

Her entire focus was on Tiger, and Tiger alone. Everyone else was nonessential.

Carly's warmth entered his body wherever hers touched his, and her breath on his face was like sweet summer air. Tiger's pain lessened, and his breathing became easier.

The touch of a mate.

Carly moved in his embrace, trying to take a step back. Tiger wasn't ready to let her go. He held tighter, but Carly wriggled, twisting her arm around to touch the slat that still dangled from his wrist.

"Can someone take this off him?"

Connor sprang forward, lifting the bar that hung like a lead weight. He chortled. "They made the cuff and chain to withstand Shifter strength, but not the bed. Good job."

"Can you take it off?" Carly asked.

She was anxious, not afraid. The others wanted to bind him—Carly wanted to set him free.

"Get me a picklock, and I can open anything," Connor said.

Spike, in silence, handed Connor a stiff piece of wire. Where he'd obtained it, or what it was for, Tiger didn't know, but Connor grinned gleefully and started scraping at the handcuff. In a matter of seconds, the cuff loosened and fell from Tiger's wrist.

"That's got to feel better," Carly said. "Now, let's get you back into bed so the doctors can patch you up."

More people filled the corridor outside. Tiger tasted their fear. They shouldn't broadcast like that. A predator sensed a prey's fear, the predator homing in on and taking out the weakest. Dangerous.

"If he can't calm down, we need to chain him up again, ma'am," one of the black-clad men said. He was the commander, the leader of his tiny band. He had a weather-beaten face, though he was still young, for a human, and scarred. He'd been in battles. The man had shorn off all but a blond stubble of hair, his eyes were a light blue, and he had an air of authority. Not as much as Liam or any Shifter, but for a human, he was strong.

"He's calm," Liam said. "See? Lass, if you can get him back to bed, and to *stay still*, we can fix him up in a trice."

Tiger kept his arms around Carly. "I am healed."

Carly ran her hand down the front of his torso. Tiger couldn't stop his flinch of pain as she touched the raw wounds.

"Bullshit," she said clearly. "You're bleeding all over the place. Back to bed with you, mister."

"Better step back from him," the human leader said, his voice as hard as Liam's. "He's a danger to everyone in the facility and needs to be contained."

Carly turned around, still within Tiger's arms, to glare at the human. "What is with you? You need to leave him alone for two minutes. No wonder he's so upset."

She turned, sliding her arm around Tiger's waist, and

started guiding him to the bed. Tiger went without resist-
ing. Now, if she'd get into the bed *with* him and snuggle up
against his side, Tiger would be healed in no time. And he
wouldn't be afraid.

The other Shifters watched in awe as Tiger, calm and
quiet, walked with Carly back to the bed. He'd stopped
bleeding for now, but his gown was covered with blood,
and blood stained the sheets.

He didn't care. Tiger lowered himself onto the uncomfortable bed, then put his hand on Carly's wrist and tugged
her toward him.

Carly gave him a puzzled look, her gray green eyes red-
rimmed with crying. Tiger tugged harder. Carly lost her
balance and landed, sitting, on the bed next to him, her
warm hip against his side.

She gave a little laugh. "They can't work on you if I'm in
the bed with you, silly. I'm flattered, but I'll be in the way."

"Need you," Tiger said. He kept his voice soft, so only
she would hear, but then, Shifters had good hearing.

"Let her go," Liam said. "She's done enough. Thank
you, lass. I don't know who you are, but you're a bloody
miracle worker."

"She's my mate," Tiger said, his voice still not working
right, but it grew firmer as he tightened his grip on her.
"She stays."

CHAPTER FOUR

Carly's eyes widened. "What exactly are you talking about?"

"It doesn't work that way," Liam said quickly, over her words. "It's a bit different in Shiftertown, laddie. I've explained it to you."

Tiger closed his eyes. Liam, Sean, and Connor had told him about the mating rules—the mate-claim signaled to all other Shifters that the female was off-limits to all other males. The subsequent ceremonies performed by the clan leader, one under sunlight, one under the light of the full moon, bound the mates together under the eyes of the Father God and Mother Goddess.

But the Father God and Mother Goddess had never found Tiger in the basement of the experiment station during his nearly forty years of captivity. Why should Tiger wait for them to acknowledge his mate?

Dylan, Liam's father and a stickler for the rules of Shifters, had admitted to Tiger one day that the rituals were artificial, put into place at a time when Shifters had fought each other nearly to extinction. To avoid Shifter males battling each other to the death over every female, they'd come up with scent-marking and the mate-claim, and the sun and moon ceremonies performed by the clan leader.

Tiger had listened, wanting to learn everything he could about who and what he was. But he knew—and Dylan knew—that the rules didn't mean anything. A Shifter recognized his mate when he met her. He scented her, he saw her, he felt her heat, and he *knew*.

Carly was Tiger's mate. No doubt about it.

With steady hands, Tiger ripped open his annoying hospital gown and tossed the shreds to the floor. The sheets around his waist bared his chest and abdomen, tanned from working shirtless on cars with Connor. Red circles of bullet holes pockmarked his chest and stomach, blood smeared around them.

The holes had already half closed. Tiger pointed at them.

"The touch of a mate," he said to Liam. "Heals, you said. Iona said."

"Shifters are good at healing themselves," Liam answered, but with less conviction. "And you're a very strong Shifter."

A super Shifter, Iona, the woman who'd rescued him, had called him. Iona had been wonderful, and Tiger would always be fond of her. But she hadn't been his mate.

"Stop this before you confuse me more." Carly pulled away from Tiger and stood up. "You're saying I closed that up?" She pointed at a wound, red and angry. "Those holes still look pretty bad to me."

"They're not."

Tiger noted that everyone in the room stood a certain distance from the bed, as though an unseen barrier kept them back. They were afraid of coming too close to his mate, he thought in satisfaction. They were acknowledging her.

"I don't believe you," Carly said. "You look terrible, and I feel just awful for getting you hurt on top of everything else. So you let the doctors do their thing. *Please?*"

Tiger closed his hand around hers again. "Only if you stay."

She gave him the perplexed look again, then she let out her breath. "Oh, why not? I'm sure I'll be fired on top of everything else today. What the hell."

"We'll see you don't lose by helping us, lass," Liam said, in the reassuring way only he could. "Thank you."

"Least I can do. My mama always said a person should acknowledge everything she's responsible for, even if she didn't mean it." She paused. "Wish Ethan's mama had taught him that too."

Tiger felt her pain through her grip on his hand, and his anger surged again. He remembered the surprise and then outrage on Ethan's face when Carly had bounded through the door to find him sexing another woman. The man had blamed *Carly*. But a male didn't cheat on his mate. No matter what.

Which meant Carly had never truly been Ethan's mate, not even in the human understanding of the bond. With Ethan's act of betrayal, Carly was free of him. Free for Tiger to claim.

Another voice joined the throng. "Is he sedated?"

Tiger recognized the doctor who, through the first haze of Tiger's rage and pain, had extracted what bullets remained in Tiger's flesh. Tiger had come awake on the table and started to change in his panic, which had led to his being chained to the bed again.

Stupid clinic should have let Connor be there to calm him down. Then Tiger might not have flashed back to the sterile experiment rooms in what humans called Area 51, might not have been completely terrified.

"He'll be all right," Liam said, using his most charming, most Irish tones. "He just needed a bit of calming, as you can see."

"Then I need him in the OR to finish."

The doctor started to walk away, leaving the three nurses and another man in white scrubs looking unhappy.

"No," Tiger said. Everything in him tensed again.

Carly's brow puckered as she ran a soothing hand along Tiger's wrist. "It's okay. He just wants to sew you up."

"He does it here. I don't go back to that room."

"Why not? It's where he'll have all the stuff he needs to put you back together, and sterilized so you won't get an infection."

She sounded so reasonable, so calming. And yet, she hadn't seen the rooms they'd taken him to in the stone building in the desert, where needles and probes had pierced his flesh, where electrodes had crackled through his brain and under his skin. The experimenters wanted to see how much he could stand, so they put him through everything imaginable.

"It makes him remember bad things," Connor said.

The cub, the youngest of them here, understood. Connor had always understood Tiger more than the others had.

Carly called after the doctor. "Wait. Why can't you work on him in here?"

The doctor, looking harassed, turned back. "Because the light is bad, and I need my equipment."

"Bring it in. It's either that or have all these people fighting to get him to your operating room again."

The doctor ran a practiced eye over Tiger. "If you guarantee he'll sit there and let me finish, I'll do it. I'll give him something for the pain, but it's still going to hurt. If not, I'm putting him under heavy sedation, very heavy, you understand? Most people die under that kind of sedation, even Shifters."

"He'll be good." Carly beamed a smile at the man. "Promise. Right?" she asked Tiger.

Tiger closed his hand around Carly's wrist, feeling it slender and fragile, bones covered with silken skin. "If you stay."

"I'll stay." Carly turned her smile on him, and suddenly the world was right.

Tiger said nothing. He stroked his hand up and down Carly's forearm, mesmerized by the softness of her, the sweet scent. The doctor walked away, still annoyed. The other Shifters remained outside a certain perimeter around the bed, as did the soldiers behind them.

It didn't matter. Carly had said she'd stay with him. Tiger would make sure it was forever.

Carly watched the doctor clean Tiger's wounds, medicate them, suture the biggest ones, and steri-tape the others, with bandages for all. Tiger lay quietly while he worked, making no noise, holding Carly's hand but not squeezing it.

No way could Carly have withstood someone poking and prodding tender wounds without sedation. She'd have flinched, fought, cried out, or at least snarled some swear words. Tiger did nothing, said nothing, didn't move. The commander of the soldiers watched him, but kept his men back.

When the doctor finally walked out, leaving the cleanup to the nurses, Tiger pushed the sheets aside and rolled out of bed, stark naked except for his bandages. Carly tried not to look, but it was sure hard not to. He was a big man, and not just tall and wide. He was big all over. *All* over. She averted her gaze, but she had to force herself. He was . . . mesmerizing.

"Where do you think you're going?" she asked him.

"Home." The word came out with strength, but also with a wistfulness.

"You can barely walk."

"I can do it."

Tiger looked stronger, that was true. But, crap, he'd been *shot*. In the stomach.

Liam, who apparently was Sean's brother, started to put his hand on Tiger's shoulder, then lifted it away before he touched him. He turned to the head soldier. "You can release him to my custody now. He'll be fine."

The soldier frowned, light-colored brows drawing down. "Give me a minute." He turned away, signaling his men to keep watch, pulled out a cell phone, and made a call quietly in the corner.

"We can take it from here," Liam said to the nurses. "He's good at healing himself, truly."

"He can't do any lifting, bending, running, anything stressful," the head nurse said in a severe tone. "He has to keep the wounds clean, the dressings changed, and he has to take all the antibiotics. Every single pill. Can you get him to do all that?" She looked at Carly.

"Me?" Carly said, touching her chest. "I don't—"

"We'll look after him just fine." Liam took the piece of paper with the prescription and gave the nurse a smile that would make any woman melt. The nurse, middle-aged, hard-faced, experienced with difficult patients, held out a few seconds before she thawed.

"All right, then," she said, her tone softer. "You call if there are any problems." Now she spoke to Liam and Liam alone.

The soldier turned back, his frown even more formidable. "My commander told me to let you take him," he said to Liam. The man obviously disagreed—strongly—with his commander, but he didn't look the type to disobey orders. "But if there's any more trouble with him, I'll have to take him in."

"Right you are," Liam said, not sounding worried.

Tiger was already heading out of the room, pulling Carly behind him. Connor stepped in front of them and held up an armful of folded clothes that smelled newly washed. "You're forgetting something."

The nurses didn't hide their need to stare at Tiger's body. They'd seen their fair share of naked flesh, but Tiger was different.

He was all muscle, with a liquid tan on his torso and arms, pale below the belt. Large all over, but not too bulging, tight and strong rather than overly bulked. Tiger wore his nakedness casually—Carly noticed that the other Shifters hadn't seemed to remember he was unclothed until Connor had stopped him at the door.

Tiger slid on the jeans and T-shirt without bothering

with underwear. Connor insisted Tiger put on the combat boots he'd brought instead of going barefoot, and Tiger growled impatiently as he tugged them on.

Tiger kept hold of Carly's hand as they walked through the corridor, down the elevator, and out to the parking lot. Patients and hospital staff stopped what they were doing and stared as the contingent of Shifters moved through.

Liam led, giving a smile and a nod to everyone he passed. The tall tattooed man with the shaved head followed him, drawing more attention. Behind him came Tiger and Carly, then Connor and Sean bringing up the rear. Kids stared, women's lips parted, men moved to stand protectively in front of women and children.

No one said a word, but again, body language spoke volumes. The Shifters were feared. Even tamed, controlled, and regulated, humans sensed the violence barely contained. Humans pretended to despise or be fascinated by the creatures, but the adult humans who watched these Shifters walk by and out of the building exhibited basic, watchful fear.

Carly had never thought much about Shifters one way or the other. She knew the ones in Austin lived in the Shiftertown, which was out by the old airport, but she rarely had cause to drive that way in the course of her day-to-day life.

"Look at this car, Liam," Connor said when they reached the Corvette. "Isn't it awesome?"

"And not mine," Carly said. "I need to take it back to Ethan's."

She stopped, the words sticking in her throat. Carly never wanted to drive up his driveway again, to see the house that she was supposed to have moved into next week. She'd never look at it again without experiencing a vision of Ethan, pants around his ankles, thrusting hard and fast into the woman on the counter.

A knife-edge of pain went through her heart. She gasped for breath, and then Tiger's hand was on her arm, turning her to him. He laid a large hand gently between her breasts, right over the hurt.

Carly looked up through tears at him. His golden eyes held sympathy, understanding. "You were never his," he said.

"I guess not." Carly tried to laugh. Tiger's hand was warm, his touch over her heart soothing. The image of Ethan blurred, the pain still there but moving away from her immediate focus.

Connor broke in. "Hey, if you need me to drive the car back, I'll do it." He held out his hand. "I'll be careful. Honest. Or, I can wreck it for you, if you want."

"Sean will take it," Liam said sternly. He looked around the little group. "And Spike." His smile came back as he observed the six-foot-six, tightly muscled man with the shaved head and tatts all over his body.

Sean laughed. "Good choice. Can't wait to watch this."

Carly too would love to see Ethan's face when first the handsome Sean and then the edgy biker-from-hell Spike emerged from Ethan's beloved 'Vette.

Carly had to turn from Tiger to hand the keys to Sean. Tiger stayed next to her, not even a step away. "Be careful," Carly said to Sean. "Ethan has powerful friends. I don't want him arresting you for stealing the car, or for scaring him."

"Don't you worry about that, lass," Sean said, closing his hand around the keys. "I'll keep Spike on a leash."

Spike growled, a wildcat sound, and showed his teeth in a smile.

"Sure I can't come with you?" Connor asked hopefully.

"No," Liam said. "I'm giving Carly a lift home—or wherever she wants to go—and you're taking Tiger back to Shiftertown."

"Carly stays with me." Tiger's growl cut over Liam's order. His warmth covered Carly's side, straight through the white dress that wasn't so white anymore.

"Hmm." Liam didn't jump to tell Tiger to let her go. The others hung back as well, as though hesitating to come between a dog and his treat.

I guess it's up to me.

"Tiger, honey, I have to go." Carly rubbed his forearm, then rubbed it again, liking the feel of tight skin over steel. "I'm sorry I dragged you into my problems, and that you suffered for them."

Tiger stared down at her as though her words were meaningless to him. The stare was intense, unnerving.

"I'll come see how you're doing tomorrow, all right?" Carly said.

"Stay with me." The words were a statement, not a request.

"I can't. I have to go home. Look at me, I'm a mess. Then I have to find Armand and explain to him why I left him in the lurch today of all days. If I'm lucky, he'll be sympathetic and give me a few dollars severance pay when he fires me."

Again, Tiger's eyes didn't register the gist of her words, only that she was speaking. When she finished, he tilted his head, like a cat examining its prey. "I will take you."

"No, you won't." Carly tapped his chest gently, avoiding the bandages under the shirt. "You'll go home and rest, like the nurses said, and take your medication. If you run around the city, you'll open the wounds again and need another clean shirt. I said I'd come see how you were doing, and I'm not lying. Least I can do." She stood on tiptoe and kissed his cheek, tasting the bristle of whiskers. "I like you, Tiger."

Tiger's eyes softened as he looked down at her. Carly was aware of the others listening, poised, amazingly still. No human being could stand that still.

Tiger touched his cheek where Carly had kissed him, then he touched her cheek. His fingers were featherlight, though she'd seen him break apart the bed in the hospital as though it were paper.

"Connor," Tiger said, the deep rumble in his voice again. "Go with her."

"I said *I'd* take her home," Liam broke in.

"No." Tiger's word was harsh. "Not you. Not anyone but Connor."

Liam studied Tiger a moment, then switched his gaze to Connor, who was trying his best to look innocent and neutral. Finally Liam nodded. "All right. Connor."

"Keep her safe," Tiger said sternly.

Connor relaxed from his watchful stance. "You got it, big guy," he said to Tiger. "This means I get to take your bike, right, Sean?"

Sean got in on the growling, looking annoyed, but he pulled out his keys and tossed them to Connor. "Not a scratch, not a speck of dirt."

"Would I let you down, Uncle Sean? Come on, Carly, it's a sweet ride."

They expected her to go home on the back of a motorcycle? In this dress? Well, it was a day for the bizarre.

Tiger didn't let Carly go that easily. He pulled her close, leaned into her, and buried his face in her hair again. She thought maybe he'd try to kiss her, right there in the parking lot, and wondered what she'd do if he did. Being kissed by Tiger would be . . .

She had no idea, but her body went hot and shivery at the same time. He was strong, powerful, and a little bit crazy.

Tiger straightened up. He didn't kiss her, but he traced her cheek, staring down into her eyes again before he finally lifted his hand away.

Connor took that as a cue to walk toward the row of motorcycles parked in front of the clinic, gesturing for Carly to follow him.

"See you, Tiger," Carly said, then walked off after Connor. Her shoes were killing her, so she paused to take them off and sling them from her fingers. She'd be more comfortable riding without them.

When she looked back over her shoulder, she saw Tiger's gaze still fixed on her; he stood motionless while the others made moves to go. Carly gave him a little wave and turned to follow Connor again, but she felt Tiger's stare on her back the whole way.

* * *

"Why did Tiger want *you* to bring me home, and not Liam?" Carly asked as she let Connor into her house.

She tried not to look at the suitcases she'd pulled out of the closet so she could pack to move in with Ethan. Good thing she hadn't had time to start moving her stuff into storage, even though she'd already put a lot into boxes. Ethan had encouraged her to hang on to her house and rent it out—it wouldn't be as good as owning a commercial property, but it would bring her some real income, he'd said. He didn't consider being an art gallery assistant a viable or long-lasting occupation.

"Hmm?" Connor asked. He contemplated the few small paintings on the living room wall that artists had given Carly as gifts. "Why me? Because I'm a cub. Not a threat."

"A cub?" Carly looked him up and down. "You said that before. You can't be much younger than I am."

"Just turned twenty-two. That's cub age for a Shifter. When I hit about twenty-eight, or maybe later, I'll start my Transition, which I'm so not looking forward to, trust me. But after that, I'll be full grown, ready to find my own mate. *That* part I'm looking forward to."

Carly saw a young man, college-aged, lanky but tough, as tall as his uncles if not as bulked. When he was twenty-eight and looking for his mate, women were going to line up for him. She was surprised they weren't following him around now, drooling.

"But I'm not a Shifter," she said. "Why should you have to wait six years before you go out with a human woman?'

"I don't. But I'm not in a hurry. Not having reached my Transition means I don't have the mating frenzy yet. So, sure, I could go out with you, or whatever human girl took my fancy, and we could kiss and cuddle, and even have sex. But I wouldn't feel the need to scent-mark you, hide you from all other males, and have sex with you until we both couldn't walk, or until you started a cub. Whichever came first."

Carly stopped. Her shoes still hung from her fingers, her feet enjoying the cool of her tile floor. "That's what Shifters do?"

"Yep. Females as well as males."

"So, Tiger was afraid that if Liam drove me home he might . . ."

"Drag you off to bed and sex you 'til you screamed? Aye, he was. Even though Liam has a mate of his own, and a little cub—Katriona; she's so cute—to Tiger, he's just another full-grown Shifter male, not to be trusted."

"What about Tiger? I guess I don't have to worry about this mating frenzy with him—he's just been shot."

"I don't know." Connor shook his head. "I can't tell you lies, Carly. Tiger's my friend, and I want to help him, but he's dangerous. And tough. And not quite right in the head." He touched his temple.

"He didn't seem that scary to me. Although . . . see what a great judge of character I was about Ethan." Carly heaved a sigh and walked on into her bedroom. "Be right back."

She closed the door so she could shimmy out of the dress and into some comfortable shorts and a top. In her bathroom, she washed her face and hands, remembering that she'd expected to come home and cry and cry. Worry about poor Tiger had erased that need, but now that her immediate adrenaline rush had gone, she felt shaky and weak. And hungry.

"Want me to order some pizza?" she asked Connor as she walked out. "I'm starving. You can take one home with you. Least I can do."

Connor had lounged back in her living room armchair and was flipping channels with the remote. "Oh, I'm not going home. When Tiger said, *keep her safe*, he meant twenty-four seven. Or at least until I take you back to Shiftertown."

CHAPTER FIVE

As Carly stared at him, Connor looked away and skimmed through more channels. "Hey, you've got the sports package. Sweet."

Carly grabbed the remote from him and clicked off the TV. "Twenty-four seven?"

"Come on, lass. I don't get these channels at home. Shifters aren't allowed. Been forever since I saw a decent football match."

"You're to stay with me until I go back and visit Tiger? I said I would. Doesn't he believe me?"

Connor let out a slow sigh. "He believes you. If you'd lied, he'd know—if you lie about anything, he'll know. He wants you protected. He's old-fashioned, is Tiger, but he's not wrong. I got the job because, like I said, I'm a cub and right now the only Shifter he trusts with you."

"He wants me protected from what? My mama raised me to take care of myself, and I made it to twenty-six without a bodyguard. Why do I suddenly need to be protected?"

"Because he's *Tiger*. He gets a little . . . focused. Besides, he scent-marked you. While that technically means other males have to back off, there are enough asshole Shifters out there who still might try to steal you, now that they know you're friendly to Shifters."

"Friendly to Shifters? I didn't *know* any Shifters until today."

Connor gave her a tight grin. "And you didn't run away screaming. That puts you ahead of most human women, except the groupies. And they don't necessarily want a Shifter for a mate—they're just in it for the titillation."

"There are Shifter *groupies*?"

"Sure. They come to the bar Liam manages, or to the dance clubs, wanting to be with Shifters. Men and women alike. Shifters are usually game for a little grope in the corner, so the groupies go away happy. But they don't want to move in with us."

"Does Tiger think I'm one of those?"

"Don't think so. Tiger doesn't understand the groupies. He's not interested. Besides, most of them take one look at him and flee the other way."

"Why?" Carly sank to the sofa, still holding the remote. "Tiger's big, so I suppose that could scare people, but he was nice to me. I know he went crazy in that hospital room, but he had three guys pointing guns at him after they'd chained him to the bed. I'd go crazy too."

"He's . . ." Connor moved his hands as though trying to find the right words. "He's different from other Shifters. More . . . intense."

"Since I don't know much about Shifters at all, how am I supposed to tell?"

"People did bad things to him before he came to live with us. I can't tell you about them until Liam says it's okay, but trust me—bad things."

Carly thought about the pain she'd seen in his eyes, wells of it that went deep. More pain than what he'd suffered today, much more. "Poor guy."

"Huh. That poor guy is strong as a truck, lass. Tell you what, let me hang out and watch a match or three, and when you're ready to go to Shiftertown, I'll take you. I'm not in a hurry, give it a day, a week. As long as Tiger thinks I'm looking after you, he'll be cool."

"You'd stay with me for a week, would you?" Carly asked, standing up again. "Watching my television and eating my pizza? Don't you have school or something? Or a job?"

Connor shrugged. "It's summer break. My final year starts in mid-August, then I grad-ee-ate. I help out in the bar between semesters if Liam needs me, and when I want some cash, but he's good for now." Connor leaned back, crossed his booted feet, and held out his hand to her for the remote. "Plenty of time for me to be catching up on sports action."

Carly sighed and slapped the remote into his open palm. "Well, you might be able to turn into a snarling beast, but in my world, you're still a *guy*."

"Thank you." Connor clicked the TV on. "Oh, righteous." He punched the air as the soccer players on the screen did something Carly couldn't follow.

"Want a beer?" Carly asked him, an ironic note in her voice.

"Sure, if you've got one. I like a good Guinness, but I'm not picky. Nothing too watery, love. Go, go, *go!* Aw, you bastard."

He yelled at the television, and Carly ducked back into the kitchen to see what beer she had in the fridge, if any. She needed to go grocery shopping—she hadn't stocked up, because she'd thought she'd be moving out.

Everything was reminding Carly of Ethan and his infidelity. What a frigging mess. She'd have to give him back the giant diamond ring she didn't wear because she was terrified of losing it. She'd have to tell her family and all her friends that the wedding was off before it was even planned. She'd sent out invitations to a big party at Ethan's for next Saturday, to celebrate the engagement. Well, Ethan could call off that party himself. His own stupid fault.

The *why* of it kept screaming through her head. If Ethan had asked Carly to move in with him, if he'd given her a rock worth who knew how much, if they'd arranged a party to show off what a brilliant couple they were, *why* had he been screwing another woman on his kitchen counter?

Why were men so fucking stupid?

Carly popped the top off the bottle of beer she'd brought out for Connor and threw the cap into the sink with extra force. She took a gulp of beer before she realized it. Never mind. The cold, fizzing fullness of it tasted good.

She needed to call Armand and explain what had happened, but she put it off some more. Armand could bluster, even though he might be sympathetic. He had a temper and could go on and on, even when he wasn't mad at Carly.

Carly heaved another long sigh and upended the beer bottle again. Then she looked at it. "Damn it, this was supposed to be for Connor."

She turned back to the refrigerator to fetch another when the opaque square window of her kitchen door darkened, and someone knocked politely.

As Carly went to answer the door, she saw out the window that a black SUV had pulled up in front of her house, its windows so tinted she couldn't see inside.

She opened the door, beer in hand. Two men stood there, a smaller man in a suit nearly hidden behind a tall guy in black fatigues, the head soldier who'd been in Tiger's room. She remembered his light blue eyes, his shaved head with pale-colored stubble, his hard face.

"Carly Randal?" the soldier asked.

"He's not here," she said, still holding the door. "He went home."

The soldier gave her a careful look. "Who?"

"Tiger. The injured man you tried to shoot. He went home like a good boy. What do you want?"

The suited man looked around the soldier. "To speak with you, Ms. Randal." He sounded nervous, not smooth as someone who'd arrived in a sleek SUV should sound. "About Shifters."

"Why? There are plenty in Shiftertown." For some reason, Carly did not want these men in here, did not want them to find Connor in her living room. In spite of Connor being taller than she was, and strong—she'd felt his strength when she'd held on to him during the ride home—Carly sensed that here in her house, Connor was vulnerable.

Would she have thought that if he hadn't explained that he was a cub? She didn't know. All Carly did know was that she did *not* want this trigger-happy soldier to start pointing guns at Connor.

"Please, Ms. Randal," the suit said. "It's important."

"Let us in, Ms. Randal," the soldier said, his blue eyes hard. "We have a warrant."

Carly's knowledge of police procedure came mostly from television, but she thought that a warrant meant they could come in and search her place legally, whether she liked it or not. But search for what?

Worth it to battle it out in court? Or let these guys in, try to keep them in the kitchen, and see what they wanted?

If Ethan had anything to do with this, she'd . . .

Damn him, she should have told Sean to shove the Corvette off a cliff.

Carly let out an annoyed sigh, opened the door, and gestured with the beer bottle. "Can I get you anything? Probably not alcohol, huh? Coffee? If I can find my coffeemaker. I packed it already."

"No thank you," the suited man said. "Is anyone here but you?"

"Not really your business," Carly said.

Soldier was around her and through the kitchen door before she could stop him. Carly put the beer on the counter and hurried after him, but when she reached the living room, it was empty. The television still blared but was tuned to a cooking show, the running soccer players replaced by cooks madly chopping and sautéing to beat a deadline. Connor was nowhere in sight.

Soldier walked from the living room down the hall to the bedrooms. Carly called after him, "Hey, do you mind?" She'd left her dress and underwear on her bedroom floor. How embarrassing.

The soldier returned after a cursory glance at the rooms in the back. Suit had followed Carly into the living room, and now he sat down on the sofa and unsnapped a briefcase. Soldier took up a stance at the end of the couch. Carly picked up the remote and clicked off the television, but remained standing, one hand on her hip, the other holding the remote.

"So, what do y'all want?"

"Your help, Ms. Randal," the suit said. "I want you to tell me what you know about Shifters."

Carly blinked, transferring her gaze to the soldier, who remained on his feet. A black-butted pistol peeked from a holster at his hip.

"I don't know anything about Shifters," Carly answered the suit. She pointed at the soldier. "This guy was aiming at him. I bet he knows more than I do."

The suit smiled. He wasn't cold and slick, like so many businessmen in suits—Ethan's friends, for example. He had soft eyes, hands that had never seen a manicure, hair growing out of a once-good cut.

"Would you like to know more about them?" Suit asked. "Perhaps for pay? What I'm trying to do, Ms. Randal—awkwardly— is offer you a job."

"I already have a job." *Well, maybe.* "What did you have in mind?"

"I want you to find out about Shifters. Talk to them, interact with them, see what makes them tick. And then you and I sit down and talk about it."

"You mean spy on them?" Carly thought about Tiger, all shot up because of Ethan, Connor so young but promising to protect her, Liam and Sean—the hottie Irish brothers—trying to keep Tiger under control, Sean and Connor convincing her to come to the hospital with them, to see if she could help. "Seems kind of underhanded. What are you? CIA? FBI?"

The man in the suit chuckled. "No, I'm an anthropology professor. My name is Brennan, Lee Brennan. Here's my card." He plucked a pale rectangle from his briefcase and held it out to her. Sure enough, the card said he was Lee Brennan, PhD, associate professor of anthropology at the University of Texas, Austin.

"Why does an anthropology professor need a bodyguard?" she asked him.

Carly tried to hand the card back to Brennan, but he shook his head. "Keep it. My number and e-mail are there, along with the website for my project. Walker isn't my bodyguard. He's my friend, or at least, a former student. He keeps an eye out for good case studies for me and called me today after you left the hospital."

Carly sank to the edge of a chair, still holding the card and the remote. "And you thought *I'd* be a good case study?"

"Not you. The man they had to chain to the hospital bed. What was his name?"

"I don't know. I've been calling him Tiger, because I guess he's a tiger."

"And that is very unusual. The Feline types of Shifter tend more to lion, leopard, even jaguar. Tiger is rare. I don't think we've even seen a tiger in the Texas Shiftertowns."

"So you want me to make friends with him and then tell you all about him?" Carly asked. "That still seems pretty underhanded."

"Be as honest with him as you want. The Shifters have heard of me and know about my project. I am interested in this tiger, and would love to view him and Shiftertown through a fresh pair of eyes. You'd be helping me out and earning a little money at the same time."

"How much money, exactly?"

Brennan chuckled again. "That depends on my funding, and I'm always underfunded. But I do have money budgeted for a research assistant. If I use you as an outside consultant, you won't have to enroll in the university, though there will be paperwork to sign before I can get you paid. There's always paperwork. Everyone talks about the paperless society, but there's no way a giant bureaucracy will ever achieve it. There's always some form that has to be hand-signed, electronic signatures not accepted."

Carly turned his card around in her fingers. "Can I think about it?"

Brennan creeped her out a little bit, no matter that he seemed friendly and legit. Maybe because he'd showed up out of the blue, at her house, knowing exactly where she lived, when she'd never met him before. Why hadn't he called her, e-mailed her, approached her at the hospital? And who was this Walker guy, really?

"Take your time, Ms. Randal," Brennan said. "My study is ongoing, and Shifters live far longer than we do."

"Tell me something." Carly fixed Walker with a steely look. "If I take this job, will Mr. Walker follow me around, armed to the teeth? Did you think an art gallery assistant was so dangerous that you had to bring a Glock or whatever that is into my house?"

"Walker's my first name," Walker said. He was the only one of the three of them who hadn't sat down. "Captain Walker Danielson. Carrying a gun is part of my job."

"What, like *Walker, Texas Ranger*?"

His hard-faced mask slipped, and he looked a little embarrassed, as though people tried to make that joke all the time. "Not quite."

Carly assessed him again. He was kind of cute, in the I'm-a-hard-bitten-soldier kind of way, but she couldn't forget how ready he'd been to shoot Tiger.

"Are you CIA, FBI, whatever alphabet agency?"

"Department of the Interior. Shifter Bureau."

"Oh." Carly had never heard of the Shifter Bureau, but she knew that Shifters were regulated. At least, articles and TV reports reassured the public of this all the time. Again, she realized how far Shifters had been off her radar—she'd given no thought to how they were regulated, or why, or who did it.

"And your job is what?" Carly asked Walker. "Intimidation?"

"I'm an officer in the Special Forces attachment to the Shifter Bureau South," Walker answered, the red at his cheekbones vanishing. "I and my men are called in when there's a problem, such as a Shifter going crazy in a hospital."

"Walker thought I'd be interested in having a look at this Shifter," Dr. Brennan said. "He seems to be a little different from the others, and a tiger, which is odd, as I've said. I need someone to help me get close to him."

"Can't you just call the Shifters and set up an appointment?" Carly thought about Liam, who'd put the nurses in Tiger's room at their ease with one look. "I'm sure they'd give you the information or let you interview him."

Brennan looked pained. "I have talked to them—to Liam Morrissey and his father. A while ago. They made it clear that I wasn't welcome to return."

"So you want me to sneak information about them to you behind their backs?" Carly said, annoyed. "You know, I'm getting pretty tired of men who want to sneak around today."

Brennan looked puzzled, but he couldn't know what Carly was talking about. "The Morrisseys made it clear that *I* wasn't welcome in Shiftertown," Brennan said. "Not that they object to me carrying on my research from afar. But I want to respect their wishes. An assistant would be helpful, especially a female one. Women seem to get along better with Shifters than men."

From what Connor had said, the Shifters seemed to regard all males as threats. Not surprising that they hadn't liked Brennan, then.

"I'll have to think about it." Carly stood up, wanting Brennan to get the idea that the interview was over.

Brennan didn't. He sat leafing through his briefcase. "I can't fit you out with fancy equipment—digital recorders, laptops, and the like. No budget. A steno pad and pen will have to be the way to go, unless you have your own laptop. If I hire you on, you can write that off as a business expense."

"I said I'd have to think about it, Dr. Brennan."

Walker, having never sat down, glanced through the blinds to Carly's front drive. "Who's that?"

Carly went to the window to look, even though she had to lean over Brennan on the sofa to do it. She'd expected to see Connor trying to ride away on his motorcycle, but instead she saw Armand climbing out of his BMW, Yvette exiting the other side. Both were talking, loudly, in French, carrying on whatever animated conversation they'd begun inside the car.

"My boss," Carly said turning away. Armand looked angry, and Yvette was yelling at him—Carly could hear them as she made her way through the tiled foyer to open the front door. She didn't know enough French to understand what they were yelling about, but she had a pretty good idea.

"Carly!" Armand said in his earsplitting roar as soon as Carly pulled open the door. *"Ma petite."* The big bear of a man threw his arms around Carly and dragged her against his soft body. "You are all right. I heard of a shooting at Ethan's house, and you were nowhere to be found. I was so worried . . ."

Carly had held up all the way to the hospital, throughout her concern about Tiger, having Connor stick to her, even Brennan's weird request, but now, embraced by the fatherly Armand, she wanted to let go, hang on to him, and sob. Armand had been more of a father to her than her own ever had been.

"Carly, you poor thing." Yvette patted her cheek as she stepped into the house, her rings cool on Carly's hot face. "We heard about the shooting at Ethan's house on the news, and Armand said you'd been going back there, and we had to come and make sure you were all right. But others have come too. Who are these people?"

Yvette had halted in the archway to the living room, staring at Brennan and Walker. Yvette was tall and willowy, a brunette with short and sleek hair, her pencil-slim dress hugging her figure and emphasizing her long legs. At fifty, she still looked like the runway model she'd been at twenty.

Brennan's mouth was slightly open; he was finally reacting like a man instead of a data-collecting machine. Yvette had that effect on unsuspecting males. Walker, on the other hand, didn't appear to be impressed by her. He only watched Yvette and Armand, his expression unchanging.

"That's Dr. Brennan, from UT," Carly said. "And his friend Walker. They were just leaving."

Walker at least could take a hint. He shut the professor's briefcase for him, and Brennan finally got to his feet.

"You have my card," Brennan said as he straightened his tie and took up his briefcase. "Give me a call in the next few days, Ms. Randal. I want to do this. Ma'am." He gave the straight-faced Yvette a nod and a smile and then walked out the door without looking at Carly.

Walker followed him without a good-bye, but Carly saw Walker look over Armand and Yvette again, and then the rest of the house, with an assessing eye. Brennan called to him from outside, and Walker shut the door.

"Interesting people," Yvette said. She took up a tote bag that Armand had dropped when he'd embraced Carly and headed for the kitchen. "We're cooking dinner for you, after your hard day. I told Armand it wasn't your fault."

Armand released Carly, patted her shoulders, and went after his wife. "How was I to know our Carly was in danger? Tell us everything, Carly. What happened?"

"And who is *that*?" Yvette asked sharply, frozen in the act of taking a wine bottle from the brown canvas bag.

Her blue eyes were now fixed on Connor, who leaned casually against the wall next to the sliding glass door that led to the back patio.

CHAPTER SIX

C arly yelped and jammed her hand to her chest. "Connor," she said, gasping. "Don't *do* that. I thought you'd
gone."

"Not me." Connor moved to the counter with natural
grace—Feline grace, Carly supposed. "I was told to look
out for you, and I'm doing it." Connor leaned his arms on
the counter and gazed with interest at Yvette's open canvas
bag. "Are those shallots in there? And bell peppers? Our
Sean makes them into a kick ass ratatouille. Only he calls
it Irish stew."

Armand came to stand next to Yvette, and Connor
extended a young and sinewy hand at them from the end of
a well-muscled arm. "I'm Connor. Connor Morrissey. Who
are you, if you don't mind my asking?"

They kept staring at him, taking in his Collar above his
T-shirt, his good-natured tanned face, his tall Shifter body.
His eyes, cobalt blue like both his uncles', were watchful.
He and Walker had much the same look, Carly realized,
except Connor smiled.

"It's all right," Carly said quickly to Connor. "This is

Armand, my boss, and his wife, Yvette. They're friends, good friends."

"I'm seeing that." Connor leaned the slightest bit forward, inhaling a little. "Not a threat."

"Where'd you disappear to?" Carly asked nervously. "I thought Dr. Brennan and that Walker guy *were* a threat."

"Yes, and it wouldn't be so good if someone from the Shifter Bureau found a Shifter in your house, would it?" Connor asked, his friendly look unwavering. "I laid low. Not so low I couldn't get back in here if you needed me, plus I took the opportunity to call Liam." He showed the cell phone in his hand, then shoved it into his pocket. "I gave him the all clear just now, but he might overreact. Liam does sometimes." He shrugged, as though the actions of his uncle were unfathomable to him.

"Overreact how?" Carly asked.

"He might send reinforcements. His trackers. Don't worry, it will take a few minutes for them to get here, and Liam might change his mind."

"How many more?" Yvette demanded. She took three red peppers out of her bag. "I only brought so much."

Connor gestured to her. "Cook for Carly. She needs it. Ronan and Ellison aren't much into fancy food anyway. Sean's the gourmet."

Yvette took a chef's knife out of her bag. Connor watched her very closely, but Yvette only rinsed off the peppers, cored them, and started chopping them, then the shallots. Armand had water boiling on the stove, and Yvette briefly plunged tomatoes into the pot to split their skins so she could peel them and then chop them up.

Carly stood in kind of a daze while Yvette went through the soothing motions of cooking. Connor watched Yvette's every move as she oiled a sauté pan and tossed the vegetables and tomatoes into it.

Armand uncorked a bottle of dark red wine, poured a glass, and shoved it at Carly. Connor had already helped himself to the beer Carly had left on the counter when Brennan arrived.

"Tell us what happened to you," Armand said.

The wine, the warmth in the house, and the smell of one of Yvette's excellent meals in the making loosened Carly's tongue. She told them the story, without inflection, without crying, holding it all in as the words came out. She told them about giving Tiger a ride, finding Ethan with the other woman, forgetting about Tiger as she rushed away from Ethan's, and Tiger getting shot by Ethan and ending up in the hospital.

Her friends listened in shock, horror, and sympathy. Yvette took out her anger by banging the vegetables around in the pan.

"He cannot shoot people and get away with it," Armand said, thunder in his voice. "A Shifter is a person, eh? Like this one." He gestured with his wineglass at Connor. "I could never shoot him. He looks like my nephew."

"Glad to hear it." Connor winked. "I wouldn't shoot you either."

"Ethan must be arrested," Armand said.

"He'll claim self-defense," Carly said. She drained her glass and reached for the wine bottle to pour another. "That's what he did when he shot his new pool man in the leg last year. Poor kid climbed the fence because the gate hadn't been unlocked for him. Ethan saw him, said he thought he was a burglar, and shot at him. Ethan was very apologetic and paid the hospital bill, but he was never arrested for it, and the kid lost a year's worth of work. Ethan knows powerful people."

"As do I," Armand said without modesty. "I will call my lawyer. The Shifters can sue Ethan if the police will do nothing. And you shall sue him for breach of contract."

"No." Carly lifted her hands, still holding her glass of wine. "If the Shifters want to go after him, fine. But I don't want to face Ethan again. Not in a courtroom, not through lawyers. I'm done. It's over." Tears stung her eyes. No use crying, she told herself. Good riddance. "At least I found out he was a lying, cheating scumbag *before* the wedding."

The tears spilled from her eyes anyway. Today had been

horrible, *horrible*. A person didn't walk away from a two-year relationship and an engagement with a laugh and a shrug.

"Carly." Armand was there with another hug.

"He will be sorry," Yvette said matter-of-factly.

"Spike and Sean will scare the shite out of him," Connor said. "Trust me."

"He'll shoot them too," Carly said, worried.

"No, he won't. Sean's very good at talking people out of hurting anyone, including himself. And Spike just has to stand there. They'll be fine."

Carly broke away from Armand. She drained the last of her wine again and poured another glass. Armand always brought the best wine—smooth, full-bodied, a caress for the tongue. The wine went down easily and made her stomach feel better.

She raised her glass. "To Spike and Sean." Connor clinked his bottle against her glass, and Carly drank. "And to Tiger. Bless him."

Again she and Connor toasted and drank. Yvette served up the sauté with thin strips of beef she'd precooked and a smattering of mushrooms. She deglazed the pan with a little of the wine to make a tasty sauce and put everything neatly on a plate for Carly.

"The best medicine," Yvette said. "Good food, good friends. You eat now."

Carly sat on a stool next to Connor at the counter and pushed the food around the plate. Because Yvette's cooking shouldn't be sneered at, but mostly because Yvette was standing over her giving her a steely look, Carly ate.

The mixture of peppers, mushrooms, tomatoes, meat, and wine was heavenly, but it felt leaden on Carly's tongue. Life was indeed tragic when she couldn't appreciate one of Yvette's meals.

"Let's not talk about it," Carly said, pouring herself more wine. The bottle released its last drop, but Armand had brought more. "How was the exhibit opening? From the fact that you didn't instantly fire me, I take it you sold a piece?"

"Three." Armand's smile beamed out. "And interest in more. That young man is on fire."

"Good," Carly said. "Good." At least someone's day had gone well.

More food and more wine disappeared, but Carly stopped following the conversation. Exhaustion, worry, heartbreak, and too much alcohol was taking its toll, and taking it fast. Connor ate a helping of the meal and talked easily with Yvette and Armand, telling them more about the events of the day. They started discussing Brennan and Walker, speculating about what they really wanted, but Carly was finished.

She slid off the stool, ready to explain that they could all leave now so she could shower and lie down. She found her legs buckling, and only Connor's strong arms kept her from sliding to the floor.

"I'm all right," she said. "I jus' need to rest." Carly heard the slur in her words and started to laugh.

"I will put you to bed," Yvette said. "Come."

She held out her long, slim arm. Carly grabbed the wine bottle and her glass as she let Yvette take her back into her bedroom. Once inside, Carly poured another glass and spun around, laughing. "I feel so free. No more Ethan, no more sitting around his pool or taking one of his fancy cars to go shopping. Damn, I would have hated that life." Carly stopped spinning, but the room kept on going. "No, I wouldn't have. I wanted to be a pampered puddle. I mean, a pumpered poodle. A . . ."

"You lie down. You sleep. You will feel better."

Sure she would. Yvette took the bottle and glass out of Carly's hands and gently but firmly guided her to the bed.

Carly didn't remember much after that, but she supposed Yvette had gotten her to settle down and sleep, because the next thing she knew, Carly was waking up, her mouth like cotton, her head pounding, her stomach in knots.

She slid out of bed, noting that the house was dark and silent, the clock beside the bed telling her it was three in the morning. Carly staggered to the bathroom, sacrificed

Yvette's great meal to the toilet, then washed her face and got ready for the next long trek—down the hall to the kitchen. As tempting as it had been to drink from the bathroom tap, Austin water wasn't the way to go on a roiling stomach. Carly needed bottled water. Cold. Lots of it.

The rest of the house was quiet, but a nightlight shone in the kitchen. Yvette and Armand must have gone home a while ago.

Connor? A glance around the kitchen showed her that it was empty, but at least someone had done the dishes. Everything gleamed. Probably Armand had cleaned up, as he usually did after Yvette cooked. She felt a moment of gratitude toward him.

Carly pulled open the refrigerator and took out a gallon jug of water. She thought about reaching for a glass.

"To hell with it." She upended the jug and drank straight from it, swallow after swallow. She wiped her mouth, noting that she'd dribbled plenty of water onto her T-shirt, but she felt slightly better.

Not much though. She needed aspirin. Her purse in the living room was closer than the bathroom, which was all the way back down the hall.

Sipping again from the gallon jug, Carly made her way into the dark living room, navigating by the light from the kitchen. She thought she'd dropped the purse behind the chair when the weird professor and his soldier had come in, but she couldn't remember. She couldn't remember anything about yesterday except Ethan's bare butt going back and forth as he banged the woman on the counter, and . . .

Carly snapped on the lamp to look for her purse. And let out a shriek.

Tiger was sitting on her couch. Not really sitting— lounging back with his long legs stretched out in front of him. The light burnished the orange in his black hair, and his yellow eyes glittered.

Connor lay on his back on the floor, his knees up, one arm over his eyes, breathing softly. He was asleep, but Tiger was wide awake and watching Carly.

Carly realized she was in a T-shirt that came to her thighs and a pair of panties, and that was it. Her long legs were bare, and there was nothing between herself and the T-shirt but empty air.

"What in the hell are you doing here?" The words came out as a croak.

"Protecting you," Tiger said. "You are my mate."

Carly looked wildly from Tiger to Connor and back again. "Protecting me from what? And what are you doing out of bed? Weren't you supposed to rest, take your meds, and get better?"

"I am better." Tiger slid his shirt up his stomach to reveal his abdomen—the skin whole and unbroken, with only round pink scars to show where the bullets had gone in. The rest of his abdomen was as hard, flat, tanned, and well-muscled as the rest of him. The man must work out three times a day.

Carly stared in surprise. "How in the hell . . . ?"

"I heal fast. Andrea helped. So did the touch of my mate."

"Andrea? Who's Andrea?"

Connor answered from the floor, sleepy but alert. "Sean's mate. She's half Fae. Has healing magic."

"Oh. Right."

Tiger lowered his shirt. "I protect you from the man who waits outside for you."

"What man?" Carly went for the window, but suddenly Tiger was there next to her, holding her back.

"Wait." Tiger snapped off the lamp, rendering the room dark again.

How he'd gotten off the couch so fast, Carly didn't know, but he led her to the dark back window, stopping her a few feet from it, and gestured outside.

Carly saw absolutely nothing. No sinister figure waiting in the dark, no figure at all. "Where?"

"He hides well. Connor saw him and called me."

"I think it's that Walker guy," Connor said. He rose from the floor in one sinuous motion, gaining his feet without making any noise. "Or one of his squad."

"Why?" Carly glanced out the window again, but she still couldn't see Walker or anyone else. "You have to be dreaming this."

"He's there," Tiger said. "Between the shadow of the fence and the tree. He's chosen a good place. He can look in here but not be seen. At least, not by a human."

"Shifters can see in the dark," Connor said. "Especially Felines. Trust me, he's there. I called Liam, and Tiger came."

"Why on earth should Walker be watching my house?"

Carly looked once more where Tiger indicated, but she still couldn't see anything . . . No, there. Something moved.

The glint vanished as quickly as it had appeared, whoever was out there disappearing into the shadows again.

"They want to know how much you have to do with Shifters," Connor said. "Brennan asked you to spy on us, right?"

"For his research project or whatever. He's an anthropologist."

"Sure," Connor said. "All I heard from him was he wanted you to get to know us and report to him. He can dress it up, but that sounds like spying to me. He wants Shifter secrets."

"Shifters have secrets?"

Connor raised his hands and looked innocent. "Do we? I don't know what you're talking about. We're sweet and innocent. Honest."

"You're full of shit," Carly said, wanting to laugh.

"So's Brennan. He's tried to get himself into Shifter-town before. Slimy bastard, he is."

"He creeped me out a little too," Carly said. "But why does Walker need to spy on *me*? I don't know any Shifter secrets. I keep telling everyone, I'd never met any Shifters until today. I mean yesterday."

"We will ask him," Tiger said. He started for the kitchen in that fluid, silent way he moved.

Carly ran after him and seized him by the arm. "Wait, wait. What are you doing?"

Connor was across the room to them, his eyes wide as he took in Carly and Tiger. But he was alarmed more, Carly thought, because she'd grabbed hold of Tiger. Body language again. Connor was trying to protect her, but right now, not from the guy outside.

Tiger did nothing but look down at Carly with his golden eyes that no longer held outrageous pain. He'd returned to the quiet watchfulness he'd exhibited when he'd helped her fix the car on the side of the road.

"The best way to find out what he wants is to ask him," Tiger said, patience in his voice.

"But he has a gun . . ." Carly sighed and released him. "And you've already proven those don't slow you down, not for long anyway."

"He might have a tranq," Connor pointed out. "Or two."

"He does not have a tranquilizer, only a pistol," Tiger said.

Connor blinked. "And you know that how?"

"Sight and scent." Tiger spoke in clipped tones, like a soldier readying himself to confront his enemy. "Protect Carly while I find him."

Connor sighed, resigned. "You're the super Shifter. Be careful, all right? I don't want to have to explain to Liam why I lost you."

Tiger answered by fading down the hall toward Carly's bedroom. Carly followed, not nearly as silently, her bare feet pattering on the floor.

Tiger ignored Carly's bed and her clothes, which had been neatly folded over a chair—by Yvette, probably—and noiselessly pulled up the blinds on her window. Then he started taking off his clothes.

Tiger stripped all the way down, getting out of his clothes as smoothly and quietly as he did everything else. He was nicely proportional, strength showing in the sculpted muscles of his shoulders, the flat planes of his chest, the firm length of his back.

He had a great ass too, as tight and good as the rest of him. Carly had seen at the hospital what hung between his legs in front, but even so, looking at it again made her mouth a little dry. "Maybe I'm still drunk," she said. "But Tiger . . . Oh my God, you are *hot*."

Tiger barely acknowledged her, and Carly realized after a moment that he didn't know what she meant.

The next second, any words of explanation were pouring back down her throat, because Tiger changed into a . . . tiger.

He did it rapidly, easily, limbs sliding from human down into the bent haunches and massive paws of a Bengal. Fur rippled across his body, orange with black stripes, a tail extending to brush the floor.

He was gigantic, bigger than any tiger Carly had seen at a zoo. Her large bedroom was now a tight fit.

Connor sighed as he pressed his way around Tiger to the window. "He always does this. Shifts and then makes me open the windows and doors for him. Quiet now."

Connor slid up Carly's double-hung window, which gave on to the side of the house. Tiger put his paws on the sill.

"What's he doing?" Carly whispered frantically. "He won't fit."

"He will. Watch."

How the hell Tiger got out the window when he was twice the size of the opening, Carly never understood. As a little girl, she'd had a cat that could flatten herself to crawl into the two-inch-high space under her dresser, but this was even more startling.

Maybe it was the magic of being a Shifter, but damned if Tiger didn't compact himself down and squirt through the window. He landed on the other side, went into an instant predatory crouch, and slunk into the darkness. Carly lost sight of him in a matter of seconds.

"Crap, I thought he'd wait for me." Connor put his head and shoulders out the window and climbed through with far less grace than Tiger had.

"It'll be okay, right?" Carly whispered. "Walker can't hurt Tiger with his gun, and Tiger can't hurt him."

Connor landed on his feet outside. "Oh, I'd say Tiger can do whatever the hell he's wanting to."

"I mean, Tiger can't attack him. The Collar will stop him. That's what it's for, isn't it?"

"Shite." Connor's whisper was agitated. "Shite. Shite. *That's* what he's after. Stay here."

Screw that. As Connor faded into the darkness, Carly grabbed her jeans and tugged them on, then stuffed her feet into sandals. She sat on the sill, swung her legs around, slithered through the window, and landed with a thump on a patch of grass that needed mowing. Carly reflected, as she started jogging toward the backyard, that at oh dark thirty in the morning, the air was at least cool.

She heard a muffled shout and then Tiger's growl, long and low. The rage in the sound was unmistakable, a wild animal ready to kill.

"No!" Carly heard Connor's agitated voice. "Crap. No. Stop it, now. Aw, Liam's gonna *kill* me."

CHAPTER SEVEN

Snarling came out of the darkness, and Connor yelling under his breath, but nothing from the watcher.

Carly ran forward. Trying to keep out of sight meant she couldn't see what not to trip over in the darkness, so she slammed into the patio chair she'd dragged to this side of the house a few days ago for a little sunbathing. Carly cursed as she went down, got up, rubbed her sore shin, and picked her way more slowly across the yard.

She reached the pitch-blackness near the fence to find a man on the ground and Tiger fully on top of him, his huge paw ready to rip out the man's throat. Connor had his hands on Tiger's back, pulling, without result.

Tiger's Collar was silent, no sparking, nothing. The man under Tiger was Walker, his face a pale smudge in the darkness. His face was bloody, and he was out. Or dead. The man's pistol, broken into pieces, lay on the grass next to him.

Carly saw all this in a frenzied second, then she joined with Connor trying to pull Tiger off him.

Tiger snarled, his face wrinkling with his deadly growl. His claws were poised on Walker's neck, Connor's tugs and pleas doing nothing.

"Don't kill him, all right?" Connor was saying. "They'll find out, they'll get Liam, and the Goddess only knows what they'll do to you."

"What *would* they do to Tiger?" Carly asked in a frantic whisper.

"Take him, quarantine him, execute him, maybe. Today was bad enough. We can't let anyone know *anything* about Tiger."

Why not? Carly wondered. And why were Brennan and Walker this interested in him?

Not the time to ask questions, Carly sank her hands into Tiger's fur, finding it surprisingly warm and silky. He had a scruff, like her childhood cat, folds of fur loose for holding. The thought flashed through her head that he must have been adorably cute as a cub, with his mother carrying him in her mouth. Did Shifters do that?

"Tiger, listen to Connor," Carly said. "This guy's not worth the jail time, or being executed over."

Tiger's growls rippled through him, vibrating through Carly. Walker lay motionless, the bruise on the side of his head explaining why he was out. Alive, though, thank God. She could hear his ragged breathing.

"If you hurt him," Carly went on, "if they take you away, I'll never see you again. I'd hate that. I *want* to see you again."

Another huge growl rumbled, and then Tiger *changed*. The fur under Carly's hands rapidly became human flesh, and in a few seconds, Carly found herself sitting on her damp lawn with her arms around a large, well-muscled, naked man.

Tiger pulled her close, his strength undiminished, the heat of his body intense against the cooling night. His hot skin was smooth under Carly's fingers, and she couldn't resist running her hands down his back.

Tiger leaned in, and Carly thought he'd kiss her, but instead he brushed his nose along her cheekbone, then nuzzled her from forehead to chin.

Carly had never had a man nuzzle her before. She'd never realized how sensual that could be, how intimate.

She touched Tiger's cheek, which was bristly with whiskers, his golden eyes still as he watched her. Tiger turned his face against her palm, and the tip of his tongue brushed her fingers.

The heat of him, the touch of his mouth, made Carly go shaky, hot and cold, giddy. Warmth blossomed in her female spaces, as did the need to have him touch her there with his strong hands.

Lust. Must be. That and reaction to her vast hurt and anger at Ethan.

But Tiger's presence was blotting out Ethan's face, his voice, his mean sarcasm. Ethan drained rapidly away as the hot sensations of Tiger snaked through Carly's body.

Tiger nuzzled her again, his breath warm. The tip of his tongue touched her cheek, hesitant, then again, bolder, a trail of fire. Tiger drew back then, hands coming up to cup Carly's face as he studied her.

Connor cleared his throat. "So, um, does this mean you aren't going to kill him?"

Tiger's fury came back into his eyes. "He threatens my mate."

"Maybe that's true, big guy. But, like I said, if you damage him more, we aren't going to be able to cover it up."

"You won't be able to anyway," Carly said. "When Walker wakes up, he'll tell the police that Tiger knocked him out, or he'll tell the Shifter Bureau, probably both. What do we do about that?"

Connor looked down at Walker, stretched out and silent. "I don't know. But we can't kill him. No matter how we tried to hide that, someone would find him and figure out he was at one time mauled by a Shifter."

"I wasn't suggesting *killing* him," Carly said. "Sheesh. I

meant maybe putting him to bed and reasoning with him when he wakes up."

Connor huffed. "Reason with an armed Special Forces dude, who's probably trained to take out Shifters with his bare hands?"

"He didn't take out Tiger."

"Yeah, well, Tiger's different."

Tiger paid no attention to Connor. He continued to look down at Carly, smoothing back a lock of her hair with gentle fingers.

Connor groaned and scrubbed his hands through his hair. "Goddess help me, why do I have to make all these decisions? Carly, you have any duct tape?"

"Probably." Carly looked at Walker and shared Connor's dismay. "Crap."

"Hurry. Before he wakes up."

The hardest thing was convincing Tiger to let her go. Tiger rose with Carly, towering over her, a giant of a man. A *naked* giant of a man. In her yard.

"I'll be right back," she said to him. "I'm only going to the garage. You stay here, and keep out of sight. If my neighbors see you, they'll have every cop in the city up here."

Tiger took a step back into the shadows. At least he understood the danger. Carly felt Tiger's hard gaze on her back as she ran across the yard, though, remembering at the last minute to dodge the patio chair on her way to the open window.

Blood. Tiger smelled the saltiness of it, the tang that made the beast inside him want to feed. Animal triumph had shot through him when he'd smacked Walker with his paw, one blow knocking him out. His claws had raked the man's face, drawing blood, waking up the carnivore he was.

Carly's scent had blotted out the blood smell, sending Tiger's thoughts in a wildly different direction. He smelled her female need, her ongoing anger at the man Ethan, her worry about Tiger and Walker lying at his feet.

Her scent had wrapped around Tiger's senses, soothing him down from his anger. He was able to change to human, to touch her, relax into her.

Nuzzling her made him forget all about Walker and even Connor; licking her had been even better. Tiger had observed Liam and his mate—and Sean and his mate, Spike and his mate, and others—touching mouths. Kissing.

Tiger wanted to do that with Carly, but he wasn't sure how it worked. When he'd asked Connor about kissing some time ago, Connor had laughed and said that Tiger would figure it out when the time came.

Tiger wasn't so certain. He was pretty sure there was more to it than pressing lips together, and he wanted to get it right with Carly.

Now that Carly was gone, back into her house, her scent wasn't as intense, and the blood smell came back. The need to make the kill surged. The tiger in him wanted to finish this, to rip out Walker's throat for threatening Carly, slam his body down, and walk away. Quick, efficient, satisfying.

Tiger clenched his fists, his growl barely contained. Connor was right that if he hurt Walker the humans would find Tiger and take him away, and then they'd discover that his Collar was fake. Liam and his family would pay the price for that. Then Tiger's captors would put him into a cage again and experiment on him, or simply shoot him full of drugs until he died.

Tiger started to shake. He wanted to run . . . *Run, never stop. Never let them take you.*

Never see Carly again.

No. Tiger needed her and needed her touch. Only Carly.

Carly came out of the house again, this time through the back door. Her scent drifted to him from across the yard, calming the fight-or-flight instinct to where Tiger could manage it. He exhaled.

"Found it." Carly held out a roll of dull silver tape to Connor.

Connor took it. "Hurry. I think he's coming around."

He unrolled a long length of tape, then wound it around Walker's ankles and calves. Connor forestalled Carly running back for scissors by letting his fingers sprout claws and slitting the tape neatly with one Feline razor-sharp nail.

"Handy," Carly said.

Connor's fingers became all human again, and he wrapped Walker's wrists with another layer of tape. Walker swam to wakefulness, eyes focusing as Connor cut a six-inch strip of tape.

Carly took the strip from Connor. "Sorry," she said to Walker as she pasted it over his mouth.

Walker only looked at her quietly over the duct tape. No anger, no frustration, no emotion at all.

Tiger didn't like that look, one that said Walker wasn't worried about anything they did to him. Carly didn't seem to like it either. "Maybe some more tape, Connor," she said, sounding nervous.

Connor added an extra layer to Walker's legs and wrists before he handed the tape back to Carly. "Tiger, want to carry him?"

"No." The word came out harshly. With the blood smell strong, Tiger wouldn't be able to contain himself. He'd take Walker far from Carly and Connor and kill him.

Connor understood. "It's all right. He's not that big." He got to his feet, heaved the bound Walker over his shoulders, and balanced the load. Connor wasn't full-grown yet, but he was wiry and strong.

"Tiger, get dressed and meet us in the garage," Connor said. "Carly, I'm going to need the keys to your car."

Carly already had them out. Tiger ignored Connor's instructions and followed them into the house and through to the garage, not trusting Walker not to twist his way out of the bonds. The man was a fighter. He'd know how.

Inside the closed garage, Carly opened the car's back door, looked inside, and put her hands on her hips. Tiger liked when she stood that way—the stance emphasized the curve of her waist and her sweet backside.

"If we put him in there, someone will see him, won't they?" she asked Connor.

"I'm thinking they will," Connor said.

Carly heaved a sigh and clicked the remote on her key chain, and her trunk popped open.

Connor rolled the inert Walker into the trunk. Carly reached for the lid. "I'm *really* sorry," she said to Walker before she and Connor slammed the lid shut.

Only then did Tiger let himself retreat to Carly's bedroom, fetch his clothes, and carry them back with him to the garage. He also brought Carly's purse from the living room. Having lived for months in the same house with Liam and his mate, Kim, Tiger had learned that these large bags were full of things females considered essential. They fussed when they didn't have them.

Carly gave Tiger a wide smile he'd treasure for a long time. "Why, thank you, Tiger. What a sweetheart you are."

"Hey," Connor said as Tiger pulled on his clothes. "I have to wrap a guy in duct tape and stuff him into your trunk after Tiger knocks him out, and *he's* the sweetheart?"

"You're sweet too, Connor." Carly dropped a kiss onto Connor's cheek.

Tiger's growl stifled itself. If Carly had done that to any other Shifter, he'd have had said Shifter on the floor. But Connor was a cub. Not a threat. Cubs were never threats.

Carly gestured Tiger toward the backseat. "Get in."

Connor held out his hand. "You're not coming. You stay here, out of trouble."

Carly said, "No," at the same time Tiger did. Connor looked at them both in exasperation.

"You are *not* driving my car around with Walker wrapped up in the trunk," Carly said. "Besides, I need it to go to work tomorrow—today. Apparently, I still have a job."

"I'll bring it back," Connor began, but Tiger ended the discussion by getting himself into the front seat of the car.

"She comes," he said. "We protect her."

Carly smiled in triumph and slid into the driver's seat.

"Besides," she said, "You have to ride Sean's motorcycle back."

"All right," Connor said, looking weary. He shut the door for Carly. "But Liam's going to shit himself, I'm thinking."

"How did you get to my house anyway?" Carly asked Tiger as she hit the control to open the garage door. "I don't see a car outside, or another motorcycle. Connor didn't sneak out and get you while I was asleep, did he?"

"I walked."

Carly blinked at him. "You what?"

"Walked."

"Walked," she repeated. "From Shiftertown."

Tiger shrugged. "Hitched a ride a couple of times. Connor told Liam where you lived when he called. I heard."

Connor had been moving toward Sean's motorcycle, still in Carly's garage, but he swung around and leaned to look through the car's window at Tiger. "Wait a minute. Does Liam even know you're gone?"

"No one saw me," Tiger said.

"Oh, *shite*." Connor thumped his forehead to the window frame. "Goddess, Tiger, you're going to get me into *so* much trouble."

CHAPTER EIGHT

Carly waited until Connor was ready on Sean's motorcycle before she started the car. She backed out, thankful that it was still too early for even her hardiest neighbors.

She drove sedately, trying not to attract attention, following Connor as she pulled out onto the main streets.

"Where are we going?" she asked Tiger.

"Shiftertown," Tiger said. "Best place."

Carly drove on with misgivings. She wasn't exactly afraid to go to Shiftertown, but she didn't like to think what all those Shifters would do with someone from the Shifter Bureau tied up with duct tape and delivered to them.

She supposed she could drive her car straight to a police station and let Connor and Tiger suck it up, but the thought of Connor's worry over Walker, Tiger, and her changed her mind. Connor was in over his head and scared. Carly didn't have the heart to give him to the police to question and maybe arrest on top of everything else.

And she remembered what Connor said they might do to Tiger—*Take him, quarantine him, execute him, maybe.* Carly didn't want that to happen either.

Tiger stared straight ahead as Carly drove, the street-lights creating bands of light that moved across his face. What he was thinking, she couldn't guess, and Tiger didn't offer to share his thoughts. He was mysterious, even more so than the other Shifters she'd met today, and none of them had stirred her desires simply by touching her.

Carly glanced at him as she drove, and sometimes she'd catch him looking back at her, his eyes enigmatic but holding heat.

Shiftertown lay behind the old airport, in houses no one had wanted even before the airport had closed down and moved to where the Bergstrom Air Force Base used to be. When Shifters needed a place to live, the Shifter Bureau and the city had designated the area exclusively for them.

Shifters had moved to the Austin Shiftertown from all corners of the globe, because most countries didn't want Shifters living in them at all. Obviously the Morrisseys had come from Ireland. But Tiger? Carly couldn't place his accent. American but neutral. Not from Texas or anywhere in the South anyway.

The sun was just coming up as Carly drove into Shiftertown. She expected to find slums, but after she passed a few derelict stores, a boarded-up gas station, and an empty field, she found old bungalows, neatly painted with equally neat yards, bathed in early-morning sunlight. Some houses were placed one behind the other, with driveways that served both houses.

She followed Connor to a two-story bungalow that looked little different from the one next door to it. The two houses shared a driveway, which was nothing more than two strips of concrete. A small white pickup, another nice Harley, and a smaller car were parked in this driveway. Connor halted the motorcycle next to the other one, and Carly pulled over at the curb and stopped the car.

Tiger was out before she could emerge, and Connor scrambled off the bike, heading to the trunk. Tiger grabbed Carly's wrist as she was about to push the remote to pop the latch.

"No," he said in a stern voice. "He's almost free."

"What? How on earth could you possibly know that?"

"Smell is different. Connor, get Liam."

Tiger put himself between Carly and the trunk as Connor ran for the house, but Tiger made no move to dig inside and stop Walker from breaking loose.

"You know, you could just knock him out again," Carly said.

Tiger shook his head. "If I touch him again, I'll kill him. Liam will want him to stay alive."

Carly stopped, the odd phrasing striking her. "What do *you* want?"

Tiger looked down at her, his eyes becoming fixed. She read confusion in them, puzzlement. "I don't know," he said.

His perplexity touched her. Tiger knew his instincts, and was fighting them, but he was obeying orders, not thinking the problem through for himself.

Carly took his hand and squeezed it. "We'll figure this out."

Tiger went even more still, his gaze riveted to her. It was unnerving, being pinned by the yellow stare, but at the same time, Carly wanted to hold on to him even harder.

She spied movement behind Tiger and took several rapid paces back. "Too late. He's out."

Walker had kicked his way into Carly's backseat. He opened the car door on the side opposite from her and Tiger, rolling out and coming to his feet in one movement. Pieces of duct tape hung from his wrists, but he'd managed to remove everything from his legs.

Without changing expression, Walker took in his surroundings, then turned and went for the most vulnerable person within his reach—Connor.

Connor had come out of the house he'd entered, but had returned without Liam or anyone else. He'd been jogging over to the house to its right, the one that shared the driveway, when Walker caught him.

Tiger let out a roar. He gave up on self-control, launched himself over the car, and went for Walker.

"A little help here!" Carly shouted. She ran after Tiger, though she didn't know what she could do. She had no weapon, wasn't a black belt in anything, and could probably lose an arm-wrestling match with a seven-year-old boy. She was used to dealing with artists, some of whom were emotionally delicate, but she'd never had to body tackle any of them to Armand's gallery floor.

Walker had Connor in a headlock, spinning Connor around to face Tiger. The muscles in Walker's arm bulged as he held a snarling Connor around his neck, not letting go even though Connor was beginning to shift.

Tiger's hands sprouted immense claws, his face transitioning to a snarling tiger's. "Don't. Hurt. The cubs."

He went for Walker, Carly still yelling for help.

The door of the second house opened, and someone emerged, but Carly didn't clearly see who it was until a tall man who looked a lot like Sean got his hands around Walker's neck and jerked him backward.

The momentum made Walker release Connor, now a young lion with the beginnings of a black mane, who fell to all fours, panting.

The rescuer spun Walker around and delivered a tight, efficient blow behind Walker's ear. Walker had balled up his fist to punch first, but his hand went slack, and he collapsed at the newcomer's feet.

The man looked Walker over, then shifted his gaze to Carly, giving her the same assessing stare. He was an older version of Sean and Liam, with similar blue eyes, but his dark hair was going gray at the temples. The difference was in the absolute stillness this man could achieve; it was even more acute than that which she'd observed in the Shifters at the hospital, or even in Tiger.

This Shifter looked at Carly, all the way through her, as though he knew every thought inside her head—the ones now, every thought she'd had in the past, and every one she would have in the future. His nostrils moved the slightest bit.

"Who is she?" he asked, voice deadly quiet. Not asking Carly—oh, no. He wasn't even asking Tiger. The question had been directed at Connor.

The young lion shook himself. He sat down on his haunches, not turning back to human. The man's blue gaze flicked to Tiger, waiting for him to answer. But Tiger remained in place, though his face and hands became human again, still protecting Connor.

Carly stepped forward into the silence. "I'm Carly Randal," she said, trying to sound both bright and firm, as she did when arrogant people came to the gallery to sneer at brilliant paintings. "And you are?"

"He's Dylan," Tiger said. "Used to be Shiftertown leader."

"Retired, are you?" Carly asked. "That's nice."

Dylan's eyes flared with white-hot anger. Carly understood in that moment what it was like to be a rabbit under the gaze of a mountain lion right before that lion put out a paw and ended the rabbit's life.

Then Dylan's rage dissipated, and the corners of his lips quirked into a small, ironic smile. "I gave over the running of Shiftertown to my son. Who is that?" He pointed at Walker on the ground.

"His name's Walker Danielson," Carly answered. "From the Shifter Bureau, apparently."

Dylan's smile vanished. "Shite, woman. And you thought it was a good idea to haul him here wrapped in duct tape?"

Connor remained a lion, slowly blinking and looking as innocent as a youthful male lion possibly could.

"He threatened Carly," Tiger said, fury in his voice.

"So you beat him down," Dylan said. "Whose idea was the duct tape?"

"Mine," Carly said quickly. Connor was too young to have this dangerous-looking man angry at him. Dylan might not be in charge anymore, but his stance said that he hadn't stopped expecting everyone to obey him. "I didn't know what to do with him, and I didn't want him to go to the police, so I thought Shifters would know what to do." Carly gave Dylan her most charming smile, one that disarmed even the pickiest of gallery customers.

"She's lying," Tiger said.

"I know," Dylan answered. "I can smell it. Let's get him inside."

Not inside his own house, the one he'd come out of—Dylan heaved Walker up over his shoulder as though the man weighed nothing and carried him into the house next door.

No one was there. This bungalow was airy, with a gigantic kitchen and an equally large living room with a dining area fixed in one corner. A staircase rose from the middle wall of the living room, disappearing upward.

"Who lives here?" Carly asked.

"My son Liam." Dylan deposited Walker on the floor, walked unhurriedly into the kitchen, and returned with another roll of duct tape.

"And me." Connor came inside, human again, his shirt and jeans ripped from his change. "And Liam's mate, Kim. And Tiger."

Tiger stood above Walker, staring at the blood on the man's face, his fists clenched. Fighting himself again.

"Tiger," Carly said. "Come on over here with me."

Tiger's glance at her showed rigid anger and pain so deep it cut her from all the way across the room. He didn't want to look away from Walker, the potential threat, but at the same time, he was pulled to Carly.

Tiger closed his eyes, blotting out the flash of anger, but his face was fixed, the pain obvious.

Carly walked to him and took his hand. Tiger opened his eyes and looked down at her, this time fully.

Carly wanted to both run away and stay under his mesmerizing gaze. As a very small child she'd gone to a zoo where the animals had roamed freely, and the humans walked past them in caged walkways. She remembered a mountain lion that had followed her on the other side of the grille, its golden eyes directly on her. Even now, Carly had no idea whether it had been curious about her or had thought a small child would make a good midmorning snack. She'd cried in terror, and her mother had carried her out.

The feeling, buried deep in her past, flooded out again. Tiger was a wild animal, never mind that he currently had a human body and wore normal clothes and a Collar. The wildness was in his eyes, a creature untamed.

Tiger's gaze held her in place as though she were the small animal that couldn't run away. The predator had her, his prey.

He touched her face. Carly shuddered with reaction, his caress a gentle contrast to the obvious strength in him.

Tiger bent to her, as though drawn by her, everything around them forgotten. He nuzzled her as he had in her yard, and Carly caught his face in her hands, rose on tiptoe, and kissed his lips.

Tiger's world stopped. The press of Carly's lips against his cut through his jangled confusion, the need to kill falling away.

Her lips were a place of warmth, satin smooth, the softest sensation he'd ever felt. The touch of her mouth was light, yet he felt it in every part of his body. Every part—especially his cock, which was becoming tight.

Carly's lips formed a slight pucker, pressing moisture to his mouth. The gentle pressure was both featherlight and firm at the same time.

She brushed her lips over his, moving across them, ending at the corner of his mouth. Her movements were so slight, and yet Tiger thought this was the most important thing that had ever happened to him.

Carly touched her lips to the corner of his mouth again, then she lifted away, her brows drawn down over her gray green eyes.

Her scent had changed, ever so slightly, but Tiger sensed

it. She'd been nervous, worried, angry, confused. Now into
the mix came wanting. She desired Tiger. That fact spun
around and settled in a hot point deep inside him.

"What's the matter?" she asked, her puzzlement rising
again. Carly touched his face with light fingertips, then she
gave him a surprised smile. "Haven't you ever kissed anyone before?"

"No."

"You're kidding, right?"

"No."

Tiger had had a mate, the female ripped away from him
after he'd impregnated her, but they'd never kissed. It had
been animalistic, that mating, though he'd become fer-
vently attached to her, had come apart in grief when she'd
died. What Carly had just done was different from anything he'd ever experienced.

"Wow." Carly skimmed her fingertips across his lips,
drawing fire. "I don't think I've met a man who was a
virgin."

"I had a mate. She had a cub."

"Ah. Then *not* a virgin. But you've never kissed?"

"No."

"That's weird. Wait, you *had* a mate?" Carly asked, her
smile going away. "Where is she now? And your kid?"

"They died."

The words came out flat and didn't say everything he
needed them to. Words couldn't. Ever.

Carly's look became shocked, her scent tinged with compassion. "Oh, Tiger, I'm so sorry." She ran her hands over his
shoulders, as though trying to soothe the tension there. "I
didn't know. I'm sorry. I didn't mean to tease you."

"Their deaths were not your fault." Again the words fell
flat. Tiger couldn't explain, couldn't make her understand
why he wanted her to feel better.

"I mean, I'm sorry for *you*. That she died. That the child
died. That must have been awful."

"Yes."

Carly's voice softened. She exuded sympathy, even more than had Iona, or any other Shifter. "There's more to you than meets the eye, isn't there?" she asked.

Tiger wasn't sure what that meant—he knew English, but he'd learned it from scientists, who didn't so much talk *to* him as *at* him or *over* him.

When he wasn't certain, he didn't answer, but Carly didn't seem to mind. She continued to touch his face, her eyes on his, her smile returning.

"Aw, Dad, what the *fuck*?" Liam's Irish tones boomed.

Tiger saw no reason to turn from Carly as Liam banged his way into the living room where his father was wrapping more duct tape around Walker on the floor. Tiger scented Liam and his daughter, Katriona, but not Kim.

"Dad, what did you *do*?"

"Talk to your nephew and Tiger," Dylan said calmly. "The man on your rug is Shifter Bureau."

Liam went silent as he contemplated the situation. Tiger noticed that Connor had disappeared upstairs.

Liam, a talker, didn't stay silent long. "Why is he here, passed out and trussed up, and why are *you* here?" He pointed a blunt finger at Carly.

Liam's daughter, a year and a few months old, was perched on her father's shoulders, her dark curly hair and blue eyes proclaiming her the Morrissey she was. She saw Tiger and stretched out her hands.

"Tigger!"

Tigger was the name of a character in a children's story, and Katriona insisted on giving the name to Tiger. Tiger didn't mind. He turned away from Carly and walked slowly to Liam, indicating he'd take the cub if Liam was willing to hand her off. He wouldn't reach for her uninvited, no. Liam needed to make the decision.

Liam's stance exuded more annoyance than anger. He hauled Katriona from his shoulders, holding her out to Tiger before joining his father over Walker's body.

Tiger closed his hands carefully around Katriona's torso and lifted her high into the air. She squealed and laughed as she always did, then cuddled down against his chest as he held her close.

Katriona's curly hair tickled Tiger's chin as she looked around with interest at everything happening in the living room. Tiger's body unclenched, as it always did when he was around the cubs. When his instincts got out of control, a cub's presence could make his animal nature stop and his thoughts cease whirling.

"Well, aren't you the cutest thing?" Carly poked Katriona in the tummy. "What's your name, honey?"

"'Trina," she said.

"Katriona," Tiger rumbled. "She can't say the whole word yet."

"A pretty name for a pretty girl." Carly seemed delighted with Kat.

"'Nk you," Kat said.

Liam's scent broke Tiger's focus on Carly and Kat as Liam himself stopped in front of them. "*Excuse me*, if I can be interrupting this sweet little moment. Will one of you tell me what the hell is going on? Seeing as I heard Connor lock himself in his room, which means he's scared about what I'm going to do, and *that* means there's something for him to be worrying about. Isn't there?"

CHAPTER NINE

"I wouldn't know about that," Carly said. She broke into a smile again as she tickled Katriona's stomach. She couldn't know how beautiful she looked when she did that. "All I know is, his name is Walker Danielson, he was spying on me, and Tiger caught him and knocked him out. He's also friends with a professor who wants me to come and talk to you and write reports about you for him. For a research project, he said. Wants me to be his assistant. Anyway, Connor was worried Tiger would hurt Walker even more, so I thought, why not bring him to you and have you talk to him? He's from the Shifter Bureau, and y'all are Shifters."

Liam listened, his blue gaze trained on Carly's face. "And Connor wouldn't have anything to do with this, would he?"

"Connor was doing his best," Carly said. "He was scared. Give the kid a break, all right?"

Liam moved the slightest bit closer to her. "And you? Are you scared?"

Carly stepped back into Tiger, and Tiger put a hand on her shoulder. "I'm a little afraid, sure," she said. "It's not every day I slap a piece of duct tape over a man's mouth and stuff him into my trunk. And y'all are *not* reassuring. If Tiger weren't here, my knees would be knocking together. But your daughter is obnoxiously sweet."

Liam's expression softened as he glanced at Katriona. "You only say that because you're not chasing her all hours of the day and night. Mum goes to the office, and Da stays home and looks after this wee monster. I thought it was bad when she was crawling."

"Looks like Tiger makes a good babysitter."

"He does, that," Liam said. "But he spoils her rotten. Lets her get away with way too much."

"She's a Shifter, right?" Carly asked. "What does she turn into?"

"Nothing yet. Her mother's human, so Kat was born human, and she won't start shifting into her beastie until she's about three. She's a Morrissey, so she'll have mostly lion in her. Feline Shifters were bred from all big cats, but families tend toward one species or the other. Except Tiger. He seems to be all tiger, interestingly enough."

"Tigger," Kat corrected him.

"Yes, love. Is that the kind of thing your professor friend wants you to be reporting?" The dangerous glint was back in Liam's eye. But Tiger knew Liam wouldn't hurt Carly, not physically. First, because Liam only attacked true dangers, and second, because Liam would never get through Tiger to touch her.

"He's not *my* friend," Carly said. "I didn't like him, if you want to know the truth. I didn't tell him I'd work for him, because I already have a job—which reminds me, I need to go so I can get to it and not lose it. My boss cut me some slack, because my day yesterday was truly shitty, but he's not going to give me a permanent vacation."

Leaving. No. Tiger's hand tightened on Carly's shoulder. Not leaving, not for the wide world and its dangers, not without him.

Liam wasn't finished with his interrogation. "And what is this job?"

"I'm an assistant and receptionist at an art gallery. And no, that doesn't mean I sit and do my nails. I take orders and keep track of them, do the inventory, sell to walk-in customers, set up receptions and such for the artists, and set up exhibit openings, which are a lot more work than they seem, believe you me. Basically anything Armand needs help with, I do."

Liam's gaze didn't move as he took in her words, also taking in, Tiger knew, her scent, her body language, and the nuances behind them.

"All right," Liam said as Carly wound down. "You go off and get ready for work, and we'll deal with duct-tape man."

"I will go with her." No way would Tiger let her drive off alone, into danger. The professor's gun-toting friend might have been rendered harmless for now, but there might be more like Walker out there. Plus, when Walker's disappearance was discovered, Carly's house would be first on the list of places to look.

"It's all right," Carly said quickly, looking up at Tiger. "I'll be fine."

"You won't be fine. I'll go with you."

"Yes, you will," Liam said to Tiger. "But not just you. Let me see which of my trackers is in need of something to do."

"What are you talking about now? Damn it." A cell phone pealed, and Carly dug through the giant bin of her purse until she brought it out, nearly dropping it in the process. She looked at the readout, frowned in a puzzled way, and answered it.

"Hello? Who is . . . ?"

Her face changed from curiosity to outrage in the space of a second. "Are you kidding me? *Are you* . . ." She looked around at the Shifters, all of whom were watching her closely, and let out a breath. "Hang on. I have to take this." She lowered the phone as she walked out through the kitchen and onto the back porch. Tiger, bouncing Kat, went right after her.

* * *

"Say that again?" Carly yelled into the phone, pressing it against her ear. "Ethan wants to sue *me*?"

"He has a list of complaints, including bringing a Shifter in to attack him."

Carly's rage changed from the simmer to which she'd managed to lower it to a full-blown boil. *"Are you fucking kidding me?"*

The smooth voice of one of Ethan's friends, who happened to be a lawyer, continued: "You returned his car damaged and are in possession of a number of expensive items he's given you, including a sixty-thousand-dollar engagement ring."

"Sixty-thousand?" Carly thought about the ring that was tucked into her jewelry box, with no lock, no alarm system on her house. "What, is he stupid?"

"If you want, Carly, you and I can settle this. It doesn't have to go to court."

"To court? He cheats on me, and he wants to take *me* to court?"

"Now, Carly, calm down. We can—"

His voice cut off as Carly slammed her thumb on the End button. She stopped herself from flinging the phone off the porch and into the green, because it was her phone, and expensive. She settled for throwing it— hard —back into her purse, where it clattered against her sunglasses case.

She turned around to find Tiger standing three feet behind her, the glower on his face telling her he'd heard everything. Didn't matter. Ethan was a dickhead, and she didn't care who knew it.

"I have to go," Carly said. The hour was early enough that she'd have time to go home, get changed, stop at Ethan's, and drive to the gallery. The stop at Ethan's wouldn't take long.

"I'll go with you," Tiger repeated. He'd planted himself so stubbornly in her path, she'd never get around him even if she tried to force her way.

"Fine. I don't have time to argue. You might want to leave the kid, though. My language is going to get ugly."

Tiger held Katriona out, not to Liam but to Sean, who was approaching through the backyard. With him was a guy with a cowboy hat who studied Carly and Tiger in open curiosity.

Sean took Katriona into his hands with a bemused expression. Carly pushed past him and descended the porch steps, hurrying around the house and down the driveway to her own car. Tiger was right behind her, sliding into the passenger seat as Carly climbed behind the wheel and started it up.

Before she could pull from the curb, the back door opened and the cowboy dove in. He yanked his feet clear and shut the door as Carly peeled out into the street.

Other Shifters were out in the early-morning sunshine, walking or just standing in yards or on porches. Every single one stopped what they were doing and stared the predatory stare as Carly sped down the road to make her way out of Shiftertown.

"Whoa," the cowboy Shifter said as the car rocketed forward. "Maybe I should drive."

"And you are?" Carly asked, tearing around a corner and sending him down into the seat.

The man righted himself and clicked on a seat belt. "I'm Ellison Rowe. Lupine Shifter."

"Lupine?" Carly asked, distracted. She whisked the car around another corner and onto Fifty-first, heading west.

"Wolf, darlin'." Ellison clutched the back of the seat as Carly sped between two cars and around a truck. "Take it easy, sweetheart. I'm just mated. I want to live long enough to put a cub in the nursery."

"I'm *so* sorry," Carly said, putting on her sugary sweet voice. "I'm just mad at all things male right now, and would really like to know *what are you doing in my car?*"

"Liam sent me."

"To keep an eye on me?"

Ellison pointed at Tiger. "No, to keep an eye on *him*. *You* seem to have things under control."

"Then you'll have to put up with how I drive." Carly smiled at him in the rearview. "And you can help me carry things."

Ellison tossed his hat onto the seat beside him, scraped a hand through blond hair, and grinned back at her. "That's what I live for."

C arly got herself showered and dressed for work in record time, including doing her hair and makeup. She enjoyed sliding into her prettiest sheath dress, a silk moiré that was bright green to go with her eyes, plus jewelry that Ethan hadn't bought her—her earrings had come from her mother, the dangling gold necklace from her oldest sister, Althea.

She put on killer high heels that made her legs look wicked and red lipstick that made her mouth ready for kissing. But not for Ethan. Oh, no.

Carly headed out to the front room, where Tiger and Ellison were doing what Connor had enjoyed doing when he was here, watching sports on cable television. While she moved down the hall, she heard Ellison saying to Tiger, "No, see, this guy over here caught the ball, so even though *this* guy hit it well, he can't stay on first base. He's out."

A full-grown American male who didn't understand baseball? Shifter or not, that had to be a first.

Carly nearly danced into the living room, and Ellison rose swiftly from the couch. "Well, damn."

Tiger said nothing at all. His gaze roved Carly, lingering on her legs and then on the curve of her waist.

"Why, thank you," Carly said, reaching for her smaller purse to transfer into it what she needed for the day. "It's nice to be appreciated."

"Sure you don't want me to drive?" Ellison asked as they went back to the garage.

"No, I've got it. I want to." Being driven around in Ethan's expensive cars or in the limos he hired for special nights out had made her feel like a princess. But today

Carly wanted to feel powerful, like a kick-ass chick in a superhero movie.

She waited until Tiger and Ellison were settled inside the car before she opened the garage door, started up, and backed out. The neighbors wouldn't be able to miss Tiger sitting in the front seat with her, but they'd be more freaked out if they caught the whole massive bulk of him.

Ethan didn't live far away, time-wise, but his neighborhood might as well have been on another planet. People with big money lived on this hill above the river and had either inherited their riches or made money through the big corporations that had settled in Austin, or both.

When Carly pulled into Ethan's long driveway, she felt both sick to her stomach and elated. Yesterday—had it been only yesterday?—she'd driven here so secure in the knowledge that she was going to marry a rich, successful, stable man. A man not at all like her father, a man who was already planning what they'd do on their ten-year anniversary. Someone who wouldn't disappear into the night, leaving her with all his debts and nowhere to live.

Ethan's obvious indifference toward her had kicked her in the teeth. Carly still didn't know who the woman had been. Someone from work? Friend of a friend?

Did it matter? It was over. Carly had her job, she had friends and her mama and sisters, and she didn't need Ethan. And now she was making friends with Shifters and carrying around men wrapped in duct tape in the trunk of her car. Strange how the entire world could change in one crazy afternoon.

Carly still had her keys to Ethan's house. She unlocked and opened the front door, not bothering to knock.

Tiger and Ellison followed her in, Tiger in his usual silence, Ellison carrying the box of stuff Carly had brought with her. Ellison observed his surroundings with interest, but Tiger behaved as though he couldn't care less where they were. Didn't seem to mind that he was revisiting a place where he'd been shot yesterday either. Trauma like that was supposed to linger in the psyche, but Tiger walked into the house with complete indifference.

Ellison whistled. "Shit, what a spread. I could go for this."

At one time, Carly could have too. She'd loved imagining herself living in this splendor. Now the decor seemed overdone and cold.

They went through the palatial front hall with its graceful spiral staircase and on through the massive living room, toward the kitchen. The pristine furniture in the living room had been overturned, and the door to Ethan's study hung off its hinges, the doorframe splintered.

"Did you do that?" Carly asked Tiger.

Tiger nodded without speaking, but he had a satisfied glint in his eye.

"Good," Carly said,

As they strode into the huge kitchen, Ethan, phone in hand, rose from a table that held his laptop and a mess of papers. "Carly? What the hell . . . ? I need to call you back," Ethan said into the phone before he clicked it off and dropped it to the table. "Carly, what the fuck are you doing bringing *that* back in here?" He pointed an unsteady finger at Tiger. "He *attacked* me. He nearly killed me."

"And you shot him in the stomach," Carly returned. "Seven times." She motioned for Ellison to put the box on the table, which he did, letting it thump down. Carly started going through it, trying to ignore Ethan.

Why had she ever thought Ethan handsome, fun, charming? He had a rather small face, which went with the compact body he kept honed by working out with a trainer. His dark hair was perfectly cut and combed, his nails manicured. He was the epitome of the young man who'd made it.

Ethan had picked out a wife who knew how to smile at people and throw parties. Of course he had—Carly had met Ethan at the gallery when he'd come in to look at some art for his office. He'd wanted to pick out the art himself, he said, because he was the one who had to look at it all day. Carly, for some reason, had thought this showed depth of character.

She understood better now. Ethan was just fussy and didn't trust anyone. He'd wanted to marry Carly, she realized, because he'd been looking for someone who knew how to give dinner parties and impress clients. In other words, he'd wanted his own personal caterer and receptionist. In return, Carly would get to live in a big house on the river with a pool and a view and money to do whatever she wanted. She would quit her job, of course, because any job in the art world was dead-end.

All that might have been fine if Ethan had loved and cherished her, if he'd had any compassion in him, any respect. Looking back, Carly had to wonder if Ethan even liked her.

"He looks fine to me," Ethan snapped, glaring at Tiger. "Obviously I missed him or just grazed him."

"Show him, Tiger."

All this time, Carly had been hearing Tiger's low growls, which strengthened whenever she drew closer to Ethan, lessened when she moved away. She liked it—like a Geiger counter indicating when she was getting too near Ethan's tainted presence.

Tiger inched up his T-shirt to expose a stomach of a tightness Ethan tried desperately to achieve. The pink scars of the healed bullet holes pockmarked Tiger's abdomen.

"See?" Ethan said, though he sounded less certain. "They must have glanced off."

"No," Ellison said from right next to Ethan. "They didn't. Went straight inside and had to be dug out. But Shifters heal fast."

Ethan jumped. Ellison had been wandering around the room but had moved with Shifter stealth to Ethan's side while Ethan's attention had been fixed on Tiger.

"The bullets went in deep, Ethan," Carly said. "You almost killed him. You're lucky he has a hell of a metabolism."

"Well, you'd know about that," Ethan said. "Are you

sleeping with both these guys now? Maybe at the same time? I didn't realize you had a thing for Shifters. How long have you been a Shifter whore?"

Tiger's growl increased, and Ellison leaned close to Ethan. "Now, that's just not nice."

Carly slammed what she'd taken out of the box to the table. "No, let him talk. He's trying to make this my fault. I never cheated on you, Ethan. Never. I caught you, and you can't change that, but you think that if you can make out that *I'm* the slut, you're not in the wrong. But you are. I was loyal to you and did everything you wanted, but that didn't count for shit with you, did it? Not when you got horny on your coffee break."

Ethan looked slightly shocked, as though he hadn't believed Carly would have the guts to say such things to him. She'd had the guts all right, but she'd been raised to keep the peace, not spread venom. That didn't mean Carly was weak; it meant she was polite.

"She's not important to me, Carly," Ethan tried. God, she'd had no idea he could sound so whiny. "We can talk about this."

"Oh, it's way too late for that, honey," Carly said. "You shouldn't have had your lawyer friend call me and threaten me. You want everything back you ever gave me? Fine. Here it is. Including the ring you wasted sixty-thousand dollars on."

Carly took it out of its box and threw it at him, laughing as Ethan scrambled to catch it. "And the necklace from Tiffany's, and the sound system I never liked." She threw these at him too, Ethan flailing after each one.

Ellison, next to him, folded his arms over his broad chest and grinned. Tiger didn't move, as though he understood that Carly needed to do this, as though he enjoyed watching her kick at Ethan the only way she knew how.

Carly threw trinkets, souvenirs, and the digital photo frame full of happy pictures of herself and Ethan at him. Finally she picked up the box itself and threw the whole thing.

"*That's* everything you've ever given me. Except the heartburn from your fancy restaurants, and the worry that I wasn't good enough for your snotty friends. I'd love to throw those at you too."

Ethan caught the box and slammed it back to the table. "You're right. I gave you *everything*, Carly. You were just a stupid receptionist with no future until you met me. I even gave you that dress. You only look so good because I took you to the best stores."

Carly clutched the dress's bodice. "No, you didn't. I remember. You didn't like it and refused to buy it, so I put it on my own credit card. It's mine."

"But I paid that credit card for you. I've been paying all your bills, Carly. You wouldn't have shit right now if it wasn't for me."

Carly's vision tinged with red. Through the haze she saw the image of Ethan banging away at the woman on the counter, her legs around Ethan's bare hips. Ethan had been wearing a business shirt, the tails of it just hiding his buns, and his pants with their fine leather belt had fallen around his ankles. He'd looked absolutely ridiculous.

How many times had Carly congratulated herself that she'd snared him as she'd run her hands over Ethan's honed body? Liking that he kept himself in shape, was so good-looking, and she was going to marry him?

Next to Tiger, and even Ellison, whom she'd only just met, Ethan was fading to nothing. He had the charisma of a flea. And he'd done his damnedest to make sure Carly felt lucky that he'd noticed her.

Carly's rage boiled over. She yanked open the zipper on the silk dress and shoved the garment down over her hips. In her underwear and heels, she stepped out of the dress and balled it up.

"You want this back? Here it is." She threw the wadded-up dress at Ethan, hitting him square in the chest. "Wait, did you pay for the lingerie too? Fine, you can have it."

As Carly unsnapped and stripped off her bra, Ellison's

gray wolf eyes widened, and he swung around on the heels of his cowboy boots and stared at the wall. "Turning my back, turning my back."

Tiger pushed himself between Carly and Ethan. *"Don't look at her."* His growl filled the room, vibrating against the glass kitchen cabinets. One had broken, Carly saw.

Carly threw the bra down on the table and planted her hand on her hips; she was still in her mile-high, leopard-print heels. Those were *hers,* and she wasn't giving them back. "No, let him look, Tiger. I want him to see what he's never getting again. *Ever.*"

Ethan's terrified gaze wasn't for Carly. Fear was evident in his wide eyes, in the fleck of spittle on his lips as he was caught and pinned by Tiger's stare. He knew damn well he'd shot Tiger full on, and now Tiger stood here healthy and whole, ready for payback.

Carly saw Ethan's hand snake for his cell phone, but Ellison was there, clamping his wrist. "Don't think so," Ellison said. "Now the lady has given you back what you gave her, fair and square. You let her walk out of here, and you don't bother her again."

Ethan's voice was shaky, but his arrogance still came through. "She can pay me for the Corvette, though."

"What?" Carly demanded, her voice rising. "I sent your stupid car back to you without a scratch."

"And those Shifters sprayed in it. It smells like cat piss. I'll have to have it detailed."

"Sean and Spike?" Ellison asked in surprise. "They couldn't have. Shifters don't spray. Must have been a regular cat that got inside it. A tomcat pissed off about something."

"What are you talking about?" Ethan snapped. "That guy with all the tattoos ruined my car!"

"Nah." Ellison, who still had Ethan's wrist, leaned close. "You know how Spike marks his territory? He doesn't spray. He kills his enemies and grinds their bones and blood into the soil. He leaves just enough scent to explain to everyone else not to cross the line with him."

Ethan's face was gray, his pupils pinpricks. He'd pass out any second. "Spike? Tiger? What kind of names do you people have?"

"Yeah, I know, Ellison is a real strange one. What was my mom thinking? Carly, even though it's a crime to cover you up, you're going to have to put something on before we leave. If you get arrested for driving around like that, Liam will kill me."

"No problem," Carly said, folding her arms over her breasts. "I have a bunch of stuff here that I bet he was going to burn. Be right down." She turned away, then looked back at Ethan over her shoulder. "Sorry, Ethan. The panties are mine."

CHAPTER TEN

Carly skimmed up the spiral staircase, fuming, not letting herself think. She'd grab her stuff and get the hell out of this house. She might even burn the clothes she'd left here, because she didn't want any reminders of Ethan the Asshole.

Tiger, of course, followed her.

Carly went, not to the room she'd slept in with Ethan whenever she'd stayed over, but to the dressing room off his bedroom that also opened into the hall. *I mean, who the hell has a dressing room?*

Ethan did, and it looked like the best-fitted dressing room from *GQ*. Walnut paneling covered the walls that were filled with drawers and shelves. He had a separate armoire for his suits, a sofa with a side table, and a little wet bar where Ethan could mix himself a drink while he dressed for his night on the town.

The dressing room was like a walk-in closet on steroids. Carly had thought it the coolest thing when she'd first seen it. Now it looked overdone and ostentatious, like the rest of Ethan's life.

Ethan had condescended to let Carly have an empty drawer in a corner near the sofa. She went to it and started yanking out her stuff, pausing to slide a T-shirt over her nudity.

Tiger's arms came around her from behind, his hands on the wall pinning her in place. Carly turned around, his warmth like a shelter. Tiger lowered his head to her T-shirt and sniffed.

"This reeks of him."

"Yes, I know." Carly heaved a small sigh. "But there's nothing I can do about it right now. I have a backup dress at the gallery, but even so, I'm going to be late, *again*."

Tiger didn't let her go. He brushed his nose from her neck across her shoulder, nuzzling her as he had earlier this morning, the absolute strength of him fixing her in place.

He raised his head and looked into her eyes. Carly had the sensation of being studied, thoroughly, much more so even than when Dylan had looked at her. Tiger might not know how to kiss, but he could look into a person and see everything.

His T-shirt stretched over a body that had stopped Carly in her tracks when she'd first seen it. And the second time, and the third. Tiger was made of muscle, but that didn't stop him from moving so quietly his prey never knew he was on it until too late.

"You really are a tiger," Carly said softly.

Tiger's expression didn't change, and he didn't answer. Stupid thing to say. Of course he knew what he was. More than Carly knew what she was.

Tiger cupped her face in his big hand, thumb tracing her cheekbone. The tenderness in the touch made her heart squeeze.

Carly moved closer to him, wanting his warmth. She was in only a T-shirt, panties, and heels, no match for the frigid breeze of Ethan's air-conditioning.

Tiger seemed to know what she needed. He pressed her back into the wall, his body over hers but never crushing. His warm weight stopped her shivering, and his hand moved from the curve of her waist to her breast, heating, soothing.

Carly tugged him down and kissed him. As before, he didn't move his mouth in response, but that didn't matter. Carly seamed his lips with her tongue, feeling his jerk of surprise when her tongue touched his.

His hands moved on her then, molding to her waist, her back, her buttocks. Tiger licked her lips in return, copying her movements. They played like that, a kiss and not a kiss, while Tiger ran his hands along her body, learning her.

Carly caressed his back, finding every plane of it, the solidity of his shoulders, the strength of his spine, the compact mound of his buttocks. At the same time, Tiger touched her mouth with little licks, tasting her while she tasted the bite of him.

Tiger rumbled in his throat, for all the world as if he was purring. He was a wild thing, containing himself for her. The incredible power he'd shown breaking apart the hospital bed, shredding Walker's gun, surviving wounds that would kill any other man in seconds, was dampened down so he wouldn't hurt Carly.

The sweetness of that made her ache.

Tiger opened her mouth more with his exploring, until the kiss turned real, Carly hungrily imbibing him. His hands were everywhere, on her hips, breasts, buttocks, moving down her waist, around to her front, between her legs to cup her. The thin panties did nothing to keep out the hardness of his hand, and heat knifed through her.

"No," she said breathlessly, pulling away.

Tiger's eyes opened, flooding with confusion and also pain. Pain?

"I mean, not here." Carly pressed her hand to his cheek. "Not in Ethan's . . ."

Then again, why not? Ethan had been happy to screw someone else in the kitchen where Carly had cooked, where Yvette and Armand had once prepared Ethan one of their exquisite meals. She shuddered even thinking about it.

Carly started to pull Tiger back down to her. Why not wrap her legs around this gorgeous man, give herself the best sex of her life in Ethan's oversized dressing room?

Oversized like his ego, compensating for a lack of size elsewhere.

"Because I don't want it to be about him," Carly finished.

Tiger's brows drew down. "Don't want what to be about who?"

"You and me." Carly looked into his interesting eyes. "I want you and me to be about you and me. Not a rebound, not revenge, not about Ethan."

"Why would it be?"

The question was genuine. She realized that to Tiger, in this moment, Ethan didn't exist, wasn't important. *What a great way to look at the world.*

Carly smiled and caressed his cheek. "I like the way you think. But *I* don't want a reminder of him. All right? I want this to happen somewhere . . . special."

Tiger slid his hand from between her legs, heady friction, to rest on her belly. "Special."

"Special." Carly kissed his lips again. "Like a romantic hotel room, or in my house with the lights low and the music on, after we've had some fine wine."

From the look on his face, Tiger had no idea what she was talking about. He didn't know how to kiss, he'd never put together sex with a rose-petal-strewn bed and a good vintage. And yet, being in Ethan's dressing room, half-naked with Tiger while he touched her all over, was by far the most sensual encounter she'd ever had.

"You never brought a girl flowers and candy?" Carly nuzzled his cheek as he'd nuzzled her. Nice. The bristles of his whiskers tickled her nose, his skin warm.

"They threw my mate in to me, and took her away when we were done."

The grating words made Carly jerk upright. The pain was back in Tiger's golden eyes, the bewilderment of trying to follow Carly's teasing words mixing with bad things from his past.

"What?" *Threw her in and took her away?* What was he talking about? "Who's *they*?"

"The people who kept me in the cage, until Iona let me out."

Tiger's words were stark, matching his bleak look. "Who the hell kept you in a cage?" Carly tasted rage. What had happened to him?

"The researchers who made me."

"Researchers?" Like Dr. Brennan, the slimy anthropologist? With his bodyguard backup?

Was that what they wanted? To put Shifters like Tiger and Ellison with his cowboy hat into cages?

"Well, I don't know who Iona is, but I'm glad she let you go," Carly said. "Good for her."

"She took me out, and Liam brought me here, to his Shiftertown. Liam's trying to teach me to be normal."

The ironic twist on the last word caught at her. "What's normal?" Carly asked with half a laugh. "Ethan is considered normal. And he's a total bastard." She cupped Tiger's face, losing her smile. "Don't be normal, Tiger. Promise me?"

Tiger closed a light hand around Carly's wrist. He gave her the intense look again, as though he were trying to read every thought inside her, as though he were looking for something to hold on to.

Carly rose on tiptoe and kissed him again, loving his warmth, the amazing power of him. Tiger's golden eyes half closed as he nuzzled while she kissed, nipped while she licked. Wanting snaked through her, hotter than ever.

The door creaked open and someone cleared his throat.

"Sorry to interrupt y'all." Ellison's over-the-top Texas accent preceded him inside. "But Ethan passed out a little bit ago. Maybe I was holding his wrist too hard? Should be careful about that. Unfortunately, he's coming around, and he's back to wanting to call the cops. I say we get while the getting's good."

Carly started to turn away, to follow Ellison, but Tiger stepped to her, not letting her move. He studied her in his slow way, as though memorizing her and every detail of this moment.

Finally, Tiger caressed her wrist with his thumb and eased back, releasing her. He never looked away.

Heart thumping, Carly grabbed up all her clothes and stuffed them into a tote bag, sliding into a pair of shorts so she'd be decent enough to drive. Though Ellison had again turned his back, Tiger watched her, the heated look that roved her body making Carly want to hurry up and find that romantic hotel room.

"I'll drive," Ellison said, taking away the keys Carly had brought out from her purse.

Tiger liked the arrangement. Before Carly could walk around to the front passenger door, Tiger wrapped his arm around her waist and pulled her into the backseat with him.

Ellison didn't wait for them to straighten themselves out. He gunned the car as soon as the doors closed, heading away from the cloying house and back to the fresh but humid air of Austin.

Tiger didn't like Ethan's smell on the clothes Carly had insisted on bringing with her, including the ones she wore. But he could always build a bonfire when they got back to Shiftertown—Shifters liked bonfires—and burn them all. Andrea could lend Carly some clothes for now. The two women looked to be about the same build, as far as Tiger could tell. Kim was too short; Shifter women like Glory, far too tall.

"You know, I like humans," Ellison said as he drove. "My mate is human—you'd like her, Carly. Maria's fiery and sweet, kind of like you. But that human Ethan is a piece of work."

"I know." Carly sounded sad under her anger. "It's humiliating. I was going to marry him."

"That's the advantage of being Shifter," Ellison said. "You can smell if someone is a shithead right off the bat. And that guy really stinks."

"No kidding. Where were you when I needed your sniffer two years ago?"

"Right here in Austin, sweetie." Ellison winked at her in the mirror. "You should have come to Shiftertown more often."

"I didn't know anything about Shifters before yesterday. Never thought about them much." Carly grimaced. "Sorry, no offense."

Tiger saw Ellison's grin in the rearview mirror. "None taken."

Carly smiled back at him, and her wide, red-lipped mouth made Tiger's need bite him. He reached for her and scooped her around to face him, positioning her knees alongside his thighs on the seat. Carly looked surprised but didn't pull away, and rested her hands on his shoulders.

"Quit," she said. "This is dangerous."

"I'll drive carefully," Ellison said, stepping on the gas.

Tiger wound his arms around Carly's waist. "I'll keep you safe. You can forget about the human. You're my mate now."

He saw Ellison glance in the rearview at them again, but his smile was gone. Carly looked puzzled.

"I'm happy to forget about Ethan. But you . . . You need to learn how to romance a girl."

Ellison barked a laugh. "Good luck with that."

"You don't even know how to kiss." Carly leaned close, bathing Tiger in her good scent.

Tiger knew that if he could lose himself in this woman— this strange woman with her laughter when he didn't understand what was funny; her long, luscious legs; her smile that lit fires in his heart—then he'd never be afraid again. The nightmares, the frustration when other Shifters expected him to make the right response, the ever-present fear that he'd be plucked out of this relative peace and put back into a cage, all of that would vanish. The fears ate at him every day, except yesterday, and today—all the times he'd been with Carly.

Her presence soothed everything feral in him, the wild instincts that the researchers had bred into Tiger and that Liam was trying to ease out of him. Tiger had never been soothed in his life. But his body relaxed when he was around Carly, as though he'd never realized his muscles had been pulled tight until the tightness was gone.

Tiger touched Carly's lips, liking the amazing softness of them. "In that room, that wasn't kissing?"

"Well, it was." Her face went pink, so pretty. "But not sweet kissing."

"You have different kinds of kissing?"

Ellison made a noise up front. "I am *so* enjoying this conversation."

"Like this."

Carly pursed her lips and touched them to Tiger's mouth. Tiger liked that, her lips soft and warm, the press light, yet it made his body heat with need.

Carly pulled away. "See, you're supposed to kiss back. When you don't move your lips, I think you're not enjoying it."

How the hell could she think that? Tiger wanted her, wanted to strip off the shorts and open his jeans and have her right here. Who cared about the cars around them, and Ellison in the driver's seat? Tiger should be inside Carly, where he belonged.

He hadn't understood why she hadn't wanted to take what they were doing to its natural completeness back in the house. She'd said it would be about Ethan, even though Ellison had the man contained downstairs. Carly seemed to think the place they did it was important. Another thing Tiger didn't understand.

Ethan was nothing. The man was a liar and a fraud, weak and ineffectual. If he'd been a Shifter in the wild, he'd have been dead a long time ago. His existence inside the house or out of it made no difference to Tiger being with Carly.

But it was important to Carly, and so he'd stopped.

Females could be fussy, both Liam and Connor had explained, and the male who wanted one had to learn how to please her. Women could afford to be choosy because males were prevalent in Shifter societies and females were scarce. Males competed with each other for the females, and females sat back and picked the best ones.

Of course, in the old days, before Collars and Shifter-towns, Liam had said, a Shifter male could choose his female by locking her away and having sex with her until she agreed she was his mate and filled his house with cubs.

Either way made no sense to Tiger. Mates were bonded to each other, no need for enticing each other or trapping each other. They were already one.

"I'll show you." Carly formed her lips into a pucker again, waiting for Tiger to imitate her.

He pulled his lips into the round shape Carly made, but instead of kissing him, she burst out laughing.

"I'm sorry," she said, wiping tears from her eyes. "But you look so funny."

Tiger relaxed his mouth, liking her laughter so much that her words didn't sting. He put his hand behind her neck and pulled her down to him.

"Kiss me," he said.

Her laughter died, her eyes went soft, and Carly touched her lips to his mouth. This time, Tiger shaped his lips to match hers, meeting hers pressure for pressure.

"Oh," she said, her breath brushing his skin. "That's nice."

Much more than nice. Tiger touched his lips to hers again, learning how to add and release the pressure as she did. It wasn't the same as when he'd tasted the inside of her mouth, but good. Very good.

He slid his hands down Carly's spine, finding a gap between the waistband of her shorts and her warm back. From there he could dip his fingers inside, brushing the waistband of the panties with the tiny polka dots. Tiger remembered her walking away from Ethan in nothing but her high heels and panties, her legs gorgeous, bare back straight.

He'd already been rock hard from watching her slide off the dress and throw off the bra, and the little wriggle in her hips when she'd walked off in fury had spiraled the mating frenzy through him. Tiger couldn't help but follow her.

He'd told himself he was protecting her, but Tiger knew his reason for going after her had been far more basic.

The skin of her buttocks was smooth, hot from the weather and from being enclosed in the shorts. Tiger wanted to push the shorts out of his way, but he couldn't because it was so tight in this little car. When he got Carly back to Shiftertown, he'd peel the clothes from her and touch her all over.

Carly drew back from the kiss. "What are you doing?"

"Touching you."

Tiger brought one hand up between them and cupped her breast, easily feeling it through the thin shirt. He lightly pinched her nipple, watching it firm to a point. Carly drew in a little breath, her eyes fixing on him.

"You shouldn't do that," she whispered.

"Why not?"

She leaned closer. "It makes me want to do bad things."

Good. The things wouldn't be bad though. Sex was never bad with a mate. "Do them with me," Tiger said, fingers going lower on her buttocks.

In the front Ellison reached to the middle of the dashboard. "I'm turning on the radio. Right now." He pushed buttons until a country song filled the car, a man and a woman singing about kissing each other. Ellison chuckled. "I guess that was just my luck."

The song seemed to galvanize Carly. She wrapped her arms around him as the strains of the music went on, and kissed his lips again.

Tiger returned the kiss, learning how to match what she did. He tugged at her nipple while their lips met and parted, met again.

Ellison pulled up at a stoplight. A man in a truck next to them looked over, then he started to whoop and honk. Carly lifted her head, her face bright red.

Tiger didn't care. Let them, as Ellison liked to say, eat their hearts out.

Ellison pulled away through the intersection, and the truck beside them turned off, the man giving a thumbs-up sign as he went.

Carly unwound herself from Tiger, pried his hands from her body, and sat down next to him. "How embarrassing. Sorry, Ellison."

Ellison was grinning. "Hey, Shifters don't care. I once came out of a bar to find my back-door neighbor and his human girlfriend going at it, full throttle, on the hood of my pickup. I had to wait 'til they were done. My neighbor said he was being discreet by using my truck instead of a total stranger's."

"Nice of him," Carly said. "So Shifters really *don't* care about romantic hotel rooms, rose petals, and champagne?"

"We can," Ellison answered. "But when the mating frenzy hits, all we need is a surface that doesn't give too much."

"Mating frenzy," Carly repeated. "Connor mentioned that."

"Every Shifter has it. That crazed need to lock yourself in a room with your mate and go for it as much as and for as long as you can. We don't come out for days, sometimes."

"Days." She sounded hesitant.

"Ellison." Tiger thought of the phrase Liam and Connor used so often. "Shut it."

"Goddess, now you're starting to sound like a Morrissey," Ellison said, never losing his good-natured drawl. "You've been living with them way too long."

"Why *do* you live with them?" Carly asked Tiger. "You don't want a place of your own?"

Ellison answered before Tiger could. "Shifters don't have a choice. Only so many houses in Shiftertown, and we're not allowed to live outside it. In my house, there's my mate, Maria, Deni—she's my sister—and Deni's two sons, and hopefully a cub of my own soon." His voice warmed when he spoke of the potential cub. "Tiger's from . . . out of town, and there weren't many houses with room for him when he arrived. Liam's is one of the largest houses, and after Sean and his mate moved in with Dylan and Glory, Liam had an extra bedroom."

"And no one else wanted me living in their house," Tiger finished.

CHAPTER ELEVEN

He spoke the bare truth, but Carly stared at him, aghast. "Why not? Did they say that?"

"They didn't have to," Tiger said.

Tiger closed his mouth, unsure how to explain, but Ellison spoke up. "Remember what he did in the hospital room? Yeah, I heard all about it. Plus he nearly took out that human, Walker. The other Shifters are afraid he'll do something like that."

"But that's not fair," Carly said. "In the hospital, they had you scared to death. You knocked out Walker because he was spying on me and was carrying a loaded pistol. I mean, who does that?"

The warmth in Tiger's heart escalated. Carly was looking at him in dismay, not fear, radiating anger at others for not understanding him.

They *had* scared him in the hospital—he'd been afraid he'd never see Carly again.

"And anyway," Carly went on. "If you were attacking to hurt people, your Collar would have stopped you." She pointed to the inert black and silver chain around his throat. "Shocks you when you get aggressive, right?"

Again Ellison jumped in before Tiger could speak. "You bet it does. Hurts like a mo fo."

Tiger remained silent. Carly was his mate, and he trusted her, but he didn't want to frighten her too soon with the fact that his Collar was a fake.

Carly leaned forward in the seat. "Ellison, you missed the turnoff. You take Koenig so I can get out to the gallery."

Ellison glanced back through the mirror, looking at Tiger. Tiger gave him a nod.

"Sorry." Ellison slowed and turned at the next intersection, driving north to make for the 290.

"Thanks. I really appreciate this," Carly said.

Ellison had been heading for Shiftertown, knowing Tiger wanted to be alone with her. But Tiger was curious to see this gallery where Carly worked, wanted to make sure all was well there.

Carly settled back, her scent sweet and spicy, but also conveying to Tiger her underlying nervousness. Not fear for what Tiger and Ellison could do to her—it was more subtle than that, buried deep. Carly feared to trust at all. The man Ethan had taken her trust in him away from her by blatantly sexing the other woman. His house had still smelled of that encounter, despite the cleaning solution scent over it. The house had also smelled of Tiger's blood.

Tiger had never trusted easily either. The things the researchers had done to him had made him close himself off, fearing to believe in anyone. Liam and his family were trying to instruct Tiger in how to trust, and so far, they'd not betrayed him. But when the researchers had taken away Tiger's cub and then told him it had died, Tiger's last spark of hope had died with it.

He'd watched the spark die in Carly when she'd seen Ethan and the woman. Whatever people had done to her in the past, they, like Ethan, had made promises, then withdrawn them, just as the researchers had poked things through the bars of Tiger's cage to see what he'd do. As a cub he'd needed touch and caring, and he'd received none.

And then they'd left him alone. Completely alone, abandoned, not even having the courtesy to kill him.

Tiger would never let Carly feel that alone. Never. Not even if he had to stick with her day and night until she understood.

Armand's art gallery lay outside the heart of Austin in a tiny town called Karlsberg that was being built up and gentrified. Large, historic homes mingled with new mansions, and several streets of art galleries, restaurants, and gourmet food shops attracted well-heeled tourists.

The long stretch of road where Carly had first met Tiger was again deserted as Ellison drove along it. They passed the place where the Corvette had broken down, not far past the sign saying that Karlsberg was thirty miles away.

Tiger recognized the spot too. He looked over at Carly, giving her his full stare. Nothing hinting or coy about it.

She knew she should talk to him. She should say, *I can't rush into another relationship right now. I need to figure out how I feel about my fiancé turning on me, and I have abandonment issues. Don't make me care about you, only to have my world pulled out from under me again.*

Carly would say all that if she were sensible. But no, she'd decided to kiss him, and to teach Tiger to kiss her. She'd fantasized about having crazed, intense sex in Ethan's dressing room with Tiger, and not just as payback to Ethan.

She should slow down, until she was not needy, and then assess what she was feeling for Tiger. Things were moving too fast, as fast as Ellison racing down the highway.

But Carly would feel awkward saying such things in front of Ellison, Tiger's friend and right now his watchdog. *Watch-wolf?* She'd have to wait until she and Tiger were alone, but that would be dangerous too.

Not that Ellison was paying attention to Carly right now. He kept looking into the rearview mirror, but not at Carly or Tiger. Carly saw a flash in the side-view mirror and turned around to see an SUV coming up behind them, very fast.

This wasn't unusual. People got out here on these stretches of back highway and let it all go. It was dangerous, particularly on this two-lane road, but that didn't stop people.

The SUV—black, like the one Walker and Brennan had used yesterday—zoomed closer. It pulled around their car into the oncoming lane, slackening its speed to run side by side with them. The windows were tinted, hiding the view of the driver and any passengers.

Tiger moved to look around Carly at the SUV, his gaze fixing on it.

"Ellison," he said. "Go."

"I hear you."

Ellison floored it. Carly's fairly low performance car sputtered as it leapt ahead of the SUV, then it smoothed out and sped away.

The other vehicle sped up next to them. Ellison grinned out the window at them and pressed the accelerator even harder. Carly's car zipped forward, but the other kept pace with it.

"Get away from it," Tiger said abruptly.

"Can't outrun them." Ellison took his foot from the accelerator. "Have to do this another way." He stepped on the brakes.

The SUV zoomed ahead as Ellison suddenly slowed. Carly assumed that would be the end of it, but red brake lights flashed on the SUV ahead, and it made a U-turn, driving halfway off the road to do it.

"Shit," Ellison said.

The SUV came toward them. "Go!" Tiger shouted.

Ellison said, "Hold on," right before he slammed on the brakes and spun the car to face back the way they'd come.

He jammed on the gas, racing back toward Austin, which loomed in the distance, the buildings of UT and the capitol area hugging the horizon.

"He's still coming," Carly said.

"Yeah, I see that." Ellison hunkered over the wheel, his foot down, as though he could make the car go faster by pushing it.

"Do you know who they are?" Carly asked Tiger.

"No."

But it couldn't be good. Carly's body tightened as they raced on toward the city. Ellison was going plenty fast, and they might reach town in time to lose themselves in traffic.

The black SUV put on a burst of speed—no unmodified vehicle could have decreased the distance between themselves and Carly's car so quickly. The SUV pulled up alongside them.

Another car came over the rise in the oncoming lane, straight at the black SUV. That other driver saw and swerved to move as close as possible to the shoulder, which was minuscule in this stretch.

"Son of a . . ." Ellison muttered.

The SUV pulled ahead of Ellison, clipping the front fender of Carly's car. Ellison jerked the steering wheel sideways, but too late. Carly's car jarred as the other vehicle bumped it, then Carly's car hit the drop-off on the road's shoulder, tires spinning on the dirt and grass beyond.

Ellison cranked the steering wheel, trying to pull the car out of its spin. The car skittered and danced. Tiger grabbed both headrests of the front seat, and Carly grabbed on to Tiger.

They might have made it if the SUV hadn't turned around again. The first oncoming car went past, the driver twisting to see what was happening. The SUV timed its own pass to ram the left back end of Carly's car.

The car lost hold of the pavement and rose into the air. Carly's stomach rose with it, her view of the rolling hills distorted as the car flipped once, twice. She only knew that Tiger was solid beneath her, one constant in the churning world.

The car landed on its side, slid down into a ditch, and

then came down on its tires, slanting with the ditch, half on grass, half in mud and dirty water. The engine hissed and spit and then all went quiet.

Tiger broke the window of the bent door and crawled out of the car, his large torso catching on the frame. He grunted and heaved, tearing apart half the door, but at last he pushed free.

Carly lay on the seat behind him, her eyes closed, blood on her face. Tiger's heart thrummed with panic, but when he touched her, he felt the warmth of her skin, the press of her breath. Alive if not awake.

Ellison, in the front, was likewise slumped, the steering wheel propping him up. His face sported bruises, but he too breathed.

Tiger braced himself on the side of the car, leaned back in through the window, and wrapped his arms around Carly's torso. He pulled her out, trying to be gentle, but needing to get her *out*.

He lifted her once he got her clear of the car and laid her on the grass about ten yards away. At least the grass was dry, warm from the morning sun, which was beaming brightly.

Tiger went back for Ellison. Ellison was Shifter and strong—he'd come around quickly—but Tiger had learned from Connor the dangers from gas or other liquids leaking from a car. Best to get away from the wreck until they knew it was safe.

He was halfway back to the car when the driver of the black SUV, which had stopped, got out and came toward them. For a second, Tiger thought the man was Walker, but quickly realized that he wasn't. This man wore black, like Walker, and he had a similar build and close-shaved hair, but the scent was wrong.

Like Walker, the man carried a gun. Tiger didn't know much about guns, but the one he'd broken apart last night had looked lethal, and so did this one. The man looked for a moment at Tiger, then turned and made directly for Carly.

Tiger became the Bengal in the space of three seconds. He was too far from the man, who was raising the black, square-looking gun to aim at Carly.

Tiger changed direction and sprinted for Carly. His tiger was faster than any other Shifter he'd encountered, and he landed on Carly just as the first bullets left the gun.

He felt the bullets enter him, pain blossoming, reawakening yesterday's wounds. Unlike the slow bangs of Ethan's pistol, though, this pistol shot so fast Tiger couldn't count the retorts. He only prayed the bullets didn't go through his thick tiger body and into Carly.

"Hey!" Ellison's yell cut through the pain. "Aw, *shit!*"

Two more flat shots sounded, one clanking on the car, the other thudding with a meaty sound as it went into Ellison. The shooter walked to Tiger, Tiger smelling him coming.

Walked. Deliberately. Slowly. He reached Tiger where he lay dazed and in pain, dusty black boots halting by Tiger's head. The man didn't shoot. He stopped, watched, waited.

Then two more bullets went into Tiger's back. Tiger gave up trying to know anything and let himself succumb to darkness.

CHAPTER TWELVE

"Oh my God. Oh my God. Tiger."

Tiger heard Carly's voice as he rose toward consciousness, toward a mountain of pain that waited for him. They'd shot him in the basement of the research facility, repeatedly, to see how much he could take, but they at least let him rest between bullets.

"Sean." Ellison was nearby, voice heavy. "I think you're gonna have to bring the sword. No, not for me. For Tiger."

Tiger heard the exclamation on the other end of Ellison's cell phone, which must have survived the crash and the shooting. The thing was as resilient as Tiger.

"He's waking up," Ellison said. "Who the hell was that?"

"Hell if I know." Carly's voice held tears, and two hot droplets fell onto Tiger's face. "I don't care right now. He's still alive. Thank God."

Carly's lips touched his cheek. Tiger tried to pucker his in response, showing her how much he'd learned. She didn't stop weeping, so he must not have done very well.

"Tiger, honey, don't move," Carly said. "We'll get you to a hospital. You'll be all right."

"I don't know," Ellison said. "He's amazing, but that was about fifteen rounds from an automatic weapon. It has to have torn him apart inside."

"Don't say that. He's strong. He's a fighter."

"We'll help him the best we can, trust me."

"Hang on, Tiger. Hang on."

Carly's light touch slid through Tiger's pain, making his heart beat harder, his lungs draw breath. The pain became incandescent then, but Tiger was breathing, functioning. He might not need the Sword of the Guardian yet.

An odd custom, the working part of Tiger's brain thought. The Guardian's sword pierced the heart of the dead Shifter, or the dying one, releasing the soul and turning the body to dust. The legend, Sean had told him, said that the Sword had been created to save Shifters' souls from a nasty, evil Fae prince. The Shifters' bodies had crumbled to dust, and the souls of the enslaved Shifters had been released, freed to go to the Summerland. The story reassured all Shifters that, though they might be enslaved during life, they never would be in death.

Tiger had been enslaved until last winter—he hadn't known about the seasons even to know what winter was. Now he was free, at least as free as he could be. He lived under Liam's watchful eye, had to wear a fake Collar to fool humans into thinking he was still enslaved, and had few remote places in which he could run flat out as a tiger, but it was better than what he'd had.

But now he wanted more. Freedom to be with his mate. The joy of running until *he* wanted to stop. Tiger was tired of being feared. Mistrusted. In pain. Afraid.

"Carly." Tiger barely moved his lips, but the sound of his mate's name gave him strength.

He needed to live, so he could be with her. Forty years of hell had coalesced into the moment he'd seen her backside sticking out of the red car, heard her voice, felt her smile. He'd start believing in the Goddess if he thought she'd known to bring Tiger to the road at the exact moment Carly Randal needed help.

"Carly."

"Don't talk. Don't move." Carly bent over Tiger, her face streaked with tears. "We're going to help you. They're coming."

"I don't need . . ."

Talking was too much effort. Keeping his mouth shut was a good idea.

Time must have passed, because more people were now kneeling around him. He'd expected to hear sirens. Humans loved their sirens.

"His breathing is good," Dylan said above him. "Andrea."

A smooth, feminine hand pressed to Tiger's chest, palm flat. He smelled Andrea's strange half-Shifter scent, the subtler scent of her cub clinging to her. Tiger hoped the boy had been left safely at home. That's what Shiftertowns were good for. Keeping the cubs safe.

Sean knelt near his mate, the vibrant hum of the Sword of the Guardian shimmering. Tiger had always been able to hear it, though Sean had said that was unusual.

Tiger cracked open his eyes. He could barely see, but he could make out Andrea with her hand around the Sword's blade, Sean holding its hilt. Curling wisps of silver snaked from the sword into Andrea, and out through Andrea's hand to Tiger.

"He's torn up in there," Andrea said. "A complete mess. So many of them."

Bullets, she meant. The threads of magic from Andrea hurt—hurt a lot.

Then Carly laid her hand on Tiger's forehead. The coolness of her touch spread like a balm through his battered body and tangled limbs.

Andrea's eyes popped open. "Wait. What?"

The new pain that tore through Tiger cut through Carly's touch, even his mate's presence not soothing it. Tiger groaned, then the groan turned to a roar. He balled his fists, clenching his jaw.

"What the fuck?" That was from Sean.

White-hot trails flowed through Tiger's body, paths

cutting from the embedded wounds to his skin. Tiger shifted without wanting to, becoming a snarling half-man, half-Tiger beast as the pain continued.

"What are you doing?" Carly cried. "Help him."

"I can't." Andrea pulled away, the silver threads going away with her, but Tiger barely felt the disconnection.

Blood bubbled up from his wounds, and then from new ones as the bullets that had lodged inside him pushed their way out. The bullets clicked together and rolled off him, gathering in little piles around his body.

And it *hurt*. Tiger kept growling, pain like a blast furnace. The bullets hadn't hurt this much when they'd gone *in*.

"They're closing up," Carly said, wonder in her voice. "Tiger, how the hell are you doing that?"

If Tiger knew, he'd also find a way to stop the crazy pain. He groped for Carly, and Carly grabbed his hand and held on. Tiger's beast fur receded as the agony lessened a bit, his human flesh and fingers returning.

"Andrea, what did you do?" Dylan sounded angry, but his scent betrayed his alarm.

"I didn't do anything," Andrea said. "I mean, nothing more than I normally do. I close my eyes and see the wounds as threads, and I try to untangle them. I hadn't even started—it was such a mess."

Ellison coughed. "Well, whatever it was, can you see if it will work on me?"

"*Now,* please," a new voice said. Female, small but loud—Maria, the young woman Ellison had fallen madly in love with.

Andrea and her Fae scent moved from Tiger, leaving him relatively alone with Carly. "*You* did it," Tiger whispered. "The mate's healing touch."

"No," Dylan said sharply before Carly could answer. "This was more than that. You, my friend, are becoming more of a puzzle instead of less of one."

"Whatever," Carly snapped at him. "Instead of questioning him and lecturing him, how about getting him home so he can rest? He saved my life, and I think he deserves a little quiet for that."

When Tiger woke again, he was in the big loft on the third floor of the Morrissey house, in the room where he now slept.

He liked this room, large and breezy with four windows, one on each side. After a life spent in darkness, shut away, not knowing winter from summer, sunrise from sunset, now he could see the world he'd missed. Sometimes Tiger simply sat up here, watching the Shifters move through their lives, gazing at the many human houses and buildings that surrounded Shiftertown, the cars and people that rushed through, never knowing he watched over them.

Now he woke in the large bed they'd bought for him, holding Carly's hand.

"Why didn't ambulances come?" Tiger asked. For some reason, this was what preyed on his mind. There should have been ambulances, police, and men with tranq guns, as there had been in Ethan's neighborhood on top of the hill.

Carly bent over him, her green eyes full of concern. "I don't know. Maybe the Shifters told them not to."

Tiger started to shake his head, then stopped as it started to pound. "Humans don't do what Shifters say."

"I have no idea, then. Doesn't matter. You spurted those bullets out of your body, and your wounds are already closing. Andrea says it's crazy. Dylan says that sure, you're faster at healing than most Shifters, but this is something new. Even for you."

"You were there."

"I know I was there. I saw it firsthand."

"The touch of a mate." Tiger squeezed her hand, finding himself so weak he barely moved her fingers. He hated being weak.

"Don't even look at me like I have some kind of magic powers. This isn't the movies. And anyway, Dylan said no."

"Dylan doesn't know everything." Tiger's lips twitched. "He only thinks he does."

"Yes, well, Liam said no too, and Sean, Andrea, and Ellison, and a really, really big man called Ronan, and a ten-foot blonde named Glory."

"Dylan's mate," Tiger said, his voice too faint for his comfort.

"So I gathered," Carly said. "She looked at me like she'd take a piece out of me if I wasn't nice to you."

"What happened to Walker? The shooter was dressed like Walker."

"Walker was taken to Ronan's house—I think that's what I heard. They didn't want him here when you got back."

"I need to talk to him." Tiger pushed aside the sheet and lifted his shoulders off the bed, then groaned and fell back. "I've never hurt this much before."

"I bet you never tossed bullets out of your own body before." Carly stroked his fingers, the cool of her healing running through him again. "They're pretty freaked out downstairs. Talking about you."

"Why aren't you?" Tiger asked.

"Downstairs? I wanted to make sure you were all right."

He'd meant why wasn't she freaked out, but he let it go. "Because you're my mate."

Carly frowned, which pushed her bottom lip out a little, so sexy. "About that. Connor explained to me what you mean by *mate*. We need to talk, but we can wait until you feel better."

Tiger wanted to laugh, but he decided it would be too painful. "Sean says that the four scariest words a woman can say are *we need to talk*."

"Could be. But not now. Lots of time for talking later."

"You're my mate," Tiger said. "Nothing to talk about."

"Mmm hmm. Close your mouth, sweetie. Sleep. Get better." Carly leaned down to him. Her lashes fluttered against his lips before she slid up to kiss them. "And thank you for saving my life. Those bullets went into you so they wouldn't go into me."

"Anytime," Tiger whispered. Another cool breath of her slid through him, another kiss, and Tiger fell into a vast well of sleep.

Liam Morrissey's anger climbed another ten notches before he hung up his cell phone and slammed it to the kitchen counter. He'd walked out here alone to take the call, but Dylan had followed him, ostensibly to retrieve a beer from the refrigerator.

"Who the hell blabbed to the council?" Liam asked, fists on the counter. "Dad, did you?"

Dylan shook his head in his quiet way. "I'm not leader anymore, lad. I don't talk to the others without your knowledge."

"I know. Sorry." Liam's edginess about Tiger had him looking for something to attack, but lashing out at his own father wasn't the answer. He reined in his temper, or tried to.

Dylan's stoic look made Liam feel even more ashamed. His father had accepted the changeover in leadership without a fight. Dylan had known it was time on that fateful day, even if it took away a large part of what he was. Liam hoped he was half as calm when it was his turn to step down.

"They want to meet," Liam said. "All of them."

"That was Eric?" Dylan asked.

Eric Warden led the Shiftertown in Las Vegas. His mate, Iona, had first found Tiger. Eric had helped Tiger escape, and then Liam had offered to let Tiger live in Austin, under his supervision.

Liam had questioned that decision every day since he'd made it. Not because he didn't think Tiger deserved a fair shot at life, but because he hadn't learned enough about Tiger to satisfy himself or the informal council of Shiftertown leaders that he was safe.

During his leadership, Dylan had begun the council, which was simply a gathering of the Shiftertown leaders off the radar to discuss common problems and help each other find solutions. Shifters being the way they were, these sessions often degenerated into volatile arguments, but leaders had come to know they could call each other when problems might affect more than one Shiftertown.

Eric had phoned this afternoon to say the Shiftertown leaders wanted to meet about Tiger. They'd heard about him getting shot up by the human Ethan and rampaging in the hospital room. Liam had relayed that Tiger had been shot again today, this time deliberately by an unknown assassin.

Or maybe Carly had been the target. Who the hell knew? Ellison had been out cold at the time, so he couldn't report on what had happened.

Maria, Ellison's mate, had glared at Liam in pure fury at the accident scene, as though he ought to have prevented Ellison from getting shot. The shot had gone into Ellison's leg, missing anything vital. If the assassin had planned it that way, he was a hell of a marksman.

Eric hadn't been happy at the news of the second shooting, and finished by saying that the other leaders wanted a talk as soon as possible. They'd picked Dallas as the meeting place, because it had no Shiftertown but was close enough to Austin that Liam could get back quickly if needed.

"So the shites are wanting me to leave Tiger in this state and trek up to Dallas so we can sit around a table and talk about him? I don't have any idea what's going on with him. Tiger's insisting Carly is his mate—what's going to happen when she says no, and he won't take that for an answer?"

"We'll deal with it when the time comes," Dylan, ever practical, said. "You can't miss the meeting, son. They'll send trackers down here to drag you there if necessary. You can't blame them for worrying about Tiger."

"*I'm* worried about Tiger. You think I'm not? How in the *hell* did he survive that, and then start to cure himself? What the fuck did those humans pump into him?"

"It's getting on for time to find out."

Liam shook his head. "Eric blew the lab to smithereens. We'll never find anything in it now."

"But people will remember." Dylan touched his fore-head. "It will be inside their heads. We find out who worked on the Tiger project, and we ask them."

"Revealing his whereabouts and putting him in more danger."

"We'll just have to ask in a way they can't refuse."

Liam wasn't sure what his father had in mind. Dylan had a ruthless streak that Liam had never found in himself—maybe Liam's mum, Niamh, a mischievous lady but one with a heart of gold, had bred it out of him. But then, Dylan had had to hold the family together through good times and times of peril, times of near starvation and grief, and then bring them to America to take the Collar and live in a Shift-ertown. The decisions Dylan had made would put ruthless-ness into anyone.

At least Liam's dad had found happiness again with Glory. Glory was a strong woman who didn't mind sharing her opinions, but Dylan needed someone who wouldn't take any shit from him. A lesser woman would be crushed by him, and Dylan knew that. They were happy together, which made Liam happy. His dad had gone through too much.

"Go to the meeting, son," Dylan said. "Sean and I can hold the fort."

"But can you hold Tiger?"

"Can you?" Dylan met Liam's gaze with his, not look-ing away. Dylan might not be Shiftertown leader or leader of the Morrissey clan anymore, but that didn't mean he'd weakened.

Liam scrubbed his hand over his face. "I don't know, Dad. He does what I ask him, but I know it's not because he's submissive to me. He obeys because he chooses. The day he chooses not to, I won't be able to stop him."

"Then we'd better find out everything we can. Find out *how* to stop him, if that's even possible."

Liam punched his fists into the counter. He wished Kim were home, but his wife had a job that was important to her, and he didn't want to pull her back home every time he needed a hug. He'd save up the need for when they were alone tonight, when he'd open her businesslike blouse button by button, slide off her skirt, indulge himself in the scent of her . . .

"I hope we don't have to stop him permanently," Liam made himself say. "I like Tiger, and he's good with the cubs."

"He is, aye," Dylan said. "But he's something we don't understand. And if it happens one day that he's *not* good with the cubs . . ."

"We'll deal with it when the time comes," Liam said, echoing his father's words. He bent his head and studied the patterns on the counter, the old wooden surface stained with generations of coffee mugs and his daughter's juice from this morning. "Shite, but I hate going to Dallas. I *always* get lost on those freeways."

Walker Danielson woke up again flat on his back, his wrists taped together in front of him. He'd swum into and out of wakefulness since the Shifter had taken him down to the yard in front of his neat bungalow. Walker had woken again in the living room of one of the bungalows, surrounded by men in Collars who looked as though they wouldn't mind tearing Walker apart and leaving bits of him around as a warning to others.

The desk jockeys in the Shifter Bureau thought Shifters were pushovers, contained and controlled. They congratulated themselves about it.

But Shifters were dangerous, and that Bengal tiger Shifter was even more dangerous than most. Walker's commander knew it too. When Walker had made his report about the hospital to the Bureau, he'd been told to contact Dr. Brennan and suck up to the human woman Tiger seemed to like, and see if they could make her find out more about Tiger for them.

Carly Randal. She was pretty, friendly, polite –a well-brought-up Texas girl. She hadn't bought Brennan's bullshit for one minute. She'd recognized the danger in Walker, and knew her Shifter friends couldn't let Walker go.

So now Walker woke up on the floor of yet another Shifter house, after the one called Dylan had shot tranquilizer into him, looking in no way worried about it. Dylan's gaze had told Walker that if the decision had been up to him, he would have given Walker a lethal dose.

Walker assessed his situation through half-closed eyes while he lay as motionlessly as possible, so that anyone set to watch him wouldn't realize he was awake.

They'd taken the duct tape from his mouth. That didn't mean kindness—it meant they didn't worry about who would hear him if he called out. He must be pretty deep into Shiftertown.

This living room was similar to the one in the Morrissey house. The ceiling was beamed, the windows wide casements, one open to let in the air, as hot as it was. This house was bigger than the other, the living room twice the size of the Morrisseys'. The back half of the room bore a long table with many chairs. A polished wooden staircase led upward, and a door near the table presumably led to a kitchen.

A lot of Shifters must live here, judging from the length of the table and the haphazard way the chairs had been pushed in. It looked like every chair was used.

The room appeared to be empty, as far as Walker could tell. They'd left him alone. Because Shifters were the best predators on earth, that meant they weren't afraid of him escaping. Not even with the open window.

Walker wet his lips, opening and closing his mouth a few times. He'd love some water.

But thirst was only a distraction. Walker wasn't dying. He moved his wrists, dislodging the sticky part of the tape from his skin, and set about making his way out of the bonds.

Walker closed his eyes as he worked, taking time to rest. Getting out would not be easy, and he'd need all the energy he could find.

Duct tape was easier to manipulate than plastic zip ties or metal handcuffs, unless he had something with which to pick a handcuff's lock. Tape was a matter of loosening it in order to slide out at least one hand, and from there he'd be fine.

Thank the saints he'd had a mentor who'd insisted on putting Walker through exercises like these and more. *You might think me unfeeling and my methods harsh*, the man had said. *But if you're ever in any of these situations behind enemy lines, you won't panic. You'll know exactly what to do.* He'd turned Walker into a talented escape artist.

The tape loosened and Walker wriggled one hand free. That was enough to let him unwind the other hand. He reached for the tape on his legs.

And found himself right back down on his back, a foot planted in the center of his chest. A bare, shapely foot.

Walker looked up a long, equally bare and equally shapely leg to a woman who wore denim shorts over a fine ass and a T-shirt that read "Keep Austin Weird." She had dark brown hair that glinted with lighter highlights, the hair falling a little past her shoulders in thick waves. Her face was incredible, her smile wide, her eyes brown and inviting.

She had to be more than six feet tall, and the foot on his chest spoke of strength.

"Not so fast, sunshine," she said, her smile widening. "You stay here with me."

CHAPTER THIRTEEN

Walker swallowed on his dry throat. "Who the hell are you?"

"I'm Rebecca. A bear Shifter, if you're wondering. And you're Walker." She tilted her head to consider him. "I like that name."

"So did my mom."

"Aw, that's sweet." Rebecca leaned forward, her large breasts behind the tight shirt softening and coming within reach. "Here's what's going to happen, Walker. You'll be staying here, in my living room, until Liam figures out what we should do with you. Want some water? When I took the tape off your mouth, your lips were dry. You have to be thirsty."

Walker cleared his throat. "Water would be nice."

Rebecca lifted her head, but the pressure on Walker's chest didn't ease. He wouldn't be able to dislodge her foot in a hurry.

"Olaf," Rebecca called. "Olaf, honey, bring out the water for our guest."

The kitchen door opened, and out walked a small boy

with white hair and night-dark eyes, carrying a sports bottle with both hands. The boy came to Walker without fear and held out the bottle.

Walker took it, mystified. He knew that if he tried anything, such as hitting the kid or slamming Rebecca onto her back and barreling through Olaf to get away, Rebecca would kill him. The look on her face told him no less.

Walker wouldn't use a child to help himself escape. He wasn't that way. He upended the bottle of water and drank.

They might have drugged the water to keep him groggy, but at this point, Walker didn't care. When he was more rested and no longer thirsty, he'd be better fit to get away. The water tasted normal, though, nothing added that he could taste.

Olaf watched him drink, his look grave. No child should be so quiet and serious. He didn't look anything like Rebecca, so not her son or her brother. The kid was about ten, his eyes black—not dark brown as Walker had first thought. They were the eyes of an animal, a sad animal.

Walker handed the empty bottle back to Olaf. "Thank you."

"You're welcome," Olaf said, then he turned and walked back to the kitchen, his job finished.

"Were you trying to lull me into submission with a cute kid?" Walker asked, wiping his mouth.

"Did it work?"

"I don't hurt kids."

"I'm glad. I'd have had to hurt you if you did."

"I thought so," Walker said.

In the next instant, he struck. Rebecca had been drawing a breath to continue the banter, but she let out the breath with an *oomph* as she fell.

Walker had grabbed her leg—silken skin over firm muscle—and jerked, reaching up to pin her when she came down.

Rebecca landed on his chest, a hundred sixty pounds or so of woman, her breasts soft against the harder planes of his chest.

She had great reflexes. Walker had started a roll to put her beneath him, where he'd wrap her hands in the loose tape, but he couldn't move her.

Rebecca had him pinned; his back was solid against the rug, Rebecca's hold on his shoulders perfect. Her smile didn't waver. "Not a bad attempt."

"Had to try," Walker said.

Rebecca came closer, her breath warm on his face. "You know what, Walker? I'm a Shifter woman in my fertile years. You know what that makes me?" She lowered herself closer still. "Horny. Very, very horny."

And helping her take care of that wouldn't be bad. Not bad at all. Walker's thumping heart and hardening cock would have told him that even if his brain didn't. She was a lush, female armful, very tempting.

Any man but Walker would have taken her up on the offer and let her bang him right here, surrendering to the beauty of her. But Walker never mixed sex with his missions. Sex was for celebration, for taking his ease afterward, for loving. He wanted to be in a position where he could let down his guard and enjoy himself. Stopping a mission for sex was appallingly stupid. It took only a little self-control to stay focused.

Rebecca might have good reflexes, and she might be the hottest thing he'd seen in a long, long time, but she wasn't a trained fighter. Not trained in fighting dirty.

Walker heaved himself up, and heaved fast. One lightning move and he had her off him, sliding her across the floor, out of his way. Walker rolled to his knees, then levered himself to his feet, reaching for the tape on his legs.

Rebecca landed hard, with enough impact for her to hit the bottom of the stairs, smacking her head on the post. Walker hadn't meant for that to happen, but it would slow her enough for him to get his legs free and himself out the window. Shifters could hunt him down faster than he could run away, but Walker knew how to hot-wire a car in ten seconds flat.

"Oh." Rebecca pushed her hair from her face. "Now."

Walker jerked at the tape until it came unstuck from his black fatigue pants, wishing they hadn't taken his knife. They'd wound a huge wad of tape around him, and he fought to pull it free.

Rebecca slid her shirt off over her head. She wasn't wearing a bra, but Walker didn't let himself look, not fully. What he saw from the corner of his eye was pretty good though.

Rebecca shoved down her shorts and then her panties more rapidly than Walker could unwind the tape. Her bare body came into view, curved, gorgeous, mouthwatering.

"Damn it," she said. "I did *not* want to go bear in front of you."

The last words degenerated into one long growl as Rebecca's body expanded and changed, growing fur and claws longer than any knife Walker ever carried. She shifted and grew, the growls becoming louder, until finally Walker saw exactly what kind of bear she was.

Kodiak.

Ordinary Kodiak bears were gigantic. A Shifter Kodiak, even a female, was at least twice that size. No wonder all the furniture in here was pushed against the walls.

Walker got himself free of the tape. He made it one step toward the open window before a giant bear paw brought him down. Rebecca's mouth opened to show her horrifyingly large teeth before she flipped him onto his back and held him there the most effective way she could—lying down on him.

She let him breathe, at least. Her large body kept him as well-pinned as she had in her human form, except now she was warmer and heavier, and had a lot more fur.

Rebecca nuzzled his face with her large bear nose, her dark eyes filled with amusement. She raised her head and huffed a little, and Walker swore she was laughing.

When Tiger woke again, the afternoon was waning, long blocks of light slanting through the windows. He'd learned that in this season—summer—the light lingered for a long time, so it could be eight in the evening already.

The first sensation he had was one of rightness. His body felt much better, the horrific pain gone. His headache had receded, leaving only a slight pounding to remind him of the previous hurt.

The second was stunned wonder. Much of the rightness he felt came from the fact that Carly was lying next to him, curled up under the sheet, her head on a pillow.

Tiger's bed was large, the biggest in the house. He was as bulky as Liam, though he shared height with Ronan, a Kodiak bear Shifter. Kim had gotten Tiger a bigger bed because when Tiger had first arrived, he'd been restless at night, rolling from side to side. Hard to find comfort on the small mattress that had been Connor's when his previous sleeping pallet had been the metal floor of a cage. After he'd fallen out of the smaller bed a few times, Kim had brought home the larger one.

Carly had plenty of room in the bed. The fan played near the window. It, combined with the cooling breeze from all four open windows, had made Carly pull the sheet over herself. One thigh, covered with a couple of inches of the canvas-cloth shorts she'd put on at Ethan's, poked out from beneath the sheet.

Her makeup was smeared from the accident and sleep, her hair was messed from its careful French braid. Beautiful. Tiger would explain that Carly didn't need the face paint and her hair tucked away for her to be pretty.

But she was unhurt. Tiger scented that from her, saw it in her unbroken skin. She'd been bruised and afraid, but not hurt. He let himself believe in the Goddess long enough to be thankful.

Before the crash, Carly had been teaching Tiger about kissing. When the subject had first come up, Liam had told Tiger that Liam hadn't known how to kiss either. Kim had taught him. He'd implied that not knowing how to kiss wasn't a problem for Shifters, and that was when Connor had said Tiger would learn when the time came.

Tiger brushed a wisp of hair from Carly's cheek. He knew he needed to make his way to Ronan's and question Walker. He needed to know why Walker had been sent to watch Carly, and why a man dressed in the same kind of black fatigues had shot Tiger in the back more than a dozen times.

But the house was quiet, the street outside quiet as well. Shifters would be inside eating their nightly meal, talking to their mates and cubs, mothers and fathers, sharing time with family. Later, the more nocturnal ones would be out with neighbors, playing with cubs in the long stretch of green behind the houses, or leaving Shiftertown to go to the bar Liam managed or one of the clubs in town that allowed Shifters.

Or they might go to the fight club that was held once a week, where Shifters took out their aggressions in the ring, with the rest of the Shifters betting like crazy on the outcomes.

Tiger wasn't allowed to fight in the fight club. They didn't trust him, and Tiger agreed with that. To him, fighting wasn't a game. It was survival. Kill or be killed.

Right now, his bed was the best place to be. He was hard and ready, wanting Carly. But just lightly touching her while she slept filled something in Tiger he hadn't realized was empty.

Tiger leaned over. Remembering how to pucker his lips and how to release the pressure at the correct moment, he kissed her cheek.

Carly blinked once, then again, then her smile blossomed. "Oh, hey." She slid herself to a sitting position and tucked stray locks of hair behind her ears. "I didn't mean to fall asleep."

"You stayed."

Carly shrugged. "I told Armand about the accident, and he said that under no circumstance was I to come to work. He said he'd make Yvette answer the phones and beg her to be nice to people." She laughed a little. "Yvette has the biggest heart in the world, but she doesn't suffer fools gladly.

She'll save their lives and fix them the best meal they'll ever eat, but she will give them her unvarnished opinions about them at the same time."

"Glory is the same. Except she can't cook."

Carly laughed again, drawing her knees to her chest and circling her arms around them. How wonderful, Tiger thought as he studied the softness of her thighs, to know people—who weren't researchers studying him—to know enough about them to make jokes.

"Looks like you're feeling better," Carly said.

Tiger put his hand to his abdomen. A few twinges went off at his touch, but that was all. As before, his body had closed up, was making itself whole again.

"Why did you stay?" he asked.

"I just told you. Armand said . . ."

"No." Tiger sat up with her, reflecting that he was tired of lying on his back. He propped himself on the headboard, leaning an arm on his drawn-up knee. "You could have gone home. Gone anywhere. But you stayed."

A flush of color stained her cheeks. "I was worried about you."

"Why? You saw that I was healing."

"Tiger, no one gets shot twice in as many days and heals faster the *second* time. Dylan said it was like your body was changing, like it was adapting to the circumstance."

He shrugged, and even that didn't hurt. "They wanted me to be the best fighting machine ever. Gave me drugs that hurt like hell, and surgeries, always surgeries. And then tested me and gave me more drugs. I was the only one who survived."

Carly's eyes widened. "There were more like you?"

"There were twenty-three. I was the last. Then there was only me."

She touched his arm, fingers light on his bicep. "I don't know how to answer that. How to convey how really sorry I am. It sounds lame even to say it."

The touch had been a mistake. Tiger's healing body had been content to be in her presence, to rest while he drank in her scent.

The warmth of her hand on him awakened primal needs, and the beast in him rushed to the surface. He should warn her, tell her to get out.

He couldn't make himself. Tiger was lonely, and alone, in spite of living in this house, in this room where he could watch over all of Shiftertown.

Carly was here. And he needed her.

Simple words, for a simple being. Tiger clasped Carly's wrist and lifted her hand away, but kept hold of it as he looked at her. She gazed back at him, her expression telling him she felt the change in him, his raw need.

"Tiger," she whispered. "I'm scared."

The hesitant words made Tiger stop himself, to push down the feral beast who wanted her. "Of me?" Even his voice had changed, the words harsh and flat.

"Of me." Tears moistened her eyes. "I just had a bad ending to a relationship I thought was fine. I don't want to let myself fall in love with you. With anyone." She touched his face, this second touch ripping away all restraint Tiger had put on himself. "But I think it's too late for that."

Too late. Much too late. Tiger growled like a true tiger, pushed Carly onto the bed, pinned her with his hands on her wrists, and brought his mouth down on hers.

CHAPTER FOURTEEN

Tiger's lips were hot, his mouth moving on hers, his tongue sweeping inside. He opened Carly's mouth with his as she'd shown him how to in Ethan's dressing room, brushed kisses along her lips and chin as she'd shown him how to in the car.

He held her down with hands on her wrists, his body weight on her. Tiger could have crushed her, Carly knew, but he held himself back, shaking with the effort.

Tiger pulled Carly's lower lip between his, sucking, the tiny pain sensual. He licked across her lips, then inside again, tasting her mouth.

Carly tasted him back, loving the velvet friction of his tongue. He tasted of spice and musk, the hot bite that was him. Tiger didn't close his eyes to kiss her; his golden gaze was fixed on her, watching her watch him.

When he eased away, Carly pressed kisses to his mouth, his lips smooth and warm, a little moisture behind them. Tiger kissed her again, matching her actions, his mouth deftly caressing hers.

"You're a quick learner," she said breathlessly.

"I am."

"Mmm. Modest too."

"They told me so," Tiger said. "The researchers said I learned fast."

Carly's anger surged at those faceless people who'd kept him in a cage, performed experiments on him that hurt him, trying to make a Shifter into a better fighter or whatever it was they were doing. *Kept him in a cage.* And he was the only Shifter who'd survived this torture.

"They should be arrested."

Tiger shrugged. "They went away."

The words were simple, but Carly sensed the volumes of pain behind them. They'd hurt him, then they'd deserted him. He'd had a mate, he'd said, and she'd died. Tiger's child had died as well. How could he bear it? How could anyone stand so much?

"I'm here," Carly said. Silly, because she was lying under him—where else would she be? "No matter what. If we hook up or we don't, if we're friends only—hell, if we move to opposite sides of the globe—I'll be there for you when you need me. Okay? I promise."

Tiger didn't answer, but the hunger in his eyes told her everything. He lowered his head and nuzzled her, sending white-hot tingles across her skin.

The same hunger flared in Carly. Tiger was sexy, he was gorgeous, and she needed some loving. Finding Ethan yesterday had made her feel like the most un-sexy, most unwanted woman on the planet. Ethan obviously found Carly inadequate, or why would he have needed to fulfill himself with someone else?

When Tiger looked at Carly, she felt beautiful. She knew she cleaned up well, which was why Yvette had hired her to work in the gallery. But Yvette had always maintained that Carly had girl-next-door prettiness, not siren beauty. Fresh faced and sweet, not a temptress. Perfect for the female customers who came in with their husbands to buy art for their houses or offices. Ethan, come to think of it, also hadn't regarded Carly as a siren beauty, which was what would make her the perfect businessman's wife. Women wouldn't be jealous of Carly.

Tiger looked at Carly as though she were a sex goddess in a G-string. Like he wanted to make love to her for days. He'd looked at Carly like that from the first moment he'd raked his gaze over her on the side of the road. She'd asked him if he liked what he saw, and he'd said a simple *Yes*.

"I was right about you," Carly said now. "You're a sweet-talker."

Tiger growled, not talking at all. He released her hands but only so he could push up her T-shirt and pop open the button of her shorts. The sheet fell from his backside, which was as gorgeous as the rest of him. Carly ran her hands over his buttocks, liking how firm he was, then up his torso again, hands finding the pockmarks from the bullets that had gone in, then out.

Tiger's next kisses were even hotter and more skilled; he adapted to kissing as much as his body was adapting to being shot.

Need in his eyes, he knelt back and skimmed her shorts from her. Panties next, Carly helping, then Tiger tossed them both away, though her T-shirt remained pushed up around her shoulders.

Carly lay back down, heartbeat speeding, ready for the man who excited her and was excited by her.

Her breath left her when Tiger lifted her by the waist and flipped her over, drawing her up onto her hands and knees. Tiger pulled her hips back to the stiff cock that she glimpsed before her hair tumbled into her face. *Good God . . .*

"Whoa, wait." Carly squirmed away, turning to sit on the big bed, her T-shirt falling to cover her lap. "What are you doing?"

Tiger remained on his knees, his cock pointing toward her—his long, thick, no-way-anyone-is-that-big cock. His brows drew down. "Mating."

"I know that, but why the back door? You're really . . . big. You'll kill me." Carly would die happy, but he was going to be a tight fit.

The cock dipped slightly. "If it will hurt you, then . . . I won't."

Carly saw how much it cost him to say that. Tiger wanted her. He pulsed with it. She wanted him as well, with every pump of blood through her veins.

"I mean we should take it slow," she said. "Let me get used to you. Me with the soft bed cushioning my back, you easing on top of me."

The cock went completely firm again, but the look on Tiger's face was one of confusion.

Pieces of information clicked in Carly's head—stuck in a cage, researchers, treated like an animal, given a mate. Not a girlfriend, or a wife, or a lover. A *mate*. Tiger hadn't said whether the woman had been Shifter or human.

"Are you telling me you haven't ever done it front to front?" she asked.

Tiger shook his head. "It was only the once."

"Oh." The loneliness of his words struck her to the heart. "You make me want to hug you more and more. Come here. I'll show you. You're a quick learner, I said. Now you can learn this."

Tiger came to her so rapidly that Carly laughed. She stopped laughing when he took her down to the bed.

"Now you're getting it." Her words ceased as he kissed her, his mouth firm, no longer hesitant.

Carly wrapped one leg around his thigh, caressing his calf with her bare foot. She liked how he kissed her, mouth warm, taking but giving, knowing what he wanted and what she wanted. Tiger nipped her cheek, her neck, all the while his body shook as he held himself back.

Carly guided him with one hand on his hip, parting her legs so that he could come between them. His skin was hot but smooth, his ass tight as he moved over her. Carly raised her hips a little, her one leg up and around his, encouraging him with her hands to come on inside.

Tiger's body heat covered her, and then his body. He brushed her tangled hair from her face, lips coming down in a long kiss as he slid inside her.

And stopped. Carly's eyes opened wide. She was certainly wet enough for him, slippery and wanting, but she tightened, the sudden ecstasy turning to an aching.

"Wait." She pressed her palm to Tiger's chest, feeling his heart beating triple-time.

Tiger pulled out quickly, kneeling back, the look on his face one of anguish. "I'm hurting you."

"Only because I'm not used to you."

At least Carly hoped that was the explanation. It would be a tragedy if she'd finally met a man who made her feel like this and they couldn't consummate their relationship . . . or whatever this was. For once in her life, Carly didn't stop to analyze her connection with a man. She wasn't thinking about whether he was going to run off with all her money, or whether he'd dump her after a few dates, or what it was they were building together, if anything.

She liked Tiger and wanted to be with him. Nothing more. No hidden agendas.

"How about we try it me on top of you?" she asked. "That way I can guide things, ease in however much I can take before we go on."

From the look on Tiger's face, it hadn't occurred to him that this position was possible either. Carly seriously needed to work on his education.

She got to her knees. "Lie down."

Carly pressed her hands to his chest again, and Tiger lay back on the sheets, his gaze never leaving her. The fading sunshine clearly showed the pink marks where Ethan had shot him, and more scars where the other bullets had come through. But the blood was gone, his skin whole again.

She climbed over him, positioning her knees on either side of him. His cock was still stiff and long, Tiger waiting.

Carly pulled off her T-shirt, breathing a sigh as the fabric left her now-itchy skin. She tossed the shirt aside and filled her hands with Tiger's swollen cock.

Large, but not unmanageable. She drew both hands up its sides, around the head, back down to his firm balls. His hair there was multicolored too—orange and black. She was falling in love with a man who was tiger-striped all the way down.

The thought made her smile. Carly leaned down and kissed the tip of his cock.

Two strong hands closed around her wrists. Tiger pulled her up, his eyes molten gold, his voice a growl. "Now. Do it *now.*"

Yes. Carly wanted him with every thought, every breath. Tiger wanted her too, she saw, was afraid he wouldn't be able to contain himself.

Carly felt even sexier knowing he could barely hold it in for her. The fleeting thought of a condom ran through her head, but she knew one hadn't been made that would fit Tiger. And she'd read somewhere that Shifters couldn't give humans the illnesses that humans could give one another through sex.

She leaned forward, her breasts brushing his chest, then lowered herself onto the end of his cock. The next fleeting thought was that Shifters could still get humans pregnant. But Carly was taking birth control—at Ethan's insistence—and the worry about that seemed far away and unimportant.

Then all thoughts about anything fled her head. Tiger was big. Unlike the startled halt when he'd been on top of her, this going-in was eased by Carly's slowness, her slickness, her burgeoning need.

Oh my God . . . That's . . .

I've never . . .

The words welled up as Tiger slid into her, and Carly heard some of them come out of her mouth. She lowered herself more, Tiger's cock opening her with blunt, hard pleasure.

Carly's hips rocked, her body wanting more of him. Tiger's hands went to her thighs, fingers pressing, and he let out a soft noise.

"Tiger." Carly's exclamation came out a groan. "You are fucking marvelous."

Tiger held her in complete silence. Carly stretched, her breasts feeling heavy and tight. She pressed her arms over her head, fingers flexing, her head going back as she felt him rise inside her.

She went hot all over at the same time gooseflesh rippled over her arms and legs. Her nipples darkened and tightened, one beam of sunshine snaking in from under clouds to bathe her in warmth.

No warmth compared to the scalding heat between Tiger's hips and Carly's inner thighs, sweat collecting to slide to the sheets. Perspiration gathered on Carly's face and beaded on Tiger's upper lip.

Tiger moved his hands from her thighs to the curve of her waist, holding her steady while he let his hips rock upward. Gently, gently. Tiger's body still shook; he was holding back, afraid of hurting her.

Carly's heart ached for him at the same time her inner places swelled and tightened. He was so tender, this man people feared. He'd shielded her body with his and taken what should have been a lethal barrage of bullets so Carly wouldn't be hurt.

Pleasure seeped through her, joy so hot she was sure her blood was on fire. Tiger watched her in silence, his eyes Shifter gold, his face quiet.

He was a beautiful man, strong, good-hearted, protective. She remembered him with tiny Katriona, how incredibly gentle he'd been with her.

He was as gentle with Carly now. Tiger held her, sweat trickling from under his palms down her skin, the sunlight moving from Carly's body to Tiger's face.

Breathtaking. She rested her hands on his chest now, the hard flatness of it dusted with dark hair streaked with gold and orange, his nipples as tight as hers.

The look in his eyes was one of wonder. Tiger marveled at what they did, Carly rocking on him, fire rippling from where they joined.

The fire grew, blocking all thought. The sun continued to slip away, the room changing from sunlit to flooded with red and gold, and then to twilit. She and Tiger rocked together, sealed to each other, Tiger higher in Carly than she'd imagined she could take him.

Tiger growled and clasped her shoulders, tugging her down to him. She went, kissing him while she lay full length on top of him, with him still inside her.

Tiger kissed her in return, licking into her mouth, tasting all corners of her. Carly tasted him too, learning him, loving the texture, the heat.

Their mouths were still together when Tiger's growl turned to a snarl. A wild darkness whipped through Carly, one that made her cry out, her body tight, so tight. Waves of pleasure so incredible she wanted to weep tumbled over her, and she rocked her hips against Tiger's, wanting more and more. As she hit the top of the highest wave, shouting his name in pleasure, Carly felt Tiger's seed flood inside her.

The last of the dusky light died, and darkness quickly filled the sky. Through the open windows, Carly saw stars prick out, but they couldn't compete with the beauty of Tiger's golden eyes.

"Shite, I missed the exit again." Liam stepped on the accelerator and shot down the freeway. He'd have to get off at the next exit, loop around, and try again.

"You should have let me drive," Spike said from the passenger seat of Dylan's truck.

Dylan had sent them off four hours ago in the predawn coolness, looking a little satisfied that he wouldn't be the one dealing with a table of full-of-themselves gobshite Shifter leaders and Dallas roadways.

"No, I need you to navigate," Liam said to Spike. "You're a tracker. So track."

Shifter leaders were allowed one backup person at the meetings, all acknowledging that a roomful of über-alpha

Shifter males could grow dangerous very fast. Therefore, each Shifter could bring one bodyguard, and Liam had chosen Spike.

The bodyguard had to be neutral though. Not the same clan, pack, or pride as the leader. The bodyguard also couldn't be in line to be a Shiftertown leader, so that the bodyguard didn't get any ideas of taking out the man above him while they were alone. If Spike offed Liam, Spike wouldn't win by it. Liam wouldn't win by it either, but Sean would take over the Austin Shiftertown and punish Spike.

Not that Liam had any worries about Spike. The six-foot-six, tattooed biker with the shaved pate was a jaguar who'd recently found out he had a cub. The new dad thought of little else but small Jordan and Myka, Spike's new mate.

"You missed this exit too," Spike said in his quiet way.

"*Shite*," Liam had been busy trying to get around a slow cement truck, and the off ramp had whizzed past. "They'll decide something asinine before I get there, like we all have to wear T-shirts that say 'My Other Animal is a Penguin.' And my vote would have been the tiebreaker against."

Spike didn't laugh. "Take this one," he said pointing to the left.

"What one?"

"There!" Spike shouted. "Left exit. *Now.*"

Liam dove across two lanes of traffic, earning honking and lifted fingers, and drove off the ramp. This exit looped them around and poured them back in the opposite direction, where Liam ran into a clump of traffic.

"Damn it."

"You know, you suck at driving," Spike said.

"Watch it, jaguar. And it's not true. I'm a master at handling my Harley."

Spike grinned. "Yeah, I just bet you are."

Liam said something in Irish that would have earned him Spike's fist in his throat if Spike had understood it.

Liam at last got the pickup oriented in the right direction, found the turnoff, and took it. Now it was just a matter of navigating through traffic, stoplights, and clogged one-way streets until they found the bar and pool hall where the Shifters had agreed, this time, to meet.

Never in the same place twice. Good idea from a stealth standpoint, bad for finding the damned place.

Liam parked the pickup behind the bar, approached the back door, and knocked. A greasy-looking man let them in through a tiny hall and a kitchen, pointing through to a large room that smelled of Shifters. Liam hoped the man with the oily hair wasn't the cook.

"About time," someone growled.

CHAPTER FIFTEEN

The voice of the Lupine who'd spoken—Graham McNeil—rumbled in the too-small room. Not enough air in the room either, Liam observed. They'd all soon be gagging on the smell. Alphas feeling competitive had a fine scent.

Eric Warden, a Feline and the leader of the Las Vegas Shiftertown, came forward to greet Liam. Liam pulled the man into a brief, tight hug, and Eric returned it, as strong as ever.

They kept the hug short, greeting only, even though they'd become good friends, so the other Shifter leaders might not think they were forming an alliance. Shifter leaders, as a group, were paranoid.

"Liam," Graham said behind Eric.

Graham was sort of co-leader with Eric of their Shiftertown. He condescended to return Liam's greeting embrace, but the hug shouted that Graham would be just as happy to break Liam's neck in other circumstances.

"What did you bring him for?" Liam asked Eric, jerking his thumb at Graham. "I can't believe *he's* your bodyguard."

Eric and Graham had tangled in the past. Eric's sister or

son didn't qualify to be Eric's backup, but Liam was surprised Eric would venture out alone with Graham, who'd made it no secret that he thought he'd be a better Shiftertown leader than Eric. Eric usually brought Nell, a bear Shifter and his neighbor, whose glare could stop the most formidable Shifter in his tracks.

"Didn't trust him enough to leave him behind," Eric said. He gave Liam his laid-back smile, but his jade-green eyes were sharp with watchfulness.

"Good thinking," Graham said, though his body language said, *Fuck you.*

"Besides, he's met Tiger," Eric said, ignoring Graham. "And Nell's busy with her new mate. Cormac, you know him. Those are the only reasons I'd bring Graham. Graham's afraid to fly, and he bitched about it the whole time."

"Huh," Graham said. He was a big man with flame tattoos on his arms and buzzed dark hair, his wolf-gray eyes holding more intelligence than he let people see. "If the Goddess wanted me to fly, she'd have made me a bird Shifter. An eagle."

"Penguin," Liam said.

Graham frowned at him. "Penguins don't fly."

"I know."

He growled. "Yeah, you're funny, Irishman."

"Can we start?" The Shifter who'd called this meeting was a Lupine named Bowman O'Donnell, who ran a Shiftertown in North Carolina. He stood at the head of the table, impatient, his dark eyes fixed on Liam. His bodyguard was a lean, mean-looking Feline, with tattoos of cheetahs chasing themselves around his arms.

Twenty other Shifter leaders and their bodyguards took up the rest of the room. Some slouched in seats as though they'd rather be anywhere doing anything but this; others were alert, eyes on Liam, interested.

Liam hid a sigh, trying to make himself sit down and be calm, but he knew he couldn't be. Tiger was his responsibility, and the other Shifters could scent Liam's worry about this meeting. That is, if they could smell anything in a room full of Shifter leaders trying to out-alpha one another.

Liam waved his hand in front of his nose as he took his seat. "Can we open a window?"

Several of the other Shifters chuckled. Bowman didn't look amused.

"If we do this fast, we can get out of here into fresh air," he said. "Or polluted air. Cities suck."

More laughter. Bowman's Shiftertown was in the middle of tall pine woods in the hills. Liam had visited once and had been impressed by the place's natural beauty. Bowman had gotten lucky.

"So you have a Shifter living with you who can heal himself from gunshot wounds," Bowman said. "We heard about the second shooting, and that this tiger Shifter basically grew himself a second skin."

Goddess, word spread fast. Liam and his family had said nothing, and Glory, as crazy as she was, could be trusted to keep secrets. So could Liam's trackers.

But Shifters had scent and good hearing, and Liam's neighbors weren't all so in love with the Morrisseys that they wouldn't gossip about them and their households. Shifters didn't need computers and electronic social networks to spread news far and wide. They only needed a chat on a front porch.

"He didn't grow a second skin," Liam said. "He's still in bed recovering." And doing other things, with Carly, he'd heard through the walls, but Liam chose to keep that information to himself. If these concerned Shifters thought Tiger was already mating, who the hell knew what they'd do? "He did, though, expel the bullets from his body without trying, and the wounds closed up. But he's weak and tired, not out tearing apart the world."

"He's dangerous," Bowman said. "We don't know what he is, or how those humans made him, or what he'll do. Or what he'll become."

"I agree," Liam said. He leaned back in his chair, hands resting lightly on his abdomen. "But he's a nice guy. I'm not going to kill him."

"No, but you need to put a Collar on him." Bowman didn't move, but his meaning was evident: Put a Collar on him, or we tell the humans and let them make the decision what to do.

"We talked about that, remember?" Liam said. "After I tried it. I thought the Collar was going to kill him—and he'd have killed me right then if I'd attempted it a second time. Tiger's not like a normal Shifter. The Collar might hurt him beyond repair, or it might kill him. Or it might do nothing at all."

"Yes, we *talked* about it," another of the Shifter leaders said. "Then *you* decided to fake a Collar for him. How's that working out for you?"

"It's fine as long as we keep him contained."

"But you didn't keep him contained," Bowman said. "Day before yesterday, he was in the house of a wealthy human man, tearing it up, then he went crazy in the hospital and had to have Shifter Bureau send in goons. I don't even know what happened yesterday."

"He and one of my trackers were run off the road," Liam said. "A man who looked like a Shifter Bureau goon shot him, then walked away."

"Walked away?" Bowman asked, curious.

"Didn't stick around to see if he'd made the kill. I was wondering about that."

Graham broke in. "Probably he figured no one could survive twenty bullets from a machine pistol in the back."

Bowman shot Graham a look of irritation. "Bodyguards aren't allowed to talk in Shifter council meetings."

"Screw you," Graham said clearly. "What *council*? You never invited me to these meetings when I was leader of my Shiftertown. Shifter leaders getting together to discuss things. That's fucked up."

The Feline guarding Bowman leaned forward, slanting

Graham a look of challenge. Graham laughed at him. "You want to try it with me? Bring it on, cat."

The cheetah smiled and rubbed one hand over his arm tattoos. He showed his teeth, eyes turning golden yellow.

"Enough," Bowman growled. "Can we stay on point? Liam, we need you to Collar the tiger. Keep him controlled and out of trouble."

"I told you, the Collar might kill him. I can't do that to another Shifter."

"If you don't, we will," Bowman said, and about half the leaders nodded agreement. "He attracts too much human attention to our business. If he causes more trouble, humans will start poking around to see what's going on, why he's not being controlled, why he can't be controlled. If they find the fake Collar, we're all screwed. We can't afford to have humans figuring out too much. Precarious times, Liam."

Liam sat back, growing uncomfortable. Bowman had a point. Humans thought they had Shifters corralled and tamed. Tiger, uncontrolled, might bring human scrutiny too far into Shiftertowns, where the humans could find all kinds of things Shifters wanted to keep hidden.

"We also need to find out everything we can about this tiger," Bowman went on. "Hack into the humans' research, figure out what they were up to. They created him from scratch, but how? Who did they use? The more we know, the more we can contain this. And if the tiger needs to be eliminated . . ." Bowman's gaze was all for Liam. "Then we eliminate him."

Goddess, had Dylan had to put up with shite like this? Probably. Liam wished for his father's strength, a little of his ruthlessness, and most of all, his penetrating stare, the one that could make all other Shifters back down in quiet terror.

The lion inside Liam began to growl, his hackles rising. "You aren't leader of the leaders, Bowman. Tiger's in *my* Shiftertown, and I'll decide when he's too much of a danger."

"You feel sorry for him," Bowman said. "I get that. But

it's clouding your judgment. He should have been taken out right after he was found. There's no way he can adjust, and there are cubs to think about."

"Tiger lives in my house with my cub, and he's amazing with her," Liam said. "Watches over her as well as I and her mum do. He's protective, and the cubs like him."

"You'd better hope your judgment isn't misplaced," Bowman said.

"And I am keeping an eye on him. Or I would be, if I weren't being dragged out to sit in stinky back rooms in bars with a bunch of Shifters with their knickers in a twist."

One of the other leaders stood up. "I say we put it to a vote. Liam puts a Collar on the tiger. If Liam can't handle him, we take the tiger out. All in favor?"

"A vote?" Graham asked, incredulous. "I've seen everything now."

The other Shifters, ignoring him, put up their hands. Almost all of them. Liam got to his feet.

"Screw this. You don't come into *my* Shiftertown and mess with *my* Shifters."

"And," Eric said in his calm way, "there's the problem of being able to kill Tiger at all. How do you propose to do that? A Shifter who can survive bullet wounds? When I first found him, it took two tranq shots just to make him sit down."

"Which is why we need to act now," Bowman said. "Who the hell knows what else he can do, or what he's become capable of? We need to contain or kill him before he hurts one of us."

Liam barely held on to his temper. "I agree about finding out all we can about him. But those other decisions are mine."

"Not anymore, Liam," Bowman said. "You're holding a potentially lethal weapon. If it gets out of control, it could spell the end for all Shifters. Living in Shiftertowns was a decision pushed through by advocates for Shifters, if you remember. Humans who didn't want to see us treated like lab rats or slaughtered outright. But the humans will shove us back into cages and drug us until we die if they think we can turn into whatever this tiger Shifter is. You know it, Liam."

"Yes," Liam had to say. The word tasted sour in his mouth. "But it's still my decision."

"Like I said, not anymore." Bowman stood up casually, as though they weren't talking about the life and death of one of Liam's friends. "We should go before people start wondering why so many Shifters are in town."

Meeting adjourned, in other words. Several of the leaders and their bodyguards got up and exited without saying good-bye. Others lingered, would drift away a little at a time. A mass exodus would be a bad idea.

Bowman had to pass Liam and Eric on his way out. Graham stepped enough in Bowman's way that Bowman would have to make physical contact to get around him.

"So they let a dickhead like you run a Shiftertown?" Graham said, giving Bowman his gray-eyed stare.

"I'm doing what I have to do to protect my Shifters," Bowman said, meeting his gaze without flinching. "It's my job."

"If Tiger was living in your house you might understand better, I'm thinking," Liam said.

"If he was living in my house, he'd already have a Collar." Bowman turned his body to slide past Graham without touching him. "See you, Liam. Eric."

Eric remained. He was about the same height as Liam, a little leaner, tanned from Las Vegas sunshine. He folded his arms and leaned against the back of a chair. "You can return him to our Shiftertown if you want," Eric said. "I know I kind of forced him down your throat."

"You didn't." Liam ran a hand through his hair, hoping he could get the smell of angry Shifter out of it when he got home. "I was the one with the arrogance in thinking I could control him, even without putting a Collar on him."

Eric didn't argue with him, Liam noticed. Or bother trying to make him feel better. "Want to grab a beer? Lunch?"

"No, I need to be getting back." Liam sighed and unhooked his sunglasses from his T-shirt. "And I need to think."

"I'm driving," Spike said, the first words he'd spoken since they'd walked in. He held out his hand for the keys. "If you'll be thinking the whole time, I need to do the steering."

"Call me when you want advice," Eric said. "You know I'm good at giving it." He showed his teeth in a grin while Graham rolled his eyes.

Spike, now holding the keys, walked out and had the pickup started by the time Liam finished his parting embraces with Eric, then Graham. Liam got into the truck, Spike navigated through the busy streets back to the freeway, and they headed south, Liam slumped against the door.

"You didn't mention Carly," Spike said as they sped down the 35, past downtown and Reunion Arena, and into the southern reaches of the city. "Or that he was shagging her most of the night last night."

"Shite, are all the rooms in my house bugged?"

"The windows were open. Tiger's kind of loud. I didn't hear, but Deni did. She told me. So did her cubs. And Ellison. And Connor—his bedroom's right under Tiger's. Glory mentioned it too."

"Gobshite," Liam muttered. "If it's all over Shiftertown already, Bowman must know. Or he will soon. I didn't say anything about Carly because I don't want the other leaders too worried about Tiger taking a mate. At the same time, Carly's the only person I've met who can calm him down. Connor can, sometimes, but not like Carly. I've never seen anything like it."

"If she has his cub . . ." Spike veered around a slow truck and car. "Bowman might want to kill it too."

"I know." Neither Liam nor Spike wanted to think about that, both men having cubs they loved. "Or at least Bowman might want to pen it up and watch it. Goddess, they're worse than the humans."

"They don't want Tiger's existence to make humans decide it's too dangerous to let Shifters live."

Spike never talked much—but when he did talk, he proved he was more than muscle, more than a stupid fighting Shifter, as too many Shifters thought him. Even Liam had made that mistake once.

Spike had distilled the entire meeting into that one sentence.

"I know," Liam said again. He let out a breath. "If Tiger has to die, it's going to be me who kills him. I'm not giving him to Bowman or anyone else in that room, not even Eric. I owe Tiger that much, at least."

Tiger trailed his hand down the sweet softness of Carly's belly. Early-morning sunshine had strengthened and poured into his bedroom, the summer heat coming with it.

Carly opened her eyes a crack, looked at him, and let out a little moan. "Oh, no way I can do it again. Not yet."

Tiger glided fingertips around her navel. Inside, tiny in her abdomen, new life would be stirring. He sensed it already, and the thought filled him with both a joy and a fear.

"No," Tiger said. "Now is for resting. And pancakes."

"Thank God for that." Carly rolled onto her side, facing him, snuggled against his chest. "I've never had that much sex in my life. Not in one night. Wait, I think not *ever.*"

Tiger traced her checkbone. He couldn't stop touching her. "I like front to front."

Carly laughed, shaking delightfully. "I figured that out. So do I."

He pressed a kiss to her hair. "Then, after pancakes . . . ?"

Carly's laugh started up again. She rubbed a hand across Tiger's healed side, and the caress both tickled and warmed him. "You have superstrength. I'm an ordinary human woman. You have to give me a little bit of a break, to recover. After that, we can talk."

Tiger cupped his hand around her arm. "I'd never hurt you, Carly."

He spoke nothing but the truth. Carly lifted her head and pressed a soft kiss to his lips. "I know."

Tiger lost himself in kissing her for a moment. Why hadn't anyone told him that the strange practice of pressing lips was this satisfying? No, not *satisfying*. More than that. He needed to learn new words from Connor. Hot. Sensual. Wonderful.

After a long time, Carly lifted her head and drew a breath. "Being with you is . . . I don't know. Amazing." She sounded like she was having trouble finding words too. "Now, what about those pancakes? You making them?"

Tiger laughed. He hadn't laughed out loud since . . . Had he ever? Once or twice with Connor, but never like this. The laugh filled his stomach, then his lungs, then came out between his lips, his smile stretching his face.

A new sensation. Another miracle from Carly.

"Liam cooks," he said. "Or Sean comes over. Sean's better. They won't let me near the stove. Or knives."

"You don't need knives. You have those really sharp claws I saw when you turned into a tiger."

She stopped and shivered, and Tiger's laughter dissolved. He hadn't given Carly time to process that she was with a man who could become a beast. He didn't want her to have time—time was what he didn't have. Tiger didn't know how he knew that, but he did.

They finally left the bed and pulled on clothes, Carly gasping and pressing her hands to her face when she saw herself in the mirror over his dresser. Tiger had no idea why she thought she looked awful, as she said. She was the most beautiful thing he'd ever seen.

He took her down to the second floor and to the house's one bathroom, where Carly shut him out while she ran water and kept up a conversation through the door that he couldn't make out. Didn't matter; he just liked hearing her voice.

Carly came out, her hair damp and combed, her face clean of makeup and dust. Tiger took her hand and walked her downstairs to the ground floor, where the smell of pancakes on the griddle filled the big kitchen.

The man standing at the griddle, a towel tucked into his

jeans as an apron, was Sean, not Liam. A quick scenting told Tiger Liam wasn't in the house.

Sean's mate, Andrea, sat at the kitchen table, her cub on her lap. She held the little boy's hands while he stood on her thighs, his little bare feet pressing her jeans. Kenny Morrissey was seven months old with a round, chubby face and gray eyes like his mother's.

Connor puttered around the kitchen as well, fetching things out of the refrigerator for Sean. He glared when he saw Tiger and Carly walk in.

"Goddess, how much sleeping do you think I got with your bed banging away over my head all night? I thought Liam and Kim were bad."

Carly turned cherry red. "Sorry, Connor."

"I should run up to bed right now and catch some shut-eye. Either that or I'm trading rooms with you, Tiger. That one used to be mine."

"Really sorry." Carly cleared her throat. "Mind if I have some of that juice?" She gestured to the pitcher of orange juice and glasses on the table, the movement elegant.

"Help yourself." Andrea bounced Kenny and smiled into his face. "Oh, yeah, little man. You'll be walking soon, won't you? Look at you go."

Tiger paused to touch his hand to Kenny's head, loving the light eiderdown feel of his hair.

"Want to hold him?" Andrea asked him.

For answer, Tiger slid his hands around Kenny's body and lifted him. Kenny cooed, recognizing Tiger's touch. Tiger cradled Kenny against his chest, holding him steady in the cup of his palm.

CHAPTER SIXTEEN

Cubs were magical. No matter how frustrated, confused, or crazed Tiger became, he could always be calmed by holding a cub. He wanted to protect all of them, to not let them be taken away from him or their parents, ever.

If what he suspected was true, he and Carly would have a cub of their own this time next year. The cub would have Carly's eyes and her smile, and when it became old enough, it would start shifting into a tiny tiger. The thought sent warmth through his entire body.

"Where's Liam?" he asked.

Kenny gripped Tiger's shirt, trying to stand on his arm and start climbing him. Tiger put up his other hand so the boy wouldn't fall.

Sean answered without turning from the stove. "He got a call and had to leave town. Nothing to worry about."

The words weren't exactly a lie, at least, the part about Liam having to leave town wasn't. Tiger smelled the lie in the second half of the sentence.

Nothing to worry about, my ass. "I need to talk to him."

"Well, he's needing to talk to you, Iron Man," Sean said. "When he and Spike get back."

"Spike went?" Tiger came alert. "Who's taking care of Jordan? And where are Kim and Katriona?"

The need to know where the cubs were while their fathers were out of Shiftertown rose in a wave of worry. Cubs were vulnerable. Fathers should be with them.

"Kim's at work, and Katriona is at Ellison's being baby-sat by him and Maria. Jordan is being looked after by Myka and Spike's grandmother."

"You need to bring Jordan here, or send Dylan and Glory to him." Tiger's words came out as orders, staccato, firm. "There's a danger in town—Walker—and Myka is human. Not strong enough to defend the cub against him. Neither is Spike's grandmother."

Sean turned around, spatula in hand. "Calm yourself, now. I'm not saying you're wrong, but there's no need for panicking. I'll tell Dad."

"Walker is secure?"

Sean's eyes widened a little at all the military-like talk, but he nodded. "He's still at Ronan's. Ronan and Rebecca have got him covered."

"I will talk to him too. Find out what he knows. No, I won't kill him." Tiger handed Kenny back to Andrea, making sure the baby was safely in his mother's grasp before he let go. "I'll let Ronan take care of holding him."

Connor snorted a laugh. "In a bear hug."

"If necessary," Tiger said with a straight face.

"Wow." Connor peered at him. "What have you been doing to him, Carly? I think he just made a joke."

"We will have breakfast first," Tiger said, pulling out a chair for Carly.

Carly finished draining her glass of juice. "You bet we will. I'm starving. I can't remember when I've been this hungry."

Connor burst out laughing. "Well, you would be, wouldn't you? After that all-nighter?" He winked at Carly as he carried a plate piled high with pancakes to the table. "Better eat up, Carly. I have the feeling you're going to get hungrier."

Filled with delicious pancakes—buttermilk, blueberry, and chocolate chip—Carly walked with Tiger across the yards of Shiftertown to visit the Shifter called Ronan.

Carly had told Tiger he should go to Ronan's alone while she went home, but he asked her to come with him. *Asked* her, but with a hint of need, and truthfully, Carly didn't want to go home, not yet. Her time with Tiger was crazy, but she was floating in a bubble of comfort and warmth, and she didn't want to burst it. Not yet.

She held Tiger's hand as they walked, his gentle on hers. He didn't seem to mind the other Shifters staring, but Carly did.

She saw right away that they weren't staring at her, but at Tiger. Carly might have been a fly on Tiger's back for all they noticed her. The Shifters' gazes were for Tiger, faces unmoving but bodies tense, men subtly stepping in front of the few female Shifters they passed. All looked Tiger up and down, assessing.

Tiger noticed—how could he help it? He turned his head to meet stares, and gazes dropped swiftly when he did that. Heads would lift as soon as he passed, but none of the Shifters would lock eyes with him. That would be a challenge. Tiger might turn from his path, come over, ask why they were watching him.

The Shifters were afraid of him.

No one else wanted me in their house, Tiger had said in the car before the terrible wreck. Carly remembered only bits and pieces of the crash, but she fully remembered the bleakness in Tiger's voice when he spoke the matter-of-fact words. Tiger lived in Liam's house because he had nowhere else to go.

Carly grew suddenly angry at these Shifters who watched Tiger as though he were a strange monster in their midst. She thought of how Tiger had picked up baby Kenny this morning, how delicately he'd handled the boy, how trusting Kenny had been with him, and how trusting Katriona had been with him yesterday. The little boy, Kenny, was Sean's, if Carly understood the relationships right, and Sean hadn't worried a minute. Andrea had watched, as mothers did, but she didn't worry either.

These Shifters who pulled back or looked away, afraid to confront Tiger but happy to stare, made Carly's rage boil. She hadn't said the phrase since childhood, but it seemed appropriate now.

"Take a picture," she called out. "It lasts longer."

Two Shifter men standing together—brothers from the looks of it—suddenly switched their gazes to Carly. Tiger growled, and they abruptly turned away, the two heading in opposite directions across a yard.

"You have fire, my mate," Tiger said, squeezing her hand more tightly. "And no fear."

The *mate* thing again. As soon as they figured out why Walker had been spying on Carly, and what he knew about the accident—she would sit Tiger down and have that long discussion with him.

But for now . . . Carly twined her fingers through Tiger's as they walked on in the sunshine.

Ronan's house sat well back from the street behind a garage that had been enclosed to make what looked like a guesthouse. Beyond that was a two-story house, larger than the others Carly had seen.

The door of the house popped open, and out ran a white-furred polar bear cub. Without stopping, the cub galloped straight for Tiger.

Tiger released Carly's hand, dropped into a crouch, spread his arms, and took the full impact of the bear cub's charge. Bear and man rolled over on the ground, dust and dried grass flying upward. The cub growled and snarled, but Tiger was silent as he pretended to wrestle with the little bear.

They writhed on the ground for several moments longer, the bear cub swiping black paws at Tiger, Tiger deflecting them gently. Finally Tiger was flat on his back, spread-eagled, the bear cub standing on top of him, growling his victory.

Tiger brought his arms up and started rubbing the bear, pulling him down into a hug. The cub made baby bear noises and nuzzled Tiger's face.

Then the cub turned its head and saw Carly. He climbed quickly off Tiger and romped toward her.

Carly stepped back, waiting for the cub to jump and knock her flat too, but the cub only stopped and sniffed curiously around her feet. When it lifted its head, Carly put one hand down to stroke it. She found fur soft and yet wiry, rather like Tiger's, but deeper, the pelt of a cold-weather animal.

The bear cub closed its eyes and leaned on Carly's legs, rumbling in its belly. A warm delight worked through Carly as she kept petting, the cub crooning its pleasure.

"Olaf." A petite young woman of about thirty, her dark hair streaked with red, had come out onto the porch. She carried a tiny baby in one competent arm, its shock of hair a rich red brown. "Let them come inside."

Olaf nuzzled Carly's hand one last time, then he took off across the yard, barreling past the woman and into the house.

"I'm Elizabeth," the woman said as Tiger picked him-self up off the ground and brushed grass from his jeans. "Ronan's mate. You must be Carly."

Carly walked up to the porch and stuck out her hand. "I sure am. Word travels fast."

"You have no idea." The woman was human, no Collar around her neck, cute in her cropped top and jeans, but with eyes that had seen a lot in life. The baby couldn't have been more than a couple of months old, serenely sleeping in its T-shirt.

"This is Coby," she said, a note of pride in her voice. "Our new little son. You two have come to see Walker."

Carly looked up from where she'd been gently tickling Coby's stomach. "That's right. How'd you know?"

"Shifter gossip. Faster than e-mail. Come on inside. I've got cold bottled water for you—it's a hot one today."

"That's Austin in the summer," Carly said.

"You've lived here long?" Elizabeth led the way into the house, Carly following, Tiger close behind her.

"All my life," Carly said. "Born and raised." By a great mother and three sisters who'd pulled together for survival.

"I've been here about seven years. But I love it. Been in Shiftertown less than that." Elizabeth bounced the little boy. "You get used to it."

Do you? Carly wondered.

Ronan's house was large, the floors polished hardwood with rugs, and had big, solid furniture all around. Carly guessed why the furniture was so sturdy when she saw the people sitting at the dining room table—a giant of a man and a woman who, Carly saw when she stood up, was tall, curvaceous, and absolutely gorgeous. The Collar around her neck only enhanced her sensuality.

The way she flicked her attention to Tiger made Carly's possessiveness rear its head.

Not ten minutes ago, Carly had been thinking that she should tell Tiger they needed to slow down and get to know each other before they proceeded with a relationship of any kind. But as soon as this Shifter woman so much as glanced at him, Carly wanted to glare at her and say, *Back off.*

Weird, she'd never felt that way about Ethan. Carly had never worried at all with Ethan, until it was too late.

The Shifter woman must have seen the jealous glitter in Carly's eyes, because she broke into a smile that threatened to become a laugh.

"Ronan," she said and wandered to an open door that led to a kitchen. "They're here."

"I can see that."

Ronan rose, the man larger even than Tiger. Walker sat behind him at the table, one wrist in a handcuff, the handcuff chained to a ring in the wall. Why Ronan's household had a heavy ring in the wall in the dining room, Carly wasn't sure, and she wasn't sure she wanted to know.

"Tiger," Ronan said. Unlike the Shifters they'd passed on the way, he didn't drop his gaze before Tiger or stare at him in hostile fear. "You're looking good for a Shifter who should be dead."

"I feel good too," Tiger said. He rested his hands on Carly's shoulders. "Not so surprising."

Ronan's brows went up, and he breathed in. "I see," he said. "You work fast. But we can talk about that later. You came to interrogate Walker, right? Just remember that he won't be able to talk if you break his jaw, knock him out, or rip out his throat."

Tiger nodded gravely. "I'll remember."

"How long do we have to keep him?" Ronan went on conversationally. He moved to Elizabeth and took up his son, using the same care with which Tiger had lifted Sean's cub. "I expected Liam to come for him, but I guess Liam has better things to do. Tasting new batches of Guinness or something."

Ronan spoke lightly, but Carly saw his tension. Liam had left town for an important reason, one Ronan wouldn't talk about in front of Walker, or maybe even Tiger.

Walker looked tired but whole. The bruises and scratches Tiger had left on his face were healing, and he looked all right. No one here had tortured him.

He seemed subdued though, and not because his hand was chained to the wall. Walker glanced at Rebecca, and red stained his cheekbones.

Tiger pulled out a chair and sat, leaning forward with elbows on knees. He looked into Walker's face, just looked at him. Walker returned the look with the same blank expression.

Elizabeth pressed a cold, damp bottle into Carly's hand. Carly took the bottle of water and opened it, watching Tiger and Walker while she drank.

Tiger waited, and minutes stretched by. Walker was getting nervous, or so it seemed from the sheen of perspiration on his forehead. But he said nothing and didn't move.

Ronan handed his baby back to Elizabeth and seated

himself at the head of the table, close enough so he could dive between Tiger and Walker if needed. The polar bear cub had disappeared, perhaps knowing that the dining room was about to become an interrogation cell.

Tiger said nothing. Carly couldn't see Tiger's eyes from where she stood, but Walker started sweating more, his hand twitching where it was cuffed.

"They want to know what you are," Walker said after fifteen solid minutes of silence.

Carly was the one stretched to her limit. Men enjoyed staring at each other until one of them broke, but she always believed that if you wanted to know something you just asked.

"Who wants to know?" she broke in. "The Shifter Bureau?"

Carly expected Tiger to be annoyed with her for interrupting, but he only waited with her for Walker's answer.

"Shifter Bureau," Walker said, giving Carly a nod. "And the commander of my unit. We're always on the lookout for Shifter anomalies. That order isn't classified; it's common knowledge."

"Not to me," Carly said. "Why so much interest in Tiger? He's just another Shifter, isn't he?"

Walker's tight mouth twitched. "No, he's not. And everyone in this room knows it. He can do things other Shifters can't. When he landed in the hospital, I was sent to report."

"And shoot him," Carly said testily. "You came with plenty of firepower."

"We were only to shoot if necessary. And it almost became necessary. And then you showed up." Walker's gaze moved from Tiger to rest on Carly.

Carly understood then that Walker wasn't a pushover, a man doing his job, controlled by others. He was smart— he'd seen how Carly had calmed Tiger in the hospital and gotten him back into bed, had wondered why she'd been able to make him see reason when no one else had.

"That's why you and Dr. Brennan came to see me,"

Carly said. "You were interested in *me*, not my observations on Shifters."

"We thought you could provide insight on the tiger. When you kicked Brennan out, I stayed to watch you, to see if you'd run to the Shifters and tell them everything. But the tiger showed up instead."

"He was worried about me," Carly said, because Tiger remained silent. "With good reason. You were lurking in my backyard, up to no good."

"And now I'm here." Walker gave her a wry look and raised the hand with the cuff.

"Don't let him fool you," Rebecca said, coming back into the room. "He's a master at escaping. He's gotten himself out of duct tape, a zip tie, and once from that cuff already. He put it back on to be polite."

Ronan rumbled, "Easy to pick open a cuff, hard to get past two Kodiak bears in bad moods."

"I have PMS," Rebecca said. She smiled at Walker. "Not a good time to piss me off."

"Why do you need insight on Tiger?" Carly asked. "He tore it up in the hospital because he was hurt, and because your little army was trying to take him down. I hate hospitals myself—all those machines beeping and people poking at you and sticking you with needles filled with who knows what. You know Tiger wasn't trying to attack anyone there, because his Collar would have shocked him. That's what it's for."

Walker glanced back at Tiger, his gaze going to Tiger's Collar. Tiger hadn't taken his eyes from Walker for one second.

"Collar shocks hurt like hell," Rebecca said. She leaned forward so her breasts clearly filled the V neckline of her T-shirt. "We avoid it, trust me."

"Another question for you," Carly said. "What about the attack on us yesterday? The black SUV chasing us and the spectacular crash at the end? We could have all been killed. And then Tiger gets shot, repeatedly. Was that meant for me? Or him? Both of us?"

"I don't know," Walker said. "You already had me here, remember?"

"The SUV was similar to what brought you to my house, and the shooter wore the same outfit." Carly indicated Walker's black T-shirt and pants, combat boots completing the ensemble.

"The Bureau might have sent someone to find out what happened to me when I disappeared," Walker said. "But I don't think they would have ordered a hit. They don't work that way. We're interested in Shifters while they're alive; we're not interested in killing them."

Tiger finally spoke. He leaned forward and said, "Tell me everything your bureau knows about me, and why they are looking." It was a command, not a request.

Walker didn't answer right away. Tiger returned to watching him with his Shifter stare, but Walker looked back without flinching.

"You told me you were in a Special Forces unit attached to Shifter Bureau South," Carly said, again unable to wait for Tiger to win the stare down. "What does that mean? What does the Shifter Bureau do, exactly?"

"Welfare of Shifters," Walker said. He talked readily when given questions he felt comfortable answering. "Set up twenty years ago to look into the problem of integrating the Shifters with humans, and to liaise with Congress and other departments who regulate Shifters."

"They created the Shiftertowns, you mean," Carly said.

"Necessary to protect and reassure the general public that dangerous people weren't moving into their neighborhoods or becoming threats to their children. If the Shifters lived apart for a time, proving they can do so peacefully, they'll be more accepted when it's time for them to integrate with the rest of the population."

"Sure," Carly said, wrinkling her nose. "Like that idea has worked so well in the past. All right, you've given me the spiel, the mission statement, but what do *you* do, in your Special Forces unit? Spy on Shifters?"

"Oversight. Make sure Shifters aren't living outside the

parameters that would cause danger to humans, or that humans aren't causing danger to Shifters."

"Outside the parameters," Rebecca said casually. "Like a bear with PMS?"

Walker's twitch of the lips returned. "Like Shifters with Collars that malfunction, or Shifters not on our radar until a few months ago. Or a Shifter name in the database that doesn't match any Shifter I've eyeballed, and a Shifter living here that no one calls by name." His gaze returned pointedly to Tiger.

"What name?" Carly asked. "In the database? Wait, there's a database?"

"The name is Rory Sylvester," Walker said. "Any ideas?"

Tiger didn't change expression. Carly shook her head. "I haven't met enough Shifters to know."

"Someone has a sense of humor," Walker said while the bears and Elizabeth remained silent. "*Felis silvestris* is a wildcat. *Rory* . . . maybe for *roaring?* Whoever inserted that name thought he—or she—was being funny."

"Doesn't the Shifter Bureau input the records?" Carly asked. "The name had to come from somewhere."

"I know it did," Walker said. "I look at the databases every day. When the name popped up overnight, and no one at the Bureau admitted to entering it, I decided I wanted to know who it belonged to."

"I don't like that name," Tiger said flatly, breaking in. "It isn't mine."

CHAPTER SEVENTEEN

Walker was the only human Tiger had met so far who didn't immediately look away from him. Except Carly, of course. She looked at him fully, with no fear, no submission.

"We're on the same side," Walker said to Tiger, holding his gaze, ignoring Tiger's statement about the name. "We're trying to figure out who you are, where you came from, and why you can do what you do. You should be dead, but you're walking around. Not even in pain."

No, Walker was wrong about the pain. Tiger's pain had been immense, and he was still sore. Being with Carly helped, but the healing wasn't instantaneous.

"Why do you want to know who I am?" Tiger asked. "I'm nobody. I live with Liam and help Connor fix Shifters' cars."

"You're not nobody. You're different. And I mean more than you being the only Bengal tiger around."

Tiger sat straight in his chair, liking that Carly was so near. Her presence, her scent, the lingering feeling of being inside her, gave him strength. "When you find out all about me, what will you do?"

Walker shrugged. "Don't know. Whatever my commander and the Shifter Bureau decides."

"That doesn't sound good," Carly said.

"They'll study you, probably," Walker said. "Find out what makes you different."

"Still not sounding good." Carly's indignation touched Tiger with a scent like wood smoke.

"We need Liam." Ronan broke in from down the table. "I don't like this."

Tiger didn't like it either. His heart beat faster, sending tingles of fear through his body, though he didn't let himself show any discomfort. "They'd experiment on me."

"Maybe," Walker said. "Not really my decision."

Carly tensed behind Tiger, the wood smoke scent turning sharp with her anger. "What do you mean *maybe*?" she demanded. "You don't experiment on a person. That's weird, and wrong."

"Like I said, not my decision."

"Then whose decision is it?" Tiger asked.

"My commanding officer's. Or the head of the Shifter Bureau. I don't know. I'm not that high in the food chain."

Carly leaned forward, resting her arm on the table. It just touched Tiger, the warmth of her stilling his fear again. "I bet you're higher than you let on," she said.

Tiger knew she was right. Walker was playing the junior man, pretending he knew only what he'd been told, giving up to them nonessential things that Shifters could have found out without much effort. Tiger was willing to bet Liam already knew most of what Walker had said.

Walker hadn't lied to them—any Shifter would have detected that. But he hadn't said everything he could have.

Tiger wasn't sure what to do now. He'd been bred to fight, not to interrogate prisoners or think up strategies. Every test on him had been about strength, endurance, stamina—not problem solving.

"Find out," he said.

Walker blinked, his blank expression finally cracking. "Sorry?"

"Go back and find out what they want to do, and why, and then tell me."

Ronan growled. "What are you talking about, Tiger? If we let him go, he'll run back to the Bureau and report this little escapade, especially the part about being chained to the wall. I don't need human cops arresting me and messing with my family, or coming to Shiftertown at all."

"They won't," Tiger said. "Walker will make sure of it, because he's interested in me for his own reasons. He reported me to his bureau because he wanted them to find out about me, but he's afraid they messed up and tried to kill me instead. He's angry at them for that, but he's still curious about me. I am too. I want to know what they know, and so does Walker."

Tiger felt their stares—Carly's, Ronan's, Rebecca's, Elizabeth's. Ronan cleared his throat. "What, now you read minds?"

"Scent," Tiger said. "What he said with his words and what he said with his scent are two different things."

"Shit," Walker said softly. "Remind me to take a shower before I talk to you again."

"Yeah, I read scent too," Ronan said to Tiger. "But I didn't catch all that or figure out what he *didn't* say."

"He wants to know about me," Tiger said. "And he wants to use me, maybe, but not for a bad reason."

Rebecca said, "Huh. That comes to you through *smell*? All I get is that he's nervous, really curious about Tiger, and wonders what it would be like to sleep with me."

Walker went beet red, and Ronan rumbled, "Becks, would you cool it? I swear, we need to get you mated. You've rejected, like what, twenty mate-claims?"

"Haven't met anyone who turns my crank. Not enough to stay with him for the rest of my life anyway." Rebecca smiled at Walker. "Shifters have long lives. I'm only a hundred."

Walker was growing more and more uncomfortable.

Tiger read his desire for Rebecca loud and clear. He didn't need to be a super Shifter to get that.

"Make a promise to me," Tiger said to Walker. "Go back to your Shifter Bureau. Find out what they know about me, and share the information only with me. In return, I'll tell you what I know about myself."

Ronan let out another growl, this one louder. "No. We wait for Liam."

For answer Tiger reached over and broke the chain that held Walker to the wall, then pulled the handcuff open from Walker's wrist.

Ronan was on his feet. "Damn it, Tiger. What are you doing? And did you have to break the chain? We need it for Scott."

Carly picked up the end of the chain and examined the place where Tiger had sheared it off. "Sheesh, who is Scott, and why in the world do you have to chain him to your wall?"

"Scott's going through his Transition," Elizabeth answered, as though chaining people up was commonplace in her house. "When his fighting instincts get too bad, we have to restrain him. It's either that or replace the furniture every day. And Scott worries he'll hurt Coby."

She cuddled the little boy, who was already waking up. Coby looked around with unfocused brown eyes at the many people gathered in his house, opened his mouth, and let out an annoyed yell.

The sound went straight into Tiger's brain and stirred a basic, primal instinct. He and Ronan moved at the same time, Elizabeth saying, "It's all right. He's just hungry. And wants attention. Don't you, little guy?"

Tiger reached Coby before Ronan did, and Elizabeth relinquished him to Tiger. As Tiger lifted the boy, Coby unscrunched his face, stopped crying, and gave a few happy kicks in the air.

"I love how Tiger can do that," Elizabeth said. "It's like magic."

Tiger nuzzled Coby's forehead, then handed him back

to his mother. "I should see Scott," he said. "Make sure he's okay."

He headed for the kitchen, where he knew Ronan's three foster cubs lingered, listening to the adults. Behind him, Ronan said, "Walker's gone."

Tiger paused at the kitchen door, but he'd already known Walker had made use of the open window to escape. "He'll be back," Tiger said.

"Shit, Tiger," Ronan snarled, his bear temper coming through. "Why are you doing this to me? Liam's going to skin me alive. I'll end up a bear rug on his living room floor."

"Walker will be back," Tiger repeated, knowing he was right. He went on into the kitchen.

Scott, a black bear Shifter in his late twenties, whose change from cub to full-grown male was making him crazy, grinned at Tiger and held up his hand. Tiger, who'd learned about high fives from both Scott and Connor, slapped his palm, then caught the young man's hand in a tight clasp.

Cherie, the female cub going on twenty-one as humans figured years, gave Tiger an impulsive hug. Olaf, who'd changed back to his ten-year-old boy form and resumed shorts, T-shirt, and sneakers, flung his arms around Tiger's leg.

Tiger sensed Carly behind him. She was watching him with wonder on her face, surprise at his camaraderie with the cubs coming through her scent, but her smile warming his world.

"I'm going to work today," Carly said as they walked back to Liam's house. "It's Saturday, we get a lot of tourist traffic, I wasn't hurt in the wreck, and I need the paycheck."

"Too dangerous," Tiger said. He held her hand again, and again the other Shifters shot him looks of wariness. Carly stared right back at them and squeezed Tiger's hand.

"Too bad," Carly said to Tiger. "I'm going."

"Then I go with you."

Carly pictured the giant Tiger standing in the gallery

while yuppie tourists strolled around him, trying to look at paintings around the pillar of Tiger. He wouldn't fit in there, among slender people who shopped for art as casually as they shopped for postcards.

Or maybe he would. Tiger had raw strength and wild beauty that was the stuff of art.

"Fine by me," Carly said. "But I'm going."

She expected Tiger to argue more, but he said nothing as they walked on, hand in hand, through the sunshine.

They arrived back at the Morrisseys' to find Liam and Spike climbing tiredly out of a small pickup. Spike lifted a hand in greeting to Tiger but said nothing at all as he turned and jogged away down the street.

Liam gave Tiger a sharp look and motioned for him and Carly to follow him into the house.

Sean and Andrea had gone, but Connor was there, wiping the kitchen counters with a large blue dishcloth. "I love Sean's pancakes," Connor said when they came in. "But damn, he makes a mess."

Liam glanced at him but kept the frown on his face, his gaze moving back to Carly and Tiger. Wherever he'd gone, whatever he'd done outside of Shiftertown, he'd returned in a black mood.

"Well, I have to be going," Carly said into the tension. "Don't worry about me. Tiger's coming along to keep me safe."

"No." Liam's word was flat, final. "Tiger's not leaving Shiftertown."

Tiger tightened his grip on Carly's hand. "Then Carly stays."

"Oh, no, she doesn't," Carly said. "I have a million things to do. Not only do I have to work, I need to start unpacking my stuff again, and explain to everyone I know why my engagement ended, which is going to be extremely humiliating. My car's totaled, so I have to see about getting a new one, not to mention talk to my insurance company— I doubt Shifter Bureau is going to come forward and admit they deliberately wrecked my car, and pay the damages.

Plus I'll need to deal with Ethan and whatever he's going to throw at me. A full day. Can't handle all that sitting here."

"Then I go with you," Tiger stated.

The look Liam shot at Tiger made Carly's next words die on her lips. Before this, whenever Liam had pinned Tiger, his gaze had been steady and strong, the stare of a man no one messed with. But this look held depths of rage.

Liam's eyes flicked from sinful blue to almost opaque silver, and he took on the stillness Carly had observed in the Shifters before. In one instant, Liam changed from tired man weary from whatever journey he'd taken to a dangerous enemy ready to strike.

Tiger growled in response. The same rumble that had shaken Ethan's house flowed from Tiger's throat, the kitchen windows humming with it. Connor looked up, eyes wide.

Liam's face elongated until it was the muzzle of a lion, the hair on his head flowing into a formidable black mane. Tiger kept his hands clenched but didn't change, his low tiger growl going on and on.

Tiger's growl was matched by Liam's, both blending into it and vibrating the air. Connor tried to flatten himself against the counter, as though fearing they'd turn and see him, weak and vulnerable, and strike.

Another growl sounded at the back door. Dylan stood in the opening, still in human form, but his eyes were the same white-hot color as Liam's.

Carly took a step back, then another and another, silently and steadily making her way back to the door to the living room. She understood how Connor felt, hoping the Shifters wouldn't turn around, see her, and send that building pool of aggression toward her.

Connor slid around the edges of the kitchen, his back to the wall, to join her. His eyes had taken on the same white-blue hue as the others', but with fear, not rage. When Connor reached Carly, he grabbed her by the wrist, pulled her out of the kitchen, and started heading for the front door.

"Wait," Carly said, trying to stop.

Connor shook his head. "If they start tearing it up in there, the best place for us to be is *not* here."

"But they can't really fight each other, can they? The Collars stop them. Right?"

Her words died into uncertainty as Connor stared down at her. "Carly, you're naive. My granddad's a killer. So is Tiger, and the Collars don't change that. Do you know what's going on in there? Liam's trying to make Tiger back down and obey him, but Tiger's saying he won't. Dylan came because he sensed Tiger was snapping Liam's control. Liam hasn't really ever been able to control Tiger, and it's been harder since Tiger met you."

Carly's mouth went dry. "Oh, sure, blame this on me."

"No, not your fault. Tiger's decided you're his mate, and that makes him stronger than ever. Shifters will do anything to protect their mates, including defy their leaders if they have to. And I don't think Tiger has ever recognized Liam as his leader. I'm thinking he's been obeying Liam just to be nice."

"But I never said I'd be his mate," Carly said, her throat tight. "We're not even dating. Last night was . . ." She broke off, her face heating. "We'd been hurt and scared, and we were celebrating being alive."

"Not in Tiger's mind. He's convinced you're meant to be together—forever. Probably he's reacting this way because his mate died, and his cub. The researchers threw them together, then dragged them apart, wouldn't even let him say a proper good-bye when they died. I bet that's why he's clinging on to you, afraid that will happen again."

"I know about his mate. He told me, the poor guy."

They peeked through the open door to the kitchen where the "poor guy" was facing Dylan and Liam, his powerful hands clenched to fists, the snarling match still going on. No sign of sparks from any Collars, no signs of pain. Just Shifters facing each other down, violence hovering in the air.

"What can I do?" Carly asked, twining her fingers together in worry. "There has to be something."

"You could reject the mate-claim," Connor said. "If Tiger is told he's no longer obligated to protect you, he might calm down."

"*Might* calm down?"

"That's all I've got."

Carly drew a breath. "All right. What do I do?"

Dylan was going to kill him. Tiger scented that without doubt. The former Shiftertown leader had run out of patience, and now he was here to protect his son. To Dylan Tiger was a danger, an aberration. They could kill him, have Sean send his body to dust, then hack into the human databases again and wipe out his presence. No trouble at all.

Liam would be sorry, Tiger sensed, but relieved. Liam had never known what to do with Tiger, had been looking after him only as a favor to Eric and Iona. Dylan had never been happy with Tiger here at all.

"Tiger." Carly was in the room again, with Connor behind her. The scent of his mate twined around him, giving him strength. Tiger knew he could defeat both Liam and Dylan, and protect her and Connor.

He scented Carly's terror as well, which made him shift his stance slightly, making sure neither Dylan nor Liam could get past him to her.

Carly stepped closer to Tiger. She shouldn't do that—Dylan was unpredictable, and Carly moving made her harder to guard.

Tiger was so focused on where Carly was and how to keep the other two Shifter males away from her that he was completely unprepared when Carly cleared her throat and then stated in a loud voice, "Tiger, I reject your mate-claim."

CHAPTER EIGHTEEN

Liam blinked, and his growl cut off. He let his face return to human, rubbing it a little after the change.

Dylan had never shifted, but his eyes didn't calm. He looked away from Tiger and pinned Carly, which Tiger didn't like. Tiger renewed his growl and stepped more solidly in front of his mate.

"Thank you, lass," Liam said, releasing a breath. "Tiger, let her go. I'll have Sean go with her today to make sure Walker or the Bureau doesn't try anything more with her. Yes, I heard already about you releasing Walker."

They didn't understand. These Shifters who thought they ruled with wisdom and experience had forgotten what it was to be Shifter. Tiger had never lived outside the basement in the place the humans called Area 51, and he'd lived only forty years, but he knew he was Shifter, wild, and different.

"The words she says mean nothing," Tiger said. "She is my true mate."

Carly made a noise of exasperation. "Oh, come on, Tiger. I'm only trying to help."

"She rejected your claim in front of witnesses, son," Liam said. "That makes her free of you."

"She is free." If Tiger explained carefully, maybe they'd get it. "But she is also my mate, and I will protect her from you."

"Damn it." Liam's anger returned. "I'm the one trying to protect *you*. The other Shifter leaders are ready to get rid of you, the Shifter Bureau is delving into who you really are, you're claiming a mate who doesn't want to be claimed, and you're threatening me. You don't threaten a leader unless you're challenging for dominance, and you don't want to go down that road."

"I don't want to lead this Shiftertown." Tiger couldn't keep the disgust from his voice. "Shifters shouldn't have leaders. I don't want to live here either. I want out."

"Too bad," Liam said. "If you leave Shiftertown, you'll be hunted down. Slaughtered. Not given a chance. At least here, I can give you a chance."

"Then stay away from my mate."

"Shite, Tiger. *I don't want your mate.* And she's not your mate. You scent-marked her, and you claimed her, but you can only complete the mating ceremonies with her consent. You know that."

"Your words and rituals are not important. Carly is my mate. Doesn't matter what words I say, or she says, doesn't matter if she wants to run away and never see me again." Tiger touched his fist to his chest. "The mating is real. She's of my heart."

Carly's voice cut through Tiger's words. "Damn, I knew you were a sweet-talker the minute I met you."

Tiger turned his back on Liam and Dylan to face Carly. He heard Dylan's growl, the man taking Tiger deliberately turning away as a slap. Tiger didn't care. Hierarchy meant nothing to him. Protect the mate, protect the cubs—nothing else mattered.

"You are my mate," Tiger said to Carly. "Even if you run from me, if I never see you again, you will always be the mate of my heart."

Carly's face softened. She was looking at him as she had on the highway, one hand on her hip, her gaze roving him. Her eyes, so beautiful with their gray on green, met his. "You're flattering, I'll give you that."

She came to him, her scent filling him, calming him. Tiger forgot about Liam trying to challenge him, Dylan ready to kill, even Connor waiting anxiously in the doorway. Carly was Tiger's world.

He smoothed her hair and pressed a light kiss to her lips. Kissing was a fine thing.

"I really have to go," Carly said. "Stay here and talk to Liam about whatever he needs to say to you, or he might burst a blood vessel. But I promise, I'll come back, and we'll have that long talk."

Tiger touched her face. He didn't want to let her out of his sight, not without protection. But he didn't want the Morrissey brothers, or their dad, anywhere near her. "If I stay, Spike goes with you." He gave Liam a hard look. "I trust *him*."

Liam moved his hands out to his sides, though the grim lines didn't leave his face. "At least you're giving me that. Stay put, Tiger—please. There are some things you need to know."

Tiger made sure Carly was safely away, driven by Spike in Dylan's truck, with Connor on her other side. Tiger didn't fully believe the two of them could keep her safe, but he also knew that the strike yesterday had been against him, not Carly. The man had shot at Carly so Tiger would protect her.

He thought of the way the man had stood next to Tiger after he'd fired the first shots, watching. The man had been waiting for something. Testing him. And he hadn't killed Tiger, had left him and all the others alive.

"There's no easy way to put this," Liam said when they walked back into the house. Dylan followed them to the kitchen—Tiger knew the man would stay until satisfied that Tiger was no longer a threat. "The other Shifter leaders want me to put a Collar on you. A real one."

Tiger touched the silver and black chain with the Celtic knot at his throat that Sean and Liam had manufactured. Unlike real Collars, this one wasn't laced with Fae magic and microchips. Who the Fae was that had turned out the new Collars, happy to help the humans subjugate Shifters, Tiger had to wonder. And why someone like Dylan hadn't killed him, Tiger wondered as well.

"I won't wear the Collar."

"You don't have a choice," Liam said. "They're scared of you. They want you to take a Collar or else for us to kill you."

"You can't kill me." Tiger knew that. None of them could.

"I don't want to," Liam said. "I want to help you. But you have to cooperate."

"I can't take a Collar," Tiger repeated. "I can't do what I'm made to do if I have a Collar."

Liam had been reaching for the refrigerator, probably to take the edge off their tension with Guinness, but he stopped. "Now that's interesting. What were you made to do?"

"I don't know. But I know the Collar will prevent me."

"I see." Liam opened the refrigerator and reached inside, coming out with, yes, a dark brown bottle with *Guinness Stout* on the label. "What do you *think* it might be?"

"They never told me. But the way I recovered from the shooting must be a part of it. The second time faster than the first. I'm changing." He let out a breath. "It's tiring. I've never felt this tired before."

Liam lowered the beer, not drinking. "You also had a lot of sex, my friend. Hours of it. Can't blame you—she's a lovely lady. As far as I know, that's the first sex you've had since you arrived. Sure you're not just exhausted from pleasure? It can wipe you out—in a different way from fighting. And much more fun."

"Being with Carly didn't tire me." Tiger warmed, remembering rolling her onto her back, still inside her, with her pliant to take him. He'd loved her slowly, kissing her while she kissed him. He'd never wanted to stop, never wanted to leave the bed. Real life had been far away, unimportant. "The healing though. That burned."

"I'm sure." Liam shook his head. "I wish we had a Shifter healer here to look at you. Andrea's good, but her talent is natural, not learned. She hasn't made a study of Shifters."

"But we know someone who might tell us what's going on inside him," Dylan said. "If it's magical."

Liam flicked his gaze to his father, then his eyes took on a faraway look as he considered. "True. If he'll talk to us. We'll need Sean. And Andrea."

"Good thing they stayed home," Dylan said in his dry voice.

"Aye," Liam said. "Tiger, there's someone I want you to meet."

Sean and Andrea met them on the strip of green behind the houses, in the clump of trees that Tiger avoided for some reason. He'd never thought about why he didn't like to go there, but something in him made him steer around it whenever he walked down the long common ground.

Sean had brought his sword. Tiger eyed it in its sheath on Sean's back. A few months ago, he'd watched Sean drive the blade of the sword into the body of an elderly Shifter, the man sighing in relief as his last breath went out of him. His body had crumbled to dust, and the Shifters who'd gathered for the parting ceremony had said prayers, both grieving and thanking Sean for freeing the man's soul.

Tiger wasn't sure how a sword could do that, but he saw again the threads that connected it to Sean, and connected Sean to Andrea, as he had when Andrea had started healing him after the accident. Sean unsheathed the sword, which rang faintly, and Tiger stepped back, well out of its reach.

Sean pointed the sword forward, holding it toward nothing. Andrea put her hand over his on its hilt.

"Dad," she said.

"Open up, it's the in-laws," Sean added.

"He's not big on humor," Andrea said in her calm way.

Sean grinned. "I know. That's why I do it."

A light slit the air. Tiger growled and stepped back again, hackles rising. In the ten months he'd been here, he'd never seen this. He'd never smelled the acrid stench that came out of the slit, which had Liam wrinkling his nose, and Sean looking stoic.

A figure appeared in the opening. He was tall, thin, almost angular. White hair hung over his shoulder in a long braid, and he wore a shirt of linked rings over white leather, a black cloak rolling back from his shoulders.

"What?" he snapped. His voice was rich and full, with a hint of Irish.

"Nice to see you too." Andrea released the sword and went to the man, enclosing him in her embrace.

The man's sharp face softened as he allowed the hug, closing his arms around her in return. "Andrea. Child. Let me look at you."

"I haven't changed since the last time," Andrea said.

"Give an old man the delight of seeing his daughter. How's the wee one?"

"Kenny's fine. Growing fast."

"Don't bother telling me he looks like me or has my nose. He'll be mostly Shifter." The man glanced at Sean. "Will smell like one too."

"Better than the stench of Fae," Sean said, but with no rancor behind the words.

"I'll ignore that," Andrea said. "Father, Liam wants you to meet Tiger. Tiger, Fionn Cillian, my father. My real father. He's a Fae."

The Fae moved his gaze from Andrea to Tiger. He stiffened, his stance becoming defensive, a warrior reacting to a threat. "What *is* that?"

"His name's Tiger," Andrea said. "Because, you know, he's a tiger."

"I'd never have guessed." Fionn took in Tiger's multicolored hair, his build, his golden eyes. "No Fae made that."

"That's why we're curious," Liam said. "Can you tell us *how* he was made? Or maybe, how he wasn't?"

"Why don't you ask his parents? Presumably pure tiger."

"He doesn't have parents," Liam said. "He was concocted in a lab. None of us, including Tiger, know how."

"I'd have to touch him to find out," Fionn said. "And I don't want to come near him. He's ready to rip my head off. I can see it in him."

"He'll behave," Andrea said. "Won't you?" She slanted Tiger a warning glance, and Tiger made her happy by nodding.

Fionn's lips thinned. "You dragged me across a dimension for me to put my hand on a tiger Shifter? What do I get in return?"

"An hour with your grandson," Andrea said.

Fionn's face softened. "You fight dirty, daughter. All right."

He stepped through the opening without any problem, the cold, nostril-curling smell clinging to his cloak. Fionn stopped in front of Tiger, the man tall enough to look at him eye to eye.

"Don't try anything," Fionn warned. "I might not be able to turn into a beast, but I've trained as a fighter for more years than anyone here has been alive. Hold still."

Fionn stripped off a skin-fitting leather glove and pressed his bare, long-fingered hand to Tiger's chest.

Something snapped through Tiger like an electric shock, shooting through his chest in a bite of pain. His mind whipped back to the dark basement, where researchers had shocked him, jolt after jolt, Tiger screaming, not even aware that he'd opened his mouth.

He brought up his hand to smack Fionn away, but Fionn had jerked back well before Tiger moved.

"What the hell?" Fionn growled. "I told you not to attack me."

Tiger opened his eyes. The lab disappeared, and he drew a breath of humid Austin air, now tinged with Faerie. "I didn't," he said, voice rasping. "You shocked me."

"No, my friend. I don't carry a thousand volts in my body. I'm Fae. I don't even like the human concept of electricity. That was all you. Throwing me out."

Tiger stared. He'd not consciously reacted to Fionn's touch.

"It wasn't Fae magic that surged up," Fionn said. "In fact, there's not a glimmer of Fae magic in his entire body. I got that much."

"There's Fae magic in all Shifters," Dylan said. "Passed down through the generations. It's what formed us in the first place."

"Not this one." Fionn shook out his hand and slid his glove back on in quick jerks. "I don't know what he is. Now, take me to Kenny."

He put his hand on Andrea's shoulder and walked off with her, finished with Tiger. Which left Tiger in the middle of the three Morrisseys.

"I can't take the Collar," Tiger said before any of them could speak. It would incapacitate him, maybe kill him, and he couldn't let it. Not yet.

The sensations in his body and mind confused him and made him angry. Without a word, he turned from them and started down the green.

He headed for Spike's house. Spike had gone with Carly, which left Jordan alone with his mother and grandmother again. Dylan should have stayed with them. Tiger would make sure they were all right, as well as see if looking after Jordan would soothe his jangled nerves. He had to think, and he had to make some decisions.

The simple cell phone Liam urged him to carry at all times buzzed on his belt. Tiger snatched it up, hoping it was Carly, not Liam demanding he return home.

The number was not one he recognized. He clicked on the phone as Connor had taught him and growled, "Yes?"

"It's Walker. Get somewhere you can talk to me alone. I've got a lot to tell you."

CHAPTER NINETEEN

Carly answered the phone at the small desk tucked away in a corner of Armand's gallery, all but hidden so customers wouldn't see that they worried about anything as gauche as business.

Connor was napping in the back office after having complained some more about last night's lack of sleep. Spike and his tatts had earned the interest of an artist who'd come to see Armand, and the artist was looking Spike over, having him stand in sunlight and so forth.

"Gallery d'Armand," Carly said in her best quiet but friendly tones. "How may I help you this afternoon?"

"I need you to get away from Connor and Spike," Tiger's voice was almost a whisper. "And meet me." He gave directions to a spot in the warehouse area south of Ben White, near the freeway.

Get away from Connor and Spike? Carly didn't dare glance behind her at Spike, who might read in her body language that she was suddenly nervous. "I'm not sure I can," she said.

"Talk to me like I am a shopper. Don't change your voice."

A shopper. He meant a gallery patron. Carly drew a breath. "Well, I'm certain we could accommodate you, sir," she said briskly, "though it might be a little bit of a challenge."

"Don't take Dylan's truck. The Bureau men know what it looks like." A hesitation. "So do the Shifters."

He wanted to evade Shifters too? Shifters like Liam? What the hell had happened?

Carly couldn't ask with Spike behind her, even though he was all the way across the gallery. She'd learned by now that Shifters had great hearing.

Tiger's voice was quiet, but she read the agitation in him. He was asking her to make a choice.

Liam had been adamant that Tiger not leave Shiftertown, and Carly had seen the rage between Liam, Tiger, and Dylan. Tiger wasn't the most normal of guys, even for a Shifter—she'd seen that in the way others treated him and in the way the others lived their lives. Liam, Sean, Spike, Ronan—they had children, families, friends, a defined place in the Shifter world. In the same way, Carly had a loving mother and three great sisters, friends, and a job with Armand and Yvette, a childless couple who treated her like a daughter.

Tiger had no one. In the warmth of the Shifter community, the Shifters either feared him or watched him, ready to stop him when he went over the top. Tiger was alone in a crowd.

What Carly had observed in the three days she'd known him was that every time Tiger went berserk, it was to defend himself or someone else. Couldn't they see how gentle he was with the kids, how much the kids liked him? No child trusted a person they'd seen hurt others.

Carly's father had been a bad person. Difficult for a twelve-year-old girl to understand when her father leaves without a word. An adolescent takes it personally, and

Carly did. She'd spent a long time wondering what had been wrong with her before realizing that she hadn't done anything wrong at all.

Thinking back over what life had been like with her father—his alcoholic tempers and compulsive gambling, his daylong harangues at her mother—Carly had come to the adult conclusion that he'd had a lot of problems he hadn't bothered to acknowledge, problems that had made Carly's home life hell for twelve years.

Tiger was absolutely nothing like him.

All this went through Carly's head in the few seconds Tiger waited for her answer.

Carly could turn around and call out for Spike, telling him that Tiger was running from Shiftertown for whatever reason. Or she could believe that Tiger had a very good reason for wanting her to meet him and to keep Spike and Connor from finding out and following.

She chose.

"I'll take care of it," Carly said, speaking in her helpful-assistant tones. "Don't you worry." She heard Tiger's breath of relief, and she decided to risk a question. "And how did you find the number for our gallery? Were you referred?"

Tiger sounded puzzled as he answered. "Phone book." And he hung up.

Carly bit her lip as she reached into the desk drawer where she kept her purse and pretended to look for something. Connor was in the office, where a back door led to the small parking area on the alley. She knew she'd never get past him without waking him up. If she went out the front, past Spike, even with the excuse of going out for gelato or whatever, Spike would follow her.

She felt Spike's gaze on her. Carly pulled a lipstick from her purse, frowned at it, and said, "Yvette, I'm just going to the ladies'."

Yvette, who'd been in low-voiced conversation on the other side of the gallery with Armand, nodded. Carly's palms sweated as she dipped her hand into Yvette's purse resting next to hers and took out Yvette's car keys. Carly slid them noiselessly into her own purse, then took up the purse and put it over her shoulder.

She walked as casually as she could through the alcove that held two very nice but small restrooms and one broom closet. Neither bathroom had windows, so the movie staple of the woman or man climbing out the bathroom window to escape everything from a bad date to death by assassins was out. Beyond the broom closet, however, was the emergency exit.

Armand, fortunately, didn't have a fire alarm rigged up to the door. But if Carly opened it, the glare of the sun outside might shine back down the hall.

She had to risk it. Carly waited until several loud vehicles passed in front of the shop. Spike turned to glance at them. At the same time, Carly opened the back door a little, slid through, and closed the door as quietly as she could.

Yvette's car was five feet away. Now to hope that Connor hadn't woken up and was looking out the office window.

Carly got into the car, closing the door so it only clicked. She set her purse on the passenger seat, put on her seat belt, and started the engine.

No one came flying out through the office door or the emergency exit. Carly backed the car out of its parking spot as slowly as she dared, then drove down the alley.

She passed the backs of four more shops before she turned onto a small driveway that led out to the main street. From here she turned right, even though she needed to go left to get back to Austin. She didn't want to risk driving past the gallery and its wide plate-glass windows.

Carly had to drive around a few blocks, once down a street that was still dirt, before she emerged onto the main road again. Then she drove as fast as she dared. At any moment, Spike would figure out that she was taking way too long in the ladies' room, or Yvette would go in and find her not there. Spike and Connor would leap into Dylan's truck, and they'd be on her ass in minutes.

There was only one paved road, a two-lane highway,

that led back into Austin, so she couldn't take a circuitous route to lose any pursuit. If Carly drove too fast, she might get pulled over, giving Spike a chance to catch up. Too slowly, and he'd catch up anyway.

Despite her fears, the road behind her remained clear. Carly breathed easier when she reached the tangle of Austin traffic and turned from the narrow highway to the 290, approaching the heart of Austin from the north and east. She went south on I-35 and got off on a frontage road near Ben White, driving onto back roads that led around the warehouses.

These were active warehouses with trucks and men working, some of whom stared at Carly as she went by in Yvette's Fusion. Good thing Yvette had come to the gallery independent of Armand, and Carly hadn't had to use the BMW. *That* would have been remembered.

She saw Tiger waiting in the shadow of a warehouse, right where he said he'd be. He'd covered his striped hair with a baseball cap, and she couldn't see his Collar under the high-necked T-shirt he wore under a flannel shirt. Lounging against the side of the building, he looked like just another Texas boy waiting to go back to work.

Carly pulled over. She popped the locks on the doors, and Tiger slid inside, lifting Carly's large purse and settling it on his lap.

"We need to go somewhere and talk. Somewhere safe, where they won't find us."

"All rightee." Carly's fingers shook. "You're scaring me, Tiger. What happened? How did you get here?"

"I talked to Walker. He drove me a ways, and I walked the rest. Do you know where to go? Not your house."

Carly thought rapidly. "Yes. Yes, I do. It's a bit of a drive."

"Good. But not in this car. Park it, and we'll take another."

Carly stared at him. "You want me to *steal* a car? It's one thing to borrow Yvette's—I can convince her I needed it—but you're talking about grand theft."

"You'll be found in this one. Park it."

She stared at him a moment longer, then she shook her head. "I can't believe I'm doing this."

Carly put the car in gear and drove it around the corner from the warehouses to the line of chain hotels that faced the freeway. She parked Yvette's car in a back lot among similar-looking vehicles, locked the car, and dropped the keys into her purse.

She and Tiger walked through the lot, Carly trying to match Tiger's ability to look purposeful and nonchalant at the same time. He didn't bother telling Carly why he'd called her out there, what had happened, what was wrong. Any question was met by silence.

Tiger stopped by a car that looked a bit older and well used, and stood with his back to it while he tried the door handle. That car was locked, but a few rows and a couple more tries later, he found another well-used one that was unlocked.

"What do we do now?" Carly asked. "Hot-wire it?"

The parking lot was deserted except for the vehicles. The sun beat down, reflecting on the metal, fiberglass, and asphalt. Beyond the squat hotels, the freeway ran heavy, the day drawing to its close.

"Connor taught me," Tiger said.

He opened the driver's-side door, but Carly forestalled him. "I'll do it. I can't think what they'd do to a Shifter if you were caught driving a hot-wired car."

His gaze flicked to her. "You know how?"

"I was a rebellious teen, and I hung out with other rebellious teens. We weren't all that bad, but we were mischievous." Carly slid into the driver's seat while Tiger went around the other side.

"Lucky us," Carly said. "He left the keys in it." She laughed a little as she moved the worn gearshift and brushed at least a year's worth of crumbs off the dashboard. "Maybe he doesn't care about it being stolen."

"He?" Tiger asked, his brows drawn. "How do you know a male owns this?"

"Because only a guy would let his car get this dirty. The windows are tinted, that's good. If I could only roll . . . mine . . . all the way . . . up." The window stuck three quarters of the way, and Carly stopped trying. But the stuck window proved to be convenient, because the air-conditioning didn't work.

Carly drove carefully out of the lot, and as she had when she left the gallery, she avoided driving past the fronts of the hotels. She went back into the warehouse area, then onto Ben White again, heading west.

The car held the stench of old cigarettes, old coffee, mud, and other things Carly didn't want to identify. When she could move down the road at a decent speed, air blew through the half-open windows, even if the air was oven hot. When she had to stop for a light or for backed-up traffic, however, the stuffiness made her gag. Perspiration trickled down her face and between her shoulder blades.

Tiger wouldn't talk. He pulled his hat down over his eyes and slouched against the door as though he wasn't worried as Carly made her way through the streets.

At one point, Carly's cell phone rang. She wasn't moving at the time, stuck in a merge of cars coming off Mopac. She grabbed the phone from her purse, but the number had no name attached to it, and she didn't recognize the number.

"Connor," Tiger said looking at it.

"This phone has a GPS tracker," Carly said. "If they can use that to locate us, we're screwed." On the other hand, she had no intention of throwing an expensive smartphone out the window. Whoever picked it up would have access to all her contacts and maybe her bank account, she didn't know. Or maybe they'd so helpfully call all her friends and family until she was found.

Tiger yanked the phone from her and ended her inner debate by closing his massive hand around it. The ringtone squeaked and went silent, and bits of black plastic rained down to join the junk on the floorboards. Tiger sifted through the wreckage until he found the chips, and he broke those too.

"Well, I guess that's one solution," Carly said. The traffic started, and she drove on, her mouth dry.

"You have any more cell phones?" Tiger asked. "Or gadgets? Connor says other things have locators in them."

"Not with me. They're at the house."

"Good." Tiger went back into his relaxed state against the door, and Carly hoped the door was solid enough to take his bulk.

She drove on, winding through streets, heading for the Bee Cave area. No one seemed to be following her, though the few people they passed in more affluent neighborhoods turned heads as the old car sputtered by.

Carly turned off a little north of Bee Cave into a neighborhood that was fairly new, with large houses and winding streets. She made it to the house she needed as shadows were lengthening, afternoon finally turning to evening.

"Hang on," she said, opening the car door in the driveway. "I'll run in and open up the garage. We can't leave this pile of junk on the street. It will definitely be noticed."

Tiger was alert now, his eyes changing to the golden sparkle they took on when he was thinking about changing into the tiger. "Who lives here?"

"My sisters. Don't worry, they're in Mexico. I have the keys. I'll hurry."

Before Tiger could argue, she shut the door and tripped up the small flight of steps through the landscaping to the front door. A key on her ring fit the locks, and Carly pushed her way inside.

A beeping sound startled her, and for one panicked moment, Carly forgot the alarm code. Her fingers knew it, though, and soon the alarm was off.

Carly went out through a back passage to the garage and punched the control to open the garage door. Then she drove the car into the garage, Tiger still in it, turned off the ignition, and closed the garage door.

She coughed and waved her hand in front of her face. "This thing really stinks."

Tiger didn't answer. He followed Carly as she got out of

the car, entered the house again, and led him through the back passage to the main part of the house.

"Your sisters live here?" Tiger stopped to look around the giant kitchen and the high-ceilinged living room beyond. "How many?"

"My two oldest sisters. They and my mom and my other sister all went to Mexico to shop. I didn't go because Armand needed me for the exhibit opening." Carly huffed. "See how well that worked out."

"So much room for two people," Tiger said, turning to take in the echoing space.

"True, but they earned it. My sisters run a decorating business together. Althea and Zoë, that is. The one just above me in age, Janine, is married and a teacher. I'm the youngest."

Tiger pulled off his baseball hat and dropped it onto a chair, combing his fingers through his hair, ruffling it and making it look sexy. The black and orange strands no longer seemed odd to her.

"Why don't you live here with them?" he asked. "It would be safer for you."

Carly opened the refrigerator. Sneaking out of the gallery, stealing a car, and fleeing across Austin—very slowly—had given her an appetite.

"Like I said, I'm the youngest. I wanted to go out on my own, see if I could do it without everyone looking over my shoulder and telling me what to do. We're close, my sisters and me, but they do tend to be a bit overprotective, and at times, downright bossy. Ooh, pasta salad." She drew out a plastic container, popped the lid off, sniffed it. "Seems okay. Someone needs to eat this before it goes bad." Carly plopped it onto the counter, then dove back into the refrigerator. "There's plenty of lunch meat in here. Want me to make you a sandwich? And while I'm at it, you can explain to me why you told me to steal Yvette's car and duck out of the gallery without alerting Spike or Connor."

Tiger sat on a stool on the other side of the breakfast bar, which was open to the rest of the room, and leaned his arms on the counter.

"I will tell you everything, Carly. From the beginning. Stop, and listen."

His face was grave, mouth turned down. Carly ceased her flustered puttering, dropped the fork she'd taken up into the pasta salad, and waited for him to start.

Tiger's position, leaning forward toward her, made his T-shirt open at the neck, but the shadows were such that Carly still couldn't see his Collar.

Then she frowned. She reached out, hooked one finger around the ribbed neckline, and pulled it down. Her heart beat faster.

Tiger wasn't wearing a Collar at all. His skin bore a thin red crease across his throat, but the Collar had gone.

CHAPTER TWENTY

Tiger saw the fear flare in Carly's eyes as she realized she was alone with an un-Collared Shifter, nothing to control him, nothing to restrain him.

Her lips parted as she reached to him and brushed one fingertip across the abraded skin. Her touch, that one caring stroke, untightened something inside him.

"You took it off?" she asked in wonder. "Looks like that was painful."

"Yes." He didn't lie. Removing the false Collar had hurt, because Liam had made it to embed into Tiger's skin, so it would better resemble the real ones. "But not as much as it could have, because I never had a Collar on at all."

Carly stared at him for a heartbeat then her brows drew together. "What are you talking about? It was right there." She brushed her fingertip across the line again.

"It was a fake." *Full disclosure,* that was the term he'd heard. If Carly was to trust him and help him, Tiger had to give her all the information he could. Nothing held back. "I will tell you all of the truth. When I'm done, if you want me to leave, I will. You'll never see me again, and I'll make sure you aren't bothered because of anything I asked you to do today."

Carly's eyes widened. "I think it's a little late for that. I just parked a stolen car in my sisters' garage."

"They made me in a research lab in a place the humans call Area 51," Tiger said, ignoring her and plunging straight in. "They were trying to create Shifters artificially. Shifters are born Shifter—they aren't humans who turn into Shifters because they're bitten or whatever, like in the movies Connor laughs at. I don't know how they made me—they might have used Shifter DNA, or only animal and human. They never told me. I was the twenty-third Shifter they made. The others all died when I was still a cub."

He told her about the long days he'd been left alone in his cage, then taken out only to be shot full of chemicals or given electric shocks or other things, then observed to see how he reacted. His reaction had usually been screaming agony. Tiger told her about the days they'd chain him to a treadmill and make him run for forty-eight hours without a break. They'd alternately starve him and force-feed him to see what he could take, then they'd enact an interrogation scenario, torturing him when he couldn't answer their questions.

Carly watched him with her beautiful green eyes as Tiger revealed the horrors in his flat voice. They'd let him see his cub once, he related, before they took it away. When Tiger had asked to see his boy again, begged them, they'd told Tiger the cub had died. The grief of that had been worse than any torture they could ever manufacture.

Tiger had talked until his voice grew hoarse, he who rarely said many sentences together. "Walker said that when Eric destroyed the building in Area 51, it was investigated, and the investigators found files and notes that didn't get burned. At first they thought I'd died either in the experiments or in the explosion, but Walker kept an eye out. When he found out there was a Shifter in Austin who came from nowhere, he started watching me. Today he told me that the Shifter Bureau wants to start the research again, officially.

The Area 51 people were trying to create Shifter soldiers, off-book. Shifter Bureau now wants to see if the project is still viable, if they can make Shifters who will be controlled soldiers, using me as the prototype."

Carly had gone very still, her gaze fixed on him in shock as he'd told the tale. Now rage flared in her eyes. "Dear God. I'm guessing they aren't asking you to volunteer."

Tiger shrugged. "Officially, I don't exist. I'm not a reg- istered, Collared Shifter. Feral Shifters, un-Collared, can legally be hunted and killed."

She planted her fists on the counter. "This is all bullshit."

"As a research subject, I'm perfect, because it doesn't matter if I die."

"It damn well does matter," Carly snapped. "And *Walker* told you all this? Why, because you were nice and let him go?"

"He doesn't like what the idea has been turned into. The Shifter Bureau sent a soldier out to wreck the car and shoot me as part of the experiment. The mission risked civilians, and Walker doesn't like that."

"How sweet of him. Well, consider me risked. Along with Ellison. And they had you shot in cold blood. Why didn't they scoop you up and take you with them right then, if they wanted to watch what would happen to you?"

"They thought they could scoop me up anytime they wanted, and they didn't want to pay for the medical care."

"Let the Shifters foot the bill and spend the time taking care of you while the Shifter Bureau sits back and watches?"

"But now they're ready to take me in. I'm pretty sure Liam will let them—and he won't be given a choice."

"Why would Liam let them take you?" Carly asked. "He seems pretty protective of the Shifters, at least from what I've seen."

"The other Shifter leaders want him to put a real Collar on me. Or kill me. Liam's choice. Except he told *me* to make the choice. He might see handing me to the Shifter Bureau and their special team as a way out of the problem."

Carly blinked. "Liam told you to choose between putting on a Collar or letting him kill you? What the *hell*?"

"Liam's job as Shiftertown leader is to protect all Shifters. I'm a threat, a danger to the Shifters in his Shiftertown. He has to contain the danger any way he can."

"Tiger." Carly pointed a polished fingernail at his face. "Don't you even sit there and tell me that he's right. If Liam's supposed to protect all Shifters, that means *all* Shifters. Individually. You as well as all the others. None of this *needs of the many* crap."

She was so beautiful, her eyes flashing, her face pink with anger and indignation. Carly was angry *for* him, at Liam and the Bureau, not at Tiger.

When Walker had called him and told him the Shifter Bureau wanted to start experimenting on him again, Tiger's instincts had told him to run and never stop running. He could have simply disappeared, using his incredible ability to survive to see him through.

But Tiger had a mate now. He couldn't go and never see Carly again. He knew he risked exposure and capture by calling her and coming here with her, but Tiger needed her. He needed to breathe in Carly's scent, and touch her skin, if only one last time.

Carly came around the counter and leaned on it beside him. The stance pushed her breasts toward him through her thin dress and washed him in her scent.

"So, what are we going to do?" she asked. "You can't go back to Shiftertown, obviously—that's why you had me give Spike and Connor the slip. I'm betting the guy who shot you before will be after you too."

"The Bureau doesn't realize I'm gone yet. Walker met me on the edge of Shiftertown and gave me a ride halfway to where I met you and told me to disappear. I didn't tell him I was going to call you."

"I'm glad you did." Carly leaned to him and slid her arms around Tiger's shoulders, her warmth soothing the shaking deep inside him. "We should be safe here for a while, but eventually they'll start checking with my friends and relatives. I'll have to pull some cash if we're going on the road, because credit cards are too easily tracked. And we have to get a different car. *That* one won't hold up fifty miles. I bet the guy left his keys in it hoping it would be stolen."

She wanted to come with him. Tiger sat in stunned silence as he realized that Carly was calmly planning how they could get away from Austin and anyone after him.

But the cruel fact was that Tiger could move faster and farther without her, could cover his tracks in ways she couldn't imagine. He'd survive, but he'd have to do it alone.

Alone. Without his mate. Or his cub.

Tiger touched Carly's lips. "You are my mate. You always will be and no other. But you will stay here and be safe, and I will go. Once I am gone, and they know you don't know where I am, they will leave you alone."

"No." Carly jerked away from him, rising and taking away her warmth. "You're not running out on me."

"Keeping you safe," Tiger said catching her wrist in his big hand. "I can run for days without stopping, I can live for days without food and sleep. You can't."

"But you can't run forever," Carly said. "The best thing to do is to hide in plain sight. As long as I can get my money in cash before we go, we can go anywhere. Mexico—I've always wanted a trip to Mazatlán, or Cabo. Once your neck heals, and if you hide your hair or dye it, we'll fit right in. A young couple in a rental on a Baja beach. Sounds good to me."

"It's that easy to leave the country?" Tiger asked. He was skeptical. There were papers and cards for humans, and Shifters were forbidden international travel.

"They don't pay much attention to a young woman hell-bent on shopping at every bazaar in a border town, or buying bikinis in Baja. You, Mr. Stealthy, can go cross-country when we get close enough to the border, and I'll pick you up on the other side. Once we're settled in Cabo, I'm sure I can find some enterprising person to make me a new ID."

"You'd never be able to come back," Tiger said. "Or see your family again. Taking a Shifter out of the country is illegal. You'd be arrested, maybe imprisoned."

Tiger saw Carly's indecision when he mentioned her family. The hope that had flickered within him for a few moments withered and died.

"I wouldn't be *taking* you out," Carly said. "*Meeting* you in a different country is a different thing."

Tiger shook his head. "Too risky for you." And for their cub.

Carly straightened and planted her hands on her hips. "Now, you listen to me, Tiger. I'm not letting you go."

"I treasure you." Tiger looked up into Carly's eyes. "If the world changes, if Shifters are freed, then I'll be back. I will always come back to you, my mate. No matter how long it takes."

Damn him. Tiger sat there looking at her with those beautiful eyes, telling her he was leaving.

He couldn't leave. She'd just found him.

Carly flashed back to the day she'd realized her father was never coming back. The pain, like a kick in the stomach, had flattened her for weeks. She'd gone to school in a daze, barely able to talk to anyone, unable to study or focus on homework. She'd started flunking her classes, which had made things worse; then had come the counseling.

Carly had struggled for years before she figured out how to go on living, how to push the anger and grief to the back of her mind so she could pay attention to what was in front of her.

"My dad left us when we were kids," she said in a hard voice. "He left my mama and four teenage girls with no money and a mountain of debts. He just walked out."

Tiger said nothing. His golden eyes fixed on her, and his hand around her wrist was warm. But he was still leaving.

"I agreed to marry Ethan because I thought he was safe," Carly went on. "He wasn't anything like my dad.

Ethan wasn't a wild drinker or a gambler, he brought home a paycheck, he owned a house, he didn't have debts, and I knew he'd never walk out and leave me to solve his problems. Ethan prides himself on being Mr. Responsible. I was right about all that, but I was wrong about Ethan respecting me or truly caring about me."

Carly leaned down to Tiger, her breath coming fast. "Then I met *you*. And I realized that all my life I'd been looking for safety. A good job, a nice place to live, friends I can trust, the right husband—anything to keep me from that feeling of falling with nothing to catch me."

"But I'm not safe," Tiger said. "Nothing about me is safe."

"I know." Carly started to laugh, but in a crazy way, not finding anything funny. "And *wham*, I realized that safety shouldn't be the most important thing in my life." She poked his chest. "*You* make me want to be wild and take chances and grab happiness while I have it. With Ethan I was content, and I admit, a little bit smug. But with you, I'm hot and happy, excited whenever I see you or hear your voice. You walk into a room, and I'm glad. When I woke up with you this morning, I knew it was the best morning of my life. I want more mornings like that, and I want each one to be even better than the last. I lost my dad, I lost the safety of marriage to Ethan, and for about the third time this week, I've probably lost my job. On top of it all, I sure as hell don't want to lose *you*."

Tiger watched her with the close stare of a predator. His tiger-striped hair was a mess, his face stubbled with whiskers and still marked with a few bruises from the accident. His black T-shirt under the flannel shirt was marked with sweat, his arms, exposed by pushed-up sleeves, corded with muscle dusted with golden hair.

He was absolutely nothing like the clean-cut, perfectly groomed man Carly was supposed to date, and then marry.

"You'll never be safe if you stay with me," Tiger said.

"And I say screw it." Carly shook off his grasp but only to plop herself onto the slant of his lap. "I'm not going through my boring, safe life wondering whatever happened to you—wondering what would have happened to *me* if I'd grabbed you and held on to you with both hands. Don't you get it, Tiger? I want *you*."

Tiger kept looking at her. Whatever he was thinking or feeling, Carly had no idea, but she saw the emptiness behind his eyes. Her heart ached from his story of torture and terror, for his life of knowing nothing but anger and fear.

She leaned down to kiss him. Carly intended the kiss to be gentle, to show him how much she cared, but as soon as their lips touched, Tiger slid his strong hand behind her neck, and the kiss turned fierce.

Carly surrendered to his strength, letting his arms take her weight, as he slanted his mouth over hers, exploring, tasting. She ran her fingertips over the line where the false Collar had been, the ridge of skin already smoothing.

Tiger's hand went to the back of her dress, tugging at the zipper. The little cap sleeves that just covered Carly's shoulders came down quickly, Tiger's hands warming her skin, the dress loosening.

Carly tilted her head back while Tiger kissed her neck then traveled down her throat with little nips. He pressed his mouth below the hollow of her throat as the dress eased down to reveal her breasts.

Carly had put on a lace and satin bra this morning, ivory to match the sheath dress Yvette had given her. She'd wanted to be pretty today, all the way to her skin. Tiger made her feel beautiful. Carly, who considered herself all lips and eyes, with a little too much curve on the bottom and not enough on top.

Tiger fumbled at the catch of her bra, but Carly was happy to reach back and release it for him. Last night, they'd been so crazed to make love to each other that they hadn't gone slowly, hadn't savored.

Tiger savored her now. He pushed Carly's body upward so he could lick between her breasts, then tilted his head back to kiss her mouth as she gazed down at him.

"You are beautiful," he said. "My mate."

When he said *mate,* a warmth grew in her heart until it almost hurt. At the same time the warmth brought a flush of happiness, the like of which Carly had never felt before.

Tiger smiled, which made his eyes heat. "Do you see it? The mate bond?"

He moved his fingers to her breastbone, directly over the warmth. When Carly looked at him in confusion, not knowing what he was talking about, his smile grew.

"Doesn't matter," he said. "*I* can see it. Like silver threads that bind us, my heart to yours." He traced the air between them. "It's like the threads on Sean's sword, and in Andrea when she heals. But better. The Fae is wrong. This is magic."

Carly still didn't know what in the hell he was talking about, but if Tiger meant he felt about her the way Carly felt about him, fine.

She pressed her hand to his chest, liking how his heart beat strong and hard beneath her fingertips. "How do Shifters pledge themselves to each other?" she asked. "Humans say *'til death do us part.*"

Tiger growled. "I don't want to talk about death. Shifters say *under sun and moon, I claim you as mate.* But we don't need to say anything."

"I want to. I like pledges. What is the Shifter woman supposed to say in return?"

"That she accepts the claim, under the Father God and Mother Goddess. But Shifters want the mate-claim to be witnessed."

"I'll witness it." Carly smiled as she touched his face. "Tiger, I accept you as mate."

Carly thought Tiger would growl again that they didn't need to say anything—men were always embarrassed by rituals—but his smile spread.

"Yes," he said, his look one of complete triumph. "*Yes.* My mate. My *mate.*"

Tiger dragged Carly up off the stool with him, kisses falling like fire on her neck, breasts, over her heart. He licked his way to her nipple, tasting it, pulling the tip into a point.

Carly ran her hand through his hair, loving the rough silk feel of it. The black locks were smoother than the orange, she observed distractedly. The rest of her focused on the fire of his mouth, the sharp tug of his teeth. Sweet goodness.

Tiger's breath was hot on her skin, his own body temperature hotter than a human's. He was a strange and exotic man, touching her so skillfully as he nuzzled and licked until she was crazy from it.

"Upstairs," she murmured. "We should go upstairs."

"Not yet."

Tiger lifted her as he stood up, sitting her on the counter. He placed his hands on either side of her, closing her in, his mouth everywhere on her exposed skin.

Two days ago, Carly hadn't wanted to go near kitchen counters or even think about what could be done on them. Today, she wrapped her legs around Tiger, pulling him to her.

She pushed his flannel shirt from his shoulders—how he could stand wearing flannel in this heat, she didn't know, but he was Tiger. The T-shirt next. Carly enjoyed herself pushing it upward over his tight torso, until he tore it off over his head in impatience.

He had a fine body. Firm, muscled, tanned, like liquid bronze over a sculpture of perfect proportions. Carly ran her hands over him, seeing that the bullet scars had lessened further in the course of the day. Soon his skin would be whole and tight again.

Unless the Shifter Bureau took him away, or the Shifters decided to kill him or make him wear that stupid Collar.

Idiots. If the Collar Tiger had been wearing was fake, and still he'd stopped himself from killing Walker and the assassin, not to mention Ethan, then obviously Tiger didn't need the damn thing.

It wasn't the Collar keeping Tiger careful when he held the cubs or careful with Carly. It was *Tiger*.

She ran her fingers around the healing line where the fake Collar had been. Tiger looked into Carly's eyes, the wanting in him stark.

Carly popped the button of his jeans. Tiger growled low in his throat, bunched her dress in his hands, and skimmed it off over her head. Carly sped his zipper down, finding behind it silky red boxers with black hearts on them.

Carly pushed his jeans down his hips, laughing. "Where did you get *those*?"

"Glory. From Elizabeth's store." Tiger kissed her again, letting her laugh against his mouth. "Connor said it was a joke, but I didn't have anything else to wear."

CHAPTER TWENTY-ONE

Tiger loved her laughter. This woman could find the joy in anything. She shook delightfully as Tiger kissed her. "I'll try to find you some with tiger stripes," she said. "Or maybe paw prints."

As she went on laughing, the warmth of the mate bond again filled Tiger's heart.

At the same time, another pang of loss reached out and gripped him. Connor and Kim had laughed so hard when Glory brought Tiger the gift of the underwear, and even Dylan had looked amused. They'd included Tiger in their family, he realized, in their jokes, even if he didn't understand them. For a fleeting moment, he'd belonged. Now he had to leave that behind, as well as Carly.

The mate of his heart. Tiger needed her more with every breath.

Maybe her crazy plan to run away with him would work. Maybe they could hole up together in a Mexican beach town and live out their lives.

But Tiger had seen the flash of sorrow in Carly's eyes when he'd said Carly would have to leave her family behind. She loved them. She had ties here, in this house where she was so comfortable.

Tiger would have to say good-bye to her. But not now. Now he would feast on her, imbibing all she had to give so he could savor the memory when he was away. He'd leave her behind so she could be safe, but he'd leave something else as well. His cub, a part of himself, for her.

Tiger snaked his hand beneath the elastic of her panties and jerked them from her bottom, pushing them down her legs to fall on the floor. While Carly ran her hands down his bare back, nibbling his bottom lip, he pushed down his jeans and then the boxers, letting them pool around his ankles.

He still wore his motorcycle boots, but so what? He didn't have time to sit down and pull everything off. Better traction on the floor anyway.

Tiger lifted Carly's hips and settled her on the edge of the counter, winding her legs around him. Her eyes widened and she started to protest, her hands on his chest, but Tiger also knew he would never make it upstairs with her. Maybe to the kitchen table, maybe all the way to the stairs if they ran, but he needed Carly *now*.

He opened her with his hand, finding her hot and wet with wanting, then he slid inside her, inch by slow inch. It killed him to go slowly, but Carly was still getting used to him, and the last thing in the world Tiger wanted to do was hurt her.

Carly made a soft sound of pleasure, her eyes half closing. She was tight, gripping, and Tiger's thoughts became incoherent. All he knew was Carly, her heat, her body pliant in his arms, the threads of the mate bond that stretched from his heart to hers.

Those threads could never be severed. No matter how far Tiger went from her, the bonds would be there, invisible, magic, unbreakable.

Carly cried out, and Tiger slid the rest of the way into her. She rocked back, and Tiger lifted her hips, steadying her on his hardness. She was slick, taking him yet squeezing him, and Tiger lost himself in nothing but sensation.

His hips moved, starting the back-and-forth rhythm that felt so incredible. Carly held on to his wrists, her green gaze locked to him, her body rocking with his. She cried his name, the sound of it echoing in the large room, wrapping around him like the magic of the mate bond.

Here was where he needed to be, inside this woman, where all was beauty and wildness. And home.

Tiger thrust into her, filling her all the way, Carly's eyes widening. She pulled him to her with her feet in their high-heeled shoes on his buttocks, this sex raw and fierce. Tiger loved it— he loved *her*.

Need you. Love you. Tiger began the rhythm again, faster, faster, the slapping sound as they came together exciting. Carly dug her fingers into his wrists, her spike heels pressing his backside.

Tiger shouted her name, white-hot fire pouring through him. The rightness of being with his mate, and feeling like this, made him know that this was the most precious moment he might ever have for the rest of his life.

Under him Carly pulsed and rocked, her pleasure consuming her. She laughed wildly as she found her release, coming up to wrap her arms around him and hold on to him.

Together, entwined, *mated*. Tiger gathered him to her, both of them breathless, and kissed her in the sweetness of afterglow.

Walker stood in front of the desk of his commanding officer, Lieutenant Colonel Mark Sheldon, and was glad Sheldon wasn't a Shifter. Walker was good at keeping his body language neutral, but Shifters could read even the minutest twitch of a finger.

"And now I hear the Shifter is missing," Sheldon was saying. "What the hell happened?"

Sheldon's voice was quiet and cold. The command of

the Special Forces attachment to the Shifter Bureau was pretty much a shit assignment. Sheldon, though, was ruthless enough to turn it into something he could use for promotion, for a bigger command. Sheldon had ambition.

Walker's assignment as XO in the unit probably meant he'd been sidelined, but he didn't care. He'd seen too much in his life, done too much, and had too much anger in him. Sitting on the sidelines for a while was what he needed. And now he had to sit back and watch his commanding officer show his true dickhead colors.

"I want that Shifter found, locked into the facility, and tested every which way," Sheldon said. "If he resists, and you have to drag in his corpse, do it. The researchers will harvest what they need from him. But I want the Shifter."

Walker listened without changing expression. When Sheldon moved back to his desk, done with his diatribe, Walker cleared his throat.

"Respectfully, sir."

Sheldon looked up abruptly, his eyes so cold they burned. "Captain? I'd be interested to hear your opinion."

The words were a hard sneer. Walker held on to his purpose, though the LTC's eyes could make even senior officers decide they needed to walk another direction instead of have to pass him.

"With respect, sir, the mission is to find out all we can about why this Shifter was singled out, what research was carried out on him, and if that research or the Shifter himself can be used to help our troops in the field. Not to kill him."

"Is it?" Sheldon asked. He gave Walker a full minute of his obey-me-or-die stare. "Let me explain something, Danielson. That Shifter could hold secrets that could save our troops, our army, and our missions overseas. You know that—you've read the research. *Our* mission, yours and mine, is to get that Shifter back and extract everything we can from him. *Your* mission is to bring him to me. By any means possible. Dead or alive."

Walker hid a twitch of nervousness. The trouble with Sheldon is that he was usually right, but the way he was right spoke of a mercilessness that made Walker's blood cold. "Sir."

"Get out, Danielson."

"Sir." Walker gave Sheldon a perfect salute and went.

That Shifter could hold secrets that could save our troops, our army, and our missions overseas. Sheldon's words, but his eyes had told a different story. Sheldon was playing his own game.

What Walker needed to do now was figure out how to keep the tiger Shifter safe and discover what the true purpose of his creation was. All this without screwing up Walker's own life.

He walked to the mess hall in the tiny camp on the south side of Austin where the small unit trained constantly, though it rarely was called out to do anything with Shifters. The Shifters in Austin, where the Shifter Bureau South was located, never gave anyone any trouble. The only incidents had been a Shifter accused of murdering a human woman a few years ago—proved innocent—and now Tiger's violence in the hospital.

Which had stopped the moment Carly Randal had walked into the room and said his name. There was something in that, and not just because Carly was cute.

Of course, Rebecca stripping down to change into a bear had pretty much floored Walker. Women could make a man feel like he'd been punched in the gut.

Because the camp was small, there was no separate dining facility for the few officers; everyone ate together in one mess hall. Sheldon either went out to lunch or ate in the small private room off the main cafeteria. Walker usually ate in the main mess when he had a meal in camp, mostly because he couldn't imagine conducting casual lunchtime conversation with LTC Sheldon. Plus he knew his men didn't mind seeing an officer eating lunch like a human being once in a while.

Walker scanned the score of men who were either already eating or standing in line with their trays, until he found the sergeant he was looking for.

Crosby was a sergeant who was very good at obeying orders to the letter, which was how he'd made it all the way to E-5. God help the army if he ever made it to staff sergeant or higher. Crosby had a square head, made more square by his buzzed hair, and a rectangular shaped body replete with muscle. He was the best at all the fitness tests and the first one out for PT every morning.

Crosby rose to his feet as Walker deposited his full tray opposite him. The sergeant was alone, isolated from the rest of the fatigue-clad lunchers, because no one liked him.

"As you were, Sergeant," Walker said, sitting down. "If you stand up while I eat, your food will get cold."

Crosby plunked back down again, but he didn't eat. "Sir."

"Nice shot taking down the Shifter," Walker said as he stirred his unidentifiable soup. "Why'd you keep shooting him once he was on the ground?"

Crosby looked puzzled. "Told to, sir. Put as many rounds into him as it took but make sure he was alive when I walked away."

Aha. Walker hadn't been certain which of the soldiers had been sent out to run Tiger off the road and shoot him, but he'd strongly suspected it had been Crosby. Crosby had just confirmed it.

"How did you know where the Shifter would be going that day?"

"Didn't. Was told to follow and take the best opportunity. That's a lonely stretch out there." He didn't change expression, but Walker saw in the man's eyes that he was pleased with his ingenuity. "Orders came straight from the LTC, sir."

Which Crosby would never question. "In the execution of those orders, you know you endangered civilians."

Crosby's puzzled look returned. "Sir? I waited until they were well away from other humans—no houses out there, no other cars. The only ones endangered were another Shifter who could have attacked me and the Shifter groupie."

Walker bit back his retort, suppressing his natural

disgust at Crosby in the interest of getting more info. He suddenly wished Rebecca or Ronan had been here to hear Crosby dismiss Ellison and Carly. Rebecca would have whacked Crosby's head off with one swipe of her paw. For that matter, Walker would love to see Crosby's face when confronted with the gigantic form of Rebecca as a Kodiak bear.

"The Shifter lived," Walker said. "Is up walking around."

Crosby nodded. "I know, sir. LTC wanted him shot to find out how much he could take."

"I guess the LTC found out," Walker said. "Even if the Shifter had to suffer a lot."

"Yes, sir." Crosby kept his hands on the table, his expression remaining blank.

"My original training was as a medic," Walker said, abandoning the soup and moving around mashed potatoes that didn't look much different from the soup. "For a special forces A-Team."

Crosby's look now turned to respect. "Infiltration. Love to be picked for one of those missions."

Walker didn't answer. A-Teams were small and often cut off from any support behind enemy lines for long stretches of time. The men in them needed to be able to adapt and react, think and judge, far from any chains of command. Crosby was an unthinking machine, ready to let someone in charge point him and shoot. He wouldn't be much use in a situation in which he needed to take initiative, or even to take over.

"I've seen pretty bad injuries," Walker said. "But never saw anyone walk away from something like what you did to the tiger."

"The Shifter's pretty strong."

Walker patiently ate another bite of potatoes. "If you get any more orders concerning the tiger Shifter—any Shifter— mention it to me before you go, okay? I like to keep track of my men in case I need someone for a mission."

"Yes, sir." Crosby never asked questions.

"Enjoy your lunch, Sergeant."

Walker rose with his tray, and Crosby jumped to his feet at attention. "Yes, sir."

Walker left the room, carrying the tray to the private room, which was mercifully empty. He sat down and ate every bite of his hot lunch, as he'd learned to, but his mind was a long way from the food.

Carly lay in warm sunshine in her sisters' guest room, feathering kisses across Tiger's bare chest.

He was awake, lying on his back with his hands behind his head, sunlight dancing on the orange and black in his hair. The bedsheets were on the floor, their only cover the sunshine.

"I never knew it could feel that good," Carly said.

"I didn't know either." The words rumbled in Tiger's chest, touched with wonder.

Carly traced lazy circles across his chest, her fingers finding and tugging at his flat nipple. "I only met you a few days ago. And now I can't imagine how I got through my life before you were in it."

Tiger unlaced his hand and pressed it between Carly's breasts. "You feel the mate bond. It's strong between us."

His hand was warm, her heart beating faster beneath it. "I don't know what a mate bond is. Or a mate-claim, or what the sun and moon have to do with any of it. I only know that my world turned upside down when I met you. And I'm glad it did."

Tiger stroked between her breasts with light fingertips, then drew them out, as though following patterns in the air only he could see.

"I'm glad we did it on the counter," she said. "Kind of exorcized it."

Tiger's brows furrowed. "Hmm?"

"You know, because that's where I caught Ethan." Ethan seemed insignificant and far away now. "But from now on when I think about doing it on a kitchen counter, I'll remember how amazing it was with you."

"Good." Tiger's voice held a hint of a growl. "You should only think of me."

"Conceited." Carly smiled as she leaned down and kissed his lips. Tiger's return kiss was gentle but tinged with heat.

He was getting better at kissing, learning to use lips and tongue to draw out sensual pleasure. Tiger hadn't liked to stop kissing her, even to shed the rest of his clothes before carrying her up here.

More kissing as they entered the bedroom, and Tiger laid her down and climbed back inside her. He'd loved her again until she thought she'd pass out from the intensity of it, and even now, he didn't look tired.

Carly loved it, but she'd also known, when he'd looked down into her eyes, that he was saying good-bye.

Carly looked down at him now and touched his cheek. "Don't leave without me," she said softly. "I just found you, Tiger. I'm not ready to let you go."

He took on his stubborn look. "It's safer if you stay."

"Screw safer." Carly sat up, her hair tumbling forward. "I told you, I chased safety because I thought it would make up for what my dad did to us. But it doesn't. It just means your life goes nowhere. And anyway, I don't believe any more that there's any such thing as safety. I fooled myself into believing it, that's all."

He looked at her as though not paying attention to a word she said. "I can move faster without you."

"That's probably true. But you don't know where to go, or how to live as a human. You'll give yourself away as soon as you try to buy food or find a car or a place to sleep. And if anyone sees you change into a Tiger—*sheesh*. Every hunter will be after you with a shotgun. Sure, you can throw bullets out of your body, but I bet *too* many blasts, and you're dead."

"Cutting off my head would probably work too," Tiger said, face straight.

"It's not funny. You need me, and you know it."

Tiger again moved his fingertips through the air, his

eyes on what he touched, whatever it was. "I need to protect you. I didn't protect my mate before, or my cub."

"From what you've told me, you didn't have a chance. The researchers locked you away from them and wouldn't let you see them. Well, *I* don't want to be kept away from you."

Tiger's face went hard. "You have so much here. Your family. All that will be gone if you run away with me."

"I understand the risks," Carly said angrily.

"I think you don't."

Carly's retort cut off as she heard the noise of a car below, then the slamming of doors.

Tiger was off the bed in a single second, moving to the window without a sound. He kept to the shadows, looking out.

"It is not the soldiers for the Bureau," he said in a low voice. "Or Shifters."

Carly heard voices now, shrill and laughing, and her heart sank. "Shit, what are they doing home already? They're supposed to be gone until next week. And, crap, we left our clothes downstairs."

She scrambled off the bed, throwing open the closet to grab for the spare T-shirts and jeans she left here. Tiger was out of luck though.

"Stay here," Carly said to him. "I'll talk my way out of this somehow. We can sneak you downstairs and out later."

Tiger remained by the window, hidden to all below. Carly thought he looked wistful somehow, as he watched her sisters as they jabbered in their shrill voices, their mother answering as loudly.

Carly hurried down the stairs in her bare feet. The staircase spilled out into the wide foyer that was open to the kitchen. She hit the bottom step, ready to dash in and grab all the clothes, when her sisters and mother walked in through the back door, hands full of boxes, bags, clothes on hangers.

"Carly?" Althea, her oldest sister, said in surprise. "I

hope that's not *your* piece-of-crap car in the garage. I almost slammed into it."

"Never mind about the car," Zoë, the second oldest, said. She grabbed a wooden spoon from the counter and used it to lift the red boxers covered with black hearts from the kitchen floor. "Whose are *these*? Carly, you bad, *bad* girl."

CHAPTER TWENTY-TWO

"**P**ut those down. It's not what you think."

"No?" Zoë raised her brows at Carly over the underwear. "I think it's a pair of men's sexy underwear on our kitchen floor. Or were you playing dress-up? And you didn't invite us?"

The Randal next youngest to Carly, Janine Randal-Johnson, respectably married with a kid, said, "Those don't look like something Ethan would wear."

Carly put her hands on her hips. "And you'd know all about Ethan's underwear how?"

"Janine's right," Zoë said. "These don't look like the boulder holders of a man who wears suits in a hundred degree weather and knows every chichi restaurant in Austin. So who is he, Carly? And *where* is he? Upstairs?"

Zoë started for the stairs, carrying the underwear like a banner. Carly stepped in front of her, grabbed the underwear, and blocked Zoë's way up. "No!"

"So, not Ethan," Althea said. "Carly, good for *you*."

"Oh, Carly," Janine said, sounding sad. She alone of Carly's sisters had thought Ethan a good catch.

"Would you pipe down?" Carly said. "No, it's not Ethan. Ethan and I . . . broke up."

Such a tame term for the volatile events of the last few days.

"Carly, why didn't you call me?" Carly's mother, Rosalie, went around Zoë and pulled Carly into a hug. "Did you have an argument? Honey, you can tell us."

"She doesn't have to tell us anything." Zoë moved back to the kitchen, where she and Althea shared a double high five. "Ding-dong, the bitch is dead. By the bitch, I mean Ethan."

"Zoë," Rosalie said sternly. "This isn't funny. Carly's broken up with the man she was going to marry. She obviously met someone on the rebound. You need to talk to us, sweetie."

"Couldn't you have worked it out?" Janine asked. "I mean, Ethan's filthy rich. Make him buy you a car or something. Better than that hunk of junk—please don't tell me that's the new boyfriend's car."

"Ew," Althea said. "What did you do, pick up a guy at a pool hall? Please tell me you made him bathe. And that he didn't use my good bath towels."

"Will you all please shut up!" Carly yelled. She backed up, holding Tiger's underwear close, one hand up, stiff, to stave them off. "I caught Ethan screwing another woman, and I threw the engagement ring at him. End of story."

They stared at her, openmouthed, Zoë's and Althea's expressions changing from glee to stark surprise. Carly realized after a few heartbeats that they weren't staring at her, they were staring past her, up the stairs, at someone else.

She swung around and saw him a few steps behind her, one of Althea's precious towels tucked around his waist, the towel barely large enough to fit around him.

Moments stretched while Tiger stared down at them, and Carly's sisters and mother stared up at Tiger.

"Okay," Janine said after a beat of silence. "I'll admit it. You traded up."

* * *

How it happened that Tiger ended up dressed again and seated in the middle of the couch in the family room, Althea and Zoë on either side of him, Carly couldn't remember. The time seemed to buzz by her like a fly against glass.

Althea and Zoë each held a large balloonlike glass of red wine, and her mother had poured herself and Carly each one as Rosalie cleaned up the kitchen and started prepping for dinner. Janine sat at the kitchen table looking on, but she wanted only bottled water after the long trip.

They'd returned from shopping early, Carly's mother said, because they'd run out of money. That was just like Carly's sisters. While Carly and Janine had both reacted to their father's desertion by wanting to be careful, Althea and Zoë had compensated by living as largely as possible— traveling, shopping, being expansive and generous. They'd been older, though, when their father had gone, already planning their decorating business together as soon as they finished their fine arts degrees. Life had been good to them business-wise, enabling them to buy this big house and go on shopping sprees whenever they wanted.

In love, though, they'd not been as lucky. Althea had gotten married during college and divorced two years later, saying she didn't want a husband who expected her to give up her dreams so she could wait on him hand and foot. Zoë had run through a series of boyfriends, none of whom had lasted long. Janine had, happily, married the sweetest guy—Simon—and now had a son who'd inherited his father's sunny disposition.

Without exception, the sisters were interested in Tiger. He held a beer between his big hands, quietly watching, but not looking unhappy, as Althea and Zoë plied him with questions.

"So, where you from? Not Texas, I take it."

"Nevada," Tiger answered.

"What part?"

"Around Las Vegas."

"Ooh, that sounds fun. How about a road trip there, Carly?"

"You just got home," Carly said to Althea. "And give him a break."

Zoë took up the gauntlet on his other side. "So, how did you and Carly meet?"

"Carly gave me a ride," Tiger said.

"Then she really did pick you up." Zoë laughed. "Great dye job on your hair, by the way. I might try it. What do you do for a living?"

Tiger contemplated a moment, then answered, "I fix cars."

Carly let out her pent-up breath. He was telling the truth but in a way they wouldn't question it.

"You didn't do such a hot job on the one in the garage," Zoë said.

"That's not mine. We borrowed it."

Althea looked at him in confusion. "Then where's your car, Carly? If you picked him up?"

"I didn't pick him up *today*," Carly said. "My car got wrecked."

"What?" All four Randal women shrieked, but not in synch. They demanded to know what happened, and Carly had to wait until they quieted before she gave them a truncated version of events, including Tiger being there when she'd caught Ethan. She told them that Tiger's name was Bram, the first name that popped into her head for some reason.

Carly ended by saying she'd brought Tiger here today, where she thought they'd have a little peace and quiet. Her pointed look was met with oblivious stares.

"What a romantic story," Zoë said, sighing happily. "A chance meeting, Ethan being a bastard, this guy scaring the crap out of Ethan."

Tiger didn't answer her, because he was looking over at Janine. "You have a little one."

Janine brightened, as she did whenever someone mentioned her son. "Did Carly tell you? Yes, a little boy. He's almost two."

"I mean you have another little one." Tiger pointed at her abdomen. "Soon."

Another chorus of *What?* rang around the kitchen, and this one Carly joined. Janine blushed as red as Althea's wine.

"How did you know?" Janine asked, stammering a little. "I'm about two months. I was going to tell y'all—I got the message when we were driving, but I wanted to wait until we were with Simon."

Althea and Zoë abandoned Tiger to surround Janine with hugs, kisses, and exclamations of delight. Carly's mom left the sink, gave Carly a quick hug on the way, and went to Janine.

"Congratulations, Janine," Carly said, warming all over. Another addition to the family, another niece or nephew to cuddle. Janine deserved the happiness.

Carly saw Tiger watching her. She knew what was going on in his head—if she ran with him, she'd have to leave her sisters and Janine's new baby. She'd likely never get to see the newest Randal-Johnson.

The lump in her throat was hard. Carly lifted her untouched glass of wine to her lips, tears stinging her eyes.

"Carly is also having a little one," Tiger said.

Althea's and Zoë's voices shut off with a snap. All eyes turned now to Carly.

"Oh my God," Althea said. "Ethan's? What a mess. I thought you were on birth control."

"I am," Carly said, her body numb. "I don't know what he's talking about."

Tiger rose from the couch and walked to Carly, putting his hands on the kitchen counter and looking over it to her. "The babe is mine. But it's there. Only a day old."

Carly tried to answer, but her mouth wouldn't work. Tiger seemed to know things he couldn't possibly, so she didn't scoff at him, tell him he was wrong, that it was too soon to know.

She looked at the wineglass she'd raised and quickly set it down.

"If that's true, you'd better get off birth control right away," Janine said. "It could damage the baby, and you."

"I'm not . . ." Carly stopped. She and Tiger had been having wild and wicked sex, making love more often in the last two days than she had with Ethan collectively over two years.

Shifter sperm, especially Tiger's, was probably stronger than a human's. Even if her birth control was meant to keep eggs from falling where they could be fertilized, she wouldn't be surprised if one of Tiger's sperm had found one and dragged it out of hiding.

The girls had gone back to talking to Janine, perhaps thinking Tiger was joking. Carly knew he wasn't. Tears slid from the corners of her eyes, and Tiger reached out and brushed one away.

At five A.M., Tiger had silently slid open the window of the guest room, preparing to climb out, when he heard Carly's whisper, felt her touch.

"No."

"I'm going." Tiger's answering whisper held a hint of growl.

"And I'm coming with you."

Carly. Tiger briefly closed his eyes. If he left her behind, she and his cub would be safe. Liam would protect the cub—Tiger trusted him for that at least.

And if he left Carly behind, Tiger might never see his cub. A fist around his heart tightened.

He remembered the glimpse he'd had of his son—a tiny mite wrapped in a blanket, with a thin down of black hair on his head, touched with the faintest brush of orange. The surge of pride and love Tiger had felt had never been equaled, nor had the surge of grief when they'd told him the cub hadn't survived.

That Carly was pregnant, he had no doubt. He saw the

glow inside her. A Shifter cub, not a full-blood human, not the offspring of the dickhead Ethan. The cub was Tiger's.

"I'm coming with you," Carly said stubbornly. "I have money, you don't. I know how to travel and live in the world. You don't."

"I will run as a tiger, hunt."

"Oh, sure, because no one will notice a Bengal running through the Texas flatlands. You have transportation? I don't call that thing in the garage transportation."

"Walker is waiting for me."

Carly seized his arm. "Wait. What? You can trust him? How do you know he's waiting?"

"We arranged it while you were sleeping."

"That's it. I'm definitely coming. I even packed." She reached into the shadows beside the bed and pulled up a shoulder bag to go with her purse. "Let's go meet Walker."

Tiger stopped arguing—this was taking too much time. He would let Carly come with him until he could convince her to go back home. *Play it by ear,* he'd heard Connor say. How anyone could play an instrument with their ears, Tiger didn't understand, but Connor had explained that the saying meant *decide as we go along.* Tiger was good at doing that.

Carly smiled her triumph when Tiger nodded, closed the window, and gestured for her to follow him out of the room and downstairs. Janine and Carly's mother had gone home long ago, and Althea and Zoë were fast asleep in their respective rooms—Tiger could hear their quiet breathing behind the doors.

The house was dark except for a night-light in the kitchen. Althea hadn't set the alarm so they could open windows to the softer air of the night, and now the door opened and closed without a sound.

Slinging Carly's bag over his shoulder and taking her hand, Tiger led her down the walk to the street, keeping to the shadows of trees and shrubs. The night was pleasantly cool, the humid highs of the afternoon gone.

If Tiger hadn't been planning to hide for the rest of his

life, the walk would be pleasant. Carly's warmth stretched to him from her hand, and the new life inside her called out to him.

Carly didn't speak. She didn't look back either, or cry. She was resilient, his mate.

At the bottom of the street and around the corner lay a twenty-four-hour convenience store. Tiger scanned the lot with its few cars, and the man who was crushing out a cigarette and walking inside. Tiger didn't see Walker, but Walker, like Shifters, knew how to keep out of sight.

Tiger kept Carly in the shadows as he looked around, but he didn't scent Walker. He smelled the musty smell of humans inside the store, the tang of exhaust as cars went by, the dregs of the man's cigarette, and the sudden, sharp smell of fear.

Beside him, Carly gasped. "Oh my God, that guy's robbing the store."

Tiger looked to where she did, and saw the store clerk taking things out of the register with quick, jerky movements. The man who'd put out the cigarette was now holding up a long weapon.

Carly hissed in frustration. "And damn it, you crushed my cell phone."

Tiger silently lowered the shoulder bag to the ground. "Stay here."

"*Tiger,*" Carly whispered frantically as Tiger pulled on the baseball cap over his hair and started across the small parking lot. She didn't follow though. She was that sensible.

Tiger kept to the sticky shadows of the building, walking through noisome trash until he slid inside the front door. The clerk saw him but made no indication.

Tiger moved noiselessly up behind the lanky man holding a shotgun. Why did humans like guns? Did they fear so much to fight close to?

He stood right behind the robber, who never heard or sensed him until he felt Tiger's body warmth. Then the robber jerked, and the gun went off, but not before Tiger had grabbed the weapon and yanked the barrel to point upward. The clerk dove behind the counter, and the slug lodged in the ceiling.

Tiger jerked the weapon out of the robber's hand and snapped it in two. At the same time he kicked the robber's feet out from under him, sending the startled man to the stained floor.

The robber started up, a knife in his hand, so Tiger broke his hand. Screaming in pain, the man collapsed to the floor again.

Tiger broke the shotgun into a few more pieces and poured the bullets onto the man's chest.

"You can call the police now," Tiger said to the clerk.

The clerk climbed up from behind the counter and leaned on it. "Thanks, man," he said, gasping. "I thought I wasn't ever going to see my kids again."

"Go home and hug them," Tiger said. "You should work somewhere safer."

The clerk shrugged, giving him a scared smile. "No choice."

"There's a bar just outside Shiftertown. Go there and tell Liam to hire you. Tell him Rory sent you."

"Liam. Right." The clerk was wide-eyed and terrified.

Tiger looked at the robber, who was holding his hand and spewing curses and threats. Tiger leaned down, carefully raised the man's head by his hair, then thumped it against the floor with just enough force to knock him out. Then he walked out of the store.

Carly waited for him where he'd left her, her eyes wide with worry. "Tiger, don't *do* that. You nearly gave me a heart attack."

Tiger looked her over. "I think you are too young for them."

"I don't mean . . . Never mind. I hear sirens. We need to leave."

"The clerk called the police. I think he will be all right, and maybe find a safer job."

Carly studied him, one hand on her hip, which gave her

the sexy, saucy look. "You know, if you go around saving everyone in the world, you'll never stay off the radar. I mean," she added hastily as he started to ask what she meant, "you'll be found."

Tiger frowned at her. "But those people would be safe."

Carly drew a breath to answer, then she shook her head. "Tiger." She touched his face, her eyes filled with something he didn't understand. "What am I going to do with you?"

"Raise our cub."

She gave him a worried look. "You can't possibly know I'm pregnant. Janine, yes, if she's already two months gone, but it doesn't work that way."

Humans, who'd invented everything from traveling to the moon to cures for deadly diseases, could sometimes be so blind

Tiger pressed his hand to her abdomen. "I *know*. You hold our cub."

Carly's eyes filled with sudden tears. She pulled Tiger down to her and kissed him, the kiss slow, warm, and loving.

Tiger drank in the sensation of her lips and tongue, the taste of her, her warmth. He eased away, smoothing her hair.

"Walker is here," he said.

CHAPTER TWENTY-THREE

Walker picked them up in a dark blue SUV that looked as though its best years were behind it. His gaze fixed on Carly as Tiger climbed into the backseat and pulled Carly in beside him.

"You didn't say anything about bringing her," Walker said.

"She didn't give him a choice," Carly said, slamming the door and fishing for a seat belt. "Is this your SUV? If anyone finds out you're helping Tiger, they'll be looking for it."

"I bought it today," Walker said. "Used, for cash. You can thank me later."

"I'll thank you now." Carly leaned against Tiger. "Where are we going?"

"Away." Walker put the SUV in gear and pulled from the dark curb where he'd halted. "There's water in the cooler, and enough food for a couple of days. Sandwiches and chips and stuff. I figured he wouldn't remember to pack food."

"Tiger didn't pack anything," Carly said. She closed her eyes, happy for the downtime.

"I don't need anything," Tiger said.

His chest rumbled pleasantly, and Carly snuggled into the vibrations. He was an incredible man—an incredible *Shifter*. Strong and sometimes terrifying, but he'd gone inside the store to help the clerk without a second thought. Before that, he'd pulled Carly from a wrecked car, then kept bullets from hitting her. She'd come out of the incident without a scratch.

And his reward for being so amazing? People shooting at him and wanting to Collar him, cage him, test him, torture him.

Well, not on Carly's watch. She'd find a place to keep him safe where no one could hurt him.

The cynical voice inside Carly, the one she kept silent most of the time, told her that things would not be that easy. Tiger was right about the trouble she called down upon herself for going away with him or even helping him get away. She might never see her family again.

Carly suppressed that dart of pain. She'd help Tiger, and deal with the rest of her life later.

Walker was talking to Tiger. "My commander ordered the hit on you, I figured out. To see what you'd do, and to see how well you'd heal. I told you that I got curious when I read up on the Area 51 experiments and then found a new Shifter wandering around. I reported to my lieutenant colonel, because it's his command, and unfortunately, he got interested."

"Why unfortunately?" Carly asked.

"Because he sees Tiger as his ticket to promotion and a way out of the Shifter Bureau attachment. If he's found a new weapon—a person who can move with stealth and survive enemy fire—he'll be a hero. He's the one who wants Tiger found, imprisoned, and tested, and he wants to breed more of him."

"Breed." Tiger's word held anger.

"Yep. Breed. You heard me."

"He would take the cubs." The rage in Tiger's voice was fierce.

"And have people cut into your brain and maybe shoot you full of holes again to see how fast you can heal."

"He must not touch the cubs." Tiger pulled Carly closer, his arm as strong as iron.

"That's why I'm driving you away," Walker said. "I'll face my court-martial like a man."

Carly thought about everything Tiger had told her Walker had told *him*. Every single person she'd met wanted to control or use Tiger in some way—even Liam, talking about putting a real Collar on him. And now they were trusting Walker not to take them right back to his commander.

Tiger didn't seem worried, though. And because Tiger had been right about pretty much everything since she'd met him, Carly decided she would need to trust *him*. Not that she had much choice right now.

Walker and Tiger fell silent as Walker navigated the dark streets out of town. Carly leaned against Tiger, worn out and worried, but warmed by Tiger and his arm around her.

Walker drove them a long way west, where Tiger had never been. When he'd come to Austin, Tiger had been flown in a private cargo plane by a man named Marlo, a friend to Shifters in the Las Vegas Shiftertown.

Flying had been an interesting experience. Tiger had seen mountains rippling below him, then flatlands neatly sectioned into fields, and precise circles of green Marlo said came from circular irrigation systems. Those had dissolved into squares of brown dust with narrow roads that ended in dots. Oil wells, Marlo had said in answer to Tiger's questions, pumping the veins of West Texas.

This drive took them farther south and west, ever west. By the time the sun came up behind them, they were in a wide plain of nothing. Brown land with tufts of brown grasses and scrub stretched as far as Tiger could see, the green hills of Austin and the river country far behind. The sky was clear overhead, not a cloud in it, and already the temperature was climbing.

Tiger didn't mind. He looked from horizon to horizon, drinking it in. He loved seeing anything new, loved the amazing variety of the world.

Carly lay against his side, sleeping, her feet tucked up on the seat. The mate bond that connected them shimmered in the sunlight. Carly couldn't see it, but Tiger knew she could feel it.

Another bond stretched between the two of them and the new life inside Carly. Tiger let out a protective growl. The Shifter Bureau could never get his cubs.

Tiger would not let his cubs—anyone's cubs, for that matter—live through the hell he had. No cages, no needles, no shocks, no experiments. He might die trying to save them, but that didn't matter. He would make sure his cub would live and grow up like the other cubs in Shiftertown—safe, protected, happy.

As the sun climbed, Carly woke and stretched. She gave Tiger a quick kiss on his cheek, then rummaged in the cooler Walker had brought and pulled out a bottle of water, droplets of moisture clinging to it. Carly offered it to Walker and to Tiger, who both declined, then she opened the bottle herself and drank.

Tiger watched her lips purse over the bottle's mouth, her throat move in her swallow, her eyes close as the cool water slid over her tongue. Tiger clenched his fist and made himself only watch, not touch.

Carly waved her hand in front of her face. "I bet it's already ninety out there. Been a while since this truck's AC has had a tune-up, I'm guessing."

"Probably," Walker said. "Open the window."

"I might. When I'm hot enough to put up with swallowing half the dust of Texas."

Tiger hadn't noticed the temperature, but Carly was perspiring. He'd never had to worry about another person before. If he let her stay with him, would she be cool enough where they ended up? Or warm enough? Safe enough? Comfortable? Happy? Would their cub be?

Carly rested her head on his shoulder again. "You look like you're thinking deep thoughts."

"I want to take care of you," Tiger said. "Hoping I know how."

Carly patted his arm. "Don't you worry about that. I'm very good at taking care of myself. I've had a pretty good sleep, Walker. I can drive when you need a rest."

"Thanks," Walker said. "I'll take you up on that in a little while."

"I'm not tired," Tiger said.

"Mmm." Carly slanted a glance up at him. "You know how to drive?"

He hesitated. "Connor was teaching me."

"I see." Another pat, this one on his chest, and she left her hand there. "I think Walker and I should handle it."

Tiger liked that she didn't move her hand from over his heart. She leaned her head on his shoulder, continuing to drink the water, her tongue coming out to wipe it from her lips.

Tiger leaned to kiss her, licking the moisture from her mouth. She smiled when they broke apart, and the need inside Tiger threatened to choke him.

They drove on. Tiger checked behind them constantly, as did Walker. No cars followed, no flashing lights appeared, and no police vehicle they passed, waiting for speeders, paid them any attention. Walker drove calmly, not going too fast but also not being overly cautious, which would also attract attention. The man would make a good Shifter.

Carly insisted on stopping at a rest area where she could use the bathroom, countering the two males' annoyed stares by saying she didn't have outdoor plumbing and couldn't pop behind the nearest bush. Not that there were many out here anyway, and she had no intention of getting foot-long stickers in her privates.

Tiger hated every second she was out of his sight in the

restroom. He didn't relax until she came out, purse over her shoulder, and walked briskly again to the SUV.

Carly took over driving then, competently steering onto the freeway. Walker rode in front with her, both he and Carly wanting Tiger to stay in the back. He was too big and too conspicuous, Walker said, even if he hid his multicolored hair under the baseball cap.

"Will you really be court-martialed?" Carly asked Walker. "Are you—what's the term—AWOL?"

"No, I had some leave coming. I won't be AWOL for a week. But unless I can convince whoever tries me that Sheldon is a cruel bastard and endangered people's lives, they might decide to make an example of me."

"I'm sorry." Carly sounded sad. "You shouldn't have gotten dragged into this."

"Doesn't matter. I believe in doing what I think is right." Walker shrugged bulky shoulders. "I've had a good run."

"You can't be much older than I am."

"You grow up fast doing what I do."

As Tiger listened, a recently learned emotion welled up inside him, one he'd never experienced in the research lab. Tiger had felt something like it for Iona when he finally realized she meant to release him from the research building and let him go, and again for Liam for taking him in and giving him a home. He felt it also for Connor for trying to teach Tiger how to live in the world. Now for Walker for helping at a cost to himself.

Tiger had a word now to put to the feeling: gratitude.

"Take this exit," Walker told Carly as a green sign loomed up. "No more easy freeway."

Carly smoothly steered off the road and followed Walker's instructions to turn left onto the empty, narrow road at the end of the ramp. This road, a little rougher, no shoulder beyond the white stripe at its edge, stretched straight and long southward, going as far as Tiger could see.

They were still on this road as the sun moved slowly westward, but they'd left behind flatlands for small mountain ridges that hugged the horizon and made the road bend around them. Carly had switched with Walker again, but she remained in the front, her sunglasses on against the glare.

She looked as neat and edible as she had when Tiger had first met her—she standing on the side of the road in pristine white, one hand holding her cell phone, fingers of the other splayed on her shapely hip.

Some instinct buried inside him had told Tiger that she was his mate. No other.

And Tiger had been right. No woman not a mate of the heart would be so determined to help him, so ready to endanger herself to help him get away.

Tiger wouldn't let her endanger herself much longer.

The afternoon grew hot, then hotter. Walker turned off on another road that led into rocky hills and canyons. The road became dirt, the SUV shaking over ruts and washboard grading.

After about an hour or so on this road, traveling at a crawl, Walker pulled over. There was nothing out here except heated sky and rock, with trees and scrub clinging to the sides of the canyons. No other cars, no buildings, nothing.

"Carly, how good are you at reading maps?" Walker asked.

"Pretty good," Carly said. "I go on road trips with my sisters. They talk instead of watching the road, and they never pay attention to their GPS, if they even turn it on. So I navigate. Put it another way, I yell at them to not miss the turn."

"No GPS service in this truck," Walker said. "And it's best if you don't turn on your cell phone. If you can read a map, I'll show you. If not, I'll just tell you."

"No trouble about my cell phone. It's broken." She shot a look at Tiger. "Show me the map."

Tiger waited while Walker spread out a map on the seat and pointed out the roads she needed to take to lead her back to the freeway and on to El Paso. She'd cross the bor-

der there and take more back roads to where she could pick
up Tiger.

"And you'll be . . . ?" Carly asked him.

"With Tiger."

"Oh," she said. "Good." Carly glanced over the seat
again at Tiger. "Someone to take care of you."

Tiger wasn't sure having Walker come along was the
best idea. He knew he'd end up taking care of Walker, not
the other way around.

Tiger opened the back door and stepped out of the SUV.
He flexed his cramped muscles—he didn't like being confined for long stretches of time.

He sniffed the air, smelling nothing but grasses, wind,
earth. No pollution, no scent of humans touching the
breeze. Clean, fresh, beautiful. A wild place, which called
to his heart. He wanted to shift and run, never stop running.

He heard Carly leave the SUV, her sneakers crunching
on the gravel of the road. Tiger went around the vehicle to
her, catching her before she made it to him.

Her eyes were luminous in the sunlight, which burned
her hair with golden highlights. "See you soon," Carly said
softly.

Tiger pushed her against the side of the SUV, his body
hemming hers in. He put his fingers under her chin, turning her face to his.

"Mate of my heart," he said. "You always will be. No
matter what."

Carly's eyes shone with tears. "Remember when I said I
thought I was falling in love with you? Well, I think I have.
All the way."

Tiger slid his arm behind her back and pulled her
against him, the length of her body along his. He studied
her, memorizing her face, her green eyes with the silver
gray flecks.

He kissed her, a light touch of lips, fixing her taste in his
mind. *Always Carly. Always mine.*

Tiger kissed her again, this kiss deepening. Carly made

a noise in her throat as her body fitted itself inside the curve of his.

Her body was soft where he was firm, rounded where Tiger was flat with muscle. He loved every part of her. The memory of Carly's warmth would wrap him when he was cold, the thought of her kiss would feed him when he was hungry.

He pressed her back into the warm metal of the SUV, wanting to climb inside her and never come out. Mating frenzy. Here and now.

Tiger kissed her, and Carly kissed him back. His mouth moved on hers, their tongues tangling. The soft sounds Carly made had his cock growing harder, every moment with her making him want to have her one more time.

Walker cleared his throat on the other side of the SUV.

Tiger eased away from Carly, his heart pounding, his temperature soaring, the beast in him angry. He didn't trust himself to speak as he took one step back and forced his hands to slide from her sides.

Carly looked up at him, her eyes moist, then she reached out and brushed a finger across his burning cheek. "I'll see you, Tiger. In about five or so hours. Depending on how long it takes me to cross. And then we'll have time."

Time. Yes.

In the cage, he'd had nothing but time. Wasted time. Now Tiger wanted to hang on to every bit of time—with her.

"We'll fix this," Carly said. "All right?"

Yes, Tiger would fix it. He had to. The thought of being without Carly was tearing him apart.

He took another step back. Carly swallowed and looked away, walking quickly around the back of the SUV to the drivers' side. Tiger followed her, Walker stepping aside so that Tiger could help Carly into the SUV and close its door.

"Be careful," she told him through the open window. "I want to see you again."

Tiger didn't answer. He leaned in through the window and kissed her again.

Touching her face one last time, Tiger stepped back, waiting while she started up the SUV, then watched her turn it around and head back down the washboard road.

Walker buckled his utility belt around him. "You all right?"

Tiger kept his eyes on the SUV, watching the lights flare as Carly slowed to go down a wash. A line of dust in Carly's wake spiraled into the solid-blue sky.

CHAPTER TWENTY-FOUR

Tiger's chest felt hollow, as though someone had kicked him repeatedly. He needed Carly with him every second—every moment away from her was one too long.

"Tiger?" Walker said.

"Fine." Tiger made himself turn away. "We should go." Better get there and meet up with her again as quickly as he could.

"Follow me, and don't deviate," Walker said. "We're going into a dangerous area—drug runners and coyotes use it. Coyotes meaning the guys who run people across the border in exchange for their life savings, not the mangy animals that howl."

Tiger had heard of these coyotes, and the drug runners who shot those who got in their way. But they were the least of his worries. In fact, he'd make sure that they needed to worry about *him*.

He paused for a moment to remove his clothes while Walker discreetly looked the other way. Once undressed, Tiger packed his clothes into a waterproof belt pack Walker had brought for him, handed it to Walker, and shifted to his tiger.

The world changed. Scents and sound rushed at him, the beast gleeful to be in open country, far from the confinement of Shiftertown. Tiger stretched, shaking himself out.

Walker had gone wide-eyed, his scent betraying his startled wariness at watching Tiger's change. Then Walker swallowed his misgivings, came to Tiger, and hooked the belt with Tiger's clothes around his middle.

The appendage felt a little strange, but Tiger would have to get used to it. He raised his head, sniffed the wind, and followed Walker down the hill, slinking into the shadows of the rocky hills.

Carly breathed a sigh of relief when the SUV hit pavement. The jarring and rattling stopped, and the ride became smooth.

She didn't pass many cars as she turned onto the highway, heading back up toward the I-10. Even if she didn't have a map, the chances of getting lost out here were minimal. There were only a few paved roads that went anywhere.

The distance gave her time to think. Too much time. She knew she had the option of turning right at the 10 instead of left, and heading back to Austin. The Shifters would pry out of her that she'd driven Tiger this far, but then they'd go after him themselves, or alert the Shifter Bureau. They'd leave her alone, not needing her anymore.

Carly could go back to her life. She'd find Yvette's car where she'd left it at the chain hotel and take it back to her, finding some way to apologize. She could go back to dealing with her broken engagement and figuring out how to keep Ethan from ruining her life. She might have to find another job, but maybe she could sell her house and move in with Althea and Zoë for a while until she got herself sorted out.

If Yvette didn't fire her, Carly would go back to the

trivia of day-to-day work, trying to convince people with large disposable incomes that they wanted to use their money for quality artwork. After work, she'd pick up something at the grocery store on the way home, and while away nights in front of the television.

Carly realized now that she hadn't spent all that much time with Ethan, even after their engagement, and that they'd only gotten together when *he* wanted to. She'd been too caught up in planning the rest of her life to notice.

Back to a world where people captured a wild, beautiful man to study him, dissect him, trap him, bind him. Tiger deserved to be free, and Carly was going to make sure he was.

When she turned onto the freeway—choosing to head west, not east—blue and red lights flashed behind her and a sheriff's car signaled her to pull over. Heart in her throat, Carly slowed and stopped on the freeway's shoulder, waiting for an eighteen-wheeler to lumber by before she lowered the window. A sheriff's deputy walked up from behind and leaned to look into the window.

"License and registration, ma'am," he said.

"Is there a problem, officer?" Carly kept her smile in place as she plucked her license out of her wallet and reached into the glove compartment to find the registration. Her mouth went dry when she didn't see the registration paper at first, but there it was, tucked under a packet of tissues.

She handed both license and registration to the deputy, glad she'd slid the maps Walker had given her inside her purse. "I know I wasn't speeding. I'm careful about that."

The deputy peered for a time at the license, then the registration. "This isn't your vehicle, ma'am."

"No, it's not. My boyfriend's. He let me borrow it for the weekend."

"Mind if I ask where you were coming from down that highway? You're a long way from Austin."

"Marfa." A lie. "I have friends there." The truth. "It's so pretty." Also the truth.

"And now you're heading for . . ."

"El Paso. More friends. We're going to Juárez, to bargain hunt."

Carly did her best to look like an empty-headed girl who lived to visit her friends and spend money.

"You still never said why you pulled me over." Carly smiled again as she took back her license.

"Looking for someone." The officer gazed, keen-eyed, into the SUV's interior, over the backseat and the space behind it. He straightened up. "You have a nice afternoon, Ms. Randal. You're about seventy-five miles from El Paso. Drive safely."

"Thank you. I will." Keeping her pleasant tones, Carly rolled up the window and pulled slowly away and back into traffic.

Looking for someone. Her heart thumped. The officer hadn't been about to tell her who. Obviously not Walker, because his name was on the registration. And not her. That left Tiger.

Carly sped up a little, making sure she didn't exceed the limit enough to get pulled over again, and headed for the horizon and the city of El Paso.

Tigers liked water. When they reached the Rio Grande, Tiger had no problem wading into the muddy stream, the water cool under his paws. Scrub and trees were green here, fed by the main river and little rivulets that made the ground soggy.

Tiger came out the other side and shook himself off. Walker took more time, holding his belt above his head as he waded then swam the deepest parts. Tiger waited, the beast in him pleased by the open country, the vast sky overhead. In such a place he could run through the night, sleep under trees during the day. If bad men were out here hurting people, Tiger could take them out, as he had done the robber at the convenience store. That was what he was meant to do, he thought. Crush bad guys.

"This way," Walker said once he was settled.

He led Tiger on across wild land, pushing through tough brush and trees to forge a path. They were going north and west, Tiger could tell, to meet Carly, which made his heart sing. She wouldn't have been good on this cross-country walk, but she had the comfort of the SUV, and its relative safety. Tiger looked forward to seeing her again, if this all worked, if only for a little while.

They saw no one. Tiger had half hoped the hills would be teeming with people who needed taking down, but it wasn't to be. His fighting blood was up, his need to run, strike, do what he was meant to do.

At one point a plane flew overhead, high enough up to be a small smudge against the late afternoon sky. Walker ducked under the spread of a tree, and Tiger lowered himself to the ground, letting shadows camouflage him. The plane went straight on, not circling or returning.

Tiger rose and moved on, following Walker's guidance, feeling the mate bond pull him back to Carly.

Carly drove over one of the bridges that connected El Paso to the Mexican city of Juárez, crossing the border after a wait of about an hour or so. The sun was setting, and plenty of cars were on the streets on both sides, people going home or leaving the cities after the weekend.

Carly knew Walker had picked El Paso as the place she should cross because the cities on both sides were busy, plenty of Americans crossed back and forth daily, and families lived on either side, crossing one way or another for visits. She'd navigated crazy traffic in Juárez before, and she drove out of that city after a time, heading south for the town of Chihuahua.

Now she began to feel a bit uncomfortable. The afternoon was waning into evening, and she was alone, in another country, in a vehicle that was better than most she passed on the road. Carjackings weren't unusual. She'd be safer not to stop until she reached the meeting point.

The sun sank as she drove south then turned down a lonely stretch of road that Walker had marked. Carly had to drive slowly, through ruts and along ungraded stretches, down dry washes where her tires spun in soft earth.

The thirty miles of this road took Carly well over an hour as the sun slipped over the horizon. Twilight didn't linger long in the desert, and soon it was dark.

Carly parked at the designated meeting point and killed the engine and lights. She peered at the empty darkness, a flat plain of desert. In the dark, she could see no more than that, and she couldn't see Tiger or Walker either.

No matter. She'd sit here until they came. Tiger and Walker were the kind of men who'd make double sure and triple sure the way was clear before they showed themselves.

Or, if they didn't come by morning, Carly could turn around and head back to Austin. She knew why Tiger had agreed to split up—he'd been giving Carly the chance to go home and leave him if she decided that course was best. Splitting up also gave Tiger the choice whether or not to come back for Carly. As he'd told her, he could move faster without her.

The watch Carly kept in her purse let her keep track of time, which crawled slowly. Agony. The longest day of her life to this point had been the one when she'd realized her father had left for good. This one might just beat it.

Carly caught movement out the back window. Tiger? She turned to look, but remained inside the SUV. Could be anyone out here.

Her heart pounded until her head hurt as whoever it was moved slowly forward. Stealthily. Like a Shifter.

But the Shifter who looked into the window wasn't Tiger. He had a shaved head and tattoos down his neck and a look of fury in his brown eyes. Spike.

Behind him was Sean, then Ellison with his cowboy hat. The large bear Ronan was approaching the other side of the SUV with Dylan, and Carly's rearview mirror showed her Liam walking nonchalantly toward her out of the darkness.

Tiger stopped, scenting the Shifters well before he saw them surrounding the SUV that waited in the spot Walker had chosen.

Liam, Dylan, Sean, the trackers. Tiger also smelled an airplane, far away, but near enough for Tiger's enhanced senses to catch the scent. That explained how the Shifters had managed to be there first, in the plane that had flown over them. Tiger hadn't known enough about airplanes, and it hadn't flown low enough, for him to recognize it as Marlo's.

Tiger shifted to become his human form, sliding his now-loose belt from his waist. He went to Walker. "I need you to take care of Carly," he said before Walker could speak. "And my cub."

"I'll get you to safety," Walker said in a low voice. "But we have to go now."

Tiger shook his head. "You'll be too slow. Promise me. Don't let them hurt her, or take the cub."

Walker assessed Tiger, then gave him a nod, not an argument. "I promise."

"Thank you, Walker Danielson."

Tiger put his hands on Walker's shoulders and pulled him into a quick embrace, Shifter fashion. Walker's scent betrayed his discomfort, but he took the hug, thumping Tiger on the shoulders in return.

Tiger resumed his belt and pouch and shifted to the Bengal again.

Every one of Tiger's instincts and his heart fought him as he turned and slunk off into the darkness. But the best way to help Carly was for Tiger to disappear. Liam would see that Carly came to no harm, and so would Walker. Tiger had to take care of what he needed to, as much as it killed him to do it.

* * *

"We'll find him," Liam said to Carly.

Carly sat on the open back bed of the SUV, arms folded, Rebecca the bear Shifter next to her. Liam stood with his hands in the pockets of a leather jacket, the desert night having turned cold. Rebecca had laid a blanket around Carly's shoulders, but Carly barely acknowledged the gesture.

"Where'd you leave him, Walker?" Liam asked. His voice was quiet, but Carly sensed the anger behind it, tight, ready to strike.

Spike and Ellison had found Walker in the desert, striding toward them, the man alone. Walker gave Liam a stoic look now and pointed into the darkness. "Over there. But he'll be long gone by now. He's not an average Shifter."

Liam nodded in agreement, but he peered into the desert as though he could see behind every tumbleweed, which he possibly could. "Ronan, Dad, Spike. See what you can do."

The three Shifters at once walked away into the dark, without looking at Carly. Spike was furious with her, she knew, though he'd not said a word. After his first glare of rage, Spike had stepped back, out of the way, and let Liam take over.

Liam swiveled his gaze to Carly. "Where is he heading?"

"I haven't the faintest idea," Carly said. "We planned to meet up here, and beyond that, we hadn't decided."

Liam made a noise that was a cross between a grunt and a growl. "Damn it, Carly, I'm trying to *help* him."

"The last time Tiger heard, you wanted to either put a Collar on him or kill him," Carly said. "Real helpful."

"And last time I checked, *this* guy wanted to lock Tiger back into a research center." Liam jerked a thumb at Walker, who remained as silent as the Shifters. "And now he's Tiger's best friend?"

"Walker changed his mind," Carly said.

"And you trust him?"

"If he'd been lying to Tiger, Tiger would have known."

"Aye, that's true enough. But shite." Liam turned on Walker. "Why didn't you come to me? Tiger's *my* responsibility. Anything he does can have a backlash on all Shifters, everywhere."

"Not really my problem," Walker said. "I want to find out what Tiger is and what he can do, what his original mission was."

"Why?" Liam asked. "Why so interested? Other than following orders from the Shifter Bureau?"

"I have my reasons."

Walker could be as stubbornly obtuse as Liam. Carly believed now that Walker didn't wish to see Tiger locked away again, but he kept going on about wanting to know what Tiger had been made for. Walker wanted Tiger away from the Shifter Bureau, true, but for his own agenda. He'd said nothing about his motives during the ride, and neither had Tiger, but whatever he'd told Tiger must have satisfied.

"Rebecca," Liam said. "Can you give me a minute alone with Carly?"

Rebecca rose, obedient, but she gave Liam a warning look as she walked away. "Don't hurt her or upset her. Kim gave me those orders. Don't make her mad at me. Hey, Walker." Rebecca smiled at the man and slid her hand through the crook of his arm. She was taller than he was by about an inch. "How about a moonlight stroll?"

Walker's stance became suddenly nervous, but he walked away with Rebecca. Ellison followed them, limping a little, still recovering from being shot, while Sean moved off into the desert, watching the darkness.

Liam settled himself comfortably next to Carly, resting his hands on his knees. With his worn jeans, leather coat, and dusting of unshaven dark whiskers, he might be a biker sitting back for some rest before continuing on the road.

"Do you know how we tracked you down?" Liam asked, his voice calm.

"I know you're going to tell me," Carly said.

"Connor was watching the morning news. There was a local story about a man who'd gone into a convenience store and stopped a robbery in progress. The hero broke the robber's gun into about ten pieces, knocked the guy down, and then broke his hand. And knocked him out. The amazed clerk described his rescuer as a very large man, hugely strong, and wearing a baseball cap. And then this superhero disappeared. Tiger was gone, no one knew where, and you'd vanished out of your gallery—don't think Spike didn't get an earful about that. How brainless would I have to be not to figure out who this hero was?"

"He couldn't help himself," Carly said. "It's who he is."

"The clerk, who's now Tiger's biggest fan, volunteered to me that he saw him getting into a dark SUV. Easy for our Sean to look at traffic cams for that hour and find likely SUVs and their plates. Easy for him to hack into the title records database to find that Walker Danielson had bought a vehicle with that description only yesterday."

"I got pulled over on the freeway," Carly said, her voice flat.

"Aye. I asked my friends in counties all over the state to look for the SUV but not to make it official. And not to arrest anyone, but to tell me where the SUV was and where it was heading. Another friend at the Bridge of the Americas gave me another clue, and my Shifter friend Eric has access to a plane."

"Who else did you tell?" Carly asked. "The Shifter Bureau?"

"Now, why would we be doing that?" Liam gave her an incredulous look. "No, lass, I told no one."

"And no one will wonder why half of Shiftertown left Austin tonight?"

"The few of us here are a long way from half of Shiftertown. Most of Shiftertown goes out at night anyway. Bars, dance clubs, the fight club. It's not unusual to have Shifters prowling the town until two thirty in the morning, which is our curfew. Many of us come from nocturnal breeds."

Carly listened impatiently. "What about the Shifters who want you to put a Collar on Tiger?"

"Carly." Liam rubbed his hands on his thighs. "I agreed to look after Tiger because I felt for him. No one should do to a Shifter what was done to him. I'm trying to protect him. And I'm trying to protect him from himself."

"Mmm hmm."

"I know you don't believe me, lass. He can wind you around his finger, can Tiger. He's got a way with him, as my mum used to say. But what happens if he attacks someone, like he did the robber? If I'm not around when daft humans try to arrest him, what will Tiger do to *them*? Or the authorities might try to kill him, which would cause even more havoc. I'm not in favor of putting a Collar on Tiger, or terminating him either, trust me. But we need to control him somehow."

"Why do you need to control him at all?" Carly demanded. "Why can't you leave him alone?"

Liam blew out his breath. "If you haven't noticed, Tiger is dangerous. Look at the havoc he's wreaked only the last few days."

"All in self-defense and in defense of others. He told me that if you put the Collar on him, it will probably kill him."

Liam looked off into the distance of the starry night. "I admit that when we tried the first time, I thought it would kill him. That's why I took it off."

"And you want to put it back on? What kind of logic is that?"

"Mmm." Liam fell silent for a long time as the cool breeze from the desert and the hills beyond flowed to them. The SUV's settling engine emitted a pop and a small hiss.

"I'm going to tell you something," Liam said. "I need to swear you to secrecy on it, but if it helps get you to believe me and help me, then it's worth it. I'm trying to find a way so that no Shifter has to wear a Collar ever again."

Carly gave him her grudging interest. "How are you doing that?"

"Experiments. Me and Dad and Sean. On ourselves—not

anyone else. I'd like to get Connor out of his before his Transition. I made Tiger a fake Collar, which was good enough to fool the humans. So far, we haven't been successful at removing Collars, but what I'd like to do is see if we can make one that's even more realistic, say delivers a mild shock or the show of one when a Shifter starts an attack. Tiger would be perfect for this. I could learn how to tone down the Collars, or make better fake ones, and the other Shifter leaders would get off my back about Tiger."

"Experiment on him," Carly said.

"Yes, but in this case, I'd be searching for ways to *not* hurt him."

Liam argued a good case, and his charming voice made Carly want to believe him.

"That's all very nice," she said. "But still, all I'm hearing is about how people want to use Tiger. Walker is helping him, but he's still trying to figure out what Tiger is and how he can be useful. You think Tiger's the perfect guinea pig, and you believe you're being nice by taking him home and sitting on him while you try out your Collars. You all want him for your own benefit. You don't want him for himself."

"I like him, Carly," Liam said in a patient voice. "I want to see him happy. I can't believe he'll be happy running wild in northern Mexico, having to hunt for his food."

"How do you know?" Carly glared up at him. "Have you ever once asked Tiger what *he* wants?"

Her eyes blurred with sudden tears. Having Carly near him had made Tiger calm and happy. Knowing she'd started a cub had made him happy.

"He's a hard one to understand, I admit," Liam said. "I truly want to find him to keep him from harm. And to keep others from being harmed by him."

Carly wiped her eyes. "He won't attack. Not unless someone deserves it."

"And how can we be sure he'll understand whether someone deserves it? Or when that line won't be clear for him?"

"He knows." Carly met Liam's gaze without fear, and she spoke with conviction. "You could trust him, Liam. Let him go. Let him be free."

Liam let out another long breath. "Love, if the humans find out I've lost a Shifter, hell will rain down upon me."

Carly had no sympathy, not anymore. "Liam," she said, "suck it up."

CHAPTER TWENTY-FIVE

Liam stared at Carly in shock, then he started to laugh. "Are you related to my wife, by chance? When Kim knows she's right, can she ever scold."

"Are you saying I'm right?"

"I'm saying you can shake your finger in a man's face and get your point across." Liam stood up. "Sean," he called, "bring back the others, will you?"

Sean turned around from the edge of the brush, moonlight shimmering on the sword slung across his back. "Why? Do we know where he's gone?"

"No, we don't. Go get Marlo, will you? Pass on the word that we're going home."

Sean stopped in surprise. "We are? You didn't answer me why."

"We're letting Tiger go."

Carly jumped up from her seat, shedding the blanket. "Thank you, Liam."

"Go?" Spike snarled out of the darkness and then appeared, stark naked from a shift and covered with tattoos. "Are you saying you brought us all the way out here, away from our cubs and mates, to hunt him, and now we're going to let him go?"

"Yes," Liam said calmly. He shot Carly an amused glance. "Suck it up, Spike."

"Shit." Spike turned around and walked away, his back as covered with tatts as his front. The dragon across his back was impressive.

"I'm thinking Iona won't be best pleased," Sean said.

"I know," Liam answered. "I expect I'll get more scolding from her. But Carly has shamed me. Tiger needs to be left alone, without interference from any of us, to be his own . . . tiger. Besides, you think we have a snowball's chance of finding him when he's alone and not wanting to be found? If any Shifter can take care of himself in the wild, it's Tiger."

"Shite," Sean said softly. "I'm already worried about him."

"Me too. But I have the feeling that if he wants to be found again, he will be."

"Damn it." Sean started to walk away, off to find the others.

"Sean?" Carly called after him. "*Rory?* Really? He didn't like the name."

Sean turned around, walking backward while he spoke. "A bit of a joke."

Carly held her thumb and forefinger up, half an inch apart. "A *little* bit."

"'Twas what Andrea said." Sean chuckled as he turned around again and vanished into the desert.

Marlo, a lanky man with thin hair who looked every bit as dangerous as any drug runner, flew them back to an airstrip outside of Austin in his small plane. All except Walker.

"I'm going to keep looking for him," Walker told Carly in his quiet way before she let the others take her to the plane.

Carly stared at him in dismay and anger. "I just talked Liam into letting him go. Why can't you leave him alone?"

"Because I need to ask him for his help. If he can give it."

"Help for what?"

Walker gave her an evasive look. "I have unfinished business. Tiger might be able to help me, I don't know. Not until I find him." When Carly continued to glare, Walker spread his hands. "I can't hurt him, Carly. Not even with this." He patted the pistol on his belt. "He can kill me a damn sight faster than I could him."

That was true. Carly dropped her anger, stepped to Walker, and touched a kiss to his hard cheek. "If you find him, tell him I love him." She sank back and squeezed his hands. "And don't go AWOL."

"Hope I don't have to."

Walker left her then to start up the SUV. He drove away, the headlights cutting through the darkness. His red taillights grew smaller and smaller, but could be seen for many miles, glowing back at them.

W hat was normal? Carly couldn't find it anymore.
Normal wasn't waking up alone in her house, brushing her teeth, donning her cute dresses, and driving to work. It wasn't collecting money for her wrecked car from her insurance company and having Althea help her pick out a new car. It wasn't pizza after work at what Zoë called the house of the Weird Sisters, or even meeting up with Liam's mate, Kim, at a coffee house and catching up on how the Shifters were doing.

They'd never heard anything from Tiger. After a week, Walker returned, came to Carly's house, and told her he'd never found a trace of him. While Carly was glad for Tiger's sake, her hunger to hear something of him turned to stark sorrow. She knew she'd never see Tiger again.

Walker returned to his unit to be chewed out by his

commander, because the tiger-man had disappeared while Walker had been on leave. Liam Morrissey was called in to the Shifter Bureau and questioned, and his house searched, but finally the Bureau concluded that Liam was as stumped as they were. Tiger had vanished, and Liam had no idea how he'd gotten out or where he was now.

That at least was true. Carly heard all this from Kim on one of their coffee visits, but it didn't make her feel better.

Carly's heart remained like lead in her chest, and about four weeks after Tiger's disappearance, her morning sickness started, confirming Tiger's claim that Carly was pregnant. Her doctor doubly confirmed it, but Carly decided not to announce the pregnancy just yet.

Yvette's car, fortunately, had still been in the parking lot, intact, when Carly had returned to Austin, and Carly had driven it to Armand's, leaving before she could do more than give the stunned Yvette the keys. Carly took the car she and Tiger had liberated to the Barton Creek Square mall and left it in a heavily crowded parking lot, walked away from it, and took a taxi home.

She'd thought Yvette would tell Armand to kick Carly out on her ass for taking her car and bolting in the middle of a busy workday, but Yvette never did. Carly didn't find out why until she went to work one morning about a month after her return, fighting her morning sickness with soda crackers and weak tea. In an hour or two, however, she knew she'd be ravenous.

"You did it for a man," Yvette said as she stirred her latte, the odor of the coffee making Carly's nausea rise. "During my modeling days, when I was in so much demand from all the photographers and fashion houses, I met Armand. He was poor, a struggling artist—he had nothing. I had everything—career, money, luxurious apartment, rich boyfriends. But I'd never met anyone like Armand. I was enchanted with him. I posed for him, and he told me his troubles. We became friends and then lovers. But because he was so very poor, he did jobs for the wrong people, put himself in debt to them. He tried to pay with his art when they came to collect, but they were philistines and did not want it. Armand came to me one night and said he had to leave the country. He wanted to go to America, and wanted me to go with him. We'd change our names so the bad people wouldn't follow him. Start fresh." Yvette shrugged. "So I did."

Carly listened, the coffee's scent becoming less sickening and more desirable. A latte with thick, luscious cream started to sound like heaven. She couldn't have it, of course, but she could breathe in the aroma.

"You walked away from your life," Carly said as Yvette fell silent. Yvette's casual *So I did* meant she'd given up her career, her home, her family, and started over again in the States, all for Armand's sake.

"We had to flee in the night," Yvette said after a dainty sip of her latte. "I took whatever cash I could find and got us out of the country and to New York. Even that was too conspicuous, so we came to Texas, to Dallas first and then to Austin. I never modeled again. Except for Armand."

"You must have loved him very much to do that."

"Oh, I did. Still do. So you borrowing my car to help a man you love get away is understandable to me. My surprise is that you didn't stay away with him."

Carly's eyes stung with tears. "He didn't give me the choice."

Yvette's usual expression was cool and distant, she an elegant statue who looked with hauteur upon the world. When she saw Carly's tears now, the hauteur melted away, Yvette's eyes softened, and she gathered Carly into an embrace. "You poor darling." She kissed the top of Carly's head. "The heart, it is a fragile thing."

Carly let herself relax against Yvette's strong shoulder. She hadn't broken down and cried, truly cried, since she'd come home. No time, Carly had told herself. And now she had a child coming. She had to be strong, like her mother had been strong for her.

But for a few minutes, she didn't want to be strong. She let herself cry, heartbroken.

Armand came in as Carly's sobs were quieting, and Carly straightened up, wiping her eyes. Yvette went to Armand and kissed his cheek. "Darling, I was just telling Carly our love story."

Armand smiled, his goodness beaming from him. Carly saw why beautiful, elegant Yvette had fallen in love with this bearlike, rather homely man, and loved him still. Armand dropped a kiss onto his wife's lips and squeezed her with one arm around her waist.

"I couldn't believe my luck, Carly," he said. "A nobody like me landing an angel like my Yvette. But my father always told me to seize the day, and I did. No regrets."

"No regrets," Yvette responded, and they looked into each other's eyes. *No regrets* must have been a catchphrase with them, because their faces softened, and years fell away.

Carly sniffled. "You two are so wonderful." She grabbed a tissue and wiped her eyes again. "I'm going for coffee."

By the time she returned, Yvette and Armand were businesslike once again. Carly cleared her throat and sucked down her decaf latte—*ah, sweet, warm cream.*

"Armand," she said. "I want to do something for the Shifter kids. I thought maybe a visit to the gallery, maybe an art class from you. You teach art classes for kids at community centers, right? Would you be willing to do one for Shifters?"

Armand looked surprised. "Are Shifter children interested in learning art?"

"I don't see why not. They're not allowed to do so many things, but no one has anything against them becoming artists. I checked. I thought some of the kids might enjoy it. Just a thought."

"A very good thought. We will arrange it."

Yvette said nothing, but Carly knew she approved. Yvette never kept strong opinions to herself.

Carly went back to work, more contented. A little bit. If she was carrying a Shifter cub, she wanted to learn all about Shifter kids. Besides, if she could put a little happiness into the eyes of a kid like Olaf, it would be totally worth it.

Lieutenant Colonel Sheldon looked Sergeant Crosby up and down as Crosby stood at stiff attention in front of Sheldon's desk.

The young man was a machine, Sheldon thought, nothing more. Not like Walker Danielson, who had an idea or two in his head. Danielson was a good XO, but Sheldon preferred Crosby, who did what he was told and didn't ask questions. No matter what Sheldon wanted him to do, Crosby figured the fact that Sheldon wanted it done was a good enough reason to do it.

Sheldon did not want to give up on the Shifter. The tiger was different, and the research on him had turned up astounding conclusions. Sheldon had seen great potential for either training the tiger or creating new Shifters from him—a body of soldiers who didn't need much food, water, or sleep, who ran straight at enemy fire without quailing, and whose bodies adapted to survive that enemy fire. Shifter soldiers who could be controlled by the shock Collars they already had.

If Sheldon could produce one of these Shifter soldiers—or better still, a platoon of them—it would make his career. Promotion, commendations, field commands—all would come his way.

Sheldon didn't know *how* more Shifters could be created, either through artificial insemination or the usual way, but he didn't care. That was for the scientists in their white lab coats to piece together. He just wanted it done.

But now the Tiger had gone. Walker Danielson thought Sheldon didn't realize that Walker must have something to do with the disappearance. Sheldon was keeping Walker on a long leash, and when he needed to, he'd reel him in.

Meanwhile Sergeant Crosby stood at attention like a vacant statue, awaiting orders. Sheldon had sent the PFC who was his clerk off to stock up on needless supplies so he

could be sure of speaking to Crosby alone and uninter-
rupted.

"DNA," Sheldon said. "We leave it everywhere we go."

Crosby said nothing, though he clearly didn't know
what the hell Sheldon was talking about.

But if Sheldon could get some of the tiger's DNA, his
scientists could do something with it, like analyze its chain
or make clones of this tiger person. Again, Sheldon didn't
know how those things worked; he only knew that if you
wanted something done, you gathered people smart enough
to do it and told them what you expected. If a person didn't
fulfill your expectations, you fired them and found another,
until you'd pulled together a crack team.

"I need the tiger's DNA. I want you to search Carly
Randal's house, top to bottom, for anything of the tiger's—
a strand of hair, his clothes, a hat. If you find nothing there,
search the house in which he used to live, in Shiftertown."

Crosby's eyes widened, the statue flickering the slightest bit. "In Shiftertown, sir?"

"The woman's house is the least dangerous, which is
why I'm sending you there first. But you can handle Shifters, Crosby. You're trained for it."

"Yes, sir," Crosby said.

"Fine. That's your assignment. Dismissed. Oh, and
Crosby—don't mention a word of this to Captain Danielson. On your honor."

"I won't, sir." Crosby saluted, turned on his heels, and
marched out of the room.

Of course he wouldn't, Sheldon thought as Crosby
banged the outer door shut. Crosby never disobeyed. If
Sheldon told Crosby to shoot himself in his own head,
Crosby would probably do it, no questions asked.

The evening after Carly had had her talk with Yvette, she
went home, cooked a large meal, ate it, then went
upstairs to take a bath.

She thought over Yvette's story, how the woman had

willingly turned her back on a potentially brilliant career to help the outcast man she loved. A sweet, romantic tale. Yvette had made her choice, and thirty years later, she still was content with her decision.

Tears filled Carly's eyes as she lay back in the warm bath. Outside, a torrential rain poured down from clouds that had been threatening the city all day. The rain pattered on the roof and beat on the windows, rain rolling down the panes in streaks like tears.

She remembered Tiger saying good-bye, how he'd looked straight into her eyes.

Mate of my heart. You always will be. No matter what.

Carly's stubborn resolve fled as though blown away by the gusts outside. She put her hand over her face and cried.

The watcher waited until the lights went out in Carly's house, then he eased back into the shadows and took up his vigil.

CHAPTER TWENTY-SIX

C arly needed more food. She'd had dinner, a snack after her bath, and then something at bedtime to tide her over. She woke after midnight, stomach growling.

"Geez, you eat a lot, kid," she said, touching her abdomen. "I bet you'll be just like your dad."

That thought brought fresh tears, which Carly had believed she was *done with,* and also a fear. Tiger was such an unusual Shifter. What if Carly's human body wasn't strong enough to carry his child?

She needed to talk to Liam, to tell him, ask his advice. At the same time, Carly feared to. What would the Shifters do when they learned she was pregnant? Ask her to get rid of the baby? Or to go ahead and have the baby but leave it with them to raise?

Carly refused to contemplate either choice. This cub belonged to Tiger and to her, no one else. She wouldn't give it up to be confined, watched, tested, chained, tranquilized, drugged—all the things they'd done to Tiger.

As soon as she made it to the dark kitchen, she knew there was someone else in the house. A breath of air, a scent, a sound . . . She wasn't sure what she sensed, but something had alerted her.

Carly reached for the light switch. At the same time, a male body barreled at her, a punch landed across her face, and Carly tumbled, insensible, to the floor.

She dreamed. She saw Tiger, his hard face and golden eyes, jaw covered with half-grown beard. He fought with a faceless assailant, then he was standing over Carly, touching her, lifting her.

Carly was safe in his arms, her mate holding her and keeping her warm. The dream dissolved, and Carly woke in her bed, the sun rising.

Carly's silk pajamas, top and bottoms, hugged her with warmth, possibly why she'd dreamed of Tiger. But no, she'd gone down to the kitchen, hadn't she? Her stomach felt hollow. Had she eaten or not?

Morning sickness was rearing its ugly head. Didn't matter if Carly had eaten or not—it was coming back.

She made it to the bathroom and lost her load, then she went to the sink to wash her hands and rinse her mouth, as Carly did every morning these days. She raised her head and looked into the mirror . . . and saw the bandages stuck to the side of her face.

"What the hell?" Carly peeled back the tape and found a cut surrounded by a nice bruise right below her left eye.

Flashes of memory returned—Carly going downstairs for yet another snack, sensing someone, trying to turn on the light. The punch, the fall, and then Tiger over her.

Tiger.

No, couldn't be. But who, then, had bandaged her face and put her to bed? She couldn't have done this good a bandaging job in her sleep.

Carly ran from the room and out into her kitchen. She looked wildly around, but she saw nothing out of place. No one here, and no evidence of anyone being there in the night.

Wait, yes there was. Her back door was unlocked. The lock wasn't broken, but someone had unlocked it, either using a key or by picking it, then had closed it nicely without relocking it. Carly clearly remembered checking the doors before she went to bed, as she did every night, and the door had been locked.

In the living room, she found that a sofa pillow was missing from her couch.

Carly stared at the sofa, hands on her hips. What kind of thief picked his way into a house, knocked out a helpless woman, stole her sofa cushion, bandaged her up, and left again, politely closing the door?

Bizarre. She drew a breath, wincing as her bruised cheekbone moved. She let out the breath, locked the kitchen door, and went back to her room to get ready for work.

Connor sat up in bed and yelled. The intruder in the predawn hour was stealthy, almost Shifter stealthy, but he'd made a sound that penetrated Connor's sleep.

Connor was in Tiger's bed, in Tiger's loft room, which used to be Connor's. He hadn't needed to move back in here now that Tiger was gone, but for some reason, Connor felt safer here, as though Tiger's presence had gifted the room with some kind of protective mojo.

Until this morning. The man was a bulky black smudge in the lighter gray of the morning, in black fatigues, with a blackened face and a black knit hat. The only color on him was a couple of Tiger's shirts he had bunched in his hands.

Connor's Shifter took over. His body fought the sudden change, which hurt like hell, and the shirt and underwear he'd slept in tore away. By the time he became his young lion form, the intruder had rushed out the door to the tiny landing.

Connor crouched down on the bed on four paws, and sprang from there to the doorway. Not fast enough. The intruder was down the stairs, and there was Kim, with Katriona, in his path.

Kim screamed but had the sense to move out of the way.

Connor leapt from halfway up the stairs onto the intruder below.

Who rolled out of the way and kept on going down the next flight of stairs. Liam and Sean were coming in the back door by the time Connor made it to the bottom, both running. The human man swung around and charged out the front, Sean and Liam after him.

Connor ran behind them, his tail, which he could never manage, waving in his rage. He galloped out onto the porch and down the steps to find the intruder on his back, having been taken down by Dylan.

Spike was there too, probably for an early tracker meeting or something. The human man looked up at the ring of Shifters around him——Liam, Sean, Dylan, Glory, Andrea, Spike, and Connor, panting behind them.

"Who is this?" Liam's voice held a savage growl, rage working its way up from a deep well. Liam could be laid-back and charm the devil, but Connor knew that his uncle had an ocean of anger, hurt, and grief in him, mostly about the death of Connor's dad, Kenny. Liam had worked through that, and he had Kim now, but when he was very angry, that old bitterness and rage seeped through him to make him a deadly enemy.

The man on the ground kept his mouth shut. Sean reached down, wiped the black off the man's face with a tissue, and remained staring down at him. "No idea who that is," Sean said.

"Some kind of pervert, looks like," Glory said. She ripped Tiger's shirts out of the man's hands. "Stealing Shifter clothes. What were you going to do next, break in and steal my bras?"

"Glory," Andrea said to her aunt in her calm tones like still water.

"Doesn't matter," Glory said, showing her teeth in a smile. "I don't wear any."

The man looked back and forth among them, his expression stoic, but his scent betrayed his alarm. No outright fear though, Connor thought. Strange. The alarm was because he'd been caught.

"What do we do with him?" Liam's question was not so much a question, or at least, it was rhetorical. From Liam's scent and the way his eyes had gone Shifter white blue, he'd already decided what he wanted to do.

"You can't kill him, son," Dylan said quickly. "Not worth the price."

Liam's rage rose, the scent of it hot. "He came into my house. He endangered my mate, my cub, and my brother's cub." Liam had become ultra-protective of Connor, Kenny's son, again going back to taking the blame for Kenny's death.

The intruder now started to exude some fear. Liam wasn't the pushover he appeared to be, and Dylan, a man who looked even more frightening than Liam, was trying to calm *Liam.*

Spike growled in agreement with Liam. Spike, recently discovering he was a father, had become a fierce protector of cubs.

"Hold it together," Sean said, his voice the calmest, but also with an underlying hint of feral anger. "How about we make an example of him?" His smile was frightening. "Sounds like fun."

"Aye," Dylan said.

Connor shifted—painfully—back to his human form, too furious to mind being naked in front of his enemy. "Let me help. He scared the shite out of me."

Andrea moved to Connor's side and slid an arm around his waist. Connor's shakes and pain started to lessen a little. Sean's mate could make people feel better just by being near them—her healer's touch, Connor supposed.

"Kim okay?" Andrea asked him.

"I think so."

Andrea glanced at the house, gave Connor's shoulder a squeeze, and turned away. "I'll just go make sure." She ran lightly up the porch steps and into the house, and Connor moved within the circle of Shifters.

"I have an idea," Liam said, his smile flashing out, but the fury still in his eyes. "Sure, Connor, you can help."

"Great," Connor said. He looked down at the man, who was smelling more and more of worry. "But wait for me a few seconds. I'm gonna need pants."

Crosby found his wrists and ankles wrapped in duct tape, then he was loaded into the bed of a pickup between the shaved-headed tattooed guy and the older guy with the eyes of steel. The two Morrissey brothers and the kid Crosby had woken rode in the truck's cab. A family outing, Crosby thought with grim humor.

They took Crosby to a dirty street in a warehouse district, parking the pickup next to a line of Dumpsters. The Morrisseys piled out of the cab, selected a Dumpster, opened it, and returned to the truck.

All five of the Shifters grabbed Crosby by the legs and arms and lifted him out of the truck.

"One," Liam Morrissey said as they swung Crosby back, then forward. "Two. *Threeee.*"

Crosby felt himself go airborne and land with perfect precision inside the Dumpster, on top of a pile of foul-smelling, slimy trash. He heard the Shifters walk away, laughing, and the truck start.

But they didn't drive away. As Crosby lay motionlessly, waiting for them to go, the square of sky above him darkened and Liam alone looked in and down at Crosby.

"If I see you in or near Shiftertown again," he said in a voice that held the quiet fury of a wild animal, "I will kill you." His laughter was gone, and much of his Irish accent too. All that was left was the calm conviction of a man not afraid to kill. "No one will ever find you. I'll guarantee that."

Crosby believed him. Liam reached for the lid of the Dumpster. He stared a while longer at Crosby, his eyes that strange blue-white, hard to look at. Crosby did his best to appear subdued and nonthreatening.

Liam at last let the lid fall with a clang, shutting out light and fresh air. The truck's door slammed, and this time, the truck drove away.

Crosby started working on the tape around his wrists. Liam's threat didn't bother him, because Crosby had no intention of ever going back to Shiftertown again. He was done with them.

He finished making his way out of the tape, reached under his shirt, and pulled out the thin undershirt he'd managed to stuff inside before the Shifters had caught him and thrown him down. The shirt had belonged to the tiger, and all Crosby had to do was take it to his commander. Mission over.

The art class for the Shifter kids was held in a community center near the gallery. Armand had arranged everything with his usual efficiency.

Carly and Armand started off with a tour of the gallery, showing the cubs the different styles of the artists, from representational art and sculpture to the abstract. Armand talked about texture and how to view a picture with rich texture from the side to get the full effect.

At the community center, Armand demonstrated various techniques, explaining that creating art was not always about simple drawing or blotching paint on canvas. He showed them how etchings were printed, and let the kids pull sheets through the printer to reveal the picture of a wildcat he'd prepared.

Next Armand stood them in front of easels and showed them how to hold pencils and paintbrushes, and then let them choose the medium they liked best for their own projects. Armand was very good at teaching kids how to make art fun.

Carly watched them with interest. Ten Shifter kids had come, from Cherie, nearly twenty-one, to Jordan, Spike's son, aged four. Cherie enjoyed herself drawing tall, long-legged angular women who looked a little like Yvette.

Jordan happily dragged a brush loaded with paint all over his page, leaving thick red and yellow splotches, which he looked very proud of.

Carly thought the cub with most potential was the little polar bear Olaf. He'd chosen watercolors, and had at first painted his entire sheet of watercolor paper black. Once that dried, he scraped away the dried paint with a palette knife to reveal patterns of the white paper underneath, like a negative. The lines resembled large bears, but they were incomplete, featureless. Olaf contemplated them with the dark-eyed seriousness with which Carly had seen him observe the rest of the world.

"That's very nice, Olaf," she said after Armand had bustled out of the room, going for more supplies. "Unique. Can you tell me about it?"

Olaf kept studying the painting-drawing, palette knife in hand. "My parents," he said.

Who were dead, Ronan's mate, Elizabeth, had told Carly. Ronan had discovered Olaf, an orphaned Shifter cub no one knew what to do with, and had taken him in.

Poor kid. Carly opened her mouth to praise his painting again when she smelled smoke.

Cherie smelled it too. She raised her head, her nose wrinkling, her sudden fear showing Carly how young she still was by Shifter standards. Cherie was looking around for an adult Shifter, someone to keep her safe.

Carly saw the ceiling above Cherie give. She grabbed the girl and yanked her out of the way just as a fireball came down and flames exploded through the room.

CHAPTER TWENTY-SEVEN

The room in which Armand taught was in the middle of the two-story building, and had no windows. The explosion shattered the lights, turning the bright space to night, lit by roiling gas-fed flames. Cubs screamed, easels clattered to the floor, and little pots of turpentine popped under the heat, feeding the fire.

Out! They had to get out.

Confusion and noise took over. Carly inhaled smoke and heat, and she gasped for breath, coughing. Dimly she remembered that when people died in a fire, it was often from smoke inhalation, long before the flames reached them.

But she couldn't see to find the doors, couldn't remember where the doors were. If the building had emergency systems, like lit-up exit signs or sprinklers, she saw no sign of them.

They were trapped.

Carly heard the high-pitched keening of Jordan, calling desperately for his daddy, Cherie's sobs of terror, and cries and calls from the other kids. Nothing at all from Olaf.

Stop. Wait. Carly closed her eyes, blotting out the horror. She needed to remember what the room had looked like moments before the explosion. Where everyone was. Who'd been there, who hadn't.

Armand had stepped out to fetch more supplies. Spike and Ellison, who'd accompanied the children, had been wandering in and out of the building. Carly knew enough about Shifters by now to know that they were watching out for danger. But the danger had been inside the room, in the ceiling above it, not outside.

Spike and Ellison, and Armand, would see the flames or the smoke. They'd come and call for help. Meanwhile, Carly had to find the door and get the cubs out.

Oblong room, doors at either end. She and Olaf had been in the center of it, Carly facing the east door, Olaf staring at his picture. Carly had leapt to jerk Cherie out of the way of the falling ceiling, but had Olaf moved in time?

"Olaf!"

Olaf still made no noise, and bile rose in Carly's throat. She couldn't breathe, she had to get out, to save the cub inside her.

Her fire-safety training, which Armand made all his employees take, cut through her fear. Smoke rose. "Down! Everybody down! Crawl toward the walls, find the doors!"

Carly's voice, ringing with authority, cut through the screaming. The cubs, used to obeying the alpha Shifters, dropped to the floor, their yelling dying to whimpering.

Carly got to her hands and knees and started across the room, groping for any of the cubs along the way. After a few moments, she found her hands full of soft but wiry fur, then the white face of a small polar bear looked out of the hell at her.

"Olaf." Carly exhaled in relief, then regretted breathing out. Breathing in hurt. "Find the door, Olaf. Or at least the wall. Can you do that?"

Olaf turned around and started walking but stopped abruptly when Carly let go of him, and waited. Carly caught on after a second—Olaf wanted to lead her to safety.

Carly held on to his fur again and let him pull her along, she half crawling alongside him. She passed another cub on the way and scooped him up, setting him on Olaf's strong back.

Olaf made it to the wall, then put his shoulder to it and slid along the wall until he found the door. Lungs nearly bursting, Carly pushed at the door, but it wouldn't move. Jammed? Or locked?

"Cherie!"

Cherie could turn into a grizzly bear. If the door was stuck, even a half-grown grizzly would be of more use than a human, a polar bear cub, and another child paralyzed with fear.

"Cherie, we need you!"

Cherie didn't answer. Olaf made a little growl in his throat, then he scampered back into the fire. Carly shouted after him, but in a few seconds, Olaf returned, his mouth around Cherie's hand.

Carly rose, seized Cherie by the arms, and pulled her down to the floor with the rest of them. She put her hands on Cherie's shoulders and looked into her face. "Cherie, you need to shift. I need someone strong to push open the door."

"The door won't open?" Cherie's eyes were unfocused, the girl clearly terrified.

"Please." Carly shook her. "I need you to be a bear right now. Shift!"

Cherie stared at Carly a moment longer in incomprehension, then she nodded. Shaking fingers fumbled at her blouse, and Carly had to help her pull it off. By the time Cherie had shed enough clothes, the young woman's instincts took over, and she began to change.

It was painful for her, Carly saw, Cherie letting out noises of anguish as her face elongated into the bear's, her hands and feet curving to accommodate grizzly claws.

Carly scrambled back as Cherie grew and changed until a grizzly, easily as large as a wild one, stood next to them. Cherie rose on her hind legs, growling, and pounded on the door with her massive paws. The door at last broke under her onslaught, spilling her, Carly, and the cubs out into the corridor.

But instead of the refuge Carly pictured, she saw more fire. Flames licked down the walls, the way out of the building blocked.

"Damn it!"

At least there was more air out here. For now.

The studio lay on the second floor, but there were other rooms up here, rooms with windows. If Carly could gather the cubs into one of them, she could open a window where the fire department might reach them and get them down. Even better if she could find a fire escape.

Carly hurried down the hall, trying the doors she could reach. All were locked.

Shit, what was wrong with this place? No sprinklers, no alarms, locked doors, no marked exits . . .

But there *were* sprinklers. Carly glimpsed them in the ceiling, and she saw the alarms on the walls waiting to be pulled. Everything going wrong at the same time was too much of a coincidence.

This fire had been set deliberately, the cubs and Carly trapped inside the room on purpose.

Carly would have to save her fury at whoever would be twisted enough to set fire to a building with kids inside for later. Right now they had to get out.

"Cherie!" she called. Cherie came to her at once, the large bear shivering as she leaned on Carly. Looking for reassurance, Carly realized. And for someone to tell her what to do.

Carly put her arm around the bear's shoulders, giving her a half hug. "We'll get out of this, Cherie. And you're going to help me. Can you break that glass? There's a fire extinguisher."

What a small extinguisher would do against a giant rampage of flame, Carly didn't know, but it couldn't hurt, and it would give Cherie something constructive to do.

Cherie bounded to the extinguisher, her tread shaking

the floor. With one blow of her large paw, she shattered the glass case. Carly snatched up the extinguisher inside, bigger and heavier than the one they kcpt at the gallery, and cranked it on.

The extinguisher, at least, worked. Fire retardant spewed from its hose, keeping the advancing flames from reaching this part of the hall. Carly dragged the thing back into the studio from which cubs were still straggling out, spraying what she could.

She yelled at Cherie to start trying to break down the other doors. Cherie obeyed, the tiles vibrating under Carly's feet every time Cherie's heavy body hit a door.

Carly kept spraying the studio. She was coughing though, not finding air. The cubs surrounded Carly, holding each other, holding her. She did a head count and nearly cried with relief when she counted eight—nine and ten were Cherie and Olaf in the hall.

Her effort with the fire extinguisher was working somewhat, tamping down the immediate flames. Carly led the cubs out of the studio again, squirting at fire as she went, taking the kids to where Cherie was still trying to open a door.

All the doors seemed to be sealed shut, or bolted. They were steel doors, and Cherie was denting them, but none had broken open.

But they had a chance. Carly kept spraying, Cherie kept beating at the doors, Olaf trying to help. The rest of the cubs huddled around Carly, Jordan holding on to one of her legs.

All would have been well, Carly thought, if not for the next explosion that ripped down the hall, shooting another inferno into the corridor.

He barreled through them all, the barricades, the firefighters, the police who tried to stop him. He broke anything in his way, including the front door that already sagged from its hinges, and leapt into a fiery nightmare.

It was black-dark and hot, smoke pouring through the corridor. He'd never been in this building before, never been near it until he'd followed Carly and Armand here today.

No matter. Tiger's well-honed sense of smell told him the cubs were above him, trapped on the second floor. It also told him the jaguar and large gray wolf at the end of the hall were frustrated by the barricade that blocked their way up the stairs.

The debris included part of the walls, the pipes, the ceiling. Spike and Ellison were trying to climb over it, but with every leap or step, the pile shifted, sending them down again.

Tiger growled, shaking the air. Ellison and Spike swung around, wolf and jaguar staring in surprise before turning back to the task of climbing up the blockage.

Tiger bounded past them. He stretched his big body and leapt up the mounded debris, finding holds that had eluded the other two, until he made it to the top. From here, it was a short leap to the next floor, but Spike and Ellison were snarling beneath him.

Tiger slid a few inches back toward them, speaking in growls. *Grab on, assholes. Hurry up.*

Ellison's wolf understood, and he reached up to clamp his mouth around the base of Tiger's tail. Spike, behind him, wrapped his jaguar paws around Ellison.

Tiger leapt. He used claws and paws to scramble up through the hole to the next floor, the weight of the other two barely slowing him. When they reached level flooring, Spike and Ellison dropped off, and all three faced a corridor littered with burning beams.

Tiger ran. His body stretched and bunched as he plowed through the flaming mess, closing his eyes against the black smoke. He knew where Carly was without having to look. The mate bond was taut like a stretched rubber band, pulling him straight to her.

He found Carly on her back on the floor, inches from a burning beam, her body still. Tiger roared, shaking loose more debris, and cubs screamed.

The jaguar ran by. Jordan shouted, opening his arms. Spike caught Jordan's shirt with his teeth, flipping the little boy up and onto his back.

Cherie in her grizzly form was hunkered next to Carly, and she raised her muzzle in a mournful howl. Olaf, in his human form, sat on Carly's other side, holding Carly's hand.

Tiger's heart pounded as he slid to a halt, but he knew Carly wasn't dead. The mate bond was still there, as was the bond to her cub.

But she was unconscious, Carly's face ashen in the light of the fire. Cherie rocked next to her, moaning.

Tiger nuzzled Carly's face, taking her scent, sending reassurances through the bond. Then he turned and grabbed at the handle of the nearest door, the heat of it singeing his paws.

Olaf, serious-faced, said, "We tried to open the doors. They're blocked. Is Carly dying?"

Tiger saw where Cherie had dented two of the steel doors. He grabbed for the handle of one of the bent ones, but the door handle snapped off, and Tiger slipped to the floor.

He stood again, shaking himself out, letting rage take over. Cherie couldn't budge the door, but Cherie hadn't been created in a lab where breaking through doors had been part of her training. After a while, the researchers had had to make Tiger's cage doors about two feet thick.

Tiger backed up, lunged, and hit the door with all four paws, full force. The door groaned under the onslaught, bent some more, then broke from the wall and skittered inside the room. Tiger rode the door through the flames, through burning tables and chairs, and slammed into a wall under a window. The shades were down, but Tiger ripped the shades from the wall and then yanked the window out of the wall as well.

Firemen below yelled, signaling the ladder truck to move its position. Tiger dropped the window and ran back through broken glass to the corridor.

He grabbed Ellison by the scruff of the neck and dragged him to Carly. Ellison, catching on, shifted to human, his skin breaking into sweat from the fire's heat. Ellison lifted Carly over his shoulders and ran with her to the window.

No time to wait to see whether the ladder trucks came for her—Tiger had to get the others out.

Spike ran by with Jordan on him as well as one other cub, and into the room with the open window. The cubs scrambled from his back to the windowsill.

Tiger growled at Cherie. She shook herself, recognizing the commander in Tiger. Three more of the cubs fit on her back, and she ran through the burning door to the next room.

Four cubs remained, including Olaf. Tiger lowered himself and they climbed onto him, clinging to his fur. A sweat-streaked fireman appeared at the window, reaching for Carly, and then another fireman came behind him. Spike and Ellison stayed with the cubs, helping and calming them, while the firemen lifted them out.

They'd make it.

As soon as the thought formed in Tiger's head, another explosion sounded, blasting Tiger and his load of cubs back into the hall. The steel doorframe of the doorway to safety folded in on itself as the wall broke apart and fell.

The explosion had come from above, and now the corridor's ceiling collapsed, burying Tiger and all four cubs under burning wreckage.

CHAPTER TWENTY-EIGHT

Carly swam to wakefulness, and thought she was being smothered. She grabbed for the thing that pressed her face and found a plastic mound, then saw the dark face of an EMT behind it.

"Take it easy," the man said. "You're fine. You just need oxygen. You're pregnant, aren't you?" Carly nodded, the mask moving with her. "We'll get you to a hospital and have both you and the baby checked out. All right?"

Carly lifted the mask from her mouth. "Where are the others?"

The EMT pressed the mask back into place. "They're coming out. Your boss said there were ten kids. That right?"

Carly nodded again, tears leaking from her eyes.

"Some crazy tiger ran in there after them." The EMT shook his head. "I guess he was one of those Shifters. We couldn't stop him."

Tiger? Carly couldn't shout questions with the oxygen mask over her face. More tears came. Tiger had returned. And he was saving the cubs.

She made herself relax, to breathe the healing oxygen

and not move. Tiger would come out, he'd have the cubs, and all would be well.

There was a *whump,* and firemen shouting, and a huge plume of flame and smoke shot from the building's roof, high into the blue of the afternoon sky. Every window showed fire, and a part of the building collapsed.

Carly screamed. She ripped off the mask and tried to scramble from the stretcher. The EMT, a strong Hispanic man with muscles almost as big as a Shifter's, pushed her back down. "No, you stay *here.*"

"Did they get out?" Carly yelled. "Did they get out?"

"I don't know. We'll find out, okay?"

Carly clutched the padded sides of the stretcher, staring at the building until her eyes ached. Ellison and Spike were on the ground, human now, leading Cherie and the cubs to the parking lot. Other Shifters had arrived, Liam and Dylan, Sean and Ronan. Ronan ran for Cherie, now a human girl again, and caught her in his arms. He led her away, snatching the blanket a fireman brought them and wrapping it around her.

Cubs: one, two, three, four, five, and Cherie. Six. The rest must be inside with Tiger.

Carly scrambled off the stretcher again, holding the mask to her face. She could barely see through smoke and tears, or through the crowd of people and emergency vehicles. All she could make out was that the small community center was now a flaming wreck, collapsing on itself, with Tiger and the cubs inside.

Shouting sounded at the front of the building. The rest of the med team started that way, running, running.

Smoke billowed from the front door, and people scattered. Through the opening, parting the smoke and haloed by flame, ran Tiger. His fur was blackened, body moving fast, children clinging to his back.

He stopped as the medics ran forward, Tiger dropping flat on his belly so the kids—three of them—could drop from his back. The medics swept them up, and Liam and Dylan surrounded the kids and EMTs.

Only three cubs.

Carly threw down the oxygen mask and darted away from the EMT, running, stumbling, toward the entrance and Tiger.

Tiger was already climbing to his feet as she sprinted forward. "Olaf!" she yelled. "Where's Olaf?"

She had to stop as coughing wracked her, more gook in her lungs coming out. Ronan released Cherie and pushed her at Sean.

Tiger had turned for the building even before Carly had shouted about Olaf. Another explosion lit up the world, the community center now nothing but flames surrounding a shell.

Tiger ran right into it.

Carly collapsed, sitting down hard on the ground. Tiger's body was outlined in flame for a brief instant, then he was gone.

There was no longer any up or down, backward or forward. There was only flame, and the melting floor searing Tiger's feet, his fur burning. Trying to see was useless, so Tiger closed his eyes.

Numbers whirled across the insides of his eyelids— coordinates, angles, distances. Every piece of data about the building as it had stood condensed itself into formula, and danced before him.

Tiger had known exactly when Olaf had fallen, but Tiger hadn't been able to stop his forward momentum to snatch him up. The other cubs had been falling too, sliding, coughing. Tiger had put on a burst of speed to take them to safety.

The new explosion complicated things, but Tiger moved unerringly through the flames, eyes closed, stopping at the small limp body of the polar bear cub. He reached down and gently picked up Olaf by the scruff of his neck.

Then Tiger turned and ran. Fire tried to stop him. It

burned him, his fur singeing with an acrid stench, his sinews melting. But Tiger kept going.

The door wasn't where he'd left it. Tiger closed his eyes again, relaxing his mind, letting the numbers come. Why they were there, and how Tiger understood them, he didn't know, but it didn't matter. With the strings of numbers to guide him, Tiger ran directly to the last door in the building that existed and out into daylight.

A giant Kodiak bear caught Olaf as he fell from Tiger's numb grip. The Kodiak turned into Ronan, who lifted the unconscious Olaf into his arms and ran with him toward a medical team.

Tiger collapsed. His lungs were liquid, his coat gone, fire dissolving his skin. He couldn't move, couldn't breathe, couldn't make a sound.

He heard Carly's voice—*my mate*—and dragged open his eyes. He saw Carly, her hair scraggly and singed, her clothes burned, blood on her arms and legs. But she was safe.

Tiger let out a sigh. Carly was too far away from him, but she was safe.

Tiger focused then on his immediate surroundings, and found the barrels of a dozen automatic weapons pointed at his head.

Tiger groaned. He couldn't move. He lay supine in his human form, chained down, too exhausted to shift to the tiger.

They'd chained him like this in the hospital, and before that, in the research facility where he'd been made. Only this time, there was no leaping up in rage, no breaking the chains. Tiger was weak, and he was dying. But then, he'd been burned to death today.

Was it still today? Or had days and nights passed? Tiger had no idea.

The cubs were safe. Carly was safe. Nothing else mattered.

At one point, men in white masks came and drew blood out of Tiger's arm, and scraped skin cells from his armpit, the only place he hadn't burned.

Most of his skin was gone. Tiger was surprised he could see or hear, but those senses seemed to function, though his left eye, when he pried it open, showed him nothing but a milk-white fog.

He had his sense of smell too, because he could smell himself, and it wasn't good. Taste, he wasn't certain, except for the dry sourness in his mouth. They gave him no water but pumped fluids into his veins through an IV.

Tiger definitely had his sense of feeling. He was in excruciating pain.

He wasn't sure who was keeping him prisoner this time, but it must be Shifter Bureau. The men who'd come for him had looked like they were from Walker's unit.

But it no longer mattered. Carly was safe. His cub was safe. Tiger had seen the magical threads of the mate bond shimmering between them—intact and still strong.

More time passed. More blood, more skin cells taken, a change of the IV drip bag. Tiger couldn't make his mouth work to ask what the white-coated medics were doing to him or why.

He drifted to troubled sleep. The next time he opened his eyes, two researchers were standing over him. Past and present melded, and Tiger started to think he'd dreamed being released from the research lab, and everything that had happened since.

"A couple more samples," one said. "Then he's done."

"Done?"

"Terminated. He's beyond saving."

"Shame," the other man said. "Would have been interesting to study him."

"Orders are orders," the first man said. "But we can dissect him. See what's inside."

"That'll work."

Tiger wanted to leap up and onto them, to tear them down. But he lay inert, his body refusing to obey.

He needed Carly. Wanted her so much. She hadn't been a dream. Carly was very real.

Tiger fought to rise, to get out of this place before they killed him, to get to Carly, but he managed only to fall asleep again.

He saw Carly, her red lips and wide smile, her sexy legs, the way she closed her beautiful eyes when she leaned in to kiss him. The position let Tiger see her soft breasts behind the neckline of whatever dress she wore that day, made him want to cup her in his hands, lick her, close his mouth over her breast. She made such pretty noises when he did that.

Carly, he tried to say. A faint croak issued from his throat.

Tiger forced the name out. "Carly."

"Sorry, my friend." He thought Walker leaned over him. "I'm not as pretty. But now I know what you are." The man wore a look of triumph. "Or at least, what you're for."

Oh goody, Tiger wanted to say in Connor's most withering tones. *I'd been so worried about that.*

"I've brought someone to see you."

Tiger's heart squeezed with fear. No. Not Carly. This place wasn't safe. She couldn't be here.

The person who walked forward at Walker's gesture wasn't Carly, but Liam.

"You were a bit of a hero out there," Liam said, his smart-ass Irish grin in place. "I'm thinking my humble home won't be big enough to hold you now, but I'm going to take you there anyway. Carly, now, she told me to bring you back with me, or not to bother coming back at all."

Carly sat on the edge of the big bed in the attic room of Liam's house and looked down at Tiger. She feared to touch him, since what was left of his skin was black and brittle. Any human, probably any other Shifter, would be dead by now.

It was night, Tiger's room lit by one small lamp. The

rest of the house had gone to bed, but Carly hadn't wanted to leave Tiger alone in the dark.

The usually quiet Olaf had been regaling everyone in sight, repeatedly for the last couple of days, about how he'd thought he was dead, and then Tiger ran in through the flames and rescued him. Ran in, straight to him, Olaf said in awe, and out again.

Olaf had begged for paper and paints so he could draw Carly a picture, and Armand happily supplied them. Olaf had submerged himself in art, painting a picture of a huge tiger carrying a little polar bear, both surrounded by flames. No more abstract images without faces—Olaf's tiger had Tiger's face and ferocious snarl.

"You're a hero," Carly said softly to Tiger now. "The newspapers and TV are full of it. Especially after the convenience store clerk recognized you and said you were the guy who'd stopped the robbery too. A Shifter superhero. You'll probably end up in a graphic novel."

Tiger didn't answer. He hadn't for the day and night he'd lain here. He hadn't healed either. No change in him at all.

"Ethan is leaving me alone," Carly said. "Armand's lawyer talked to Ethan's lawyer, and Ethan's been advised that since he did cheat on me, and because you're so popular right now, he should leave you alone. And me. That's good. I don't care if I never see Ethan again."

Tiger lay silently, breaking Carly's heart.

She gave in to tiredness and stretched out beside him. She was fine, despite the ordeal, fortunately. The medics, the emergency room doctor, and then her own doctor had confirmed that though she had cuts and bruises, and would have a sore throat for a while, she'd suffered no worse damage. Her child was fine too. Thank God.

Carly propped herself on her elbow. Tiger's face was half-black, one eye closed tightly, the other resting more naturally, unburned. His lips were partially burned, only one side of them pink and strong. He'd been burned as a tiger, but she supposed his human form retained the relative placement of the burns.

"My doctor was pleased at how resilient our little guy is. Or girl. I don't know yet." Carly touched her abdomen. "He—or she—will be strong, like their daddy."

Tiger remained silent, unmoving. Not even a finger twitch. He was breathing, shallowly, and that was all.

Andrea had been by twice to work her healing magic on him, which was likely why Tiger was breathing at all, but Andrea had said she'd done all she could. Nature had to take its course.

"My mother was so excited when she heard the story," Carly said. "She hadn't realized you were a Shifter—but then, you didn't have your Collar when you met her. All my sisters are happy, in fact. They keep calling me. I had to tell them to stop it and give me a break. They want to throw us a party when you're better. Yvette and Armand do too, and with the way Yvette cooks, you know it will be good."

Carly didn't expect Tiger to answer. She talked because she needed to talk.

"Liam rescued you, you know. Walker got clearance for Liam to go to the camp and see you. Not, of course, for Liam to pick you up and haul you away. They sneaked you out in Walker's truck. He's here, by the way. Walker, I mean. He's excited about you too, keeps saying he needs to talk to you, and won't tell the rest of us about what. He's also pretty sure he'll face a disciplinary hearing, but he said he's not worried."

No sound. A light breeze made the shade tap at the window, and far away a Shifter wolf howled. Here, all was silence.

Carly remembered their night in this bed, the two of them learning the wonder of each other's bodies. Her child had been conceived then.

She thought about Tiger's hard, male beauty, the way his eyes went dark when he was ready to come, how he held her tenderly, just stopping himself from giving her raw, rough sex.

The feeling of him inside her, deep and tight, with Carly rocking on him, then him driving into her, had been mo-

mentous. In all her life, Carly had never experienced anything like it.

In the night, they'd touched, kissed, licked, tasted. He'd
loved her slowly, first on top of her. Then they'd rolled onto
their sides, Carly's leg around his hip, while Tiger eased
inside her again. He'd liked that position, where he could
smooth back her hair, kiss her forehead, slide his hand
down to cup her breast.

Now the beautiful man lay immobile, almost unrecog-
nizable. He must be in terrible pain.

"I wish you weren't hurt so bad," Carly said. "I'm scared."

The word broke on a sob. One tear dropped and touched
his burned skin.

Tiger made a small noise, a grunt or a sigh. Carly leaned
forward, half-afraid, half-hopeful, but the sound wasn't
repeated.

"You told me that a mate's touch healed." Carly held her
fingertips above his face. "But I'm afraid to touch you now."
She let her finger brush the unburned part of his lips, the
lightest stroke. "So I'll just tell you that I've decided I'm
definitely your mate."

No response. Carly touched the corner of his mouth
again, marveling that the unburned part of his lips could be
warm and soft despite his terrible hurts. "Mate of my
heart," she whispered.

She lay down beside him again, pulling a sheet over herself, careful not to let the fabric touch him. Carly didn't
think she'd sleep, but her exhaustion and worry caught up
to her, and she drifted off.

Crosby slid in through the open window, landed noiselessly on the floor, and had his target in visual. These
bungalows were too easy to break into, windows in the upper
floors in reach from the porch roofs, handholds galore.
Scouting this house the last time had made this entry even
easier.

Without changing position, Crosby eased his gun out of its holster.

The woman was on the bed with the Shifter, but it didn't matter. She wasn't the target. Crosby would finish this mission, return to camp, report in, and either sleep or carry on with his next assignment.

He crept to the bed, quietly eased a pillow from the foot of it to use as a silencer, put the pillow over Tiger's chest, and started to squeeze the trigger.

His wristbone shattered as a hugely strong hand closed around it, the gun twisting away to shoot the wall. The pillow fell and the gun went off loudly.

The woman, Carly, screamed and shot out of bed. What held Crosby's wrist was the tiger, half-burned, looking more like a corpse than a human. One of his eyes was white and unseeing, the other yellow with rage.

The tiger Shifter spoke, his voice raw and broken. "Don't. Hurt. My mate."

Crosby tried to jerk away, and agony shocked through him. He couldn't draw breath to explain that no, he wasn't here to hurt the woman. Only the tiger.

The door slammed open, nearly tearing off its hinges, and the Shifter called Liam came in. Crosby remembered what Liam had said about catching Crosby in Shiftertown again, and he felt fear. Crosby never felt fear. This was new.

"Tiger," the woman was saying, but not in alarm. In surprise, probably because the half-dead tiger was still alive.

Liam closed his hand around the back of Crosby's neck. Crosby still held his Glock, but he couldn't turn it or fire it, because his fingers didn't work.

Liam twisted the gun from Crosby's inert hand. "Tiger, let him go. I'll take care of this."

"Who the hell *is* he?" Carly shouted at Liam. "How did he get in?"

Crosby felt disgust. If any woman had snapped a demand like that at Crosby, he'd backhand her. Shifters really should control their women better.

"He's more determined than I thought," Liam said grimly. "Tiger, I said let him go. You need to save your strength."

The tiger's fury didn't abate, but he opened his hand and released Crosby's wrist. Without the clamp of the tiger's fingers, Crosby's wrist went slack, and the broken bones shot white-hot pain through him.

"You're awake," Carly said to the tiger, joy in her voice. "Moving. Stronger."

Tiger looked at her, then the light of rage left his eyes, and he fell back to the bed. "The touch of a mate," he said, then his eyes closed.

Carly shot Crosby a look of fury. "Bastard. If you've made him worse . . ."

Stupid bitch. "My orders are to kill him," Crosby said. "He's dying anyway."

"Then why try to kill him?" Carly snapped.

"A good question," Liam said, his grip strengthening on Crosby's neck. "Do you know the answer?"

Crosby did, because the LTC had told him. "We have enough DNA samples. The tiger Shifter is useless now. He needs to die and be taken back to camp for cremation. He can't be allowed to fall into enemy hands." No reason to keep it a secret. The LTC hadn't said the info was classified.

Liam shook him a little. "And by enemy hands, you mean . . . ?"

"Anyone not Lieutenant Colonel Sheldon," said a new voice. Captain Walker Danielson, the insubordinate, disrespectful asshole, entered the room. Not that Crosby would ever call anyone of senior rank that out loud.

"Anyone who might get the glory for learning what Tiger is and what he can do," the captain continued.

"No, sir," Crosby said crisply. "Enemy intelligence. Enemy armies. Enemy governments."

"Them too," the captain answered in the tone that always sounded like he was making fun of Crosby. Crosby hated that.

"The tiger can't fall into hostile hands," Crosby repeated.

"That's why I'm here," Walker said. "Dismissed, Sergeant."

"Respectfully, sir, my orders are from the LTC. Above your head, sir."

Walker shrugged and addressed Liam. "It's your house. Escort him out. I don't want to know what you do."

"Aye, and I wasn't going to tell you." Liam turned Crosby and marched him out the door, the hand around Crosby's neck immovable.

CHAPTER TWENTY-NINE

Liam took Crosby down the stairs, out of the house, and along the yards behind the Shifters' houses. No other Shifters were in sight, windows and doors closed up tight.

Liam walked Crosby to a stand of trees that formed a sort of ring. A mist floated there, and only there, but Crosby was interested solely in the pain in his wrist and in planning how to get away from Liam to complete his mission. He couldn't return to Sheldon to confess a failure.

A second Shifter creature emerged, walking through the mists. Dylan, Liam's father. Dylan was more problematic. He was older and more experienced than his son, and his eyes told Crosby he'd do what it took to stop him.

"I told you before, son," Dylan said to Liam. "You can't kill him. You have too many others depending on you."

"I know." Liam squeezed Crosby's neck, fingers biting down with terrible strength. "But maybe we can make an exception this once?"

"No."

More pressure on Crosby's neck. At any moment, a

vertebra would burst. "You know that this asshole started the fire."

Dylan gave Liam a nod. "Yes."

"Then you know why I need to kill the gobshite." Liam's voice was low, not carrying, but fierce, bearing a note of rage Crosby hadn't heard from him before.

Dylan turned his gaze to Crosby. "What was your purpose?"

Liam snarled. "Does it matter?"

"I want to know." Dylan fixed Crosby with a steady stare, his eyes as cold as icebergs. "Speak."

Crosby shrugged the best he could. "I was told to smoke out the tiger Shifter. My commander suspected he was hanging around the area. He said if we put his woman in danger, he'd come." Crosby felt a bit smug. "He was right."

"But there were cubs in the community center," Dylan said in his chill voice. "Children. Babies."

"Not children," Crosby corrected him. Crosby would never hurt a kid, or a female, unless they deserved it. "They were only Shifter get, the woman a Shifter whore."

One of Crosby's vertebrae crackled this time. "You're dying for that," Liam said. "Sorry, Dad."

"No." Dylan's word was quiet but rang with authority.

Father and son studied each other for a long time. Finally Liam sighed and released Crosby's neck. Crosby's knees buckled, but he was pulled upright by the equally strong hand of Dylan.

"All right." Liam looked at his father again, then without further word, he turned his back and walked away.

Mists from the trees swirled around Crosby and Dylan, cutting off Liam, cutting off Shiftertown.

"You won't die for what you just said," Dylan said in a mild tone. "Not for ignorant words."

Crosby started to relax. If Dylan was adamant about keeping him alive, then Crosby might be able to get away, get back into the house, and somehow kill the tiger, and then worry about escaping. The mission came first.

Dylan's hand clamped down on Crosby's neck, harder than Liam's had. Dylan's mouth came close to Crosby's ear. "You'll die for nearly killing our cubs. For that, may the Goddess help you." He turned his head and stared straight into the mists. "Fionn!"

The mists thickened, and a slit of light about ten feet high snapped open. A tall man, with limbs so long they looked as though they'd been stretched, appeared in the opening. The man was dressed like an old-fashioned warrior, with long white braids, chain mail, leather, and furs.

"Come," he said.

Dylan shoved Crosby through the slit and followed.

The air became clammy and damp, and also brighter, as though the sun had suddenly risen. The ground was spongy underfoot, no more Texas dryness.

Crosby knew he was in a different place, more like the jungles of Central America, but cold. What the fuck? The slit in the air disappeared. No way back, no more Austin, no more Shiftertown.

Dylan spun Crosby to face him. Dylan's eyes had gone white, the hand holding Crosby changing to the paws of a huge cat.

"I'm trying to teach my son mercy and restraint," Dylan said to Crosby, his voice guttural. "Because I don't have any myself."

"There's no law against vengeance here," the tall man said in a tone of satisfaction. "In fact, it's required."

"For the cubs," Dylan said, and finally Crosby thought to give in to his fear.

He beheld the nightmare that was the truth of Dylan, and that was the last thing he ever saw.

Tiger didn't move again or speak for the rest of the night. Carly slept fitfully, even after reassurances that Crosby had been dealt with. Having a gun go off next to her when she'd been sound asleep had not been a happy experience.

Morning light streamed through the windows, touching

Tiger's face with gentle fingers. The air was cooler now as August waned toward September. The pressing heat of summer had broken.

Carly thought Tiger looked better. The unburned part of his face was flushed instead of deathly pale, and his scalp where his hair had burned was pink instead of black.

Tiger opened his eyes. Maybe the rosy hue of sunrise made his hurt eye look a little clearer—golden instead of white.

"Tiger?" Carly whispered.

Tiger turned his his head the tiniest bit. His face drew down, the movement painful. "Carly." His voice was barely audible, a rasp.

"I'm here."

"Touch me."

Carly blinked, clenching her hand. "I don't want to hurt you."

"Touch . . . me." He exhaled the last word, his eyes closing again.

Carly swallowed and brushed her fingertips over the clear part of his face. As it had been last night, the unburned part of his lips was satin smooth, his face smooth too, every whisker singed away.

She ran her hand down his neck, finding the unhurt patches, across his shoulder and down the slice of chest that was firm flesh. Back to his face again, then she slowly, carefully bent over him and kissed the corner of his mouth.

"Carly," he whispered. Was his voice stronger? "Mate of my heart."

"Yes." Carly kissed him again. "You said we had a mate bond. I believe you now." She put her hand to her chest. "I feel it. I swear I do."

Tiger closed his raw-red fingers around hers and guided her hand to a space between her chest and his. "There."

Carly thought she felt something, a faint tingle that moved from her hand up her arm to warm her behind her breastbone.

"Is that the mate bond?"

Tiger gave her a slow nod, his eyes warming. He moved his hand and hers together over her abdomen. "My cub. *Our* cub. Another bond."

"I can't wait to meet him." Carly said, carefully caressing his fingers. "Or her."

"The bonds heal me," Tiger whispered. "Magic."

Carly smiled. "There's no such thing."

"Shifters have Fae magic. Fionn said I had none, but there is something. I see the magic, the bonds, the threads." He touched his own eyes, his voice gaining a little strength as he spoke. "I can see things in the dark. Know where they are. I saw Olaf."

"When you went back into the building, I thought both of you would be dead." She swallowed on the last words, the remembered dread filling her throat.

"I saw him," Tiger said. "When I closed my eyes, my brain told me where he was. And he was—in the exact spot."

"Your brain told you," Carly repeated. "What does that mean?"

"I don't know. But I can see things that are true, even when others can't."

"Like when you knew my sister was pregnant," Carly said slowly. "And when you knew I was, when it had been only a day."

Tiger gave her another nod. "I saw it, the life inside you, and knew we had created it. And the day I first met you, you standing on the side of the road, I saw the mate bond. I knew you for my mate, and my world changed."

Carly gave him a little smile. "So you kept telling me."

"I saw what was there. Before it was clear to anyone else." Tiger lifted her hand to his lips and kissed it. "That is my magic."

"But no one ever believes you. Not even me. What good does it do you?"

"It doesn't matter," Tiger said. "*I* know."

No, it didn't matter. Tiger was always proved right in the end. As much as the other Shifters thought him frightening, ignorant of Shifter ways, and not one of them, Tiger was . . . Tiger. He was unique, amazing, smarter than anyone would ever understand.

"All right, then, hotshot," Carly said. "Why don't you know your own name?"

Tiger let out a breath. "Maybe I do know it. Maybe I've known all this time."

"Tigger," Carly said, straight-faced.

Tiger rumbled a laugh. "I'd like it."

"So, not Rory?"

"What is your saying? *Not only no, but . . .*"

"All right, all right." Carly waved her hands. "What is it, then?"

Tiger touched Carly's face, and that touch was definitely stronger. "You have always called me Tiger. And you are my mate. So . . . that is my name."

Carly gave a soft laugh. "Wait, you want to go the rest your life being called *Tiger*? It will look weird on the birth certificate. Mother, Carly Randal. Father, Tiger."

"Father. That will be the best name. Or Dad."

Carly caught her breath. She pictured a cute kid, like Jordan or Olaf, looking up at Tiger with his same golden eyes, and saying "Daddy." She wanted to cry.

"Mate of my heart," Tiger said, tugging her closer. "Come here and kiss me."

Carly leaned to him and kissed the corner of his lips again, trying to be careful.

Tiger slid his good arm around her neck and pulled her down for a true and thorough kiss. Nothing wrong with his mouth.

When he eased away, Carly looked down into the face that she loved, no matter what. Tiger's left eye was definitely clearer, the golden iris coming into view. Both eyes fixed on Carly, strength returning.

"The touch of a mate," Tiger said. "Heals. Which means you need to keep kissing me."

Carly laughed as he pulled her back down, then she gave herself over to healing him the only way she knew how.

* * *

Tiger did mend, inside and out, but it took days, and it was painful. But Andrea confirmed that though Tiger had been as near to death as anyone could get, his thread of life barely intact, he would make it.

Andrea came over many times in the next few days, she and Sean lending healing strength through her gift and the Guardian's sword. At least Tiger didn't have to worry about seeing the big sword coming toward his heart to send him to the afterlife. Not yet.

One morning about a week later, Tiger opened his eyes to find Carly at his side. She'd insisted on sleeping with him every night, and she slept now, her head on one hand, her sleek hair in fine strands on the pillow.

Tiger immediately knew he was well. His skin was whole—the pain that lingered was like the remnants of a sunburn. He'd gotten his first sunburn this spring, a new and interesting sensation.

Tiger had slept without covers, but a thin sheet hugged Carly's breasts, her dusky areolas showing through the pale cloth. Her hip rose in a sweet curve, legs stretched out and touching Tiger's.

Tiger gently pushed Carly onto her back, peeling the sheet from her and replacing its drape with his body. His ready cock nudged between her legs.

Carly stirred, woke, smiled. "Hey there. I guess you're feeling better."

Tiger wanted to tell her he loved her, that he loved waking up next to her, that he was grateful beyond words for what she'd done for him, but his throat closed up, and he couldn't speak. His need climbed, the mating frenzy tapping him.

Carly stretched, saying "Hmm," then she brought her arms around him. "I've missed you."

That, Tiger could respond to. His voice rasped. "I missed you every day, every hour, every second."

"Then why did you go? What were you doing all this time? I was going crazy without you."

Tiger's fears, which had been dulled by pain, rose again. "I wanted you to be safe. So that if they came for me, they wouldn't hurt you. But I couldn't stay away. I had to protect you, to watch over you."

"That *was* you in my house, saving me and bandaging me up." Carly touched her face, where the bruises had been. "And what was with stealing my sofa cushion? Which I found in my yard, unsalvageable."

"The man Crosby took it," Tiger said. "He dropped it when he ran."

"He broke into my house to steal a cushion. What a weirdo."

"Connor said he broke in here too, stealing my shirts. He was looking for something that might have traces of my DNA, I'm thinking."

"And you slept on my sofa that one time. How could he have known that? Unless . . ."

"He was spying through the window. I sensed Walker that night, but . . ." Tiger thought about it. If Crosby had been outside Carly's living room window, he'd have known. "He could have been spying far away, if he was looking for an opportunity to shoot me. Some rifles have good scopes."

Carly's amusement died. "And then he tried to kill you." Tiger had come very close to death that night Crosby had snuck in, but whatever had been bred into him had made him wake up, alert, in time to stop the shot.

Carly wrapped her arms around him. "I hate how close to losing you I came."

"And I came too close to losing you," Tiger said. "I almost didn't make it in time."

"But you did. You saved us all."

Tiger looked down at Carly, her green eyes, her fine-boned face, her wide-lipped smile. Desperation tugged at his heart. "I can't lose you."

"I'm right here, love," she whispered.

Tiger kissed her again, gently at first, then letting his mouth become firmer, bolder. Carly returned the kisses with as much boldness, her arms tightening around him.

Tiger needed her. Lying here next to her for days, scenting her, feeling her, wanting her, had made him insane. He was hard with mating frenzy. She'd declared herself his mate, and Tiger had been too weak to do anything about it.

He wasn't weak anymore. Tiger parted Carly's thighs with one hand, then pushed his wide-awake cock straight inside her.

Carly's eyes opened wide, the gray sparkles in the green beautiful. "Mmm," she purred. "I *have* missed you."

Tiger's powers of speech deserted him. He only felt Carly around him, his *mate*.

The mating frenzy reached up and closed its fist around him. Thought fled. There was only Carly, her scent, her heat, the dampness of her skin, the scalding moisture that gripped his cock.

Carly, always Carly. The beautiful woman who'd healed him with her touch. She'd saved Tiger, given him his name.

The room filled with the sounds of their lovemaking, their quick breaths and little moans, the creak of the sturdy bed, the slide of skin on skin, their mouths coming together.

Tiger pumped into her in a hard, fast rhythm, his body knowing what to do. Carly rose beneath him, legs coming around him, her bare feet pressing him. She took him easily now, fitting around him. Her eyes were half-closed, lips parted with pleasure.

As Tiger wound up toward his climax, she did too. Carly's movements became jerkier, her hips rolling with his, her quick cries fueling his frenzy.

Tiger's growl vibrated the air. His fingers grew claws, then quickly receded, Tiger wanting to be a man when he was with this woman.

Carly crushed against him as she rose into him, crying his name. Tiger held her close, the frenzy erasing all pain, including the sunburnlike tingle. Being inside her took away all sorrow, all grief, all hurt. He had so much hurt, and Carly was dissolving it.

"Carly," he cried as the white-hot point of climax clenched him and didn't let go. *"I love you."*

"I love you," Carly's reply came, loud and clear. Tiger kept driving into her, both of them seeking, rocking, holding, loving.

Then they crashed onto the bed, the morning sunlight kissing their skin. Tiger rumpled Carly's hair and let kisses fall on her warm face, her neck, her breasts.

Carly gathered him into her, laying his head on her chest with a happy sigh. "My Tiger," she murmured, her voice broken. "I very much love you too."

When they straggled down to breakfast, Tiger's first since he'd come home, Sean was there, making a special batch of pancakes, with Connor assisting. Walker waited at the kitchen table, looking content. Smug even.

Carly felt warm, stretched, satisfied. She'd thought Tiger would tire soon after his first foray back into lovemaking, but she'd been proved wrong very quickly. Tiger was healing fast, and with the healing came his stamina.

Carly sat down at the table, gently, a bit sore, and reached for the pitcher of orange juice.

Walker nodded at Carly, then looked up at Tiger. "Thank you," he said. "For the promotion and the command."

Carly blinked while Tiger sat down with his usual stoicism and accepted the glass of juice Carly handed him. He'd resumed the fake Collar before coming downstairs, preserving the illusion.

"Promotion? Command?" Carly asked Walker, when it became clear Tiger wouldn't speak.

"Because of Tiger, I get to trade my captain's bars for gold leaves. And assume command of the detachment to the Shifter Bureau. Lieutenant Colonel Sheldon has disappeared."

Tiger set down the glass he'd just drained. "Disappeared where?"

"If I knew, I wouldn't have said *disappeared*. Seems that someone tipped off Shifter Bureau, the army, and the media that Sheldon ordered the fire to be set in the community center. He's public enemy number one. Post vacant, and I was offered it, as I was XO and knew all about the training and projects at the camp anyway."

"Someone tipped them off, eh?" Sean said at the stove. "I have to be wondering who did that."

"Couldn't say," Liam said, coming into the room. "These rumors, how do they get started?"

He and Sean shared a conspiratorial grin.

"Anyway, I'm now in charge of all research concerning the tiger Shifter," Walker said. "Who's not to be harmed, by the way, because he's become a freaking superhero." Walker leaned forward, looking Tiger in the eyes, a gleam of excitement in his. "And I've figured out, my friend, what you were made for."

CHAPTER THIRTY

Tiger lifted his head, waiting, his heart beating rapidly, but Walker only sat there, hands around his coffee cup, grinning.

"What?" Carly asked, fists on the table, her impatience heightening her scent. "Don't keep us in suspense."

Walker cleared his throat and moved his coffee cup on the placemat. "Sheldon thought Tiger was a weapon. A perfect soldier who never gets tired, heals right away, and doesn't need to eat, drink, or sleep for long stretches of time. As I mentioned, Sheldon wanted to use Tiger as a prototype. He wanted to take Tiger to Afghanistan and demonstrate how well he heals from being shot up or burned. Sheldon's plan was to breed more Shifters like Tiger, except ones more easily controlled than him, using Collars and other things. He regarded Tiger as his beacon, one guiding Sheldon all the way to brigadier general and higher."

Liam sat down in his usual lazy way, holding a mug of steaming coffee. "The Fae bred us a couple thousand years ago to be the perfect soldiers," he said conversationally. "We'd fight their wars so they wouldn't lose so many Fae, who are, of course, the most important beings in the universe. The Fae found out the hard way that they couldn't control us, when we fought a war with them and won our freedom. They're still trying to control us, but in, oh, about a thousand years, they still haven't figured out how."

"But you wear Collars," Walker said.

Liam's eyes widened. "Well, now, that's true, isn't it? How about that?"

Connor snorted a laugh from the stove. "Too right."

"Anyway," Carly said. "Back to Tiger. Is that what he was made for, to be a soldier?"

"I thought so at first," Walker said. "Then I did some digging, back to the original experiments. My old friend Dr. Brennan knew a few of the people from the research team way back when. He consulted with them, as a Shifter anthropologist. I hunted up a couple who were still around and talked to them. The project had been shelved and most of the files sealed, and more was lost when the building in Area 51 burned down. But the researchers had kept their personal notes, and they gave them to me." Walker shot Tiger a look of sympathy. "They put you through hell, didn't they? Believe me, I'd never do that."

Tiger gave him slow nod. "I believe you."

"You thought so *at first*," Carly broke in, still watching Walker. "What do you think now?"

"That Tiger *wasn't* bred to be the perfect killing machine," Walker said. "Yeah, he has all those qualities I mentioned—stamina, rapid healing, a body that adapts to extreme stress." He fixed his gaze on Tiger again, the excitement still in his eyes. "But you're not a killing machine, my friend. You're not a gun to point and shoot." Walker stopped, letting them all stare at him, waiting, including Sean and Connor, who'd turned from the stove.

Kim came into the room with Katriona, dropped a kiss to Liam's cheek, and sat down next to her mate. She fixed Walker with a steely glare. "Well, come on, then. Spill."

Walker grinned. "Search and rescue." He delivered the words, then sat back and drank his coffee.

They sat in stunned silence, until Liam said, "Ah. Yes."

Tiger said nothing, but Walker's words made something click inside him. Something right.

I know what I was made for. What I'm meant to be.

Carly, though, still looked bewildered. "Search and rescue? You mean like with people trapped after a disaster or missing out in the middle of nowhere?"

"More than that," Walker said, animated. "Search and rescue, domestically, or behind enemy lines. He was going to be put in with A-Teams, to go deep into enemy territory. He'd find civilians hurt by the fighting, like kids and moms, fix them up, keep them safe. The same for civilians of allies or our civilians when war comes to them."

The sense of rightness spread through Tiger, weaving around him as strongly as the mate bond. *Yes,* his entire body said. *I was made to protect.*

Carly's surprised look fled. "Of course," she said to Tiger. "That's why you're so adamant about the cubs."

"All Shifters protect the cubs," Kim said.

"Yes, but Tiger goes above and beyond," Carly said. "He looks out for every cub in Shiftertown. Anyone who's vulnerable, actually, like the clerk in the convenience store."

"She does have a point," Liam said. He sipped coffee, looking the least surprised of everyone.

"And the cubs aren't afraid of him," Carly said. "They all adore you, Tiger. The adult Shifters look at you like you're some sort of Frankenstein's monster, but the cubs are always thrilled to see you."

"That's true," Connor said. "I'm still a cub, and I like Tiger."

"So do the little kids, like Olaf and Jordan," Carly said. "They trust Tiger completely, no matter how much the adults try to say that Tiger needs to be controlled and contained."

"That's because cubs are smart," Connor said, his expression serious.

Katriona laughed and held out her hands toward Tiger. "Tigger."

Tiger couldn't stop himself from rising, going to Katriona, and lifting her from Kim. He touched a light kiss to the little girl's forehead, sat down again next to Carly, and balanced Katriona on her little feet on his knee. In about a year, he'd be holding his own cub, with Carly at his side.

The conversation around him dimmed and became unimportant.

"See?" Walker was saying. "There's something inside Tiger that makes the kids seek him out and trust him. Makes sense if his mission is to find them and get them to safety. They'd need to trust him completely."

Liam nodded in silence. Sean had gone back to making pancakes, and Connor, after one more long, thoughtful look at Tiger, turned to help him.

"One thing I don't like about your explanation," Carly said to Walker. "You say the kids trust Tiger because there's something programmed into him, some genetics thing."

"Probably having to do with pheromones," Liam put in. "And scent and so forth."

Carly waved that away. "Maybe, but could you consider that cubs trust him because they can see he's just a wonderful guy? Caring, protective, amazing?"

Liam chuckled, lifted his coffee, and patted Kim's knee. "Spoken like a true mate."

Carly frowned at him. "I refuse to believe that Tiger's the way he is because a scientist mixed something in a test tube. People don't work that way. A lot of what makes Tiger *Tiger* is . . . Tiger."

"Exactly," Kim said. "Well said."

"All of us are a bunch of chemicals stuck together," Liam argued. "Even you, love," he finished, with a warm look at Kim.

"I don't believe that entirely," Carly said. "My sisters and I share the same genetic makeup and we're all very different. So even if people *were* created in test tubes, even clones, what would come out of each test tube would be different." Carly looked at Walker, sudden concern in her expression. "Wait, you didn't mean you wanted to make clones of Tiger, did you?"

"Sheldon did," Walker said. "I'm of the mind that we don't have the technology yet to get cloning exactly right. But studying you could tell us a lot, Tiger. And you could do your rescue thing and train others in search and rescue. We could sure use you."

"Wait a minute," Carly said. "You are *not* going to do experiments on him and torture him and treat him like a guinea pig. Tiger's a *person*. And I'm going to marry him. Or mate with him, as Shifters call it. I accepted his mate-claim."

Her announcement fell into stunned silence, and Tiger looked up. Carly had already declared to Tiger that she was his mate, but he hadn't expected her to state it to other Shifters, in terms they'd waited to hear.

Connor let out a wild whoop from across the room. He threw his spatula into the air, scattering droplets of batter, rushed to Carly, and dragged her up and into a hug.

"Another mating," he shouted as he released her. "Sun and moon. Time to par-tay. Get on with it, Liam."

"Give us a chance, Connor." Liam was out of his seat too, waiting while Kim crushed Carly in an enthusiastic embrace.

Carly had tears on her cheeks when she emerged. "I didn't realize y'all would be so happy."

"Of course we're happy." Liam caught Carly in a hard hug, ruffling her hair. "Tiger needs a mate, and you're perfect for him. Another mating means more cubs, more Shifters."

"There will be more cubs," Carly said, and she smiled. "Sooner rather than later."

Connor let out another whoop, and this time five pancakes went to the floor. Instead of scolding him, Sean shoved Connor out of the way and came to hug Carly himself.

"Now, that's a fine thing," Sean said, wrapping his arms around her.

"I thought you were up the spout," Liam said to Carly, still holding on. "I scented the change. But I was waiting for you to say."

"You waited more patiently than Tiger did." Carly laughed from within their embrace. "He blabbed to my whole family."

"A cub," Walker said thoughtfully. "Congratulations. That will be interesting."

Tiger shot Walker a fierce look. He got to his feet and hoisted Katriona to his shoulder. "I will help you, Walker," he said, taking on a hint of a growl. "But you will stay away from my cub."

Walker stared up at him, his blue eyes taking on a wary look. But then he relaxed, nodded, and stuck out his hand. "Deal."

Tiger studied Walker's hand without touching it. "And no shooting me to see how fast I heal the next time. That fucking *hurt*."

"No more worries about that," Walker said. "If you help us, you'll work *with* us, not be a test subject. I've even put in the paperwork to create a new position for you if you'll take it—Shifter Liaison to the Shifter Bureau South, Special Assignment. With a salary."

Tiger stared at him in wonder, not quite taking it in. Walker was saying he wanted to give Tiger a job, with money paid to him, which meant Liam wouldn't have to provide for Tiger's every meal. Most Shifters didn't worry much about money and were happy to share, but the idea that Tiger could pull his weight with them, as even Connor did, gave him a feeling of satisfaction, of belonging.

"Deal," Tiger said and shook Walker's hand, human-style.

Kim hugged Tiger around the waist. "I'm so happy for you, big guy."

Tiger returned Kim's hug carefully, not wanting to squash Katriona in the rejoicing. He handed the giggling Kat back to her mother, then he stepped to where Liam and

Sean still hugged Carly, took them by the backs of their necks, and peeled them away from her.

"Hands off my mate."

Sean laughed, shook off Tiger's hold with surprising strength, and returned to the kitchen.

Liam stepped back, making a gallant gesture. "She's all yours."

"Yes," Tiger said. "She is."

Carly laced her arms around Tiger's neck and pulled him down to her. "I love you," she whispered before she kissed his lips. "My mate."

Warmth flowed from her, and her words, to fill all the empty spaces inside Tiger. Nothing left out.

Walker had declared that he'd figured out what Tiger had been made for. But Tiger already knew.

He'd been made to find this woman, Carly, this mate of his heart. He'd been made for the bond that stretched between her and him, and he'd been made to bond with the child that grew inside her.

Tiger always seemed to know things before others did. Maybe that was part of his programming, a mechanism that let him find those in danger, as he had Olaf in the fire. He would work with Walker to figure out how he knew these things, and all about what he could do.

He did know, as he held Carly and kissed her back— the best new activity he'd learned since meeting her—that the child inside her was a boy. And that he'd live, and grow up, and be a tiger like his father. There would be more cubs, and Tiger and Carly, together for as long as it took.

Liam had told Tiger about the Fae spell that let humans live as long as their Shifter mates, as Kim would with Liam. Tiger would grab the Fae called Fionn and make him perform the spell on Carly right away.

Tiger saw their days stretched before them, Carly with him, and all their cubs. He pulled Carly close.

"I know what I was made for," Tiger whispered into her ear. "I was made for you."

That, and happiness. Tiger had reached for happiness in the past, only to have it shatter like a glass bubble when he closed his hand around it.

"I love you, my mate," Tiger said, touching the softness of her cheek.

"I love you, Tiger," Carly said again.

This time, as Carly smiled up at him, her green eyes the most beautiful things Tiger had ever seen, happiness stayed with him, whole and warm, and surrounded his heart.

CHAPTER THIRTY-ONE

Carly didn't thoroughly understand the Shifter mating ceremonies, though Kim and Andrea had done their best to explain the symbolism. The circle dances called the Goddess and the God to the place; the flower garland in Carly's hair represented nature, eternity, and fertility. The ritual sealed Carly and Tiger so that their union was sacred under the moon—the Mother Goddess—and under the sun—the Father God.

What Carly did understand was that the ceremony itself was brief, Liam saying, with a smile, "Under the light of the moon, the Mother Goddess, I recognize this mating."

She also understood the party into which the solemn ceremony degenerated, music blasting from Sean's back porch, the beer flowing, meat grilling, Shifters dancing, talking, laughing. Carly's mother and sisters, who'd come to Shiftertown for the event, fit right in—Althea and Zoë already had Shifter admirers. Janine and Simon, her husband, were a little more reticent, but Olaf and Jordan soon had their son playing with them, and Andrea and Sean had the couple laughing and talking.

Likewise Yvette and Armand had come for the ritual, Armand with gifts of food and his beneficence, Yvette with a wise smile for Carly for following her heart. Yvette immediately joined Liam at the grill, first discussing with him and then arguing about cooking techniques, marinades, and what should be served with what.

Liam was in a particularly good mood, even beyond his excitement at presiding over a mating. The other Shifter leaders, he'd told Carly and Tiger before the ceremony, had agreed it was a good thing that Tiger would work with the Shifter Bureau in learning about himself. The arrangement kept Tiger out of trouble—in other words, made him someone else's problem. And the Shifter leaders, particularly Bowman, Eric, and Graham, were interested in Liam testing out Collar changes on Tiger. Tiger had agreed to help in figuring out ways to get the Collars off Shifters, especially after Liam mentioned he wanted to get the cubs out of the Collars first.

As the night deepened and the food and beer were consumed, some Shifters started slinking into darkness to be alone together. Mating rituals stirred the mating frenzies, Kim had said.

Carly also understood how she and Tiger ended up in his bed under the eaves, moonlight streaming in to caress them.

They were alone in the house, Liam and company still out reveling. To thumping strains of party music coming from next door, Tiger gave himself over to Carly as though theirs would be the last coupling on earth.

Carly didn't mind, as her body rose to his, her hands gripping the sweet tightness of his buttocks to pull him inside her. She arched to him, sweat hot between them, dripping to the sheets.

Tiger wasn't silent, and tonight he wasn't gentle. Gripped by the mating frenzy, Tiger drove into her with ferocity, and Carly, bound to him, wound up into frenzy herself.

Tiger opened points of pleasure in Carly she'd never

known existed. Sounds escaped her mouth, incoherent, her throat aching with them.

Tiger filled her and loved her, his hands everywhere, his mouth a place of heat. He was one with her, and she with him, and that was all Carly wanted.

After a long time, Tiger growled, his eyes flashing golden as he neared his peak. He continued to rock into her, and she was crying out in joy by the time he spilled his seed. They fell together, spent and shaking, and the room went silent.

Carly lay in the tangle of sheets, her body scalding, with the hottest part of her the place where they were still joined. She ran her hands down Tiger's back, his skin slick with sweat. But he was whole, healed, hers. The touch of a mate.

His touch healed her in return. Carly had never felt so well, so cared for, in all her life.

Tiger would never desert her. She understood that now. Even when Tiger had been gone, he'd been taking care of her.

Because he cared. Carly's father had cared for only himself, had seen his family as an obstacle, a distraction. And so he'd left them.

Tiger saw Carly as his anchor in the roiling stream of life, and she now thought of him in the same way. Not because of a magical mate bond, but because he loved her and she loved him. Love, not programming, not magic.

"I love you," Carly whispered, her voice ragged from their lovemaking. "You know that, right?"

Tiger rose over her again, his rare smile wide, his eyes warm with afterglow. "I do know," he said. "And I know I love you, Carly. My beautiful mate."

Carly traced his cheek. She wriggled her hips at the same time, Tiger still rigid inside her. Wildness touched her again.

"You know everything, do you?" she asked, teasing.

"Yes." His kiss was lazy, warm. "I do."

"Mmm. Then you know I want to do that again."

"I want to do it too, mate of my heart. Right now."

"Yep. Right now."

"I know something else," Tiger said as he brushed kisses down her neck.

He slid out of her, the friction delightful, the anticipation of more to come even better. Tiger kissed her breasts, then moved down to press a long kiss just below her navel.

"What do you know?" Carly asked, stroking his hair, which was already growing back in, black and orange.

Tiger chuckled, his breath warm on her abdomen. "That it's a boy."

Carly laughed in delight, the sound ringing through the room. She opened her arms, and Tiger kissed his way back up her body, his welcoming heat covering her as he slid inside her again.

Right where he belonged. The mate bond wound around her heart, and his, and Carly was complete.

Turn the page for a preview of Jennifer Ashley's
next Shifters Unbound novel

WILD WOLF

Now available from Berkley Sensation!

Graham McNeil slammed his massive fist into the jaw of the attacking wolf just as his cell phone rang.

Graham got the wolf into a headlock and tried to reach for the phone, but the wolf fought and clawed, drawing blood, its breath like sour acid. Graham's Collar sparked heavy pain into his throat, while the Collar on the wolf he fought was dormant.

Was this where things were going with the ludicrous idea that all Shifters should have their pain-shocking Collars replaced with inert ones? Shifters at the bottom of the food chain would try to claw their way up, using their fake Collars as an advantage.

Like this Lupine was. The shithead was from the family of one of Graham's trackers, was supposed to be loyal to Graham. The wolf had decided today to wait in Graham's house, until Graham walked in alone, and jump him.

Idiot. Graham had territory advantage, even if he still wore his true Collar, which blasted pain into him with every heartbeat. Time to show the attacking wolf who was truly alpha.

Except that Graham's phone kept ringing against his belt. Because Shifters were only allowed to carry "dumb" phones, he didn't have a fancy ring tone to tell him who was calling. The damn thing just rang.

Graham grabbed the insubordinate Lupine by the throat and threw it against the wall. The wolf howled, but did it stay down? No.

As the wolf prepared to launch another attack, Graham yanked the phone off his belt and flipped it open. "What?"

"Graham," came the breathless voice of his more-or-less girlfriend, a human called Misty.

The picture came to him of the curvy young woman with the light brown hair she wore in ponytail while she worked at her flower shop, her soft face, and her sweet brown eyes. Graham wished with everything he had that he was with her, teasing her, kissing her, instead of trying to beat an annoying wolf into submission.

"I'm a little busy right now, sweetheart," Graham said loudly as the wolf landed on him. A wooden chair smashed under them as they both slammed against the wall—damn, he *liked* that chair. "You break my TV, you're dead," Graham snarled.

"What?"

"Not you, sweetie," Graham said into the phone. "A fucking Lupine. I'll have to call you back."

"You can't. Graham, listen, I need you. They're . . . Oh, crap."

"What?" Graham bellowed. "Slow down. What are you saying?"

"I have to go. I don't know when I can call you again."

A soft noise sounded on her end. A human being might not have heard it, but Graham's wolf hearing was gearing up as he felt the wolf inside him taking over. What the hell was happening at her house a long way from Shiftertown?

Graham's shift was coming. In a few seconds, he wouldn't be able to hold the phone, let alone talk. "Wait!" he yelled at her.

"I can't. I've got to go. Graham, I l—"

The phone clicked, and Graham was shouting at a dead line. "What? Wait! Misty! Fuck."

He threw the phone across the room and lifted the attacking wolf by the scruff of the neck. "Would you stop it, you asshole?"

The wolf snarled, teeth snapping at Graham's throat. The wolf in Graham responded. He felt his body change, muscles becoming harder and leaner, face elongating to accommodate teeth, claws jutting from fingers that quickly became paws.

With an earsplitting snarl, Graham went for the other wolf's throat, snapping his teeth around fur.

At the last minute, the alpha in him told him not to kill. Graham was this wolf's protector, not an enemy. The wolf needed to be taught its place, not destroyed.

Not that Graham wouldn't rough it up a bit. But quickly. He needed to find out what was wrong with Misty. The fear in her voice had been clear, the desperation palpable. *They're . . .* What? *Here? Coming? Killing me?*

Graham's Collar kept sparking, snapping arcs into his neck. He held on to the throat of the subordinate wolf, not letting the disadvantage of his Collar stop him.

Dominance didn't have anything to do with Collars, or pain, or fighting. Dominance was about putting full-of-themselves, arrogant Lupine Shifters in their place.

Graham got the wolf on the floor and stepped on it. He shifted to human again, breathing hard, his clothes in tatters. "Stay down." The words were hard, final.

The wolf snarled again, then became human—lanky, dark-haired, gray-eyed—typical Lupine. Except this one was female.

She looked up at him, still snarling, rage in her eyes. "This isn't over, McNeil."

"Famous last words. Your dad sent you, didn't he? Thought maybe I'd mate-claim you if you couldn't best me, right?"

The way she looked quickly away told Graham he'd hit upon the truth. She was naked, and not bad, but Graham hadn't been able to think about any other female since he'd met Misty.

He hadn't mate-claimed Misty, or even had sex with her. Graham had never had sex with a human before, and he feared he'd hurt her. Also, his position as leader of the Lupines in this Shiftertown—but not the overall leader of all the Shifters—was precarious. He couldn't afford to bring in a half-human cub that might get the Shifters beneath him worried.

But her phone call had his gut churning. Graham got to his feet. "I have to go. I want you out of here by the time I get back. No more ambushes. If you want a mate, go chase some bears. They're always horny."

Graham turned around and walked away. The best way to show a submissive that they were submissive was to indicate you didn't fear them jumping you the minute your back was turned. Making them know that if they did jump you, you'd stop them. Again.

His heart was hammering with worry, the wolf forgotten, as he detoured to his bedroom to grab clothes to replace the ones he'd shredded with his shift.

Graham left through the back door, mounted his motorcycle, started it, and rode noisily away from his house and Shiftertown.